OLIVER PÖTZSCH

The
Poisoned Pilgrim

A Hangman's Daughter Tale

Translated by
LEE CHADEAYNE

MARINER BOOKS
HOUGHTON MIFFLIN HARCOURT
BOSTON   NEW YORK

First Mariner Books edition 2013
Text copyright © 2012 by Oliver Pötzsch
English translation copyright © 2013 by Lee Chadeayne

The Poisoned Pilgrim: A Hangman's Daughter Tale was first published in 2012
by Ullstein Buchverlag GmbH as *Der Hexer und die Henkerstochter.*
Translated from German by Lee Chadeayne. First published in
English by AmazonCrossing and Mariner Books in 2013.

www.hmhbooks.com

Library of Congress Cataloging-in-Publication Data is available.
ISBN 978-0-544-11460-9

Printed in the United States of America
DOC 10 9 8 7 6 5 4 3 2 1

For Marian, Wolfgang, Martin, Vitus, Michi, and all the rest.

With hoods pulled far down over their faces and

swords swinging in an almost perfect circle . . .

Andechs Monastery

Inn

Pharmacist's house

K i e n   V a l

Road to
Erling

Monastery

1 Monks' library
2 Refectory
3 Monks' cells
4 Priory
5 Abbot's private room
  (study)
6 Prince's room
7 Library

Church

Courtyard

Courtyard

Monastery
garden

3 3 3 1

3 3

2

Ground floor

Monastery church

Monastery

Monastery garden

Brewery

Hospital

Watchmaker's house

Second floor

Courtyard

3 3 3 3 3 4 4

3
3

5

Third floor

S — N

1

Church

Courtyard

Courtyard

7

6 6 6 6

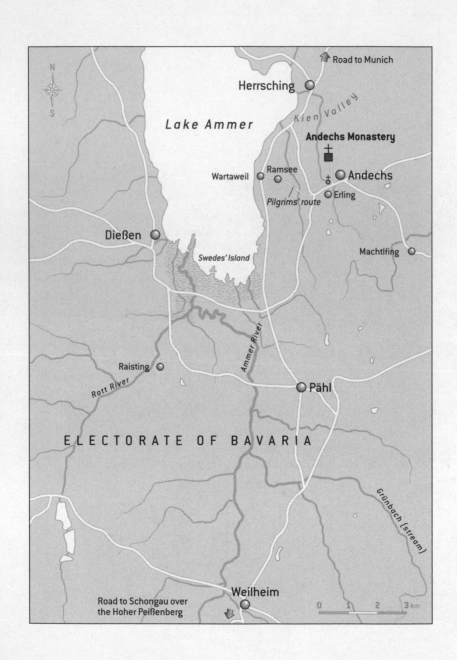

Road to Munich

Herrsching

Lake Ammer

Kien Valley

Andechs Monastery

Wartaweil   Ramsee

Andechs

Pilgrims' route

Erling

Dießen

Swedes' Island

Machtlfing

Ammer River

Raisting

Rott River

Pähl

ELECTORATE OF BAVARIA

Grünbach (stream)

Weilheim

Road to Schongau over
the Hoher Peißenberg

0   1   2   3 km

DRAMATIS PERSONAE

SCHONGAU PILGRIMS

MAGDALENA FRONWIESER (NÉE KUISL), the hangman's daughter

SIMON FRONWIESER, Schongau bathhouse medicus

KARL SEMER, presiding burgomaster of Schongau

SEBASTIAN SEMER, son of the presiding burgomaster

JAKOB SCHREEVOGL, stove fitter and Schongau alderman

BALTHASAR HEMERLE, Altenstadt carpenter

KONRAD WEBER, city priest

ANDRE LOSCH, LUKAS MÜLLER, HANS AND JOSEF TWANGLER, bricklayer's journeymen

OTHER CITIZENS OF SCHONGAU

JAKOB KUISL, hangman of Schongau

ANNA-MARIA KUISL, the hangman's wife

GEORG AND BARBARA, the hangman's twin children

PETER AND PAUL, Magdalena and Simon Fronwieser's children

MARTHA STECHLIN, midwife

THE BERCHTHOLDT BROTHERS HANS, JOSEF, AND BENEDIKT

JOHANN LECHNER, court clerk

ANDECHS MONASTERY

MAURUS RAMBECK, abbot

BROTHER JEREMIAS, prior

BROTHER ECKHART, cellarer

BROTHER LAURENTIUS, novitiate master

BROTHER BENEDIKT, cantor and librarian
BROTHER VIRGILIUS, watchmaker
BROTHER VITALIS, novitiate and watchmaker's assistant
BROTHER JOHANNES, apothecary
COELESTIN, novitiate and apothecary's assistant

ADDITIONAL CHARACTERS

MICHAEL GRAETZ, Erling knacker
MATTHIAS, knacker's journeyman
COUNT LEOPOLD VON WARTENBERG, the Wittelsbachs'
  ambassador
COUNT VON CÄSANA UND COLLE, Weilheim district judge
MASTER HANS, Weilheim executioner

PROLOGUE

DARK THUNDERCLOUDS HUNG OVERHEAD AS THE novitiate Coelestin, with a curse on his lips, marched toward his imminent death.

In the west, beyond Lake Ammer, swirling clouds towered up, the first flashes of lightning appeared, and a distant rumble of thunder could be heard. When Coelestin squinted, he could make out gray rain clouds over the monastery in Dießen, five miles away. In only a matter of minutes the storm would be raging over the Holy Mountain, and now, of all times, the fat monk of an apothecary had sent him to fetch a carp from the monastery pond for supper. Coelestin cursed again and pulled the cape of his black robe farther down over his face. What could he do? Obedience was one of the three vows of the Benedictine order, and Brother Johannes was his superior — it was that simple. An occasionally hot-tempered, often enigmatic, and above all gluttonous lay brother, but nevertheless his superior.

"Porca miseria!" As so often when he was in a bad mood, Coelestin switched to his mother tongue. He had grown up in an Italian village on the other side of the Alps, but in the turmoil of the war, his father had become a mercenary and his mother a

whore who followed army camps. Here in the monastery on the Holy Mountain, Coelestin had found a home in the pharmacy at Andechs. Even though the incessant litanies and nightly prayers sometimes got on his nerves, he felt safe here. Three times a day he got a good meal; he had a warm, dry place to sleep, and the Andechs beer was said to be one of the best in the entire Elector- ate of Bavaria. In these hard times, one could have it much worse. Nevertheless, the spindly little novitiate cursed under his breath, and not just because he would soon be as wet as the carp in the pond of the Erling Monastery.

Coelestin was afraid.

Ever since the discovery he made three days ago, fear had been eating at him like a rabid beast. What he saw was so horri- ble that his blood almost froze in his veins. It still followed him at night in his dreams, when he woke up screaming and bathed in sweat. God would never allow such a crime to go unpunished; that much was certain. To Coelestin, the dark clouds and the flashes of lightning in the sky seemed like the first harbingers of an Old Testament revenge that would soon be visited on the monastery.

Even more threatening than the heresy, actually, was the man's hateful gaze. The man had recognized Coelestin when the novitiate tried to make a hasty escape—at least that's what Coelestin thought. And the look on the novitiate's face said more than a thousand words. In recent days they had reached out to him, prodding, as if checking that Coelestin hadn't betrayed the secret.

Coelestin knew that the *other one* had powerful advocates. Why would they believe him, the little novitiate? The accusation was so monstrous that he could be considered insane. Or even worse, a character assassin. This comfortable life, with meat, beer, and a warm, dry bed, would then no doubt be gone forever.

Nevertheless, Coelestin had decided to speak up. The next

morning he would tell the monastery council what he'd seen and his conscience would finally be clear.

A loud clap of thunder rolled across the countryside, and the freezing novitiate could feel the first cool drops of rain on his face. Hastening, he tightened his hood and had soon left the last houses of Erling behind. Fields and meadows spread out before him. On the other side of a small wooded area, surrounded by fences and bushes, lay the fishpond. When Coelestin turned around, he saw storm clouds towering over the monastery up on the mountain—the home he might soon have to leave. He sighed and shuffled the last few yards to the pond, as if advancing toward his own execution.

In the meantime, drops fell faster and faster, until the surface of the pond seemed to boil up like a poisonous brew. Coelestin could see the fat gray bodies of the carp slowly coursing through the dark water by the dozens. Their hungry mouths snapped at the raindrops as if they were manna from heaven. Coelestin shuddered as a wave of disgust came over him. He'd never cared for carp. They were dumb, slimy scavengers whose flesh tasted of moss and decay. The fish reminded him of the monsters he'd seen in pictures of Jonah and the Whale: horrible creatures of the deep that swallowed whole everything that wriggled in front of them in the water.

Timidly Coelestin started down the narrow, slippery walkway and reached for a fishnet leaning on a post alongside the pier. With his hood deep down over his face, he leaned into the wall of rain and wind and moved his net back and forth listlessly in the water. If he hurried, he might be back in the monastery pharmacy before the trousers and socks under his thick black robe were soaked as well. In another life he probably would have slapped Brother Johannes across his chubby face with the carp, but for now, he was damned to prayer and obedience. This was the price he had to pay for such a comfortable life.

A slight creaking sound, almost drowned out by the thunder, caused the novitiate to pause. It sounded as if someone had stepped onto the walkway behind him. But just as Coelestin was about to turn around, something started flopping about in his net, and with a sigh of relief, he pulled in the long pole.

"Got you," he mumbled. "Let's have a look at what a big fish—"

At that instant, something heavy hit him on the back of the head.

Coelestin staggered, slipped on the rain-soaked wood of the walkway, and finally fell—fishnet and all—into the swirling water of the pond, where he thrashed around and fought to save himself. Like so many people of his time, Coelestin could skin a rabbit, identify hundreds of herbs by their smell, and recite whole sections of the Bible by heart. But one thing he couldn't do was swim.

The young novitiate shouted, waved his arms around, and kicked his skinny legs, but his own weight pulled him inexorably down. When he felt the muddy bottom beneath his feet, he pushed himself back up to the surface, gasping. In despair he reached out in all directions until he suddenly felt the pole floating in front of him on the surface. He clung to it and pulled himself up. Through the increasingly violent downpour he could see a hooded figure on the walkway holding the other end of the net.

"Oh, thank you," he groaned. "You saved my—"

At that moment the figure pushed the pole down so hard that Coelestin sank again, gurgling. When he came to the surface again, he felt the pole push him down violently once again.

"But—" he started to say as his mouth filled with murky water, which stifled his last desperate cries. Silently he sank into the pond.

As life ebbed from his body in little air bubbles, Coelestin could feel the fat, slimy carp rubbing against his cheeks and nibbling on the short hair of his tonsure. When the dying youth had finally sunk to the bottom, his mouth was as wide open as those of the fish around him that stared back at him with dumb, expressionless eyes.

The man on the walkway watched the bubbles for a while and finally, nodding contentedly, put the net back in place and set out for home.

The time had come for him to complete his work.

I

Lightning flashed from the sky like the finger of an angry god.

Simon Fronwieser saw it directly over Lake Ammer, where for a fraction of a second, it lit up the foaming waves in a sickly green. It was followed by a peal of thunder and a steady downpour—a black, soaking wall of rain that within moments drenched the two dozen or so pilgrims from Schongau. Though it was only seven in the evening, night had fallen suddenly. The medicus gripped the hand of his wife, Magdalena, tighter and, along with the others, prepared to climb the steep hill to the Andechs Monastery.

"We were lucky!" shouted Magdalena over the thundering downpour. "An hour earlier and the storm would have caught us out on the lake."

Simon nodded silently. It wouldn't be the first time a ship of pilgrims had gone down with all hands in Lake Ammer. Now, barely twenty years after the end of the Great War, the crowds of pilgrims streaming to the famous Bavarian monastery were larger than anyone could remember. In a time of hunger, storms, ravenous wolves, and marauding brigands, people were more eager than ever to find protection in the arms of the church. This longing was fed by reports of miracles, and the Andechs Monastery in particular, thirty miles southwest of Munich, was renowned for its ancient relics that possessed magic powers — as well as for its beer, which helped people to forget their worries.

When the medicus turned around again, he could just make out through the rainclouds the wind-whipped lake that they had just managed to escape. Two days earlier, he had left Schongau with Magdalena and a group from their hometown. The pilgrimage led them over the Hoher Peißenberg to Dießen on Lake Ammer, where a rickety rowboat took them to the other shore. Now they were proceeding through the forest along a steep, muddy path toward the monastery, which towered far above them in the dark clouds.

Burgomaster Karl Semer led the procession on horseback, followed on foot by his grown son and the Schongau priest, who struggled to keep a huge painted wooden cross upright in the storm. Behind him came carpenters, masons, cabinetmakers, and, finally, the young patrician Jakob Schreevogl, the only other city councilman to follow the call for the pilgrimage.

Simon assumed that both Schreevogl and the burgomaster had come less in search of spiritual salvation than for business reasons. A place like Andechs, with its thousands of hungry and thirsty pilgrims, was a gold mine. The medicus wondered what the dear Lord would have to say about this. Hadn't Jesus chased all the merchants and money lenders from the temple? Well, at least Simon's own conscience was clear. He and Magdalena had come to Andechs not to make money but only to thank God for saving their two children.

Simon couldn't help smiling when he thought of three-year-old Peter at home and his brother, Paul, who had just turned two. He wondered if the children were giving their grandfather, the Schongau hangman, a hard time at home.

When another bolt of lightning hit a nearby beech, the pilgrims screamed and threw themselves to the ground. There was a snapping and crackling as sparks jumped to other trees. In no time, the entire forest seemed to be on fire.

"Holy Mary, Mother of God!"

In the twilight, Simon could see Karl Semer fall to his knees a few paces away and cross himself several times. Alongside him, his petrified son stared open-mouthed at the burning beeches while, all around him, the other Schongauers fled into a nearby ravine. Simon's ears were ringing from the bone-jarring thunderclap that seemed to come at the same instant from right over their heads, so he could only hear his wife's voice as if through a wall of water.

"Let's get out of here. We'll be safer down there by the brook."

Simon hesitated, but his wife seized him and pulled him away just as flames shot up from two beeches and a number of small firs at the edge of the narrow path. Simon stumbled over a rotten branch, then slid down the smooth slope covered with dead leaves. Arriving at the bottom of the ravine, he stood up, groaning, and wiped a few twigs from his hair while scanning the apocalyptic scene all around.

The lightning had split the huge beech straight down the middle, and burning boughs and branches were strewn down the slope. The flames cast a flickering light on the Schongauers, who moaned, prayed, and rubbed their bruised arms and legs. Fortunately, none of them appeared injured; even the burgomaster and his son seemed to have survived the disaster unscathed. In the gathering dusk, old Semer was busy searching for his horse, which had galloped away with his baggage.

Simon felt a slight satisfaction as he watched the burgomaster running through the forest, bellowing loudly.

Hopefully the mare took off with his moneybags, he thought. *If that fat old goat shouts one more hallelujah from up there on his horse, I'm going to commit a mortal sin.*

Simon quickly dismissed this thought as unworthy of a pilgrim and quietly cursed himself for not having brought along a warmer coat. The new green woolen cape he'd bought at the Augsburg cloth market was dapper, but after the rain it hung on him like a limp rag.

"One might almost think God had some objection to our visiting the monastery today."

Simon turned to Magdalena, who was looking up at the sky as rain ran down her mud-spattered cheeks.

"Thundershowers are rather common this time of year," Simon replied, trying to sound matter-of-fact and somewhat composed again. "I don't think that—"

"It's a sign," cried a trembling voice off to one side. Sebastian Semer, son of the burgomaster, held out the fingers of his right hand in a gesture meant to ward off evil spirits. "I told you right away we should leave the woman at home." He pointed at Magdalena and Simon. "Anyone who takes a hangman's daughter and a filthy bathhouse owner along on a pilgrimage to the Holy Mountain might as well invite Beelzebub, too. The lightning is a sign from God warning us to do penance and—"

"Shut your fresh mouth, Semer boy," Magdalena scolded, narrowing her eyes. "What do you know about penance, hm? Wipe your britches off before everyone notices you've peed in your pants again."

Ashamed, Sebastian Semer stared at the dark spot on the front of his wide-cut reddish-purple petticoat breeches. Then he turned away silently, but not without casting one last angry look at Magdalena.

"Don't mind him. The little rascal is nothing but the spoiled offspring of his father."

Jakob Schreevogl now emerged from the darkness of the

forest, wearing a tight-fitting jerkin, high leather boots, and a white lace collar framing an unusual face with a Vandyke beard and a hooked nose. A fine rain trickled down his ornamented sword.

"In general I agree with you, Fronwieser." Schreevogl turned to Simon and pointed at the sky. "Such violent storms aren't unusual in June, but when the lightning strikes right beside you, it's like you're feeling God's anger."

"Or the anger of your fellow citizens," Simon added gloomily.

Almost four summers had passed since his marriage to Magdalena, and since then, a number of Schongau citizens had let Simon know just how they felt about this marriage. As the daughter of the hangman, Jakob Kuisl, Magdalena was an outcast, someone to be avoided if possible.

Simon reached for his belt to check that a little bag of healing herbs and medical instruments was still attached there. It was quite possible he'd need some of his medicines during this pilgrimage. The Schongauers had often sought his help in recent years. Memories of the Great War still haunted some of the older people, and plagues and other diseases had swept over Schongau in recent years again and again. Last winter, Simon and Magdalena's sons had also fallen ill, but God had been merciful and spared them. In the following days, Magdalena prayed many rosaries and finally convinced Simon to take a pilgrimage to the Holy Mountain with her after Pentecost, along with nearly two dozen other citizens of Schongau and Altenstadt—citizens who wanted to show their gratitude to the Lord at the famous Festival of the Three Hosts. Simon and Magdalena had left the two children in the care of their grandparents—a wise decision, in view of the last hour's events, the medicus again admitted to himself.

"It looks as if the rain will finally quench the fire." Jakob

Schreevogl pointed at the storm-ravaged beech, where only a few flames still flickered. "We should move along. Andechs can't be far off now—perhaps one or two miles. What do you think?"

Simon shrugged and looked around. The other trees were just smoldering now, but the rain had in the meantime become so heavy that the pilgrims could hardly see their hands in front of their faces in the growing dusk. The Schongauers had taken refuge beneath a nearby fir to wait out the heaviest rain. Only Karl Semer, still looking for his horse, was wandering around somewhere in the nearby forest, shouting loudly. His son had decided in the meantime to sit down and pout on an overturned tree trunk, trying to drive the cold from his bones with help of a flask he'd brought along. His Excellency Konrad Weber frowned at the young dandy but didn't interfere. The old Schongau priest was not about to pick a fight with the son of the presiding burgomaster.

Just as the pilgrims were beginning to calm down, another bolt of lightning struck not far away and once again the Schongauers ran like spooked chickens down the muddy slopes, farther into the valley below. The priest's wooden cross came to rest filthy and splintered between some rocks.

"Just stay together," Simon shouted into the thunder and rain. "Lie down on the ground. On the ground you'll be safe."

"Forget it." Magdalena shook her head and turned to leave. "They don't hear you, and even if they did, they'd hardly obey a dishonorable bathhouse owner."

Simon sighed and hurried after the others with Magdalena. Beside them, the carpenter Balthasar Hemerle carried an almost thirty-pound pilgrimage candle. Though its flame had gone out, the powerful, nearly six-foot-tall man held it up as straight as a battle flag. In comparison, Simon looked even smaller and more slender.

"Stupid peasants," Hemerle grumbled, stepping around a muddy puddle in great strides. "It's just a thunderstorm. We have to get out of this goddamned forest — fast. But if those cowards keep running around like that, we'll get completely lost."

Simon nodded silently and rushed ahead.

In the meantime darkness had descended completely under the dark canopy of trees. The medicus could see only vague shadows of some of the Schongauers, though he heard anxious cries farther off. Someone was praying loudly to the Fourteen Holy Helpers.

And in the distance now howling wolves could be heard.

Simon shuddered. The beasts had multiplied considerably in the years since the Great War and by now had become a true plague upon the land, like wild pigs. The hungry animals were no threat to a group of twenty hardy men, but for anyone wandering alone through the forests, the wolves presented a real danger.

Branches lashing his face, Simon struggled not to lose sight of at least Magdalena and the sturdy Balthasar Hemerle's pilgrimage candle. Fortunately, the carpenter was so tall that Simon could see him over the tops of bushes and even some low trees.

Suddenly the huge man stopped and Simon stumbled, almost bumping into him and Magdalena. The medicus was about to utter a curse, when he froze and felt the hair on the back of his neck stand on end.

In a small clearing directly before them stood two wolves with drooping jaws, growling at them. Their small eyes were red dots in the night, and their hind legs were tensed, ready to pounce. Their bodies were thin and scrawny, as if they hadn't found prey for a long time.

"Don't move," Balthasar Hemerle whispered. "If you run, they'll attack you from behind. And we don't know if there are any more nearby."

Slowly Simon reached for his linen pouch, where along with his medical instruments and herbs, he kept a stiletto as sharp as a razor. He wasn't sure the little knife would help against the two famished beasts. Beside him, Magdalena stared at the wolves, unmoving. A few steps away Balthasar Hemerle raised the heavy candle above him like a sword, as if he were about to smash the skull of one of the beasts.

A pilgrimage candle sullied with wolf's blood, Simon thought. *What would the abbot in the monastery have to say about that?*

"Stay calm, Balthasar," Magdalena whispered to the carpenter after a few moments of silence. "Look how they have their tails between their legs. The animals are more afraid of us than we are of them. Let's just slowly step back —"

At that moment, the larger of the two wolves lunged for Simon and Magdalena. The medicus dodged to one side and, out of the corner of his eye, saw the animal rush past. Scarcely had the wolf landed on his feet than he turned around to attack again. The animal snarled and opened his mouth wide, revealing huge white fangs dripping with saliva. Simon imagined he could see every drop individually, magnified as through a microscope. The wolf prepared to jump again.

From somewhere a shot rang out.

For an instant, Simon thought lightning had struck again nearby, but then he saw the wolf whining and writhing in agony before falling to the ground where he twitched one more time and died. Red blood flowed from a wound in his neck onto leaves on the ground. The second wolf growled once more before running off and, a second later, disappeared into the darkness.

"The Lord giveth and the Lord taketh away. Amen."

Now a broad-shouldered figure appeared between the trees holding a smoking musket in one hand and a burning lantern in the other. He wore a black habit and a hood drawn over his face. In the pouring rain, he looked like an angry forest spirit in search of poachers.

Finally, the stranger pushed back his hood. Simon found himself looking into the friendly face of a bald man with protruding ears, crooked teeth, and a bulbous nose furrowed with veins. He was probably the ugliest man Simon had ever seen.

"Allow me to introduce myself. I'm Brother Johannes from the Andechs Monastery," said the fat monk, squinting at the three lost pilgrims. "Have you by chance seen any bloodroot growing nearby?"

Rain and cold sweat pouring down his face, the medicus was too exhausted to answer. He slid to the ground alongside the trunk of a beech, mumbling a little prayer of thanks.

It appeared that in any case he'd have to dedicate another candle up on the Holy Mountain.

Half an hour later, the Schongau pilgrims, led by Brother Johannes, climbed the narrow path up to the monastery.

Everyone was filthy, their clothes ripped or tattered; some had suffered a few scratches and bruises. But otherwise, they all appeared unharmed. Even the burgomaster's horse showed up again. Right behind the fat monk, old Semer rode at the head of the procession, trying to make a dignified impression, an attempt that was not entirely successful, however, in view of his battered hat and muddy coat. In the meantime, the rain had turned to a steady drizzle as the storm moved east toward Lake Würm. The sound of thunder was faint and distant.

"We have you to thank, Brother," declared Karl Semer in a stately voice. "Had you not appeared, some of us would have gotten lost in the forest."

"What a stupid plan to leave the road with a storm coming on and take the old path to the monastery," grumbled Brother Johannes as he shifted a sack bulging with iron tools to his other shoulder. "You can count yourself lucky that I was out foraging for herbs, or the wolves and the lightning would have finished you off."

"Considering the approaching darkness I thought it was advisable to—uh—take the shorter route," the burgomaster retorted. "I'll admit that—"

"It certainly was a stupid idea." Brother Johannes turned to the pilgrims and examined the large white pilgrimage candle that the carpenter was still holding in his callused hands.

"Damned heavy cross you have there," he said, obviously impressed. "How far have you carried it?"

"We come from Schongau," said Simon, who was just behind the monk with Magdalena. The medicus's vest was filthy, the red rooster feathers on his new hat were bent, and his leather boots from Augsburg looked like they needed new soles. "We've been traveling for two days," he continued wearily. "Yesterday near Wessobrunn, we heard a pack of wolves howling, but they didn't dare to attack us."

Brother Johannes panted as he continued up the steep forest path, his lantern swinging back and forth like a will-o'-the-wisp. "You were very lucky," he mumbled. "The beasts are getting fresher. In this area they've already killed two children and a woman. And to make matters worse, we are plagued by vagrants and murderous gangs." He hastily crossed himself. "*Deus nos protegat.* May the Lord protect us in these uncertain times."

In the meantime, the forest had thinned. Before them, the Schongauers saw the warm and inviting lights of the small hamlet of Erling, located on a plateau at the foot of the Holy Mountain. Simon breathed a sigh of relief and squeezed Magdalena's hand. They had reached their goal unharmed—a blessing not shared by all in these hard times. He fervently hoped their two children were well in Schongau. But he had no doubt they were, in view of the overflowing love of their grandparents.

"I hope you all have a place to stay," Brother Johannes said. "It's no pleasure sleeping outside in the field on such damp June nights."

"We Schongau council members are staying in the monastery guest house," replied Burgomaster Semer coolly, pointing to his son and the patrician Jakob Schreevogl. "We've arranged for the others to be boarded with farmers in the area. After all, our journey is for the benefit of the community, isn't it?"

Brother Johannes chuckled. His face, already lopsided, contorted into a grimace. Once again Simon couldn't help noticing how ugly he was.

"If you mean the repair of the steeple, I must disappoint you," the monk replied. "The farmers don't give a damn about the condition of the monastery, but the abbot promised bread and meat to any resident of Erling who provides shelter to a needy mason or carpenter. So it shouldn't cost you anything."

Semer nodded contentedly and stroked his horse's mane. "Thanks be to God," he exclaimed. "I promise that if the Savior sends us good weather, the work on the church will be finished soon."

The Festival of the Three Hosts, one of the largest pilgrimages in Bavaria, was still a week off, but Abbot Maurus Rambeck had sent messengers to pilgrims in the surrounding villages asking them to come early to the Holy Mountain. More than a month ago lightning had damaged the steeple of the monastery church. The roof truss had been destroyed, as well as a large part of the south nave. Many strong hands were needed to ensure the festival could take place as planned. For this reason, the abbot had given the local craftsmen an indulgence for a year and good pay—an offer that a number of hungry men in the area were all too happy to accept. Along with the usual pilgrims, four masons and a carpenter had come from Schongau, and in Wessobrunn three plasterers joined their group.

"I myself am here—uh—on an urgent business matter," Karl Semer declared. "But I'm sure this pious group will be quite happy to help you with the construction work," he said, pointing to the bedraggled crowd from Schongau that had just begun singing an old church hymn.

In Erling, a number of windows and doors opened to reveal

village residents, who eyed the pilgrims suspiciously. A few dogs barked. These strangers could hardly expect a warm reception in town — too often strangers had brought death and destruction in recent decades. This time, at least, the villagers would be well compensated for the annoyance.

"What's that light up there?" Magdalena asked, pointing to the monastery that towered above the village like the castle of a robber baron.

"A light?" Brother Johannes stared back at her, somewhat perplexed.

"The light up there in the steeple. Didn't you just say the tower had been destroyed in the fire? There's a light burning there, though."

Now Simon, too, looked up at the steeple. Indeed a tiny light flickered above the nave just where the lightning had struck the belfry four weeks ago — more than just a weak glimmer. When the medicus looked more closely, however, the light vanished.

Johannes put his hand over his eyes and squinted. "I can't see anything," he said finally. "Probably sheet lightning. In any case, no one is up there; it would be much too dangerous in the dark. Much of the tower has already been rebuilt, but the roof truss and the stairs are still in bad shape." He shrugged. "Anyway, why would anyone be up there at this time of night? To enjoy the view?" Although he laughed briefly, Simon sensed the laugh was fake. The monk's eyes seemed to flicker before turning to the other pilgrims.

"I suggest you all spend tonight in the big barn on the Groner farm. Tomorrow we'll send you out to individual towns and houses. And now, good night." Brother Johannes rubbed his eyes tiredly. "I hope very much my young assistant has prepared the carp with watercress that I'm so fond of. Saving lost pilgrims makes one terribly hungry."

With the three aldermen, he stomped off toward the monastery and disappeared in the darkness.

"And now?" Simon asked Magdalena after a while. The other Schongauers had marched off, praying and singing, to the newly built barn next to the tavern.

Again the hangman's daughter stared up at the dark belfry; then she rubbed her hand over her face as if she were trying to shake off a bad dream.

"What else? We'll go where we belong." Sullenly she walked ahead of Simon toward the village outskirts where a single little house stood at the edge of the forest. The roof was holey and covered with moss and ivy, and a rickety cart by the door gave off a smell of decay. "Unlike the other pilgrims, at least we know someone here."

"But who?" Simon muttered. "A mangy knacker and distant relative of your father. Isn't that just great?"

He held his breath as Magdalena walked determinedly to the crooked door of the Erling knacker's house and knocked. Once again Simon thanked God they'd left the two little ones with their grandfather in Schongau.

A light flared up again in the belfry. Like a huge evil eye, it shined out into the night, searching for something in the forests of the Kien River valley. But neither Simon nor Magdalena noticed. The figure in the tower clung to a charred beam and let the wind pass through his hair. Flashes of lightning appeared on the horizon — large, small, jagged, straight. Up here, so close to heaven, the man felt most clearly God's presence. Or was it a different higher power, one much stronger than that of the good, kindly Maker who believed love could heal men but had let his own son perish on the cross?

Love.

He let out a malicious laugh. As if love could accomplish anything. Could it save a human life? Could it survive death? If so, then only as a thorn in the side, a wound that festered and wept and ate away at your insides till all that was left was an empty shell. A sack full of maggots where worms feasted.

With lifeless eyes, the man looked on the little band of pilgrims far below, struggling through the thunderstorm and the rain, singing a pious hymn, bowing down, praying. Their belief was so strong one could actually feel it, and up here in the tower he felt it the strongest—like a bolt of lightning, the finger of heaven infusing him with divine power. He had been wondering for a long time how to make his dream a reality, and now the goal was close at hand.

He placed the lantern on the floor, looked around, and got to work.

2

Damn it! keep your dirty paws away from my sacred crucibles before I send you back to bed without breakfast."

The Schongau hangman was sitting at the dining room table trying to keep his three-year-old grandson Peter from eating the ground herbs in an ancient stone vessel. The plants weren't poisonous, but Jakob Kuisl couldn't say what the effect on the boy would be of a mixture of arnica, St. John's wort, mountain lovage, and nettles. At the very least the boy would get diarrhea, which made the hangman shudder when he thought about how few clean diapers were still left.

"And tell your brother not to pester the chickens to death, or I'll chop his head off myself."

Paul, who had just turned two, was crawling through the fragrant rushes strewn under the table, reaching his little arms out at the chickens running through the room, cackling noisily.

"Good Lord in heaven!"

"You mustn't be so strict with them," said a weak voice from the bed in the next room. "Think of our Magdalena when she was little. How often did you tell her not to pluck the hens while they were alive, but she did it anyway."

"And each time she got a good licking for it." With a grin, Kuisl turned to his wife. Seeing her lying there in the bed, pale, rings under her eyes, he at once turned serious again. Anna-Maria had been suffering with a bad fever since last night. It had come over her like a cold wind, and now she lay there trembling under thick woolen blankets and a few tattered wolf and bear pelts. The herbs in the crucible, mixed with hot water and honey, would — he hoped — give her a little relief.

Kuisl eyed his wife with concern. Recent years had left their mark on her. She was approaching fifty, and though she was still a beautiful woman, her face was deeply furrowed. Her black hair, once so shiny, had become dull and interspersed with strands of gray. With only her pale head sticking out from under the blankets, she reminded Jakob of a white rose beginning to wither after a long summer.

"Try to sleep a bit, Anna," the hangman said gently. "Sleep is still the best medicine."

"Sleep? How?" She laughed softly, but the laugh quickly turned into a coughing fit. "You run around shouting so much, it's practically a sacrilege," she gasped finally. "In the meantime, the two little ones knock our stoneware pots from the shelves if you're not right there to keep an eye on them. Of course, the master of the house never sees that sort of thing."

"What the devil — "

And in fact, little Peter had climbed up onto a bench by the stove while Kuisl wasn't looking, and at that moment was pulling himself up on the rough pine shelves, reaching for a jar of last autumn's preserves. The jar slipped from his hands and landed on the ground with a crash, spilling its contents all over the floor. The hangman's house looked like the scene of a botched execution.

"Look, Grandpa, there's blood." Wide-eyed, Peter pointed to

the mess on the floor, then finally stuck his finger in it and sucked on it. "Good blood."

Kuisl clapped his hands over his head and let out another curse. Then he grabbed the two loudly protesting troublemakers by the scruff of the neck and carried them out into the yard. Once the door slammed closed, the hangman started picking the cherries up from the floor, getting the gooey mess all over him in the process.

"Let's hope they both fall in the well," he grumbled. "Damned hoodlums."

"You mustn't say things like that," his wife replied from the bed. "Magdalena and Simon would never forgive us if something happened to the little ones."

"Magdalena and Simon," Kuisl spat noisily into the reeds on the floor. "I don't want to even hear about them. Why do the two of them have to hang around the Holy Mountain? For a whole week!" He shook his head and wiped his hands on his worn leather apron. "Two rosaries in the Altenstadt basilica would have been enough. One for each of the brats."

"The Dear Lord meant only the best for us, and we should thank him," his wife scolded. "It wouldn't hurt you to go on a pilgrimage, either, what with all the blood on your hands from the people you've executed."

"If it's on my hands, then it's also on the hands of every one of the goddamned Schongau aldermen," Kuisl grumbled. "Until now I've always been good enough to hang the thieves and murderers."

"You'll have to clear that with your Savior." Anna-Maria coughed again and closed her eyes wearily. "I don't feel well enough today to fight with you."

Suddenly, footsteps could be heard outside, and then a loud pounding on the door. Kuisl opened it and found the midwife Martha Stechlin standing there holding the whining children, one in each hand.

"Are you out of your mind, Kuisl? I found these two down by the moat . . ." she started to say. Then her gaze fell on the hangman's spotted red shirt and she let out a scream. "My God," she cried. "Are you killing people now in their own homes?"

"Nonsense." Embarrassed, the hangman ran a hand through his black hair, which was just beginning to gray. "It's just cherry juice. The two brats knocked the jar over, and I threw them out of the house."

Martha laughed briefly, but then frowned. "You mustn't leave the children outside alone," she scolded. "Think of Huber's boy who drowned in the Lech this spring. And little Hans, the Altenstadt tavernkeeper's son, who broke all his bones recently when he was run over by a carriage. Why do you men always have to be so thickheaded? Idiots!"

Kuisl closed his eyes and groaned softly. Martha was, along with his wife and his daughter, the only person who could speak this way to the Schongau hangman. Usually the midwife brought the hangman a few herbs when she stopped by and, in return, took some crushed thornapple or a few ounces of human fat for her patients, or she leafed through Kuisl's books of medicine. The hangman's medical library and his expertise in healing were known far and wide.

"Is that the only reason you came?" Kuisl groused at Martha, with a furious look. "To holler at me like an old washerwoman?"

"Jackass! I'm here because of your wife, why else?" She pushed the two crying boys out of the room and took a worn leather pouch from her skirt. "I've brought along clubmoss, yarrow, and St. John's wort to reduce her fever."

"I have St. John's wort myself," the hangman said. "But, please, go ahead—help is always welcome."

He moved to the side so Martha could enter the bedroom where Anna-Maria was laid out with closed eyes. Evidently she had fallen asleep again. While the midwife cooled her patient's fevered face, she turned to Jakob. "Where are your two older children? Barbara at least could watch her nephews."

Grumbling, the hangman sat back down at the table and continued crushing the herbs in the mortar. His movements were smooth and even. "I sent Barbara to the forest to gather some melissa," he said. "Good Lord, my wife is not the only one in town with the fever. People are pestering me to death. And Georg is out cleaning the wagon used for carrying the prisoners to the gallows. It's filthy and covered with blood." Kuisl rubbed a few dry herbs between his calloused fingers and dropped them carefully into the mortar. "In any case, that's what he's supposed to be doing. If I catch the kid hanging around down by the Lech again, there'll be a whipping he won't forget for a long time."

Martha smiled serenely. "Oh, Jakob," she replied. "The lad is thirteen; at that age he has other things on his mind than sweeping and polishing. Think back on when you were a child. What did you do when you were thirteen?"

"I went to war and slit open the bellies of Swedish soldiers. I had no time for nonsense."

There was an awkward pause in which no one said anything.

"Even so, you really shouldn't leave your grandchildren outside by themselves," Martha finally said. "Down by the pond, I saw two of Berchtholdt's boys hanging around. If I were you, I'd be a bit more careful."

Sullenly resuming his work, Kuisl pushed the heavy pestle into the mortar. "What do you mean by that?"

"What do I mean?" Martha chuckled. "You know only too well. Ever since you caught the eldest Berchtholdt boy with the sacks of grain at the Stadl warehouse a few weeks ago, they've sworn bloody revenge."

"I only told him that wasn't his grain and to please keep his hands off it."

"And for that you had to break two of his fingers?"

The hangman grinned. "That will help the little bastard re-member it, at least. If I'd told the city council, the aldermen would have had him whipped and made him wear the shrew's fiddle. Basically, by doing what I did, I missed my chance to col-lect a reward."

Martha sighed. "All right, then. But in any case, you should watch out, at least for the children's sake." She looked at him very seriously. "I've looked these fellows in the eye, Jakob, and they're as evil as Lucifer."

"Oh, for God's sake." The hangman pounded the mortar so hard with his pestle that his two grandchildren, who were play-ing, looked up in shock. They knew their grandfather, and knew he could get loud and angry. Now that he seemed especially ir-ritated, it would be best for them to keep quiet.

"Bastards, all of them, these Berchtholdts," Kuisl said. "Just because their father sat on the city council as the master baker until he died, they think they can do anything they want. People like us have to haul the garbage from the streets and be nice and keep our mouths shut. If I catch that Berchtholdt punk down in the Stadl again, I'll break not just two fingers but both hands. And if he touches my grandkids . . ." His voice faltered. The hangman clenched his hands into fists and cracked his knuckles while his grandchildren stared up at him silently.

"If the Berchtholdts even harm a hair on the head of my grandkids," he continued, his voice as sharp as a razorblade, "then, as sure as my name's Jakob Kuisl, I'll smash their bones on my wheel one at a time, slit open their bellies, and hang their guts out the window of the Schongau Tower."

When he noticed the wide, anxious eyes of the two boys, a kind smile spread over his face. "And which of you scaredy cats wants to play piggyback now with his grandfather?"

• • •

Simon was awakened by coughing alongside him. When he turned around on the prickly, flea-infested bed of straw, he saw Magdalena wiping her pale face with the back of her hand.

"Damned bellyache," the hangman's daughter groaned. "My stomach has been queasy for days." She tried to get up but collapsed again, moaning, on the bench by the stove. "And I feel a bit dizzy, too."

"That's no surprise with all the smoke in here." Simon coughed and squinted at the door. It was ajar, and black clouds of smoke were coming through the cracks. "Your lousy cousin can't even afford a decent tile stove. Why do we have to spend the night with this miserable horse butcher? Just because he happens to be a cousin of your father?"

"Shh!" Magdalena put her finger to her lips as Michael Graetz entered the room. The Erling knacker was a skinny, consumptive man whom no one would suspect was even remotely related to the robust hangman of Schongau. His shirt was torn and stained with soot, his beard unkempt, and his teeth shone in his cadaverous face like pieces of black coal. Only his eyes sparkled genially as he held out two steaming bowls to his guests.

"Here, eat," he mumbled, venturing a wry smile. "Barley porridge sweetened with honey and dried pears. We have it only on holidays and when my dear aunt comes to visit."

"Thank you, Michael. But I don't think I can get any food into me this early in the morning." Shivering, Magdalena took the bowl to warm her hands. It was just after sunrise, and outside the opened shutters fog was rising from the forest floor. Somewhere nearby a goat was bleating. Though summer had arrived, the hangman's daughter was quivering.

"This is the coldest damn June I can remember," she complained.

Her cousin eyed her anxiously. "It may be cold, but from the way you look, I'd say the cold comes from inside." He quickly crossed himself. "Let's hope you haven't caught that damned fever that's plaguing this area now. The Grim Reaper already took two Erling farmers and a maid from Machtlfing this summer."

"Oh, come now," Simon scolded. "Magdalena has a stomach-ache, nothing more. A little anise and silverweed will get her back on her feet again."

The medicus glanced furtively at his wife, who had crawled back under the thin, torn blanket. The three had slept together in the same room—the horse butcher on the hard bench, Magdalena and Simon on the rickety couch in the niche by the stove. Lost in thought, Simon dished out a spoonful of the steaming porridge and sent a silent prayer to heaven. Michael Graetz was right. Magdalena had looked pale for days, and she had dark rings under her eyes. He could only hope she wasn't really coming down with a fever. The medicus knew from his own experience that people who complained of a simple cold in the morning could be near death by nightfall.

"I'll make something for you to drink," Simon said, partially to reassure himself as he took another spoonful of the porridge. It tasted amazingly good, as sweet and rich as an expensive dessert for pampered councilors. "Some medicine from anise, camomile, and perhaps a bit of bloodroot . . ." he mumbled. He looked around the room that occupied almost the entire first floor of the house. There was a rickety table, two stools, a bed, an old trunk, and a crooked homemade cross in the corner.

"I assume you don't have those herbs here in the house, do you?" Simon asked hesitantly. "Dried perhaps, or crushed into powder?"

Michael Graetz shook his head. "I have some chamomile growing in my garden, but the rest . . ." He shrugged. "Ever since my wife and my two dear children died of the Plague three years ago, I've been all alone in the house. I skin the dead cows and horses and take the hides to the tanner down in

Herrsching on Lake Ammer. It's a long, steep way, and I don't have time to plant more than a few carrots and cabbages behind the house."

"Don't worry," Magdalena said. "I'll be fine. I'll sit outside on the bench in the sun and—"

"You'll do nothing of the sort," Simon interrupted. "You'll stay right here in bed while I go and get some herbs. The only question is . . ." His face brightened. "Of course, that ugly monk we saw last night. Didn't he say he was out gathering herbs? I'll go over to the monastery and ask him. I need a few other herbs, in any case. Andre Losch has a bad cough, and Lukas in Altenstadt can't get his hand to heal." He took another quick spoonful of the tasty porridge. Then, smoothing his rumpled clothing, he headed for the door.

"Just don't try to get up." Simon raised his finger with feigned severity. "You can come over to the monastery later. Just be glad you have a bathhouse surgeon caring for you free of charge."

"All right, fine, Mr. Bathhouse Surgeon." Magdalena lay back down on the bed, exhausted. "And while you're out, bring a little rosemary and some fresh reeds for the floor. This room stinks like the inside of a dead horse. It's no wonder I feel ill."

The sun was just rising over the forest in Kien Valley as Simon left the knacker's house. Dew was rising on the meadows around Erling, and the day promised to be pleasantly warm. In the fields, farmers with scythes were harvesting the meager winter barley.

Simon buttoned his vest and trudged along the narrow path, still muddy from last night's rain, that led from the forest to the village. So far, the year had been much too cold; there had been frost as late as May. In the last few weeks, a number of storms brought torrential rain and hail across the Alpine foothills, flattening what little grain remained. Men prayed to God for drier weather in the coming months. Only those whose granaries were filled could expect to survive the coming winter.

The path passed behind a barn by the edge of town and then ascended steeply to the monastery. Behind a low wall was a huge complex of all kinds of buildings. On the right, some granaries were surrounded by apple and plum trees, while on the other side of the wide, muddy street were some low wooden houses with thick white smoke billowing out of their chimneys. In an open shed nearby, a blacksmith hammered loudly on an anvil. Beyond that were a low-lying bakery that smelled of fresh bread, a whitewashed tavern, and a large, multistoried stone building—until finally the walls of the inner monastery appeared: a labyrinth of nooks and crannies with the church towering up in the center.

Simon noticed groups of simply clad pilgrims holding walking staffs, dressed in black habits and singing and praying as they approached the monastery. It appeared they either wanted to pay an early visit to the monastery or were just hoping for a free breakfast. Other Brothers were working with dirt-stained hands in the surrounding vegetable gardens or pushing carts loaded with barrels through the narrow entrance of the monastery. Simon stopped one of them and asked for Brother Johannes.

"The apothecary?" The man grinned. "If I know the ugly bugger, he's lying in bed snoring loudly. He didn't show up for morning prayers. Well, he'll hear from the abbot about that. But you can try your luck." He pointed to a tiny, nondescript house down by the storage buildings. "But you better knock loudly, or he'll sleep till noon prayers."

Moments later Simon stood at the apothecary's house below the monastery. It was a low-lying building with narrow windows and a thick oaken door. He was about to knock when he heard voices inside. Though the sound was muffled, it was clear that two men were having a heated argument. Simon waited in front of the house, uncertain about what to do as the voices approached along with the sound of footsteps.

The next moment, the door flew open and a lanky, black-robed Benedictine stomped out. Red-faced and furious, he clutched a walking stick decorated with ivory, waving it around wildly. Simon noticed that the monk's cape concealed a small hunchback and that he was dragging one leg. The angry, pitiful cripple hobbled off and had soon disappeared amid the apple trees.

Simon was so intrigued by what he saw that he didn't notice in time that someone had crept up on him from behind. When he turned around, he found himself looking directly into the ugly countenance of the apothecary.

"What is it?" growled Brother Johannes, standing in the doorway with a suspicious look on his face. The monk seemed anxious and harried, and his swollen face was as white as soft moonlight. Clearly he'd also been troubled by the argument. Finally a look of recognition appeared in his face.

"For the love of Mary!" he cried in surprise. "Aren't you one of the lost people from Schongau last night? Listen, if you wanted to express your thanks, this is a bad time. I suggest you come—"

"My wife is ill, and I urgently need some anise and silverweed," Simon interrupted calmly. "And a few other herbs. Can you help me?"

For a moment the monk appeared about to turn away the uninvited guest, but then changed his mind. "Why not?" he grumbled. "In any case, I've got to inform the abbot at once. Then the gossiping can begin."

"What gossiping?" Simon asked. "About the argument you just had with your colleague? I didn't really hear anything, it's just that . . ."

But Brother Johannes had already disappeared in the darkness of the apothecary's house. With a shrug, Simon followed, entering a low-ceilinged room illuminated by a half dozen tallow candles. A narrow shaft of light fell through the shutters onto a huge cupboard on the opposite wall, which contained innumerable little drawers all identified by tiny hand-painted parchment labels. There was a bewitching odor of herbs — sage, rosemary, marigold, and chamomile. But he thought he detected a sweet scent, too, that briefly made him feel sick. It smelled almost like . . .

"Tell me again. What did you say you needed for your wife?" Brother Johannes asked abruptly. "Silverweed?"

"Yes, and anise," said the medicus, turning again toward the ugly monk. "She has stomach pains and feels sick all over. I hope it's nothing serious."

"God forbid. Now, let me see . . ." Brother Johannes set an eyepiece to his right eye, making his already frightening face just a bit more so. Then he walked over to the cupboard, paused a moment to think, and finally opened a drawer at eye-level. In the meantime he seemed to have forgotten his quarrel with the little monk. "Silverweed is really an excellent medicine for stomachache," he mumbled, taking out a bundle of herbs, "though I actually prefer liver compresses and a mixture of gentian, centaury, and wormwood. Do you know the doses to use with the herbs? Always remember: *dosis facit —*"

"*Venenum.* The dose makes the poison. I know." Simon nodded and stretched out his hand in a greeting. "Excuse me if I haven't introduced myself yet. My name is Simon Fronwieser. I am the bathhouse surgeon from the little town of Schongau on the other side of the Hoher Peißenberg. I lecture my patients almost every day with Paracelsus's words about the correct dosage."

"A bathhouse surgeon who speaks Latin?" Brother Johannes smiled and shook Simon's hand cordially. The monk's grip was firm, as if he'd been swinging a hammer on the anvil all his life.

With the ocular in his eye, he looked like a misshapen cyclops. "That's rather unusual. Then are you familiar with the *Macer Floridus* in which the eighty-five healing plants are listed?"

"Indeed." Simon nodded and crammed the dried herbs into his leather bag. "I studied medicine in Ingolstadt. Unfortunately, I was unable to find a position as doctor. The . . . circumstances were not favorable." He hesitated. The monk didn't have to know he'd gone broke because of his gambling debts and the money he spent on fancy clothes.

The medicus cast an approving glance around the dimly lit room. Everything here was exactly the way he wished his own office to be. The large pharmacy cupboard, heavy wooden shelves along the walls lined with pots and tinctures. A low entryway led into another room that evidently served as a laboratory. In the dim light, Simon could make out a stove with a few pieces of wood glowing inside and on the mantelpiece, some sooty flasks. In front of this, a huge marble table supported something long and misshapen, partially covered with a dirty linen cloth.

At one end of the cloth a single pale foot protruded.

"My God!" Simon gasped. "Is that—"

"My assistant, Coelestin," the Brother sighed, rubbing the sweat from his forehead. "Some farmers brought him to me shortly before sunrise today. Last night, the unfortunate fellow went to catch a carp for me in the pond down by the woods. And what does the dolt do? He falls off the walkway and drowns like a little cat. And then this charlatan Virgilius comes by and . . ." He broke off, shaking his head as if trying to shake off a bad dream.

Carefully Simon stepped into the laboratory and sniffed. Now he could explain the sweet odor he'd noticed yesterday.

The body was starting to decompose.

"May I?" the medicus asked hesitantly, pointing at the corpse beneath the shroud. Simon had always had a strange fascination with dead people. Stiff and lifeless, they were like anatomical dolls God gave the world to demonstrate the miracle of the human body.

"Go right ahead," Johannes replied, finally removing his eyepiece and securing it in his robe. "Since you are evidently a sort of colleague, a second look certainly can't harm. But there's really nothing unusual about him. I can't tell you how many drowned corpses I've seen in my life." He sighed and crossed himself. "Man is not a fish, or God would have given him gills for breathing and fins to paddle."

Curious, Simon pulled back the wet cloth and stared into the white, slightly blue face of the young Coelestin. Some compassionate villager had closed his eyes and put two rusty kreutzers on them, but his mouth was wide open like that of a carp gasping for air. Leaves and pieces of algae stuck to the thinning hair of the monk's tonsure, and green blowflies buzzed around the putrid corpse. The dead novitiate's robe hung on his body like a wet sack.

"I wanted to be alone with him a little longer," Brother Johannes said hoarsely. "He was, after all, my loyal assistant for more than two years, and we lived through many things together, beautiful and some ugly . . ." He swallowed. "But now I shall have to go up and see the abbot, so please take your herbs and—"

"There are spots there."

"What?" Annoyed, Brother Johannes turned to the medicus, who was pointing at a spot on the dead man's collarbone.

"Look, black-and-blue spots here, both on the left and right shoulders." Simon ripped open the wet robe. "And here on the breastbone as well."

"He probably got those when he fell into the water," the monk retorted. "What does that tell you?"

"Bruises on someone who fell into unresisting water?" Simon frowned. "I don't know." He began studying the body until he finally found what he was looking for on the back of Coelestin's head.

"It's just as I thought," he murmured. "A big bump. Someone clearly dealt your assistant a heavy blow, then held him under water until he drowned."

"Murder?" the Brother gasped. "Do you really think so?"

Simon shrugged. "Murder or manslaughter I can't say, but in any case there was a second person involved. Perhaps a tavern brawl? A robbery that turned to murder?"

"Nonsense. A monk doesn't get involved in brawls. Besides, why would . . ." Johannes hesitated and shook his huge head like a stubborn ox. "Of course there are still riffraff in the area. But the good Coelestin was nothing more than a simple novitiate in a thin robe! He had no money, nothing of value on him." The fat monk raised his finger and his voice took on a singsong character. "Saint Benedict put it so nicely in one of his rules. No one may own a thing. No book or writing table or writing implement — nothing. So who could have wanted to harm Coelestin?"

"Didn't he have any enemies down in town or here in the monastery?" Simon inquired.

Brother Johannes laughed so loudly his round belly bounced up and down. "Enemies? Good Lord, we are monks. We watch our tongue, we don't steal, and if heaven permits, we don't run after women, either. So why are you asking?" Suddenly his eyes narrowed to little slits. "But let me tell you something, barber surgeon. If you're so sure of yourself, then come along to see the abbot and tell him. Brother Maurus is an intelligent, well-read man. Let him decide how Coelestin met his end." Grimly he stomped out the door. "If the abbot agrees, you can use my apothecary as if it was your own," he grumbled. "You have my word on that. And now, let's go before my novitiate is completely eaten up by these damn blowflies."

Mumbling a curse, Simon ran after him. This is what he got

for talking too much. All he really wanted to do was to get back to Magdalena as fast as possible.

As the medicus turned around one last time, one of the blow-flies, buzzing noisily, flew right into Coelestin's mouth. It sounded like the corpse was softly mumbling to himself.

Magdalena was sitting on the bench in front of the knacker's house, getting angrier by the minute as she waited for Simon to return from the apothecary. He had been gone over an hour now! What could be taking him so long? He probably got involved in a long conversation with that ugly monk about mandrake root or daphne and had completely forgotten her.

Impatiently she watched Michael Graetz as he struggled to hoist a stinking horse cadaver onto his cart. Despite the arduous work, the knacker hummed a soldier's marching song and seemed completely happy with himself and the world. Beside him, a stocky young man pulled the dead nag onto the flatbed. Magdalena had learned from Graetz that this was his assistant, Matthias.

The hangman's daughter couldn't help but think of her father at home, whose job it also was to cart away dead animals. Looking at her cousin clothed in rags, Magdalena swore once more that her children would someday be better off. Peter and Paul wouldn't be dishonorable executioners, knackers, or torturers but doctors or bathhouse surgeons like their father.

The dry horse manure made her sneeze suddenly, and Michael looked at her with concern. "May Saint Blasius protect you from the fever," he mumbled.

"Nonsense!" Magdalena hissed, blowing her nose loudly on a rag she extracted from her skirt pocket. "I just had to sneeze, that's all. So stop acting as if I had the Plague."

The knacker's stocky helper grinned at her and made some inarticulate noise that sounded to Magdalena like a laugh.

"What is it?" she growled. "Is there something funny about

me? Is snot running out of my nose? Answer me, you scoundrel."

"Matthias can't answer you," Michael replied. "He doesn't have a tongue anymore."

"What?"

The knacker shrugged and looked sympathetically at the strong young man, who now was completely involved in his work. "Croatian mercenaries cut out his tongue while he was still a young lad," Michael said in a low voice. "They were trying to force his father, the innkeeper in Frieding, to tell them where he'd hidden his savings." The knacker sighed. "But the poor fellow really didn't have anything. Finally they took him away and strung him up on the gallows hill in Erling, and the boy had to watch."

Magdalena stared at the strapping assistant in horror. "Oh, Lord, I'm so sorry. I had no idea . . ."

"Don't fret. He's no doubt already forgiven you. Matthias is a good fellow, a bit shy around people, but we deal more with dead animals, in any case."

Michael laughed, and his assistant joined in with a dry coughing fit, casting a mischievous grin at Magdalena. He had a handsome face, a full head of sandy hair, and under his black smock, strong, bulging arm muscles like those of a blacksmith's assistant.

If they hadn't cut your tongue out, you would certainly be the cock of the walk, Magdalena couldn't help thinking. *I wish men would hold their tongues more often.*

"No offense," she said, standing up. "I think I'll stretch my legs a bit. Simon isn't coming back." With a last nod to the mute assistant, she started down the path toward the village just as the bells began to ring.

"Where are you going?" Michael called after her as the bells continued to ring. "Your husband said—"

"My husband doesn't tell me what to do," Magdalena

shouted. "If I were really sick, he wouldn't have taken off and be spending so much time chitchatting with the apothecary. Now attend to your dead horse and leave the living alone."

She hurried off toward the monastery that was teeming now, in the late morning, with throngs of pilgrims and workmen. The walk in the fresh air made her feel noticeably better. The odor in the knacker's house had reminded her too much of her own home in Schongau, the nasty looks and whispers of her fellow townspeople, and the feeling of being an outcast—your whole life.

Without realizing it, Magdalena had climbed the hill and was standing now on the wide square directly in front of the church. From here it was easy to see the damage the lightning strike had caused. The roof of the belfry had burned almost entirely, and there was a huge hole in the ceiling in the front of the side aisle. Masons in overalls covered with plaster, as well as sturdy-looking carpenters and day laborers, ran about everywhere hauling stone, erecting new walls, and applying plaster to the parts already finished. At the edge of the building site, Magdalena found the carpenter Balthasar Hemerle from Altenstadt involved in a deep discussion with the patrician Jakob Schreevogl.

Noticing the hangman's daughter, the Schongau alderman beckoned to her. "You look pale," Schreevogl said, concerned. "Are you well?"

"Thanks," Magdalena replied coolly. "I already have a husband and a cousin who are watching me like a hawk. That's enough." She pointed to the church belfry, which was covered with scaffolding. "It's hard to believe the damage lightning can cause," she said, shaking her head. "It doesn't look like the church will really be finished in time for the Festival of the Three Hosts."

"We're on a really tight schedule," Hemerle grumbled. "Only seven days left, just time enough to repair the worst damage." He pointed to the alderman at his side. "Master Schreevogl assured us, though, that he can deliver the new stone from his brickworks in Schongau by tomorrow."

Magdalena looked the young patrician up and down. "Then at least the lightning is good business for you, isn't it, Master Schreevogl?"

"Don't worry about that, I'm giving you a special discount," he assured them. "In Augsburg or in Landsberg I'd get a lot more. If someone has a good deal here, it's our dear burgomaster." He winked slyly and lowered his voice. "Karl Semer sold thirty barrels of Bolzano wine to the Andechs Monastery tavern, as well as wax for pilgrim candles, pickled fish from the North Sea, and petitions he had printed cheaply and wants to palm off on the pilgrims. For the Schongau mayor, the Festival of the Three Hosts is better than any Easter mass."

Magdalena whistled through her teeth. "I had no idea. I wondered what the old moneybags was doing on a pilgrimage. He insisted on our getting to the Holy Mountain last night in the middle of the thunderstorm."

"Because he was afraid the merchants from Munich and Augsburg would get there first." Schreevogl grinned. "At present that pious pilgrim is down at the tavern negotiating with the monastery's business manager. And one of the Wittelsbachers is supposedly interested in what Semer has to sell. I just have to wonder what the elector's family intends to do with all this stuff."

The hangman's daughter nodded. Mention of the previous night had awakened memories of the strange light flickering in the belfry. She shielded her eyes and looked up. "Is there any construction being done up there?" she asked curiously.

"In the belfry?" Hemerle shook his head. "The framework is complete, but we're working our way up from the bottom. There's still quite a bit of work to do up there where the lightning hit the tower. All that remains are charred beams and rubble. It's a miracle that none of the bells has come down."

Suddenly Magdalena remembered how unfriendly Brother Johannes had been the night before when she asked whether there was someone up in the belfry with a torch. What had the monk said? *Why would anyone be up there at this time of night? To enjoy the view?*

Magdalena stared up at the belfry ruins again. Even as a child, she never liked it when someone tried to hide something from her. And something deep inside warned her that Brother Johannes was not telling the whole truth. Suddenly feeling dizzy, she placed her hand on the patrician's shoulder.

"You really should lie down for a while," Schreevogl told her. "My wife, God bless her soul, had the same dark rings around her eyes at the end."

"For heaven's sake," she said angrily, "is there anyone here who thinks I'm still alive? Goodbye, gentlemen. And if one of you sees my dear husband, that good-for-nothing bathhouse surgeon, tell him he can drink his potion himself. I'm going inside now to pray."

Leaving the dazed men standing there, she walked quickly toward the monastery church. Though she was not as pious as many others in Schongau, she had nevertheless come to Andechs with the firm intention of thanking God for the preceding good years. So why not start with a prayer, especially since she felt so miserable now? Perhaps there was something after all to Simon's worries.

She passed along the south side of the church, where the fire had caused the most damage. The foundation had collapsed and was covered with soot, and sun was falling through the narrow slits in the makeshift canvas beneath the hole in the roof. Magdalena took a deep breath and entered the old Gothic building where monks had more or less put things back in place. Now, after morning mass, only a few people were inside. On the right was the high altar with two golden statues of Mary, and in the nave four smaller altars. Narrow passageways led into dark side chapels lit only by flickering candlelight. Halfway up the wall was a gallery where a half dozen plasterers were busy cleaning dirt and soot from the frescoes or replacing the burned-out gothic windows. None of the workers seemed to have noticed Magdalena yet, so she sat down in one of the back pews, closed her eyes, and prayed. She soon realized, however, that she was having trouble concentrating. Her thoughts kept turning to her husband's disappearance; Michael, her lice-ridden cousin; the storm the night before; and the light in the blackened belfry. Especially the light.

Opening her eyes, she looked around and discovered a winding staircase leading up to the balcony and from there farther up. Perhaps up into the tower?

Just a few minutes, she thought. *If I don't find the entrance to the tower after a few minutes, I'll come back and keep praying — I promise, Dear Lord.*

Magdalena left the pew on tiptoe and climbed up to the balcony. In fact, there was a low entrance there and, behind that, a newly constructed staircase leading up. The old wooden stairway had been almost completely destroyed by fire. In some places the remains of the old, worn steps were visible, but for the most part all that remained were charred stubs over the void below. Magdalena crossed herself and started up the creaking frame.

After just a few steps, she was all alone. She could hear hammering and shouting down below, but the higher she climbed the more the sounds faded. Through the empty, charred window openings that appeared at regular intervals, Magdalena could look out into the green valley of the Kien, the beech forests around the monastery, and the construction site far below. The workers looked like ants crawling around the building site, pushing tiny stones.

The makeshift staircase creaked and swayed; there was no hand railing, and Magdalena could feel herself getting dizzy again. One step at a time she climbed higher and higher. Drops of sweat ran into her eyes and she silently cursed herself for climbing the burned-out, rickety tower. She was about to turn back when she saw a square opening in the ceiling just above her. She climbed through it and had finally made it into the belfry. A cool wind blew through the blackened window openings. The view was splendid.

Several times Magdalena had climbed to the top of the Hoher Peißenberg not far from Schongau, but here she felt just a little bit closer to heaven. Far out on the horizon, the snowcapped Alps served as a background to the Bavarian foothills, with their forests, moors, and lakes. On the west side of Lake Ammer, she could see the great tower of the Augustinian monastery in Dießen, and to the left of that, the Hoher Peißenberg, which blocked the view of her hometown just a few miles beyond. Here in the church steeple, everything seemed so close at hand as to make their two-day pilgrimage look like nothing more than a leisurely stroll.

Suddenly a gust of wind tugged at her hair, and she tightened her grip on a wooden beam to keep from falling. When she had regained her balance, she turned around to get a look at the interior of the destroyed tower room.

The walls were blackened and had burst in places from the heat, but beyond the empty window frames she could see only blue sky. In the middle of the belfry, three bells that had survived the flames hung in an iron-reinforced wooden frame. The floor around it had mostly burned away, so Magdalena could see through the beams into the yawning abyss below. A new rope dangled down from the bell cage.

It occurred to Magdalena now that she'd heard the bells early that morning. Could it have been just the bell ringer checking things last night? She frowned. What in the world could he have been doing up here in the pitch black?

Magdalena decided to climb over the balcony to the bells to

get a better view of the room, taking care not to look down any more than absolutely necessary. As long as she put one foot in front of the other and kept looking straight ahead, she felt more or less secure.

Finally she reached the huge bronze bells and placed her arms around the smallest one, feeling the cool metal in her hands and breathing a sigh of relief. Her dizziness was completely gone now. It was as if the exertion had renewed her strength and cured her. As she stood up carefully to look to the other side of the room behind the bells, she spotted something strange.

Against the opposite wall, a sort of stretcher lined with metal clamps along the side leaned upended against the wall. On the ground in front of it lay some polished iron rods. Something squeaked, and looking up she saw on the ceiling directly above the stretcher a wire about the thickness of a finger, swaying in the wind like a hangman's noose.

As she approached the strange contraption, she heard a sound on her right and wheeled around.

A black form ran toward her, like a human bat that had been sleeping in the tower rafters and was now swooping down on the unexpected visitor. The figure wore a black robe and a cowl, so Magdalena couldn't see his face.

In the next instant he attacked.

Magdalena staggered, her hands lost their grip on the smooth metal bell, and she lost her balance. As she fell through an opening between the beams, something sharp scraped against her thigh. At the last moment she reached out and seized a wooden beam above her. The tendons in her wrists felt like they were going to rip out, but she held on with all her strength. As she swung wildly back and forth, she looked down, heart pounding, into the abyss beneath her. For a moment, she thought she was going to pass out, but then she heard steps on the stairs beneath her, and the figure disguised in black robes appeared again, then raced down the stairs so fast it almost appeared he was about to fly away. A moment later, the man had disappeared into the church nave.

Magdalena swung back and forth like a thin branch in the wind, knowing her strength wouldn't last much longer. Tears of anger and despair ran down her face. With a last ounce of strength, she pulled herself up to see the bell rope hanging just two arm's lengths away.

Would she be able to reach it?

Inch by inch, she worked her way forward. At one point her left hand slipped and she was barely able to hold on. When finally she got close enough, she let out a gasp and leapt for the salvation of the rope. Grabbing it tightly, she tumbled one or two yards, then started to sway back and forth.

The church bells rang wildly.

Magdalena's ears rang, too; it seemed as loud as if she were being tossed around inside the heavy, hollow bell itself as it swayed back and forth, yanking her up and down. Slowly she slid down the rope to the bottom of the tower, where several surprised workers were already looking up wide-mouthed at her, Jakob Schreevogl and Balthasar Hemerle among them.

Magdalena could see they were both shouting and trying to tell her something, but all she could hear was the thundering bells—a constant and deafening booming, clanging, clanking, and rumbling.

As if the angels were announcing the Last Judgment.

The pealing bells could also be heard in the main building of the monastery, interrupting the Andechs abbot, Maurus Rambeck, for a moment. But the occasion was too serious to pause for long.

"So do you really think it was murder?" The abbot raised his right eyebrow and cast a short glance through the window, as if in this way he might determine the reason for the ringing bells.

Simon guessed that Rambeck was about fifty, but his shaved head and black Benedictine robe made him look considerably older. After what seemed like an eternity, the abbot turned back to his visitor. "What makes you say such a dreadful thing?"

"Well . . . ah, I found bruises on the novitiate's shoulder blades and chest, Your Eminence," Simon mumbled. "And a large bump on the back of his head. Feel free to examine the corpse yourself."

"You can be sure I'll do that."

Simon looked down, silently examining the many books on the shelves all around them. Brother Johannes and he had met Maurus Rambeck in the so-called study on the second floor — a room meant exclusively for the abbot. He was sitting at a table, scrutinizing a tattered book full of strange signs that seemed vaguely familiar to Simon.

"If your theory is correct," Rambeck continued, "then it's a matter for the district court in Weilheim — something I'd like very much to spare us all. Are there any clues who the culprit might be?"

"Unfortunately not." Simon sighed. "But perhaps we should pay a visit to this fish pond, if you will permit me to say so."

"Perhaps we should do that, indeed."

The abbot ran his tongue over his plump lips, lost in thought. Maurus Rambeck was a chubby man with the jowls of an old lap dog. He radiated an easy-going nature; only his eyes revealed the quick mind behind his demeanor. As they walked toward the monastery living quarters, Johannes told Simon that the abbot had assumed his duties only a few months ago and was regarded as one of the smartest minds in Bavaria. He spoke eight languages fluently and could read twice that number. Like many educated men of his time, he had studied not only theology but philosophy, mathematics, and experimental physics at the Benedictine University in Salzburg. After serving in his youth as a simple monk in the monastery, he had been sent back to the university in Salzburg as a lecturer. His call back to Andechs had caused quite a stir in the monastery council.

"I think the whole thing is just imaginations running wild," Brother Johannes interrupted for the first time. "Believe me, Your Excellency, I've seen many corpses, and — "

"I know you've seen many corpses, my dear Brother," the abbot interrupted. "*Too* many, if you ask me . . ." he added ominously. "In addition, you've been involved with some troubling things, Brother Johannes. The rumors concerning the lightning strike and your gluttonous behavior during the time of fasting, to say nothing of the eternal arguments with Brother Virgilius. Is it true, as I have heard, that there were harsh words between the two of you just today?"

"How do you know . . ." Brother Johannes burst out. Then his shoulders sank, and he continued in a meek voice. "Very well, it's true. We argued, but it was a . . . scholarly dispute, technical really, and nothing serious."

"Scholarly?" The abbot grinned. "Remember your place, Brother. You are our apothecary, nothing more. Heal the sick and make sure that no more of your patients die. That's all I ask of you. Leave scholarly issues to the scholars." He turned back to Simon. "And now to you, bathhouse surgeon. You seem to understand something about human anatomy, perhaps even more than Brother Johannes. And why wouldn't you?" Maurus Rambeck rocked his head from side to side as if trying to decide what to do. Finally he nodded. "I'd be pleased if you'd write a short report about this incident. By tomorrow morning, let's say? Cause of death, wounds, and so forth, something for our files if we actually have to call upon the judge from the district court. And naturally we will pay you for that." He winked, and Simon thought he noticed a touch of mockery in his eyes. "And of course you should also pay a visit to this mysterious pond," he continued. "Or whatever you wish to do — it's up to you. After that, I'll decide how to proceed. And now, I wish you a good day." Maurus Rambeck pointed at the tattered book in front of him. "This Hebrew manuscript about healing herbs in ancient Egypt is most enlightening. I'd like to prepare a translation of it today. In peace and quiet." With a sigh, he looked out the window where the occasional pealing bells could still be heard. "And dear Brother Johannes, please find out why there's all that nerve-racking ringing out there. It sounds almost as if the Swedes were at our gates again."

"As you wish, Your Excellency," Brother Johannes mumbled. "I will check at once to see that everything's in order." He bowed and took leave of the abbot, but not without first casting an angry glance at Simon.

The medicus swallowed hard. It looked as though his notorious curiosity had gotten him into a heap of trouble again.

3

JAKOB KUISL CAUGHT THE MEN IN THE ZIMMER-stadl warehouse not far from the river.

They were about a dozen young punks, pimply, broad-shouldered, and practically bursting with strength and cockiness. The hangman recognized two or three carpenter's journeymen from Altenstadt and naturally the three Berchtholdt brothers. The oldest Berchtholdt boy was, as so often, the leader.

"Well, just look at that," growled Hans Berchtholdt. "The hangman's taking his little brats for a walk." He straightened up and puffed out his chest, pointing to the two children Kuisl was carrying in his huge arms. The boys were sucking sleepily on their thumbs, eyeing the angry young men as if hoping for some candy or a shiny toy.

"Leave my grandkids out of this," said Kuisl, glancing around furtively for a way to escape. But by now the youths had formed a circle around him.

The hangman had wanted to spend the morning with the children down at the river, whittling wooden boats and waterwheels. When he entered the narrow path behind the storage building, though, he noticed at once that one of the loading hatches was open. A few men were sitting there on top of stolen sacks of grain with devious expressions on their faces, while others were climbing down from the hatch on a ladder they'd nailed to the side of the building. Two lookouts approached him from the front and back, each with a glint in his eyes that reminded the hangman of hungry wolves. Apparently, Kuisl's last warning had had no effect. Berchtholdt and the others in the gang had broken into the warehouse again to steal grain.

"Just get out of here, and I won't have seen a thing," he grumbled. "I'm in a good mood today, and this time I'll let you go."

But a short look at Hans Berchtholdt told Kuisl things wouldn't be so easy this time. The young man still had his hand with two broken fingers in a sling, and his lips quivered with anger and excitement.

"I'm afraid we can't let you off so easily," Berchtholdt snarled. "It was a really stupid idea of yours to come by at this moment. Who's to say you won't report us to the council?"

"You have my word."

"The word of a hangman? To hell with that."

Laughter broke out, and the baker looked around confidently at his companions.

"So whaddya want? Maybe a sack of grain from the warehouse for your little brats, Kuisl?" Berchtholdt sneered, pointing at the grandchildren. "So maybe someday they'll become fat, filthy executioners just like their grandfather?"

"You mean so they can one day string up thieves and hoodlums like you and watch them dangle on gallows hill?" Kuisl replied calmly. "This is the second time I've caught you stealing, Berchtholdt. That's a hanging offense. Go home, all of you, or there's going to be big trouble. If the secretary learns of this, he'll make short work of you."

Hans Berchtholdt bit his lip. This wasn't the answer he expected. Clearly, this old goat was being insolent.

"And who would testify against us, eh?" he growled. "Maybe you, hangman?" His laughter sounded like a bleating goat. "A dishonorable man testifying before the city council? Do you really think the secretary would believe you? Or the whining, babbling little brats?" Again he started bleating as the other men joined in. "Where is their lousy mother, huh?" he continued in a hoarse voice. "She and that quack doctor. Shouldn't they be minding their brats themselves so that nothing happens to them? Where are they?"

"You know exactly where they are," Kuisl murmured. "So now let me through, and—"

"The whole city was against a dishonorable person going on a pilgrimage," screeched the second oldest of the Berchtholdts. At nineteen, he was bigger than most of the others and his angry red face shot forward like that of a snake. "A hangman's daughter on a pilgrimage with honorable citizens to the Holy Mountain. That's unheard of! Now look what the Lord God sent us as punishment: rain and hail and destroyed fields. And mice that eat up our seed corn."

"That doesn't give you any right to break into the warehouse and steal the grain."

"The grain belonging to those rich moneybags in Augsburg? The devil take them all. By all the fourteen saints, we're only taking what belongs to us anyway."

Kuisl sighed softly. Josef Berchtholdt had learned such narrow-mindedness from his late father. It was true that in recent days bad storms had swept over Schongau and mice had become a real plague. The vermin had practically stripped bare many of the fields. The hangman had warned his daughter about going on a pilgrimage with the other citizens—he knew it would be the subject of gossip. But as so often, she didn't want to listen. Now Kuisl was standing down here on the Lech with his grandsons, facing a mob that would have liked nothing better than to start a fight.

"Where is your hangman's sword, Kuisl?" one of the boys taunted. "Did you forget and leave it at home? Or are you going to carve yourself one here?" Again this was followed by loud, gloating laughter. Mumbling and hissing, the mob moved toward the hangman, who stood with his back to the warehouse.

"I would never have thought you'd get involved with a group like this, Berchtholdt," Kuisl growled. "Your father would turn over in his grave."

"Shut up, hangman," the baker's son shouted. "If my father were still alive he'd whip the whole Kuisl gang and drive them out of town."

"I'm the one here who whips people and drives them out of town, Berchtholdt. Don't forget that."

The hangman tried to size up the group of young men blocking his path. Kuisl was fifty-four now, no longer a spring chicken, but people still feared his anger and strength. They'd seen how he broke the bones of a bandit chief, one by one, and how he cut off the heads of condemned murderers with a single blow. Kuisl had a bloody reputation all over the region; nevertheless he could sense that his authority was beginning to crumble. Today loud words or a quick blow would no longer suffice to drive away this mob.

Especially not with two babbling, thumb-sucking kids on his arm.

"Let me tell you, Kuisl," Hans Berchtholdt hissed as a mean smile spread across his lips. "You bow your head and ask humbly for forgiveness for your daughter, that good-for-nothing hangman's girl, and we'll let the three of you go."

As raucous laughter broke out, little Peter began to cry, and it wasn't long before his younger brother joined in. Kuisl closed his eyes and tried to breathe calmly. They wanted to anger him, but he couldn't endanger the children. What could he do? He didn't want to risk a brawl because of his grandsons. Should he call for help? It was a long way up to town, and the rushing water

would no doubt drown out any sound. Should he accept Berchtholdt's demand?

Remorsefully, Kuisl bowed his head. "I plead—" he began
softly.

Hans Berchtholdt grinned, his eyes glistening like two pieces
of ice. "Humbly," he snarled. "You plead *humbly.*"

"I plead humbly," the hangman continued. He paused, then
he continued in a monotone: "I plead humbly that God will give
me the strength to endure such a big mob of stupid, blockheaded,
low-down bastards like this without bashing their heads in. Now
for the sake of the Holy Virgin let me through before I smash the
nose of the first one of you."

A horrified silence ensued. It seemed the young journeymen
couldn't believe what they'd just heard. Finally Hans Berchtholdt got control of himself again. "You'll . . . you'll regret that,"
he said softly. "There are a dozen of us, and you're an old man
with two children in his arms. Now the little bastards will learn
how their grandfather can put up with—"

He stopped suddenly, screamed, and put his hand to his forehead where blood was pouring out. Now other boys were howling and wailing as they sought refuge behind carts and barrels
while a hail of stones fell down on them. Kuisl looked around,
puzzled. Finally, up on the roof of the warehouse he spied a
crowd of children and young people tossing stones and clumps of
dirt down on the gang.

At the crest of the ridge up front stood Kuisl's thirteen-year-
old son, Georg, with a slingshot in hand.

The hangman was shocked. What was that snotty little brat
doing down here? Wasn't he supposed to be cleaning the knacker's wagon in the barn? Wasn't it enough for the two grandchildren to be in danger?

Kuisl was about to give the boy a good tongue-lashing when
he realized the possibility that his son might just have saved his

life. Again he looked up at the roof. Georg Kuisl looked very big for his age; everything about him seemed to have been hewn out of solid rock. A little fuzz was starting to form around his lips and his shirt and trousers looked much too small for his hefty body.

Just like me once, Kuisl thought. *He's almost as old as I was then in the war. My God, now my own boy has to get me out of this jam. Jakob, you're getting old . . .*

"Run, Father," Georg shouted. "Now!"

Jakob shook off his gloomy thoughts, clasped his grandchildren, and ran off. All around him the stones were still raining down. When he saw a shadowy form lunge at him, he picked up his foot and kicked his attacker, a young carpenter's journeyman, with full force in the groin. The man collapsed, groaning, just as another attacker raced toward Kuisl. The two young children in his arms were screaming now like stuck pigs. Kuisl hugged them tightly, bent down, and butted the journeyman right in the stomach; then he stood up again and ran. Behind him Hans Berchtholdt shouted as he was struck by another stone. "You'll pay for that, Kuisl," Berchtholdt shouted furiously. "You and your whole clan! Just one word to the city council, and I'll take care of your two snotty little brats."

In just a few minutes the hangman had left the dock area and arrived at the Lech Bridge, where two unsuspecting Schongau guards were standing, halberds in hand. They turned to watch the fast-approaching hangman; it appeared they had no idea of the fight going on behind the warehouse.

"My God, Kuisl," one of them cried. "You're running like the devil is on your heels."

"Not the devil, just the Berchtholdt gang," the hangman panted. "You'd better have a quick look at what's going on behind the warehouse, before the Augsburgers start asking where their wheat is."

Then and there, Kuisl decided not to let his grandchildren out of his sight again.

As Simon left the Andechs Monastery, he remembered with a start the herbs for Magdalena. He fumbled for the full leather pouch on his belt with the medicinal plants inside, then he hurried as fast as he could down to the village. He only hoped Magdalena hadn't notice how long he'd been away or he could no doubt expect trouble.

When he got to the knacker's house, he was surprised to find it empty. Only a few ragged goats were grazing in the little yard in front of the cabin, and the door stood wide open. Neither Michael Graetz, his helper, nor Magdalena was anywhere in sight.

"And I told her three times to lie down and rest," Simon muttered, perplexed. "Stubborn woman." Inwardly he prepared for a strong tongue-lashing.

After hesitating briefly, he decided to go back up to the monastery, where he might find Magdalena in the church or at the building site. Looking up, he saw a new group of pilgrims just arriving at the gate, where they were greeted by one of the monks and given a blessing. Singing and praying loudly, the pilgrims slowly made their way up to the monastery with their candles, where they no doubt planned to visit the church first. Because the Festival of the Three Hosts was only a week away, some people had already arrived and were crowding the narrow roadway.

To avoid them, Simon hurried along the wall until he found another open gate closer to the forest. Here, too, there were a number of barns — cows mooed, somewhere a pig grunted, and everywhere there was an odor of manure and beer mash. To the left of a well-worn path stood a neat little stone house that, with its freshly whitewashed walls and quaint garden of poppies and daisies, seemed out of character with the dirty farm buildings. Behind it, a steep stairway led up to the monastery.

Just as Simon was about to start up the stairs, a loud crash made him turn quickly and he saw a cloud of smoke emerge from behind one of the shutters of the stone house. Something must have exploded inside.

Without hesitating, the medicus ran toward the front door and pushed it open. Black sulfurous clouds billowed toward him, making it impossible to see.

"Is . . . is everything all right?" he called uncertainly.

He heard coughing, followed by a grating voice. "It's nothing to worry about," came the reply. "I probably used a pinch too much gunpowder, but as far as I can see, no harm is done."

When the smoke drifted out the door, what emerged was the strangest room Simon had ever seen. Along the sides were rough-hewn tables with all kinds of strange instruments piled on them. On the left, Simon saw a silver chest with a number of gear wheels turning inside it. Alongside it was the arm of a white porcelain doll, whose head at that moment was rolling across the table, bumping finally into a ticking pendulum clock decorated with tiny silver nymphs. The doll's face glared at Simon wryly; then its eyelids closed and it seemed to fall asleep. Dozens of strange metal parts lay on the tables farther back, their nature and purpose a mystery. Though it was broad daylight outside, the closed shutters allowed not a ray of sun into the room, which stank of sulfur and burned metal. Large parts of the room were still obscured by the smoke.

"Step right in," said a voice from the midst of the cloud. "There is nothing to be afraid of in this room, not even the stuffed crocodile hanging from the ceiling—a genuine rarity from the land of the pyramids, by the way."

The medicus looked up to see a wingless green dragon with a long tail hanging from a cord and turning slowly in a circle. The monster's glass eyes looked down at him indifferently.

"My God," Simon mumbled. "Where are we? At the entrance to hell?"

Someone laughed. "Rather to paradise. Science opens doors

undreamt of by those who don't close their eyes to them. Come a bit closer so I can see with whom I have the pleasure of speaking."

Simon groped his way forward in the dim light until he saw the outline of a person on his right. Glad to have finally found the strange owner of the house, he turned and reached out his hand.

"I must say, you gave me quite a shock ..." he started. But suddenly he stopped and his heart skipped a beat.

The figure in front of him was a woman. She was wearing a red ball gown, and had put up her blond hair in a bun as had been the fashion at court several hundred years before. Though she smiled at Simon with her full red lips, her face seemed lifeless and as white as a corpse. Suddenly her mouth opened wide and from somewhere inside her body came a soft, tinny melody.

It took Simon a while to realize what he heard was a glockenspiel. Tinkling and jingling, invisible hammers played the notes of an old love song.

"You ... you ... are ..." he stammered.

"An automaton, I know. I'm sorry I can't offer you the company of a real woman. On the other hand, Aurora will never turn into a cranky old shrew; she'll remain forever young and beautiful."

At this point a little man stepped out from behind the life-size doll. Startled, Simon realized this was the same crippled monk who'd been arguing with Brother Johannes just a few hours ago. Simon tried to remember the monk's name. The abbot had mentioned it in the abbot's study. "What was it? Brother ... ?"

"Brother Virgilius," the little hunchbacked man replied, reaching out one hand while supporting himself with the other on a walking stick decorated with ivory and a silver knob. A shy smile passed over his face. "Haven't we met before?"

"This morning in front of the apothecary's house," Simon

murmured. "I was there to pick up some herbs for my wife: anise, artemisia, and silverweed for stomach pains."

A shadow passed over the face of the wizened little man. He was probably over fifty, but everything about him seemed as delicate as a child. "I remember," he said in a monotone. "I hope Brother Johannes was able to help your wife. He's no doubt a good apothecary, just a bit ... short-tempered." Again a smile spread over his face. "But let's talk about something more pleasant. Do you speak Latin? Are you perhaps a friend of the sciences?"

Simon introduced himself in a few words, then pointed to the strange devices all around. "This room is the most fascinating place I've ever seen. What is your profession, if I may ask?"

"I'm a watchmaker," Brother Virgilius replied. "The monastery gives me the option of pursuing my profession and at the same time ... uh ... experimenting a bit." He winked at Simon. "A few moments ago you were the unintentional witness of a re-enactment of von Guericke's Magdeburg hemispheres experiment."

"Magdeburg hemispheres?" Simon looked at the little monk, puzzled. "I fear I don't quite understand."

Casually, Brother Virgilius pointed to a soot-stained copper globe the size of a child's head resting on a charred table behind him. "The fascinating power of a vacuum," he started to explain. "In an experiment carried out at the Reichstag in Regensburg, the inventor Otto von Guericke put two halves of a hemisphere together and pumped the air out, forming a vacuum. Sixteen horses weren't able to pull the hemispheres apart again. It's not even possible with the destructive force of gunpowder." He sighed. *"Quod erat demonstrandum.* My lily-livered assistant fled up to the attic before the explosion. Vitalis? *Viiitaaalis!"* The little monk pounded his cane impatiently on the floor until a shy young man appeared from an adjacent room. He was probably not even eighteen yet and so delicate in stature that Simon at first took him to be a girl.

"This is Vitalis, a novitiate at the monastery," Brother Virgilius introduced him brusquely. "He seldom says a word, but his fingers are so slender he can place even the smallest gear in a clock mechanism. Isn't that right, Vitalis?"

Shyly, with downcast eyes, the novitiate bowed. "I do my best," he whispered. "Is there something I can do, master?"

"If you weren't here to observe the experiment, then at least make yourself useful afterward," Virgilius growled. "I'm afraid we'll need a new table. Go and see if Brother Martin has another in his carpentry shop."

"Very well, master."

With a final bow, Vitalis left, and the monk turned again to Simon. "What do you think of my Aurora?" He pointed at the automaton. "Isn't she beautiful?"

Simon furtively eyed the doll still standing motionless beside him and smiling. Only now did he notice little wheels under the dress where feet should have been. "Indeed, a . . . a miracle of technology," he murmured, "even though I must confess I still prefer real people."

"Balderdash! Believe me, the day will come when we won't be able to distinguish between real people and automata." Brother Virgilius hobbled around the doll and turned a screw in Aurora's back, until the soft melody returned. The automaton opened its mouth and rolled through the room as if drawn by invisible threads. In the darkened room, it looked in fact like a refined lady dressed for a fancy ball in Paris.

"The glockenspiel, the mouth, and the wheels are driven by watch springs and cylinders," the monk declared proudly. "At present I'm working on making the hands moveable, as well, so Aurora can dance a bourrée. Who knows, maybe someday she'll be able to write letters and play the spinet."

"Who knows?" Simon whispered. The longer he looked at

the automaton, the more sinister it seemed. As if he were watching a vengeful spirit floating through the dark room.

"And the monastery?" he asked hesitantly. "What does the church say about your experiments?"

Brother Virgilius shrugged. "Abbot Maurus is an enlightened man who can easily distinguish between faith and science. Besides, the monastery benefits from my abilities." With a blissful smile he watched the doll make a wide circle through the room, bells tinkling. "But of course, there is also resistance."

"Brother Johannes, I assume?" asked Simon curiously.

"Brother Johannes?" The little monk turned away from his automaton and stared at Simon in disbelief.

"My apologies," replied the medicus, raising his hand, "I saw you both engaged in that violent dispute this morning."

After a moment, Virgilius's face brightened. "Of course. Johannes. You're right. As I've already said, he's an impulsive man who sometimes lacks the necessary vision. We've argued frequently in the past," he continued, lowering his eyes, "but this time I almost feared for my life. Johannes can be very hot-tempered, you know, which may have something to do with his past."

"What kind of past?" Simon inquired. At this moment the glockenspiel stopped. An ugly squeal came from inside the automaton, and Brother Virgilius rushed over to it.

"Curses," he hissed. "Probably a loose screw again in the clockwork. Can't you just for once run smoothly without breaking down, you stubborn woman?"

He undid the back of Aurora's red dress, revealing an iron plate. Mumbling softly to himself, he extracted a tiny screwdriver from beneath his robe and began to unscrew the plate on the doll's back. He seemed to have completely forgotten Simon in an instant.

"It . . . it was nice to have met you," Simon mumbled, smoothing his jacket with his hand. "I'll probably have to . . ."

"What?" Virgilius looked Simon up and down as if he were a stranger who'd just entered the room. "Oh, naturally. The pleasure was all mine, but now please excuse me; I have a lot to do. Damn!" Again he bent to inspect the automaton's back, and Simon turned to leave.

Stepping outside into the blinding bright sunlight, the medicus had to shield his eyes. He could still hear the mumbling watchmaker inside.

Moments later the soft melody of the glockenspiel began again.

Magdalena sipped on a cup of mulled wine and tried to come to grips with the terror of the last hour. Still trembling slightly, she leaned back on the hard corner bench and from there observed everything going on in the monastery tavern, which she'd entered on a whim.

At the noon hour, the inn at the foot of the Holy Mountain was packed: A few richly clad merchants had ordered a boar's leg with white bread, and its fatty juice dribbled down their beards and chins. A group of pious pilgrims sat together in one corner over a steaming bowl of stew. Smoke from tobacco and a wood fire hung heavily over the tables, and the air was full of the humming and buzzing of many conversations.

After her fall from the tower, Magdalena had to first answer worried questions from Jakob Schreevogl, the carpenter Hemerle, and a few other workers. The unexpected ringing of the bells had upset everyone on the building site, among them Brother Johannes, who eyed the hangman's daughter distrustfully. For that reason, she told the astonished men she had just climbed the tower out of curiosity and had slipped. She still didn't know whether the ugly monk had anything to do with the incident in the tower. Was it possible Johannes himself was the hooded stranger who had pushed her off the belfry?

As she came staggering down the hill from the monastery,

Magdalena saw a sign over the tavern door painted invitingly with a wine glass and entered without hesitation. Just as she was about to pour herself another cup of wine, she spied Simon in the doorway. The medicus looked around until he spotted Magdalena in the crowd.

"So this is where you're hiding out," he cried with relief when he reached her table. "I've looked for you everywhere. Weren't you going to wait at the knacker's house until I came back with the herbs?"

"Aha, and when was that going to be?" she replied angrily. "When pigs fly? I waited, but you never came back." She pointed to the pitcher of mulled wine on the table. "In any case, this medicine does more good than all the marjoram, vervain, and mint in the Priests' Corner put together. They put so many herbs in the wine here that you get better just smelling it. Now sit down and listen to what happened to me."

She briefly told him of the bizarre things she saw up in the tower and the stranger who had pushed her off the platform.

"A stretcher with metal clamps along the side and a thick wire?" Simon replied. "What in God's name could that be?"

"I have no idea. In any case, nothing that anyone's supposed to find out about — or this fellow in the robe wouldn't have tried to throw me from the belfry."

"How do you know he really wanted to throw you from the belfry?" Simon asked. "Maybe you just startled him up there, and he was trying to flee."

"Are you telling me I just imagined all that?"

Simon raised his hands apologetically. "I just don't want us to jump to any false conclusions, that's all."

Magdalena lowered her voice and looked around furtively. "If you ask me, that ugly monk Johannes has something to do with it. Do you remember the strange look he gave us yesterday when I told him about the light up in the tower? And do you remember the large sack he was carrying?"

Simon frowned. "Yes, why?"

"There were iron rods inside just like the ones I saw up in the tower, only a bit smaller."

"That's right." The medicus tapped the table nervously. "There's something fishy about that monk, but he can't have been the man in the tower. Johannes was with me and the abbot at that time."

"You went to see the abbot?"

Simon sighed. "You're not the only one who saw some strange things. If we keep going like this we'll get involved in another messy story and your father will give me a talking-to for not keeping a better eye on you. In any case, by tomorrow the bishop wants a report from me about a possible murder."

Excitedly he told Magdalena of his experiences in the apothecary's house, the abbot's study, and the house of the strange watchmaker. After he finished, the hangman's daughter just sat there silently for a long time, then picked up the clay pitcher and poured herself another cup of wine.

"An automaton that's a woman and has a glockenspiel instead of a heart." She shuddered. "You're right—this watchmaker Virgilius is really a strange character. An atrocious idea that one can make a doll come to life."

"It's not really so strange," replied Simon. "I've heard that in Paris and Rotterdam there are a lot of automata like that—singing birds, life-size drummer boys, tiny black men who strike the bells . . . In the Hanseatic City of Bremen, they say there's even an iron watchman who raises his visor to the merchants and salutes."

"Just the same, I prefer real people." Magdalena suddenly frowned and nodded toward the door. "Well, in most cases."

At that moment, the Schongau burgomaster Karl Semer and his son strode into the tavern with haughty looks on their faces. At their side was a gentleman with a Van Dyke beard wearing a white collar, a huge, wide-brimmed hat, and an ornamental

sword on his belt. Coldly he eyed the guests as if they were annoying insects. When he snapped his finger, the innkeeper approached, bowing deeply.

"Oh, God, the Semers," Simon groaned. "We're not being
spared anything today. It looks as if they've found a friend."

In the meantime, the innkeeper had approached the new
guests. "Ah, Count von Wartenberg," he murmured, bowing
so deeply it looked as if he was about to polish his guest's shoes.
"What an honor to be able to greet a representative of the
House of Wittelsbach in my modest tavern. It's been a long time
since — "

With an impatient wave of his hand, the man with the Van
Dyke silenced the stout innkeeper. "Stop buttering me up and
get me a private room," he growled. "I have something important to discuss with these two gentlemen."

"As you wish, as you wish." Bowing deeply again, the innkeeper led the count and the two Semers into a separate area of
the tavern. As young Sebastian Semer strode past Magdalena
and Simon, he gave them a fleeting, disgusted glance.

"Look, Father," he whined. "Even lowlife bathhouse surgeons and hangman's women patronize the Andechs tavern
nowadays. The Holy Mountain is not what it used to be."

Karl Semer looked down at the two Schongauers and
frowned. "I don't think the tavern keeper knows everyone pa-
tronizing his establishment, my son. In *my* tavern something like
that wouldn't happen. Dishonorable people have no place there."
Impatiently he took his son by the shoulder. "But come now, we
have more important things to do. I hear they serve an exquisite,
though expensive Tokay here — just the right thing for concluding our business."

The two disappeared into the side room with the distinguished gentleman. Simon looked over at Magdalena, who had
turned white as chalk and was biting her lip.

"This pompous Semer clan," she hissed. "Jakob Schreevogl

told me the two plan to make a killing here during the Festival of the Three Hosts. The very sight of them makes me sick."

"Don't always get so worked up." Simon passed his hand through her hair sympathetically. "In any case, there's nothing you can do to change it. I'd just like to know what the Semers have to do with a genuine nobleman from the House of Wittelsbach. If it's true they have really arrived — anyone doing business with the family of the Bavarian elector is very well-off."

Magdalena blew her nose loudly and took a last deep gulp of wine. "I expect they'll palm some cheap pilgrim's candles and prayer books off on the count, which the fine gentleman will dispose of for even more money," she murmured. She stood up, stretched, and tossed a few coins on the table. "And now, let's go. The Semers have spoiled this tavern for me, and you still have your damned report to write, too." She sighed and turned toward the door. "Damn, all I really wanted to do in Andechs was pray."

Outside, in a dark corner of the monastery garden, a figure in a black robe crouched down, observing the couple from Schongau with suspicion as they strolled down the steep pathway toward Erling. The man uttered a curse just as he had learned to do in the war. Even though God forbade it, it always made him feel better and helped to drive away the bloody scenes. Nevertheless, he remained anxious.

Ever since this bathhouse surgeon and his girl had appeared, things had been going badly. First the failed experiment, then the dead assistant and the argument with Virgilius — and what, for God's sake, was the curious woman up to in the tower? Had she become suspicious? Had she discovered something up there?

The man smiled and waved casually as a few singing pilgrims passed by, but the pilgrims drew away from him as if they could sense that nothing good would come from him. He was accustomed to people reacting fearfully when they saw him. Striking fear in the hearts of men used to be his calling, but now his face did the work. The contorted grimace of the devil in the garb of a monk. That's what they said about him when he took the vows many years ago and cast aside his old life. But he could not cast away his face.

Or his past.

Grumbling furiously to himself like a fat blowfly, Brother Johannes reentered the apothecary's house, where worry, stench, and a decomposing corpse awaited him.

He didn't know this was just the beginning.

In the meantime, Jakob Kuisl sat alongside the city moat, not far from his house, cutting little whistles out of the reeds for his grandchildren.

He'd bought some dried fruit and a few candied nuts for the children, which they were now devouring with great appetite. Their mouths were sticky with honey and their hands filthy with grime. The hangman grinned—it was good their mother couldn't see them this way.

At the thought of the children, his face suddenly darkened again. It wasn't just that his wife was sick; his grandchildren were now in danger, too. The warning from Hans Berchtholdt had been unmistakable: if Kuisl reported the warehouse theft to the Schongau secretary, the children would be in real danger. And even if he did nothing, Hans Berchtholdt was burning for revenge. Who was to say he wouldn't be lying in wait for the two little ones here along the moat or down by the river? It would just take one push, and they would disappear beneath the waves in an instant.

Grimly, the hangman took out his tobacco pouch and began stuffing his pipe. As always when he was thinking, he needed that heavenly weed, which a few friends, wagon drivers from

Augsburg, brought him every month. As the first puffs of smoke rose up, he was already feeling noticeably more relaxed, but in the next moment the sound of footsteps interrupted his reveries.

"Confound it! Can't one ever get a moment's peace around here?" Kuisl grumbled.

As he turned around, he saw his son Georg emerge from willow trees. The boy was carrying the slingshot he had used just a few hours ago to drive away the Berchtholdt brothers. And behind him came his sister Barbara, with her dark, tangled, shoulder-length locks, wearing a white blouse that barely concealed the first signs of her changing figure.

Georg and Barbara were twins, but as different as they could be. Barbara was chatty, with the same impudent tongue as her older sister, Magdalena, and promised to be just as beautiful. Georg, on the other hand, was as hefty as an unhewn piece of wood and as silent as his father. As an executioner's apprentice, the thirteen-year-old boy helped from time to time at executions and could look forward to his examination and certificate in a few years—a proper beheading.

"When Mama learns you bought candy for the two little ones again, she's going to scold," Barbara warned him, smiling as she drew closer.

"Watch out or I'll give you a proper thrashing, rascal," the hangman mumbled. "Didn't I tell Georg to clean out the knacker's wagon? And then I find him down at the warehouse with a slingshot in his hand. What were you doing down there?"

"I was going to shoot sparrows with the others," Georg replied tersely. His voice wasn't as deep as his father's, but it already sounded just as grim. "But then all I met were a few gallows birds."

"You ought to be glad he was down there, Father," Barbara interrupted. "They could hear Berchtholdt screaming way up in the Tanners' Quarter. I can't imagine what he would have done with the children if Georg hadn't come along with the others."

"Oh, nonsense. I could have handled them easily enough," the hangman grumbled.

"Twelve men?" Georg laughed. "Father, don't overdo it. You're not getting any younger."

"Young enough to deal with the Berchtholdt gang, though. In the war I killed small fry like that by the dozens. I wasn't much older than you back then, but strong enough for two. What it takes is strength and smarts."

Kuisl took a drag on his pipe and watched the smoke ascend. While Barbara went down to the moat with the two children, his son sat down alongside him on a rock and stared into the swirling water. After a while, Jakob silently handed him the pipe. Georg grinned. He knew his father would never say thank-you for anything, but this gesture was more thanks than a thousand words — it was the first time the old man had offered him a drag on his pipe. Georg closed his eyes and breathed in the sweet smoke, then puffed it out again like a little dragon.

"How's Mother?" Kuisl finally grumbled.

Georg shrugged. "She sleeps a lot. Martha made her a potion of linden blossoms and willow bark and is with her now."

"Willow bark is good; it reduces the fever."

There was another long pause before Georg finally cleared his throat. "You said before I'm just as old now as you were in the war . . ." he began, haltingly. "What did you mean by that? You never told me much about what happened then."

"Because there's nothing to tell except slashing, stabbing, and killing." The hangman spat brown tobacco juice into the meadow. "And anyone who comes back can only hope the war doesn't haunt his dreams. What is there to tell?"

"At least you got to meet Mother there," Georg interjected. "And you saw the world." He turned and pointed toward the walls of the city, visible through the trees, adding sarcastically, "Not just little stinking Schongau."

"Believe me, the world stinks just the same everywhere: it

smells of death, disease, and horseshit, and it doesn't matter whether you're in Paris or in Schongau." The hangman looked earnestly at his son. "We can only see to it that it smells a little better. Put your nose in a book, boy. It always smells better there."

Georg sighed. "You know I'm not very keen on reading. It's different with Barbara—she reads Paré and Paracelsus as if she'd written them herself. And I stutter even when I read the Lord's Prayer."

"Nonsense," Jakob hissed. "You're just lazy. A hangman who can't read isn't any better than a knacker. What are you going to live on? We hangmen don't just kill; we cure, as well. That's how we earn most of our money. And how can you heal if you can't read books?"

"I think I'm better suited for killing than for healing, Father."

The slap hit the boy so hard his lip broke open and drops of blood fell on his leather vest. Stunned, he rubbed his face; the pipe lay in front of him in the grass.

"How can you talk such nonsense?" his father growled, his face white with fury. "What do you want to do with the rest of your life—just break bones and chop off heads? Do you want to remain an outcast whom people run from and only dare to visit at night to buy a piece of hangman's rope or a little bottle of blood?" Kuisl picked up the pipe from the ground and knocked out the ashes. "Is that what you want? To sweep up other people's shit and do their dirty work? I thought I had taught you better than that."

"But . . . but what else can we do?" Georg stuttered. "We're not allowed to learn any other vocation. Hangmen remain hangmen—isn't that the way it always was? Did you ever hear of anyone who became something different?"

Suddenly Kuisl's eyes went blank, as if he were looking far back into the past. "Perhaps . . ." he murmured. "Yes, perhaps I knew someone."

The bodies twitching up in the branches of the oak ... The young regimental hangman walks down the rows of the out-laws; one after the other, he lays nooses around their necks and pulls the whimpering young men up into the treetop with his strong arms ... Only Jakob sees the tears streaming down the hangman's cheeks, the tremble coursing through his powerful, hulking body, the silently mumbled curses ... Jakob knows the man's fears all too well, for they are his own ... At night, his friend lies next to him, staring into the starless heavens, and swears an oath that Jakob himself made many years before ... In the morning, his friend is gone, and only his weapons are left behind, still lying by the fire. The captain curses like the devil and sends a search party out after the deserter, Jakob among them. At noon, when the men return shaking their heads, Jakob silently thanks God. He sharpens his sword and tries to forget ...

"By God, yes," Kuisl murmured after an eternity. "I knew someone like that, someone who tried. Heaven knows what he's doing now, but at least he tried. It's just me, stupid bastard that I am, who returned from the war to keep hanging people."

He laughed softly. Then he dragged on his pipe until a small ember began to glow bright red again.

"Damn," he finally continued, pointing with the stem of his pipe to his two grandchildren frolicking around and shouting cheerfully with Barbara in the shallow water.

"If I weren't here, then you wouldn't be, either, would you? And neither would the little bed wetters. For that alone I'll be glad to chop off a few more heads."

4

AT SUNRISE, SIMON ROSE WITH A GROAN FROM HIS
prickly straw bed in the knacker's house.

He'd worked till late in the night on his report for the abbot.
In it, he mentioned a possible murder weapon he'd discovered
the evening before by the pond. On a long net leaning against the
side of the walkway, he found drops of blood that could have
come from the back of the dead noviate's head. But Simon could
suggest neither a suspect nor a motive.

The medicus would have liked to sleep a bit longer, but Michael Graetz rose before sunrise, noisily prepared a breakfast for
his guests, and then left, whistling and singing, to visit a farmer
nearby. After that, sleep was out of the question. In any case, the
events of the previous day kept going through Simon's mind. He
sat down at the rickety table and, lost in thought, served himself
some steaming porridge.

"Can you be a bit quieter when you smack your lips, or do
you want to wake the dead?" Magdalena rubbed her eyes and
stared at Simon angrily.

"Well, at least when you grouse like that it seems you're on the road to recovery." Simon grinned and pointed at the second bowl of porridge. "Want some breakfast?"

Magdalena nodded, then stood up and dished out some porridge. She did in fact seem to have recovered and ate with an appetite that reminded Simon of a hungry wolf.

"I'll deliver my report to the abbot this morning," he said, wiping his mouth. "First, I'll stop by to see this watchmaker Virgilius. From some of the things he said, I'm guessing he knows more about Brother Johannes than he wanted to tell me yesterday."

"Do you think perhaps that Johannes killed his own apprentice?" she asked, taking another serving of porridge. "I wouldn't put anything past that ugly toad. I can feel he's covering up something."

"Actually, it's no business of ours," Simon sighed. "If only I'd kept my big mouth shut when I was talking with the abbot. But now one more visit won't make any difference. In any case, I'd like to take you along to have a look at that bizarre automaton," he said, getting up from the table. "What do you say? Do you want to come?"

"To admire my rival? Why not?" Magdalena laughed. "Watch out—if I don't like her, I'll yank out a few screws, and after that your nutty companion Virgilius won't be able to use his doll for anything but an expensive scarecrow."

Shortly thereafter they strolled through the village, up the hill toward the monastery, then took the little trail branching off to the right to the watchmaker's house. The sun had already risen above the treetops and shone brightly and warmly now on the freshly painted stone building with the little garden in front. Simon walked past the daisies and poppies and up to the door. He was about to knock when he noticed it was already ajar.

"Brother Virgilius?" he called into the room. "Are you there? I brought someone along whom I'd like you to . . ."

Noticing the stench of sulfur and gunpowder, he stopped short. He also sensed another odor, which at another time and place he might have experienced as pleasant.

The odor of grilled meat.

"What's going on?" Magdalena asked, amused. "Did you catch the monk in bed with his doll?"

"Evidently Brother Virgilius has been experimenting again," Simon murmured. "Let's hope nobody got hurt this time."

As he pushed against the door, he met with resistance, as if something heavy was right behind it. Groaning, he pushed harder, and the odor became stronger. Heavy clouds of smoke issued through the crack; then suddenly something sprang out of it like a snake.

A pale, bloated arm.

With a loud cry, Simon jumped back, stumbling and landing on his back in the middle of the daisies. Magdalena, too, stepped back, trembling and pointing to the arm that hung lifeless in the doorway at knee-height, its fingers pointing accusingly at the shocked couple.

"Someone . . . someone must be lying behind the door," Simon stuttered, as he slowly rose to his feet.

"And whoever that is, is likely dead as a doornail." Magdalena gathered her courage, struggled to open the door, and in the gradually dispersing smoke, gazed on a scene of horror. The room looked as if a demon had been unleashed in it.

Directly in front of them lay the corpse of the young assistant, Vitalis. The novitiate's head was angled oddly, as if some superhuman force had broken his neck; his shirt and parts of his trousers were burned, and beneath the clothing, burned flesh was visible on his back and legs. His arm was extended toward the door as if in a last desperate attempt to flee, and his face, seared by the flames, grimaced in fear, his mouth wide-open and eyeballs turned upward.

"My God," Simon panted. "What happened here?"

In the room itself, tables and chairs had been overturned, the valuable pendulum clock lay in pieces on the floor, and the two halves of the copper sphere had rolled into a corner. Only the crocodile dangled from the ceiling as before, staring with lifeless eyes on the chaos below.

"If Virgilius was really experimenting with gunpowder, he's blown himself up, along with everything else here, and has dissolved in a cloud of smoke." Magdalena stepped into the room and looked around warily. "In any case, he's not here."

Simon stooped down to pick up the head of a doll that had rolled in front of him, its forehead shattered and eyes smashed in. Perplexed, he was turning the porcelain head over in his hands when something crossed his mind.

The woman doll! Where in the world . . .

Simon groped about for a while in the dimly lit room, but the automaton had disappeared. In the middle of the room, however, he discovered Brother Virgilius's black robe in a large pool of blood, as well as a scorched screwdriver.

"It doesn't look like Virgilius made it out of this room alive," he murmured. A horrible thought passed through his head, so absurd that he cast it at once into the furthest corner of his mind.

Could the doll have killed its master and dragged him away? Was that even possible?

Suddenly he could feel something crunch beneath his feet. Stooping down, he picked up a broken lens inside a small, blood-stained brass ring. It took him a moment to realize what it was.

Brother Johannes's eyepiece — the one the monk had worn yesterday in the apothecary's house.

Simon was about to turn around to Magdalena when he saw two black-robed Benedictine monks in the doorway. Their faces, white as sheets, stared down in horror at the dead Vitalis at their feet.

"For the love of the Holy Virgin, what happened here?" one of them groaned, while the younger one stared at Magdalena and crossed himself.

"A witch!" he wailed, falling to his knees. "A witch has killed our dear Brother Virgilius and Vitalis. Lord in heaven, help us!"

"Uh, that's not exactly what happened," Simon replied hesitantly from out of the darkness, which made both monks scream in terror.

"A witch, the Grim Reaper, and the stench of sulfur," the older one cried out. "It's the end of the world!"

Wailing and screaming, they ran up the mountain to the monastery, where the bells had just started to ring. Simon nervously turned the destroyed eyepiece in his hand. It appeared he would have to rewrite his report.

Far below in his hideout, the man read the news his assistant had just brought him. A faint smile passed over his face. They'd found the dead assistant amid the chaos, and the watchmaker had disappeared. Now everything else would take its course.

The only thing troubling him was that sneaky bathhouse surgeon and his damned woman. Why did they have to poke their noses into everything? Had she noticed anything in the tower? And why had her husband gone to the pond yesterday to nose around? Those two were like boils that itched and ached — not really dangerous but a distraction nevertheless. The man decided he'd have to keep a better eye on them, and he knew from experience what to do with painful boils.

You cut them out.

Full of a newly regained composure, he rose and crossed to a heavy oaken table covered with books and parchments. Some of these that were from distant lands would have been unfamiliar to most people; some were written with flourishes and in runes; one even in blood. All sought answers to a secret so ancient that it went back to the very beginnings of human life and human faith — when a first fur-clothed cave dweller held in his hands a shiny stone, a little bone, or a skull and kneeled down to kiss it.

It was faith alone that breathed life into that dead thing.

The man hunched over the books, closed his eyes, and ran his fingers over the lines written in blood. The solution was hidden somewhere in these books. And he suspected even more blood would flow before it was found.

An hour later, Simon stood in front of the monastery council in what they called the Prince's Quarters on the third floor. Abbot Maurus Rambeck sat at the head of a long table, and to his right sat his deputy, the Prior Brother Jeremias, as well as the cellarer, the novitiate master, and the cantor, who was responsible for the care of the library, among other things. They all stared at Simon with dark and reproachful looks that conveyed their certainty he had something to do with the horrible murder.

Simon swallowed hard. For a moment he thought he could already feel the fire at his feet as he was being burned at the stake. At this moment he envied Magdalena, who, as a woman, was not allowed in the monastery wing. The monks had arrested her and taken her to an adjacent building, pending the outcome of his interrogation. Simon himself had had only a few minutes to speak privately with the abbot before the other members of the council appeared.

"Dear Brothers in Christ," the abbot began with a trembling voice. Simon noticed that Brother Maurus, in contrast to the last visit, now appeared extremely anxious, even confused. Nervously he passed his tongue over his bulging lips. "I've called you together here because a murder has been committed in our ranks, one so horrible and mysterious that it's difficult for me to find the right words . . ."

"The devil," interrupted the cellarer, a fat monk whose tonsure was encircled by only a few thin hairs he'd artfully combed back over his bald head. "The devil came to fetch this effeminate Vitalis, along with his master, the warlock Virgilius. I've warned him many times to stop his accursed experiments, and now he's fallen into Satan's hands."

"Brother Eckhart, I forbid you from talking that way about our fellow Brother," the abbot shouted at him. "Brother Virgilius has disappeared, and that's all we know. The blood in his shop leads us to believe there has been an accident. My God, perhaps he is just as dead as Vitalis . . ." Maurus Rambeck stopped and pressed his lips together, visibly moved.

"We must expect the worst, Maurus," murmured the cantor and librarian sitting at the far end of the table. His hair was snow-white, and deep folds in his face made him look like a withered plum cake. "The destruction suggests a deadly battle took place. But why?" Distrustfully he looked at the medicus.

"I think it's time for the bathhouse surgeon to tell us what he saw," said the scrawny prior whose hooked nose and piercing eyes reminded Simon of an eagle.

An eagle just before it plunges downward toward a terrified little mouse in the wheat field, thought Simon. *I'm lucky this Jeremias is only the abbot's deputy.*

"Who can tell us that this man from Schongau doesn't have anything to do with it?" the prior continued. "After all, Brother Martin and Brother Jakobus came upon him and that woman at the scene. And other monks have disclosed to me that the bathhouse surgeon went to visit Virgilius — and Brother Johannes — yesterday," he added ominously.

Now all five monks eyed Simon suspiciously. Their gazes seemed to pass right through him. Once more the medicus felt as if his feet were being held to the fire.

"Allow me please to explain what happened," he began hesitantly. "I . . . can explain everything."

The abbot nodded sympathetically, and Simon began his report, starting with his visit the previous day with Brother Johannes. He mentioned the latter's argument with Virgilius, and finally pulled out the blood-encrusted eyepiece he'd found on the floor in the watchmaker's workshop, which Abbot Rambeck reached for and showed to the other monks.

"This clearly belongs to Brother Johannes," he said pensively. "The Schongau bathhouse surgeon told me before our meeting about his suspicion, and I then summoned Johannes."

"And?" the old librarian asked.

Rambeck sighed. "He disappeared."

"Is it possible he's just in the forest collecting herbs?" the novitiate master interjected. He was a younger man with pleasant features and alert eyes, which were slightly red now. Simon wondered whether he'd been crying.

"Collecting herbs this early in the morning? Brother Johannes?" The cellarer Eckhart laughed derisively. "That would be the first time our dear Brother had been up that early. He usually prefers to go out in the light of the full moon and, after that, down a few pitchers of beer."

"In any case, I've sent a few men out from the village to search for him and bring him back," said Rambeck. "I'm reluctant to disturb the judge with the case until I've spoken with him. You know what that would mean."

The monks nodded silently, and Simon, too, could imagine the consequences of a visit by the local judge. A few years ago, the elector's deputy had appeared in Schongau at a witch trial, along with a large retinue and noisy soldiers. The city was still paying the bill for that months later.

"What we have here is a murder, Maurus," the prior scolded, shaking his head. "Probably even a double murder, if we can't find Virgilius." He shrugged, and Simon thought he saw quiet satisfaction in his eyes. "I'm afraid we can't avoid calling the district judge from Weilheim."

The medicus took a step forward and cleared his throat. "Excuse me, but perhaps Brother Johannes is even responsible for three deaths."

The prior frowned. "What do you mean?"

Hesitantly, Simon removed his report from his pocket and presented it to the council. He briefly explained his suspicions concerning the death of the novitiate Coelestin.

For a while, no one said a word.

Finally, the abbot spoke, his face now ashen. "Do you mean that Brother Johannes may have first killed his assistant Coelestin, then Vitalis, and possibly Virgilius as well? But . . . why?"

"We know that all too well," Brother Eckhart snapped. His bald head turned red, and little veins stood out. "Haven't the two always carried out sacrilegious experiments? Johannes *and* Virgilius? Didn't we just two weeks ago forbid Brother Johannes from studying things that only God should be concerned with? And yet he persisted." He stood up from his chair, panting heavily, and pounded the table so hard with his fist that the monks stared back at him in shock. "I'll tell you what happened: the good novitiate Coelestin wanted to prevent his master from experimenting any further with this devil's work. So Johannes simply killed him. Finally there was an argument between the two sorcerers Johannes and Virgilius; they fought with balls of fire and sulfur, until Virgilius went up in smoke at the end and went to hell, and his assistant was struck down by his enemy's magic spells."

"Nonsense," the young novitiate master mumbled. "Nobody goes up in smoke. There must be another explanation."

"Think of the wounds poor Vitalis suffered," the prior pleaded. "May his soul rest in peace. They were clearly not of natural origin."

"To know that for certain, we'd have to examine—" Simon started to object, but the old librarian interrupted, raising a trembling hand.

"Something else must be noted," he said hoarsely. "You know all these automata that Virgilius was so fond of—this woman made of metal who plays the glockenspiel."

"I do hope it has been destroyed," Brother Eckhart grumbled. "That at least would be something positive. God alone, and not man, should create life."

"Well, it's even worse," the librarian continued hesitantly. "Our Brothers Martin and Jakobus have told me that the . . . well, the automaton has disappeared."

"Disappeared?" The prior shook his head. "Just like Virgilius? But how is that possible? The doll is as large as a human and certainly very heavy. How could anyone—"

"My God," Brother Eckhart, who was still standing, raised his hands in prayer and directed his gaze theatrically to the ceiling. "Don't you understand what happened? Don't you understand the full horror of this?" His voice was trembling. "This . . . creature . . . has come to life and has seized its master. Somewhere here in the monastery a golem is stalking about. God help us!"

Excited murmurs could be heard from all sides; some of the monks crossed themselves or clung tightly to their rosaries. Simon, too, felt a shiver run up his spine. He couldn't help thinking of the automaton in the watchmaker's shop, the lifeless face and the slightly off-key melody of a glockenspiel playing inside. He could practically see the puppet in front of him as it whirred through the room.

Like a ghost gliding along weightlessly, he thought, *driven by a lust for revenge—one that never stops until its task is complete.*

The abbot stood now and pounded the table angrily with the palm of his hand, bringing Simon back to reality.

"Quiet!" he shouted. "Dear Brothers, I beg for silence."

Only gradually did quiet return to the room. The abbot took a deep breath before continuing in a broken voice. "We won't understand what has happened until . . . until Brother Johannes is back among us. We have to be grateful for every clue." Turning to Simon, he added, "I shall read your report carefully, and I'd be very grateful if you can contribute anything else to clarify this case. You've seemed quite astute thus far."

Prior Jeremias gasped. "A bathhouse surgeon, a dishonorable person, helping to solve a murder in the monastery? My dear Brother, I beg you—"

"And I beg you to be silent," Abbot Rambeck interrupted. "Dishonorable or not, this bathhouse surgeon has made more intelligent observations than all of us together. It would be stupid not to accept his help. I'm asking him to continue work on his report." Rambeck seemed to get briefly lost in thought, and his hands began to tremble again. After a brief pause, he turned back to Simon. "Ah, there's something else, Master Fronwieser. It's come to my attention that some of the pilgrims are ill. Now that our apothecary is no longer available, someone else is needed to care for them . . ."

It sounded like an order, so Simon nodded respectfully. "Naturally, Your Eminence, as you wish."

Wonderful, he thought. *Until today, I was an ordinary pilgrim, and now I must write a report about a mysterious murder and care for sick pilgrims. Why didn't I just go to Altötting with Magdalena?*

The abbot closed his eyes and made the sign of the cross. "Then let us pray to God for our dead and missing Brothers."

Simon watched each monk, one after the other, as Maurus Rambeck recited a psalm in Latin. The Brothers had folded their hands, murmuring the prayers as they lowered their eyes. It seemed each radiated an evil aura quite out of place in this cloistered atmosphere. Suddenly the prior raised his head and looked Simon directly in the eye.

The medicus winced. In Brother Jeremias's eyes Simon saw a hateful spark that rattled him to the core.

• • •

Brother Johannes ran through the forest as if the devil himself were in pursuit.

He stumbled over roots, picked himself up again breathlessly, jumped over muddy ditches, and rushed through thick underbrush. The hem of his robe had long been reduced to tatters; thistles and branches clung to the material, and his face was sweaty and mud-stained. Tears ran down his chubby cheeks and his heart pounded. Except for a linen bag with his essential belongings, he hadn't been able to save a thing.

Johannes cursed and sobbed. His former life behind him, he would have to hit the road again. He didn't know what the future held for him, only what would happen if they caught him: They'd pull out his fingernails and toenails and stretch his bones until they popped out of their sockets. Then they'd crush his thumbs, burn his wizened skin with matches, and throw him on a huge pile of wood and brush to be consumed by fire.

Brother Johannes knew all this because he was familiar with torture and executions. He had seen far too many up close; he knew what awaited a murderer and warlock.

Without stopping once to look around, the fat apothecary ran through the Kien Valley. By now it was early morning, and the sun bore down mercilessly through the boughs and branches. Like most of the other monks, Johannes had been awakened at the crack of dawn by loud wailing. Something dreadful must have happened, and he had a dark suspicion what it was. He'd secretly hurried to the watchmaker's house, only to find the bathhouse owner and his woman leaving, both of them as white as a sheet. From the bits of conversation he overheard, he pieced together what they'd discovered inside.

When he heard them mention his name, Brother Johannes knew he couldn't return. They would find out everything — the experiments, the fire in the tower, all about his former life . . .

A curse on you, Virgilius!

Thus Johannes snuck back to his little house, picked up some provisions, a blanket, and his old wooden cross, and made off toward the Kien Valley. He ran through a narrow hidden gorge, which many Erlingers had used during the Great War to escape the Swedes and was known to them as *The Ox's Gorge* . . . From time to time Johannes had to gather up the folds of his robe and wade through the Kien Brook. Somewhere in the distance, he could hear dogs barking and a horn sounding. Were they already on his heels?

He suppressed the thought and rushed forward blindly. If he could make it down to Mühlfeld or Wartaweil, perhaps he had a chance. He could find a fisherman to take him over to Dießen, and from there he could keep going toward Landsberg, where he had friends who would help him. Perhaps somewhere he would find an army he could join up with. People with his experience were always needed.

The trees in front of him were thinning out, so he could already see the lake sparkling down in the valley. His goal, the little fisherman's port not far from Mühlfeld Castle, seemed within reach. As soon as Brother Johannes stepped out of the forest, he heard a shot. A bullet whizzed by his ear, missing him by just inches. Gasping, he threw himself down in the mud.

"There he is, the filthy bastard. You were right; he fled through the Ox's Gorge."

A man stepped out from behind the trees with a smoking musket, followed by a second and a third. All were experienced hunters employed by the monastery, and Johannes knew them. In the tavern they sometimes whispered behind his back; they didn't like it that he collected herbs in their hunting grounds and scared the wildlife. To them, he was just a fat, ugly priest who ate what by rights belonged to them. A monster in a monk's cassock who terrified children.

Today was the day of reckoning.

"We heard you killed three of your Brothers, you scum," the

oldest growled, nudging the monk with his foot. His eyes gleamed with the thrill of the chase. "It was easy for you with the three priests, but we're made of different stuff." Laughing, he turned to his friends. "Well, what do you think? Do we want to see the fat toad jump again?" When the others howled their approval, he held his musket in the air and fired. A swarm of sparrows scattered, chirping angrily in the direction of the monastery.

Dazed by the noise and fearful, Brother Johannes leapt up and stumbled toward a field of barley. Behind it was the lake with little boats rocking on the waves—he could almost smell the water. As he began to run, he looked up and could see between the low-lying clouds on the horizon the monastery in Dießen. And he could hear the rustle of the grain beneath his feet as he ran.

The world is so beautiful, he thought. *Why are the people in it so cruel? Will they let me go in the end?*

When Johannes heard the dogs barking behind him, he knew it was all over.

Magdalena crouched on the floor of the filthy provision cellar, watching flies buzz about in the light from a small window. For a while she had paced around, but now she settled down in a corner where she brooded and cursed her husband for getting her into this disastrous situation.

After Simon had been taken off to see the abbot, a few grim-faced helpers had silently led Magdalena away. Since then, the hangman's daughter had been awaiting her fate in the cellar of the monastery dairy farm. There was an odor of old cheese and fermented milk in the air, and in one corner, a pile of moldy boards and broken containers made of willow bark. Otherwise the room was empty. A massive wooden door with a heavy sliding bolt was the only way in or out.

Lost in thought, Magdalena ran her hand through her hair and tried to ignore the strong odor of the old cheese baskets. She couldn't imagine they would charge her and Simon with the murder of the watchmaker's assistant just because they'd found the corpses. But she wasn't entirely sure, either. The way the two monks ran screaming from the scene made it clear to her how inflamed the mood was in the monastery. Magdalena had to admit that all the strange events—the bestial murder of the assistant, the disappearance of his master, and an automaton that had likewise vanished—all this made her also wonder if the devil was at work here.

She was just about to get up to stretch her legs a bit when she heard steps outside the door. A moment later, the bolt was pushed back, a disheveled Brother Johannes staggered in, and fell lifelessly to the floor.

"Lots of luck with the bathhouse owner's woman, you scum," jeered one of the two men standing outside in the corridor with their muskets. "But leave something for us—don't eat her up afterward the way you did the watchmaker." Laughter rang out, then the door closed with a crash.

For a while, the only sounds were the gasps of the apothecary. Finally, Magdalena bent down to him and touched him gently on the shoulder.

"How . . . how are you?" she asked hesitantly. "Do you need . . ."

Suddenly Brother Johannes raised his head and stared her in the eye without saying a word. With a muted cry, Magdalena jumped. The monk's face, already an ugly sight, was beaten black and blue, one eye was swollen shut, and blood dripped from his swollen lips onto the ground. He looked like something resurrected from the Andechs cemetery. He crawled into a corner and held his swollen nose.

"I've . . . lived through worse things," he muttered. "And this is nothing compared with what I still have coming. I know what I'm up against."

Suspiciously, Magdalena observed the monk doubled up in

the corner. Simon had found the apothecary's eyepiece at the crime site and had witnessed the argument between Johannes and the watchmaker. His entire behavior to that point made him look suspicious. He was no doubt the murderer of two of the men, if not all three. Still, as Magdalena looked at him, beaten and bloody like a wounded animal, a wave of pity came over her. She tore off a part of her skirt and handed it to him.

"Here, take this, or nobody will be able to see your pretty face again."

In the dim light, Johannes's faint grimace looked like that of a badly stitched puppet. "Thanks," he murmured. "I know I'm not the handsomest fellow."

"It still remains to be seen whether you are also a murderer." Magdalena moved back to her corner and watched Johannes dab at his face. Flies buzzed around, trying to settle on his bloody lips, and though Johannes chased them away each time, they kept coming back. Magdalena couldn't help but think of a stoic ox being whipped.

"You must be the wife of that Schongau bathhouse surgeon," the monk said after a while. By now he was looking halfway human. "Are you feeling better? Your husband said you were suffering from stomach trouble."

Magdalena laughed despairingly. "Thank you for asking, but I think that's the least of my problems at present." She sighed. "It looks like we're in the same boat. We're suspected in the murder of the watchmaker's helper."

"Don't worry, you'll be released soon." Johannes said, waving her off. "They want to get me, and no one else."

"Why? Are your accusers right?" Magdalena asked in a soft voice. "Are you a warlock and a murderer?"

The ugly monk looked her up and down. "Do you seriously believe I'd tell you that if I really was?" he said finally. "And if I'm not the murderer but nevertheless have other dark secrets, why should I tell you? Who's to say you wouldn't betray me?"

Shaking her head, Magdalena leaned back against the wall. "Whether I betray you or not makes no difference. No doubt they'll call the local judge tomorrow, then they'll take you to the torture chamber in Weilheim. They'll show you the instruments, and if you still don't confess, they'll start breaking your bones."

Brother Johannes took a deep breath. Magdalena could see how he was shaking. "It's astonishing a bathhouse owner's wife like you knows so much about these things," he murmured. "It's almost as if you'd seen a torture once yourself."

"But I haven't. I've just listened carefully to what my father has to say."

"Your father?" For the first time Johannes appeared really confused.

"He's the Schongau executioner, Jakob Kuisl."

"Jakob *Kuisl?*"

A sudden change came over the Benedictine monk. His face turned ashen, his eyes widened, and he mumbled softly to himself. After a while Magdalena could hear him praying.

"Oh Dear Lord, I have doubted, pardon me," he pleaded. "I was a fool, a doubting Thomas. But you sent me a sign, Glory to God in the Highest! This is a miracle, a miracle!"

He fell on his knees and swayed back and forth, clutching a little wooden cross hanging by a chain from his neck.

"By all the saints . . . what . . . what is wrong with you?" Magdalena asked cautiously. Had pain and fear driven the monk mad? "Is it something I said?"

Finally Broker Johannes raised his head. "You . . . you . . . are an angel," he began in solemn tones. "An angel passing through on a mission from God."

He really has gone mad. Magdalena shuddered. *Perhaps I should call the guards before he attacks me?*

She smiled uncertainly. "An . . . an angel?"

Brother Johannes nodded eagerly. "An angel sent to me to

announce Jakob's coming." He looked at her earnestly, and suddenly the maniacal expression vanished from his face.

"By God," he whispered. "Your father is the only one who can still save me."

Plumes of smoke rose into the sky above Schongau like the shadows of restless spirits.

As he had the day before, Jakob Kuisl sat beside the moat, looking down into the same green water where just a hundred years ago women who had murdered their children had been drowned. Kuisl liked this lonely place, as people very rarely wandered into it. The moat was regarded as cursed because so many poor souls had met their ends here, and the people of Schongau believed you could hear the dead crying here when the moon was full. Kuisl had never heard anything—on the contrary, the moat was a place of silent tranquility that the hangman missed all too often in town.

Kuisl needed rest. He wondered what to do about the Berchtholdt brothers. Was it advisable to go to the secretary and tell him about the thefts in the warehouse? At one time, Kuisl wouldn't have hesitated, but now his two grandchildren were there, and they were in danger. Would the Berchtholdts really attack innocent children?

No matter how hard Kuisl tried to achieve clarity, his thoughts kept returning to the past. His conversation the day before with his son Georg had awakened memories of the war—the many dead and the battles, but above all the only true friend he'd ever had in his life. Together they'd gone through hell; they'd stood together in the front lines when they were attacked. They'd been almost the same age, like brothers.

But above all, they were bound together by a fate that separated them from all others.

As Kuisl stared into the water mirroring the willows along

the bank, he suddenly had the bitter taste of gunpowder in his mouth, and in the distance he imagined he could hear shouting and the clanging armor.

It was as if he were looking through a tunnel as an indistinct image emerged at the other end.

Drums beat; flutes play; smoke and the scent of frying mutton are in the air. Eighteen-year-old Jakob wanders from campfire to campfire. As far as he can see, there are colorful tents alongside the dirty canvas-covered wagons belonging to the sutlers—the peddlers, traders, and whores who follow the army. In the foreground are the hastily dug trenches, and in the distance, the city they will storm the next day.

Will he still be alive tomorrow?

Jakob has been traveling with the army for five years. The pimply drummer boy has become a broad-shouldered man, a fearsome warrior who always stands in the frontlines with his two-handed sword. The captain awarded him a master's certificate for the long sword, and his men fear him because they know his sword is thirsty for blood, a magic blade that moans when battle begins.

A hangman's sword.

With the sword strapped to his back, he strides through the camp. The mercenaries who know him step back and cross themselves. The hangman's son is not a welcome guest here; he is respected but not loved.

When Jakob senses someone looking at him, he turns around to see the ugliest fellow he's ever met. With a face swollen like a pig's bladder, eyes bulging, and mouth crooked, the stranger crouches like a fat toad in front of a campfire. It takes Jakob a moment to realize that the stranger is smiling.

"A fine blade indeed," says the stranger. His voice sounds soft and intelligent, out of character with his face. "No doubt cost a lot. Or did you steal it?"

"What business is that of yours?" Jakob grumbles. He is about to turn away when the other reaches behind him to extract his own sword from a pile of rags. A two-hander without a point—almost seven feet long, with a blood groove and short crossguard—it looks remarkably like Jakob's sword.

"Inherited the sword from my father, who was fetched by the devil," the ugly stranger says with a grin. "In Reutlingen, where I come from, people say it shouts for blood on execution day. But ever since I was a little kid, I've never once heard it shout. It's only the others who do the shouting."

Jakob laughs softly. For the first time in a long while.

"Now the Reutlingers will have to do their dirty work by themselves," he growls. "Serves 'em right, the fat old money-bags."

As the ugly man nods and runs his huge hands over the freshly sharpened blade, Jakob knows he has found a friend for life.

The Schongau hangman tossed a stone in the moat. As little waves spread in circles, his image in the water dissolved. He stood up and headed for home, his heart pounding.

It wasn't good to awaken too many old memories.

For a long time, Magdalena could only stare at the monk in the Andechs dungeon in disbelief.

"You . . . You know my father?" she finally asked.

Brother Johannes was still kneeling in front of her. Now he crossed himself and struggled to his feet.

"Let's say I knew him," he murmured. "Better than my own brother. But I didn't know he'd gone back to Schongau and become an executioner again. We've not been in touch for more than thirty years." He laughed and raised his hands to heaven. "It's a miracle that I'm now meeting his daughter. Perhaps everything will turn out well, after all."

Magdalena looked at him skeptically. "Even if you knew him, why should everything turn out for the better now? How could my father help you?"

"You're right." Brother Johannes sighed and crouched down in his corner again.

"I'll probably wind up burned at the stake soon, but if anyone could help, it would be your father, believe me. I don't expect he's lost any of that quick mind, has he?"

Magdalena had to smile. "Nothing of his sharp mind or his pig-headedness. Was he always like that?"

"He was the most pig-headed damn guy in the whole regiment. A great fighter and smart as a whole army of Jesuits." Johannes grinned, then he began his story: "We had known each other since the battle at Breitenfeld. We were both hangmen's sons and both running away from our former lives. War is a great equalizer—there's no better place to start over again. We understood each other from the start." He laughed, causing his swollen lip to burst open again. Cursing, he wiped the blood from his mouth. "I got a job as a whipping boy and had soon worked my way up to our regiment's executioner. Your father, despite his dishonorable status, became a sergeant, something very few simple people manage to do. He was so damned clever that he figured out almost every case of theft in his regiment. Every unauthorized raid, every rape." Johannes's face darkened. "Then it was my job to string up the poor bastards. I can still see them in my dreams, twitching and thrashing about up in the trees. My God, how I hated that."

For a while, the only sounds were the chirping sparrows outside the window.

"Is that why you became a monk?" Magdalena finally asked. "Because you were no longer able to stomach the killing?"

Johannes nodded hesitantly. "Jakob . . . he . . . could simply handle death better," he continued in a halting voice. "He'd run away from home, just like me, because he didn't want to be a hangman, but really he never gave it up." He raised his hands dismissively. "Not bloodthirsty—not that—but rather an ... an ... archangel like Michael who came down to earth with his sword to vanquish evil. I couldn't do it ... the constant torturing and killing ..."

The Brother clapped his hands over his face to hide his tears. "Finally, I deserted. Without a word I just left and wandered about for years until I found a place to stay here in Andechs more than ten years ago. My apothecary's license was forged, but that didn't bother the abbot at the time. All that mattered to Father Maurus Friesenegger was that I knew about herbs. The new abbot, Maurus Rambeck, also knows about my past. But if the others learn about it ... a hangman disguised as a monk and apothecary." He laughed bitterly. "What does it matter? Nothing matters anymore."

Still on his knees, he slid across the floor to Magdalena, who to this point had been listening in silence.

"Please," he stammered. "You must tell your father I'm in trouble. He's my only hope. Tell him ... tell him ugly Nepomuk needs his help."

"Nepomuk?" Magdalena stopped short. "Is that your real name?"

"Nepomuk Volkmar. I was baptized with that name." Groaning, he rose to his feet. "The name is a curse. I renounced it when I took my vows."

At that moment, footsteps could be heard again. The door creaked and swung open, and Simon entered. He looked over at Magdalena with concern, but hardly glanced at the monk at her side.

"I'm sorry it took so long," he said, shrugging. "But the abbot had a few more questions. Now everything is clear." He smiled. "We are free to go."

"Simon," Magdalena replied, pointing to Nepomuk Volkmar. "This monk knows my father. He—"

"That won't help him now," Simon interrupted. "The Weilheim executioner is in charge of executions at Andechs, not the one from Schongau." Whispering, he continued, "Besides, I don't know what your father could do here except assure a fast, halfway bearable death."

"Simon, you don't understand. Nepomuk was—"

"What I understand is that you've been happily chatting away with a man accused of three murders and the guards outside are already looking at us suspiciously," Simon hissed. "So let's get out of here, please, before the abbot changes his mind and locks us up for complicity in this case."

Nepomuk Volkmar gave Magdalena a hopeful look. "You will tell your father, won't you?" he murmured. "You won't forsake me?"

"I'll . . ." Magdalena began as Simon pulled her out the door. The last thing Magdalena saw as the dungeon door closed slowly behind them was the ugly apothecary's battered, pleading gaze.

Then the door slammed shut.

Outside, the sun shone brightly in a blue sky as a few puffy clouds passed overhead, and the world seemed like quite a different place. The sound of singing pilgrims could be heard in the distance and butterflies fluttered over the meadows near the monastery.

Magdalena sat down on the ruins of a wall and stared at Simon angrily. "You didn't even let me finish," she hissed. "Don't you ever do that again. I'm not one of your former whores. I'm a woman, damn it—don't you forget it."

"Magdalena, it was all for your own good. The guards—"

"Now just shut your mouth and listen to me," she interrupted. "That man in there is probably my father's best friend, and unless a miracle happens, he'll be tortured as a sorcerer and murderer and burned in short order. Can you imagine what will happen if I don't tell my father about it? Can you imagine what he's going to do to you if you stop me?"

"His best friend?" the medicus asked, surprised. "How do you know that?"

Briefly, Magdalena told Simon about the monk's former life, his time as regimental executioner in the war and his friendship with her father. When she had finished, the medicus still looked skeptical.

"And you believe everything he says? Don't you think it's more likely the man is just grasping at straws?"

"He knew details of my father's life, Simon. He . . . he described them better than I could." Magdalena looked into the distance, where a new storm was approaching over Lake Ammer. "Yes, I believe him."

"Very well," said Simon, softening his tone. "Perhaps he really does know him, but that's a far cry from saying he's innocent." He held his wife firmly by the shoulder. "Magdalena, all the evidence points to his guilt. The eyepiece at the scene, the argument with the watchmaker, his behavior . . . Didn't you yourself say he was behaving strangely? Just think of those strange rods he was carrying in the forest. In the council, too, they said he's engaged in blasphemous experiments."

Magdalena gave him an astonished look. "Blasphemous experiments?"

"They . . . they didn't say anything specific," Simon replied hesitantly. "But clearly Nepomuk has often argued with Virgilius, and it no doubt had something to do with his experiments."

"That strange bier and all those wires up in the belfry," Magdalena murmured. "Could those have been one of his experiments?"

Simon shrugged. "I don't know. The monks were very guarded about that. In any case, the entire council is a group of very strange characters." He started counting them off on his fingers. "The cellarer is a fat zealot who wants nothing more than to burn the apothecary right off . . . The prior has something against me . . . And the old librarian was very cold, as if none of it mattered to him. Only the master of the novitiates seemed concerned about death. I think he'd been crying—his eyes were red, in any case."

He recounted in great detail his meeting with the abbot and the uproar that ensued when the monks heard about the automaton that had vanished.

"The stupid cellarer really believes the automaton is a sort of golem that haunts the Holy Mountain," Simon replied, shaking his head. "It's almost as if time has stood still up here. Musical automata like that are pretty common nowadays."

"A golem?" Magdalena asked. "What is that?"

"An object that springs to life when life is breathed into it." Absentmindedly Simon reached for a piece of brick and crumbled it in his hand. "I read about that once when I was a student in Ingolstadt. *Golem* is the Hebrew word for *unformed*. Some Jewish rabbis were said to be able to create a lifeless servant out of clay. It involved some very complicated rituals." He shook his head. "It's nonsense naturally, but for literalist Christians, also a perfect opportunity to depict the Jews once again as the devil incarnate. The cellarer in any case was almost foaming at the mouth, and the librarian was just as fired up. If I remember correctly, he was the first to bring it up."

"Suppose someone in the council was involved somehow in the murders?" Magdalena wondered aloud.

Simon laughed derisively. "Perhaps the abbot himself? Magdalena, give it up. It was the apothecary, without a doubt. He isn't a sorcerer—it's not that—but there's a simple reason why he committed these murders. We just haven't found out yet what that is. Jealousy toward a colleague, revenge . . . who knows?

Brother Johannes put this idea into your head and now you'll stop at nothing to try to prove his innocence."

"You didn't talk with him," Magdalena whispered. "Nepomuk is a man who has suffered a long time and is always fleeing from something because he can no longer stand the horror. A man like that would never kill three people. Besides, it wasn't Nepomuk who pushed me out of the belfry. You told me yourself that at the time he was with you visiting the abbot."

Simon sighed. "From your mouth to God's ear. So what are you going to do?"

"I'm going down to the tavern in Erling to send a message to Schongau. What else?" Magdalena jumped down from the wall and ambled away toward the village. "Expect to see my father arrive shortly to straighten things out."

"That's the last thing I need," Simon groaned. "I not only have to provide the abbot with more details on the murder, but now my father-in-law will be nosing around after me."

Magdalena turned around and grinned. "He's always known what to do, so quit whining. You could have looked for another family to marry into."

With a wink, she ran through the flowering meadows toward Erling. To the west, the distant rumble of thunder could be heard.

Somewhere deep inside the Holy Mountain a clicking and rattling could be heard.

The automaton rumbled over pebbles and stones, banging against a low beam from time to time but stoically soldiering on. The corridor it rolled through was ancient, having been hewn into the mountain long before there was a monastery, at a time when the sword alone ruled and religious beliefs were celebrated in bloody rites with burning baskets full of writhing prisoners of war or on rough, charred altars. Since then, faith had grown; it had changed form, but it had persevered. In its new form it had overthrown kingdoms and crowned emperors. Its power was greater than ever.

Like an ever-grinning, life-size nutcracker, the puppet kept opening and shutting its mouth, while its soft melody echoed through the hallways and off the rock faces, until it seemed to be playing everywhere at the same time.

Though this was a love song, here in the lonely depths of the mountain, it sounded sad.

Sad and uncanny.

5

THE SCHONGAU HANGMAN STARED AT THE LETTER in his hand and felt his pulse quicken. It was rare that a messenger brought him a message in person. Just touching an executioner could in some regions cost an honorable man his reputation and his job. So this document had to be important.

"Where does it come from?" Kuisl asked the courier, who had arrived on horseback and stood before him now looking down at the ground, crossing himself in a gesture meant to ward off evil spirits. His coat was dripping from the thunderstorm that had just passed through Schongau.

"From . . . from Andechs," the messenger mumbled. "From the Holy Mountain. The letter is from your daughter."

Kuisl grinned. "Then she surely had to pay you something extra to come down here to the hangman's house."

"I was on my way to Schongau anyway," the messenger answered hesitantly. "First thing tomorrow I head out for Augsburg. In any case, your daughter has astonishing . . . powers of persuasion. Not at all like . . ."

"Like a dull hangman's girl? Is that what you wanted to say?"

The messenger winced. "Oh, God, no! Quite the contrary. She's an extremely talkative and very attractive young lady."

"She gets that from her mother," Kuisl growled, somewhat more obligingly. "Talking all the time, even when there's absolutely nothing to talk about."

The hangman pulled out a few coins to hand to the messenger, but he waved him off. "Ah, that's not necessary," he stammered. "Your daughter and that bathhouse surgeon already paid for it. Farewell." Anxiously, he bowed and disappeared in the cold, wet twilight.

"Yeah, you can kiss my . . ." Kuisl grumbled before returning to the living room, where his wife had just had another coughing fit. Her fever hadn't worsened in the last two days, but it hadn't gone down, either. She still lay semiconscious on a bench by the oven. At least the two little ones were sleeping upstairs. Peter and Paul had been romping around all evening near their sick grandmother.

"Is there news from Magdalena?" the hangman's wife gasped. "I hope it's nothing serious."

"Whatever it is, she charmed the dickens out of the messenger." With his rough hands, Kuisl broke the simple wax seal and unfolded the letter. "So it won't be so . . ." He stopped short. Only his lips read on, silently. Finally he had to find a seat on a stool.

"What's the trouble?" his wife asked. "Did something happen?"

"No." Kuisl tore at his hair. "It's nothing, at least not what you think it is. It's something . . . else."

"Good Lord, do I always have to drag everything out of you, you stubborn damned Schongauer?"

Once more the hangman's wife started to cough violently. When she had calmed down again, Kuisl continued haltingly. "Magdalena . . . she . . . she apparently met the ugly old Nepomuk. I haven't heard a word from that bastard for almost thirty years, and then out of the blue he pops up in Andechs. I could wring the neck of that fat weasel."

"Nepomuk? *The* Nepomuk?"

The hangman nodded. "He's in a jam. It looks like he's become a monk." He spit onto the reeds on the floor, then pulled out his pipe and lit it from a burning wood chip.

"Nepomuk, a monk," he said finally. "It would be easier for a camel to pass through the eye of a needle than for a hangman to become a priest. Nepomuk was always a sly dog; he read a lot, and thought up the craziest things for the regiment to do. But he was far too soft for killing. Who knows, perhaps in another life he would really have been a good priest . . ." He stopped short. "In any case, they're trying to pin three murders on him in the monastery and accusing him of witchcraft. He's asking for me to come and help him."

Anna-Maria sat up carefully in bed. "And? What are you waiting for?"

"What am I waiting for?" The hangman laughed darkly. "For you to get better. And I can't leave my two grandchildren here all by themselves." He took a deep drag on his pipe. "I told you about the Berchtholdts. I don't trust them not to try to hurt the children while I'm away — if only to threaten me on account of the theft in the warehouse."

Anna-Maria seemed to be mulling this over. For a while, the only sound was the rattle in her lungs and the distant thunder.

"Then take them along," she said finally.

"What?" Kuisl was startled out of his gloomy thoughts.

"Peter and Paul. Take them along."

"But . . . but . . . how would I do that?" the hangman managed. "I'll save my friend from execution while I watch the children like an old nanny?"

"Magdalena and Simon are there, too. They can take care of them — they're the parents, after all."

The hangman shook his head slowly. His wife's idea was not that bad. Martha Stechlin wouldn't be able to care for his grandchildren at present; especially now, after Simon had left, the midwife was much too busy treating sick people in the area.

Anna-Maria wasn't the only one suffering from the fever, and Kuisl didn't have much faith in Georg and Barbara. They were both scatterbrains and couldn't be depended on to protect the little ones from the Berchtholdts. The only option left was his wife's . . .

"If I go," he began, "what will happen to you? You're sick, and who will take care of you when I'm not here?"

"Martha can," Anna-Maria replied. "She knows almost as much about healing as you. And Georg and Barbara are here, too. So why not—" Again, she had to cough.

The hangman gave his wife a worried look. "You're the most precious thing I have, Anna," he murmured. "I would never forgive—"

"For God's sake, get moving!" his wife shouted. "Nepomuk was once your best friend. How often you've told me about him. Do you want him to burn at the stake while you're just a few miles away brewing chamomile tea?"

"No, but—"

"Then get moving, you dolt, and take your grandchildren along." She pulled a tattered woolen blanket around her neck and closed her eyes. "And now let me sleep. You'll see; tomorrow I'll be much better."

Kuisl collapsed in a heap on a stool and stared at his sick wife. They'd been together almost thirty years. At that time, Kuisl had taken Anna-Maria from a village laid waste by his regiment near Regensburg. And even if the two quarreled and growled at each other like two old dogs, they had always been close. Their ostracism by the citizens of Schongau, their love for their children, their daily work together—all that bound them together. Kuisl would never say so, and he didn't have to, because Anna already knew that, in his own gruff way, he loved his wife more than himself.

Softly, so as not to waken Anna-Maria, Jakob stood up from the stool. He crossed to the storeroom where he kept his medi-

cine cabinet, a few torture instruments, and a trunkful of old
weapons from the war. He hesitated briefly, then opened a
weathered box he'd kept with him the last forty years. On top
was a moth-eaten soldier's uniform, its once bright colors now
pale and faded. Underneath were the sword, the matchlock musket, and two well-oiled wheel-lock pistols.

Lost in thought, Kuisl passed his hands over the barrel of the
guns while memories came rushing back. He closed his eyes and
saw himself standing in the frontlines beside Nepomuk, his best
friend, as they marched toward the Swedes . . .

*A yellow line on the horizon quickly approaching . . . Drums
and fifes, then the shouts of men breaking rank to become individual soldiers. The enemy mercenaries running toward them
with long pikes, swords, and daggers; behind them the closed
ranks of the musketeers, the flash from the muzzles, the moaning
and wailing of the injured and dying . . . Jakob smells the gunpowder; he looks over at Nepomuk, and sees the fear in his eyes.
But he sees something else: a beastly gleam, a blackness deep as
the pit of hell, and suddenly Jakob notices he's looking into a
mirror.*

What he sees there is the joy of killing.

*Jakob shakes himself, reaches for his sword, and strides out
to meet the screaming enemy. Calmly and precisely, he performs
a task he never wants to repeat.*

The job of a hangman.

Jakob slammed the trunk shut as if he could block out the
spirits he'd just awakened in this way. As he wiped his forehead,
he noticed it was damp with cold sweat.

Raindrops ran like tears down the panes of the bull's-eye glass in
the Andechs Monastery tavern.

Simon stared out into the growing gloom as a ghostly group

of singing forms ascended the mountain for evening mass. Magdalena had also decided to attend mass to thank God for the recovery of her two children the year before. That was, after all, the reason she and Simon had come to Andechs.

The medicus sighed softly. This pilgrimage was turning into a real nightmare. It wasn't just that they were once again caught up in a murder case or that his grouchy father-in-law would be arriving soon. Now more and more pilgrims were coming down with a strange fever that brought on weariness, headaches, and stomach cramps. Could this be the same sickness Magdalena had suffered?

Simon had fulfilled the abbot's request and spent the entire day treating patients in a building adjoining the monastery. Three or four cases had grown to a full dozen now, many of the patients showing red spots on their chests or grayish-yellow tongues. He treated the first patients free of charge, but in the course of the day had begun asking for a few coins, at least from the better-off patients.

Now he had turned some of his earnings into a pitcher of hot mulled wine. While Simon drank, he listened to the clatter in the kitchen and brooded. In vain he tried to make sense of the strange events of the last two days.

Just as he was pouring himself a new cup, someone touched him on the shoulder. He turned around to find himself looking directly into the grinning face of the Schongau burgomaster. In contrast to their last meeting in the tavern, Karl Semer was extremely friendly this time.

"Fronwieser!" he exclaimed, as if greeting an old friend. "It's good I've found you here. I hear that the abbot put you in charge of looking into these terrible murders. Is that correct?"

Simon grew suspicious. The burgomaster was cheerful like this only when he wanted something. "Could be," he muttered. "Why do you want to know?"

"Well . . ." Semer made a dramatic pause, then sat down next to Simon and beckoned to the innkeeper. "Some of the Tokay we had yesterday." he ordered gruffly. "Two glasses, and quick."

After the innkeeper brought the wine, bowing profusely, Semer paused, then began again in a whisper. "All these events are most unfortunate. Among the pilgrims, there's already talk of witchcraft—they say a puppet has come to life and is shuffling through the monastery killing monks." He laughed under his breath. "What nonsense. But fortunately, you have the perpetrator already, don't you? They say it's the ugly apothecary. Can we therefore—uh—reckon with a trial soon?"

"The investigation isn't yet complete," Simon replied curtly. "It's not certain Brother Johannes is really the culprit. The abbot is requesting a few days to think it over before he informs the district judge in Weilheim."

Karl Semer waved him off. "Pure waste of time, if you ask me. It was the apothecary; that's as sure as the amen in the church. It would be better to burn him now than later."

"How can you be so sure?"

"Well, I . . . have my sources." The burgomaster smiled broadly. "I know that the monster's eyepiece was found at the scene. He fled. And moreover . . ." He leaned forward with a conspiratorial look. "Since then, the prior had the apothecary's cupboard searched and found a number of forbidden medicines that suggest the practice of witchcraft—belladonna, henbane, thornapple, also that notorious red powder obtained from the mummies of executed men . . ."

Simon rolled his eyes. "Belladonna in small doses is very useful in curing fever, and henbane is something that quite a few monks have mixed in their beer in the past, and still do."

"Aha, and the red powder? Tell me about the red powder."

"Burgomaster, may I ask why you are so keen on seeing the monk burned at the stake?" Instinctively, Simon recoiled from

Semer. The medicus still hadn't touched the glass of wine in front of him.

"Isn't that obvious?" Semer hissed. "The Festival of the Three Hosts is in exactly six days, and crowds of pilgrims will be coming to the Holy Mountain. What do you think will happen if the culprit isn't caught before then?"

"Let me guess," Simon replied. "A rumor would go around about an automaton that's murdering people, fewer pilgrims would come, and you'd be left with a lot of unsold candles, votive pictures, and wine carafes. Is that right?"

The burgomaster cringed. "Who told you that . . ." he flared up, before getting control of himself again. "All I care about is the welfare of the pilgrims," he whined. "Look, Fronwieser— what would our Savior have to say about fear and terror on the Holy Mountain?" He shook his head regretfully. "It really would be best if you could convince the abbot to wrap up the case before the festival next Sunday." He looked at him solicitously. "We'll take care of you financially. I have powerful allies who are certainly ready to pay—"

Abruptly, Simon stood up from the table. "Thank you for your time, Burgomaster," he said softly. "But unfortunately I have another report to prepare for the abbot. In addition, we expect the arrival of my father-in-law tomorrow, so there's a lot to do."

Semer's face drained of color. "*Kuisl?*" he whispered. "But . . . but why is he coming here?"

"You wanted a hangman, didn't you?" Simon replied with a smile. "One is coming, and he's the best and cleverest damn hangman in the Priests' Corner. He'll certainly be able to solve these murders. And besides . . ." He shrugged. "If anyone needs to go on a pilgrimage, it's an executioner, isn't it? Now, farewell."

Simon pushed the untouched wine glass back to Semer and headed for the door. The burgomaster could only sit there, astonished.

Finally, he reached for his glass and downed the wine in one gulp.

Shaking, Magdalena pulled her thin woolen shawl tight around her shoulders. In the cold abbey, she was finding it difficult to concentrate on the prayers, and the queasy feeling of the last few days came back. All she could do was hope this feeling had nothing to do with the sickness going around the monastery these days.

In the hopelessly overcrowded building, it was as cold and damp as a cave—even on this June evening. A strong wind whistled through the roof of the south wing, which had been only temporarily patched, and gusts in the high, pointed windows were so loud they sometimes drowned out the Latin murmuring of the mass. This was of little concern to most of the pilgrims and local parishioners, however, as they couldn't understand the words in any case. But they listened reverently to the homily by Abbot Rambeck, who was performing the mass today himself.

The reason for the special mass today was the people sitting in the first rows of the congregation. Count Wartenberg sat with his family under a carved baldachin. Two pale, chubby children yawned and passed the time playing around while their young mother kept trying to quiet them. The older boy was perhaps eight, and the younger one sat sucking his thumb on the lap of the pert young countess. The count, a man in his forties with bushy eyebrows and a sharp, arrogant gaze, looked around the church as if wondering what could be confiscated next for the Wittelsbach treasury.

Though Magdalena had seen many churches, she was filled with awe by the Andechs abbey church. Some of the most important Christian relics were housed here on the Holy Mountain. The church interior was just as awe-inspiring, with numerous altars along the sides and in the nave and doors leading to additional side chapels. Mighty columns supported the high vaulted ceiling and colorful stained glass sparkled everywhere amid the candlelight.

What impressed Magdalena even more than the opulence and splendor were the candles placed all around the church, brought here by pilgrims over the course of many centuries. On the walls, innumerable votive pictures, some yellow with age, bore testimony to miraculous acts of salvation.

"Agnus Dei, qui tollis peccata mundi, miserere nobis . . ." As the abbot spoke the sacred words, worshippers all around Magdalena fell humbly to their knees. She, too, knelt and bowed her head but couldn't help glancing up at Maurus Rambeck, who appeared extremely upset. Several times, he seemed confused or lost his place, and his face was as pale as a corpse. Magdalena wondered whether this had anything to do with recent events or perhaps the presence of the noble family. She, too, was having difficulty concentrating on her prayers.

"Domine, non sum dignus, ut intres sub tectum meum. Sed tantum dic verbo, et sanabitur anima mea . . ."

While Magdalena joined in murmuring the words of invitation to Holy Communion, she glanced up to the gallery, where the church dignitaries had gathered. From Simon's descriptions of the church council, she thought she recognized the fat cellarer, as well as the white-haired librarian and the sensitive novitiate master. The latter, in fact, a relatively younger man, seemed strangely withdrawn. His eyes were red, and now and then he pulled out a silk handkerchief to wipe his face until a hook-nosed monk on his right finally poked him hard in the ribs. It took Magdalena a while to figure out this was the prior. He whispered something to the novitiate master, whereupon the latter put his handkerchief back in his pocket and mumbled a soft prayer. The other members of the council also seemed strangely tense.

Something is fishy here, Magdalena thought. *Did the death of the two young assistants and the disappearance of a Brother really upset the monks so much?*

Finally, the abbot finished, raising his hand in the benediction, and the pilgrims pressed toward the exit to the accompaniment of loud organ music. Magdalena stayed seated in the pew for a while, watching as Maurus Rambeck descended from the apsis into the nave and bowed before Count Wartenberg. They exchanged a few words; then the count turned to his family and sent them to their quarters. Finally, the count and the abbot walked up a flight of stairs to the gallery, which was empty now except for the prior who awaited them there. The three men spoke softly for a while before exiting together through a small door. Magdalena noticed how the prior kept looking around cautiously as they left.

What in all the world was going on here?

After hesitating briefly, Magdalena stood up and approached the stairway leading up to the gallery. Now after evening mass, the church was almost empty. Only a few acolytes still moved about, extinguishing the many candles. It was getting noticeably darker.

The hangman's daughter looked around again, then started up the well-worn staircase.

"Are you lost?"

Leaning on the railing above her, a broad-shouldered monk looked down suspiciously at her. It was the cellarer, and he was clearly in a bad mood. "The gallery and the choir are reserved for the monks. They're not open to visitors," he growled. "Especially not women. What are you looking for here?"

"I'm . . . I'm looking for the sacred relics," Magdalena stuttered. "I've come all the way from Lake Constance on foot to pray before them."

"Stupid woman," the monk grumbled. "Do you think the sacred treasures just stand around here where anyone could steal them?" He pointed to the little door the church officials and the count had passed through. "They are kept in the inner sanctum, where only a chosen few have access. If you wish to see the holy three hosts, you must wait till next Sunday."

"And the noble gentleman who just came up here with two of your Brothers?" asked Magdalena, affecting the voice of a simple farm girl. "He's allowed to see the treasure?"

"Count Wartenberg?" The cellarer laughed. "Naturally. As a member of the House of Wittelsbach, he always has the third key. Now get moving, before I chase you out."

"The third key?" Magdalena was clearly astonished. "Which—"

"Get out, I told you!" The monk approached her threateningly. "Curious daughters of Eve. You should all be thrown out of the church. Brood of vipers!"

Magdalena raised her hands defensively, then rushed down the stairs, crossing herself and bowing obsequiously, until she finally eluded the cellarer.

Outside the main portal, she spat hard and mumbled a curse. That fat milksop would live to regret treating her like that. Something here was fishy, and she was damn well going to find out what was behind all these strange events.

Magdalena tossed her woolen shawl around her shivering body and took a deep breath. The square in front of the monastery was deserted now. Only piles of stones and sacks of limestone and mortar betrayed that this was a busy building site by day. In the nearby forest, trees rustled in the wind and scattered drops of rain fell on the pavement.

Just as Magdalena was about to descend the wide lane to the tavern to tell Simon the latest, she heard a sound that made her stop short. It was so faint and discreet that she took it at first for the singing of a far-off nightingale. Finally, she realized what she was really hearing.

Somewhere behind the monastery, music was playing.

Magdalena started. The glockenspiel! Hadn't Simon said the automaton that vanished had a glockenspiel built into it? She couldn't help but think of the golem the monks had spoken of, the one now supposedly haunting the monastery.

What was it again that Simon said? *An object that springs to life when life is breathed into it . . . It involves some very complicated rituals . . .*

For a moment she hesitated; then she set out to find the source of the music. The sound seemed to come from the right, where an old wall separated the church square from the forest. There she found a little gate, and behind it, some weathered stairs leading to a path along the wall. On the other side, a steep gorge led down into the Kien Valley. In the distance, she could see the vague outlines of a chapel.

For a moment, Magdalena thought she couldn't hear it anymore, but then the sound returned: it was somewhere in front of her, soft, but still clearly audible. She stopped and held her breath, listening intently, and also thought she could hear a rattle and whirring. Now the melody was close, not in front of her, or behind her, but . . . beneath her.

Magdalena was transfixed. The sound seemed to be coming from somewhere inside the Holy Mountain. She looked around in the gathering twilight for a cleft in the rock, or a cave, but couldn't find anything of the sort. As she continued to search, the melody became softer, as if its source were gradually moving away.

That's when she heard something whiz by, brushing her neck, and she felt as if she'd been stung by a big horsefly. Putting her hand to her neck, she felt dampness, and when she took her hand away again, she could see blood in the moonlight.

What's going on here? Is someone shooting at me? I didn't hear a shot . . .

There was no more time to think; she heard the whooshing sound again and threw herself on the ground at the last second.

Above her, something bored into a tree trunk, and now she was sure it was a shot. She picked herself up and ran down the path, stooped over. One last time something whizzed past her and hit the wall, producing a spray of mortar, but by then Magdalena had arrived at the gate. Seized by panic, she dashed into the middle of the deserted church square, almost fearing the automaton would emerge, rattling and humming, from behind the bags of limestone, its mouth open wide and ready to devour her. But when she turned around, there was nothing—just darkness and the rustling branches in the forest behind the wall.

Breathlessly she ran down the lane toward Simon, who was just coming out of the tavern.

"Magdalena!" he cried in relief. "I've been worried. Mass has been over for a long—" That's when he got a closer look at her. "My God!" he gasped "You're bleeding. What happened?"

Magdalena reached up to her neck, still wet with blood. Something had grazed her, and the wound was very painful. The collar of her cape was also wet with blood.

"The automaton . . . is . . . somewhere beneath us . . ." she blurted out as her legs gave way. The last thing she saw was Simon bending down over her, his mouth moving up and down like that of a huge puppet, while somewhere gigantic gears were turning.

Then terrified, exhausted, and suffering from loss of blood, she fell unconscious.

6

'THE BOAT PITCHED AND TOSSED SO VIOLENTLY that Jakob Kuisl had his hands full keeping his grandchildren from drowning. Despite a blue sky, a strong wind was blowing over Lake Ammer, kicking up little whitecaps that covered the entire boat in a fine spray. The children shouted joyfully and kept trying to wriggle out of their grandfather's strong arms and jump over the side into the water.

"You've got two real rascals there. Your grandchildren?" The old ferryman grinned as he rocked back and forth to the movements of his rowing. His weathered face was red with exertion as he dipped the oars deep into the water. Since the very start of their trip in Dießen, he hadn't been silent a moment, and kept badgering the hangman nonstop with questions.

"Would you like to get out at Herrsching over there?" he continued. "Or are you going to sell them to the first traveling salesman you meet?"

"If they keep carrying on like this, I'll donate them to the monastery as little cherubs for the altar. At least then they'll have to keep still."

Kuisl bared his teeth and pushed both children gently under the rowing seat, where, giggling and sniggering, they tangled themselves in a rancid fishnet. Peter played with an old fish head while Paul reached out for a couple of crabs scuttling about in a basket. Although they weren't causing any trouble now, the hangman gave up all hope of a leisurely smoke of his pipe.

Snorting, he wiped the sweat from his forehead. He'd asked himself a dozen times whether it had been such a good idea to take his two grandchildren along to Andechs. After all, it was a matter of life or death for his best friend, who sat in the dungeon accused of murder and witchcraft. Well, as soon as they arrived up on the Holy Mountain, this foolishness would end and he could finally hand the children over to their mother. That way Magdalena would at least have something to do and stop sticking her nose into things that were none of her business.

Kuisl mulled these things over as he watched the shore in Dießen gradually recede in the distance. The tower of the monastery church now looked no longer than his hand, and behind it, he could see the Wessobrunn Highlands and Mount Hoher Peißenberg. The hangman had left Schongau early in the morning with his son Georg on two horses he'd borrowed from the well-to-do Schreevogls. Georg returned home with the horses while Kuisl looked around Dießen for a boat. The old ferryman knew nothing about Kuisl's job, and it was better that way. The men who worked on the lake were especially superstitious, and no fisherman in the world would have permitted a living, breathing hangman on his boat. With winds increasing in force, Kuisl's ferryman had already prayed several times to Saint Peter, the patron saint of fishermen and seafarers.

"Are you making a pilgrimage to Andechs with the two young lads?" the old fisherman asked now. When he got no answer, he continued fervently: "We should thank the Holy Virgin every day that we live so near this blessed place. I've been up on the Holy Mountain at least ten times, and I swear I've seen more relics than would fit in this boat."

And people still drown in the lake just the same, Kuisl thought. *A lot of good all that praying does.*

Shuddering, the hangman remembered a stormy night some years back when a ship sank in Lake Ammer and a large group of pilgrims drowned. Only two children could be saved at that time, yet people spoke of this as a miracle, as if it somehow lessened the grief over the other thirty who had drowned.

"The most precious of them are the three sacred hosts," the fisherman kept on babbling cheerfully, paying no heed to the silence of the man opposite him. "They are displayed only once a year at the Festival of the Three Hosts, but there are others, such as the Charlemagne's Victory Cross; a branch from Christ's crown of thorns; half of His kerchief; Mary's belt; the wedding dress of Saint Elizabeth; Saint Nicolas's stole, and . . ." He stopped for a moment and lowered his voice conspiratorially. "And our Savior's foreskin, taken from him by the accursed Jews at the age of — "

"Please just pay attention to your rowing, or all the beautiful relics in the world won't help us," the hangman interrupted, pointing to the sky. "It looks as if a new storm is brewing."

The ferryman winced and dipped his oars deep in the water. Indeed, a dark bank of clouds was moving toward the lake from the west.

"Damned weather," the old man cursed. "Have hardly ever seen so much as in the past few weeks. If it keeps up like this, there won't be a thing still growing in the fields. The Lord is angry at us, and I'd just like to know why."

"He's probably punishing people who never stop talking," Kuisl murmured. "Maybe you should make another pilgrimage to Andechs. At least up there you can't drown."

"But lightning can strike you dead there." The ferryman laughed and pushed his hat back on his neck. "Believe me, there's more lightning up there than anywhere else — it's almost as if the steeple attracts it. Just a few days ago I saw it hit the ruined steeple again, flashing green and blue like at the Last Judgment. I thought the whole mountain was on fire. If you ask me, it all has something to do with that new abbot who spends too much time with his nose in books instead of praying for our salvation."

While the fisherman cackled on like an old chicken, they arrived at Herrsching Bay on the other side of the lake. To the right, at the little village of Wartaweil, pilgrims departed on the strenuous route to the monastery.

The water here was noticeably calmer, and the wind had abated to a gentle breeze. Jakob Kuisl saw at least two dozen fishing boats tied to rotting piers as fishermen on the shore laboriously patched their nets. Behind them, the Holy Mountain rose up out of a forest of green beeches.

"And how are you going to get up to the monastery with the two youngsters?" the old man asked curiously. "The path is pretty steep."

"Just let me take care of that. I've hauled bigger guys off to say their prayers."

The fisherman looked at him, confused. "What do you mean by that?"

"God bless you." Kuisl handed the old man a few coins, then, despite the child's loud objections, lifted Peter into a wooden frame and, groaning, strapped the pack on his back. With an old cloth, he tied little Paul around his waist where the two-year-old watched with curiosity as the boats bobbed in the water.

"So now I'll take you to your mother," the hangman grumbled. "Just quit rubbing that fish head through my hair." Kuisl took the foul carcass from Peter's hands, tossed it in the water, and then stomped along the path to the landing site in Wartaweil.

Soon the hangman had left the few houses behind him and entered the shady forest that surrounded the monastery on all sides. He had decided to take a little-used path to avoid being annoyed again by another chatterbox on a pilgrimage. The children seemed to enjoy their grandfather's rolling strides and squealed with delight. Again and again Peter pointed out birds and squirrels poised on tree branches over the path that stared back down curiously on the teetering, six-armed monster. The three-year-old gave the animals imaginary names and sang a little song in a squeaky voice.

> *"May bug fly, your father's gone to die,*
> *your mother is in Pommer Land . . ."*

"What crazy songs your mother teaches you," Kuisl cursed, but soon he was humming along softly, too. In the meantime, the constant swaying and singing had put little Paul to sleep in his sling.

The path quickly became steeper, and as Kuisl made his way up the mountain, sweating and panting, he couldn't help thinking about how many pilgrims had taken the same path to the Holy Mountain before him. At one time there had been over forty thousand present just for Pentecost, and now, for the Festival of the Three Hosts, huge crowds were also expected. The hangman could imagine that a warlock locked up in the monastery would be troubled by all this pious activity, and for that reason he also imagined they would try to set Nepomuk's trial for the next day or so.

Deciding to take a shortcut, Kuisl hastened his steps, abandoning the narrow serpentine path up the mountain, and climbed directly up the slope. Now and then he came upon old, weathered steps—moss-covered stones—amid the beeches, but mostly he had to struggle through knee-high thickets. Ahead he saw some boulders placed in a circle that looked almost like the foundation of a tower. The hangman threw back his sweaty head and tried to guess how far it might still be to the monastery.

"Look, Grandpa, a witch. Are you going to burn her?" Peter

pointed to an especially large boulder, at least forty feet high, in a clearing to the right. A gnarled linden tree was growing on top of it, so in the shadows of the surrounding forest it looked, in fact, like a stooped old woman.

"Nonsense, lad," Kuisl growled. "That's no witch, that's a—" Only then did he realize what the boy was actually pointing at. At the foot of the rock stood the entrance to a cave. There before a small fire sat an old, gray-haired, barefoot woman wearing a dirty, torn dress tied around her waist. She rose slowly with the help of a cane and hobbled painfully toward the hangman and his grandchildren. When she finally stood face to face with Kuisl, he looked into her milky white eyes and realized she was completely blind.

"May the Lord bless you," the woman murmured, extending her withered hand. "Is it you, Brother Johannes? Have you brought me a little beechnut porridge again?"

"I . . . I'm only a pilgrim on the way to Andechs," Kuisl replied hesitantly. "Tell me, old woman, is this the way to the monastery?"

The old woman was visibly shocked, and it took a while for her to relax again.

"A burden of great sin lies upon you," she whispered. "Great sin! I can feel that. The devil's rock has led you to me, hasn't it?"

"Devil's rock?" Kuisl shook his head. "Woman, I have no time for your nonsense. I have two lads here who need their mother. So tell me . . . is this the way—"

"This is the entrance to hell," the woman hissed, pointing to the cave behind her. Her voice took on a hard tone now, and the whites of her eyes seemed to glow from the inside. "I am standing guard over it because Satan has come back to earth, but I have no power over him. He sings, he groans, he moans; I can hear him in the night when he forces his way through the bowels of the mountain with his Plague-infested body." When she reached for Kuisl with her cadaverous hand, he took an instinctive step backward. "Beware, wanderer! I can sense you follow in the footsteps of Lucifer. Who are you? A mercenary overcome by misfortune? A murderer? How many men have you killed? Tell me, how many?"

"I am the Schongau executioner," Kuisl growled. He could feel the hair standing up on the back of his neck. "Ask the city council—they keep the books. Now let me through before I kill one more person." The hangman brushed the old woman's hand aside and hurried past her.

Angrily the old woman pounded her crooked cane on the ground. "It is no accident that the Lord has sent you this way," she shouted after him. "Hear the truth, hangman! Judgment is at hand. I can hear the demons digging. They are worming their way through the world, they are reaching out through moldy leaves with their long claws. Soon they will be here, very soon. Repent, hangman! Soon misfortune will strike you like a bolt of lightning."

The children were starting to cry, and Kuisl hastened up the steep path until the old woman's voice was only a distant echo. His heart was pounding, and not just from exertion. The woman had touched something deep within him, something black, dark, in the very depths of his soul. It was as if all the dead men in the last decades, all those tortured, hanged, beheaded, or broken on the wheel had called out at the same time for revenge. He couldn't help thinking of his dream the night before, the memories of the war that had flashed through his mind.

How many men have you killed? Tell me, how many?

For the first time in a long while Jakob Kuisl felt real fear.

He shook himself and hurried along the path through the trees. Branches seemed to reach out to seize him, leaves brushed against his face, the children whined and wailed, and Peter kept pulling at his hair like an angry little gnome on his shoulders.

Kuisl staggered forward, almost falling, but finally pushed one last green branch aside. Now he looked out on a sunny clear-

ing of meadows and fields where ears of light brown barley
waved in the wind. Beyond these, in the bright light of early afternoon, lay the monastery.

The horror had vanished.

Suddenly the hangman couldn't help laughing out loud.
Like a child, he'd let himself be scared by an old woman babbling about revenge and retribution. What in the world was
wrong with him? Was he turning into an anxious child afraid of
old wives' tales? It was high time to hand the children over to
Magdalena and concentrate on his real reason for being here.

With renewed courage Kuisl hiked along the fields toward
the monastery, but in secret he decided to pray and beg for forgiveness in the coming days.

Not that he really believed in any of this, but it couldn't hurt,
either.

Magdalena was awakened by the rattling cough of an old man on
a simple wooden plank bed to her right. Gasping, the old man
spat a green clump of phlegm onto the reeds on the floor.

Disgusted, the hangman's daughter turned away. Since the
night before, she'd been laid out in a wing of the monastery — a
horse stable no longer in use, which the abbot made available for
the sick. Only a handful of patients were there in the early morning, but their numbers had increased dramatically in the last few
hours. She estimated that over two dozen moaning, snoring,
wailing pilgrims were housed now in the provisional hospital.
Wrapped in thin woolen blankets, they lay shivering in flea-
infested beds and on bales of straw on the ground. The damp old
quarters stank of manure and human excrement, while outside
they could hear pilgrims singing on their way to the monastery to
pray for a good harvest, a healthy child, or simply a peaceful year
without war, hunger, and pestilence.

Carefully Magdalena tested the fragrant herbal dressing on
her neck. The wound wasn't deep — the strange projectile had

only grazed her. Nevertheless, she had passed out briefly due to exhaustion and loss of blood. What troubled her even most was the fear of whoever was lying in wait for her the night before along the monastery wall.

That unknown person . . . and the strange melody.

Was it the same man who'd pushed her from the belfry the day before?

"Well, are you back among the living?" Simon bent over her with a smile and handed her a bowl of steaming oatmeal. "My poppy-seed potion obviously worked well. It's afternoon; with just a few interruptions, you've slept more than sixteen hours."

"I . . . I probably needed it," Magdalena replied, still a bit drowsy. "But I'm damned hungry now." She attacked the oatmeal with gusto. Not until she had wiped the last morsel away with her finger did she lean back, sighing.

"That was good," she murmured, "very good. Almost as good as the porridge my cousin makes, the scruffy knacker." Suddenly her face turned serious. "I should be glad I'm still alive and can eat at all," she added softly.

Simon caressed her sweaty forehead. "I made you a compress with shepherd's purse, horsetail, and marigold," he said, with concern in his voice. "The wound on your neck should heal well, but you were spouting all kinds of crazy things last night. What in the world happened to you?"

Magdalena sighed. "If only I knew." Then she told Simon about what she had seen during evening mass, the strange melody, about being ambushed and the shots that came from behind the wall.

"It was the same song Brother Virgilius's automaton was singing?" Simon looked at her skeptically. "Are you sure?"

Magdalena shrugged. "In any case, it was a glockenspiel, and it came from somewhere inside the mountain . . . down below." Suddenly a chill came over her again. "Do you think that automaton really killed its master and the apprentice and is now looking for other victims somewhere down there? Is it a . . . a golem?"

"Nonsense," Simon replied. "Those are nothing but horror stories. Only God can create life. But I do think these monks have something to do with it."

Magdalena grinned triumphantly. "Then do you believe now that the ugly Nepomuk is innocent? I said so right away."

"You mean Brother Johannes?" Simon handed Magdalena a pitcher of water, and she gulped it down eagerly. "If he really isn't a sorcerer, he'll be sitting just as before in the old cheese cellar," he mused. "So he can't be the one who shot at you last night. Perhaps it was just a hunter who thought you were a wild animal. It was, after all, pretty dark."

"Simon, don't be silly. Do I look like a wild boar?" Magdalena shook her head and cringed, as the wound began to sting again. "That was no hunter; it was that stranger. Sometimes I believe you think I'm just a hysterical woman."

Simon smiled. "Oh, God, no, I'd never dare to think that. But it's true that you sometimes . . . well . . . seem overstressed."

"Good heavens, I've rarely felt as clear-headed as now," Magdalena snapped. "But if you say one more time that I'm sick, I'll probably really start feeling that way."

But Simon was already lost in thought again and seemed not to have heard. "The monks are indeed behaving very strangely," he continued, haltingly. "All this talk in the monastery council about the blasphemous experiments Johannes and Virgilius were carrying out. What did the monks mean by that? And what was the abbot doing with the prior and one of the Wittelsbachs in the relics chamber so late at night? You said that Maurus Rambeck seemed very distracted during mass . . ."

"Just like the young novitiate master," Magdalena spoke up. "He looked like he'd been crying and got a poke in the ribs from the prior. And the fat cellarer was standing guard up on the balcony. If you ask me, they have a secret and are afraid someone will learn about it."

"But Count Wartenberg?" Simon frowned. "What in God's name does that Wittelsbacher nobleman have to do with it?"

"The cellarer said Wartenberg had the third key."

"The third key?" Simon shook his head, stood up, and stretched. "Things are getting more confusing just when I have my hands full here. This damned fever is like a plague." He pointed to the door where two pilgrims were just carrying in another patient, a deathly pale farmer dressed in coarse linen, whose weak moans joined the chorus of the wailing and rattling of the other patients.

"Basically this pilgrimage is one huge source of infection," Simon grumbled. "For years, both my father and I have preached that what makes people sick is not vapors escaping from the ground, but that people infect one another. Thousands will come to Andechs in the next few days and carry this fever back with them to their cities and villages. It would be better for people to stay home and pray there."

"It's too late for that now, Master Fronwieser. The best we can do is to care for the people, so they can return home healthy."

Simon turned around to see Jakob Schreevogl carrying in a child. He was weak, sweat was streaming down his forehead, and his eyes were closed.

"The parents believed that a hundred rosaries and the donation of a candle would assure their child's survival," the alderman sputtered. "Fortunately I was able to convince them to leave the boy in your care, at least during noon mass. It's a disgrace." Carefully he placed the child down on a bale of straw in the corner of the low-ceilinged vault, then looked at Simon with a tired smile. "When I see sick children, I can't help thinking of my little Clara and how you cured her back then, Fronwieser. I hope you can help this boy as well. Every child is a gift of God." The young alderman reached for his belt and took out a purse of clinking coins. "Here, take this. I actually wanted to buy an arm's-length bee's-wax candle with the money and donate a new confessional booth, but I have the feeling the coins are better off invested here."

"Thank you," Simon murmured, weighing the purse in his hands. There must have been thirty guilders in it. "I'll ask the abbot for permission to buy medicine and clean bed linens with it."

Schreevogl waved him off. "Just decide for yourself. The abbot really has other concerns at the moment. Rumors of this horrible murder are going around, and some golem is said to be haunting the monastery. If Rambeck isn't careful, his flock will be nothing but anxious sheep at the Festival of the Three Hosts." He winked at Magdalena, who had sat up in bed now. "But if I know you, you both already know more about this than I do."

"If we learn anything about the murderer, you'll be the first to know, we promise." Magdalena stretched again and stood up. She was still wavering slightly but otherwise seemed to have recovered. "And now excuse us for a moment. I'd like to . . ." She stopped short as a shadow fell over her face. Something large was standing in the doorway, blocking the sunlight. It was a man in a black overcoat with broad shoulders, carrying a crude walking stick in his callused hands, his face concealed by a wide-brimmed hat. The giant bent down and placed two little boys gingerly on the ground. They ran toward Magdalena with shouts of joy.

"Looks like Paul has finally learned to walk," the hangman grumbled. "It's about time. I thought he'd always be crawling through the house like a little worm."

"My God, Father!" Magdalena shouted, running toward her children, who embraced her warmly. She laughed out loud with relief. In all the excitement, she'd completely forgotten the letter she'd sent the day before. Now that her father and children were with her, she felt everything would turn out well.

"Spare your mother, you rascals," Kuisl scolded, raising his finger playfully. "You'll crush her. It's hard to believe that they were clinging to my coattails just a minute ago."

"Even the best grandfather can't replace a mother." Smiling, Simon came over to his father-in-law and held out his hand. As they shook, Simon could feel his bones cracking. He never ceased to be amazed at the strength of the Schongau executioner.

"It's great that you came so soon, Jakob," Simon said through clenched teeth, "but we thought it might be without the children—"

"Wouldn't that suit you just fine," Kuisl interrupted gruffly. "Leave the sick grandmother with two screaming youngsters and enjoy your vacation. Nothing doing—Magdalena can just take care of her own little rascals."

"Mother is sick?" Magdalena approached her father anxiously with her two children in her arms. "But why did you then—"

"What am I to do? Abandon my friend?" Kuisl said crossly. "Anyway, I don't think it's anything serious, just a stupid cough like so many in Schongau have nowadays. I wanted to stay, but . . ." He stopped short, then continued gruffly. "Your mother is a tough woman. She practically threw me out of the house when she heard about Nepomuk."

"Nepomuk? Your friend?" Jakob Schreevogl, who had been standing quietly alongside them until then, gave the hangman a bewildered look. "I'm afraid I don't understand. And just what are you doing in Andechs, Kuisl? Has the executioner come on a pilgrimage?"

"Ah . . . I'm afraid that's a long story, my dear councilor," Magdalena interrupted. "I'll tell you about it another time, but for now we have a favor to ask."

"And what would that be?"

Magdalena pointed at the coughing and wailing patients all

around them. "Could you watch Simon's patients for about an hour? The Kuisl family has a few things to discuss."

The patrician was dumbfounded. "Me? But I have no idea how—"

"It's very simple." Magdalena handed Schreevogl a rag and a bucket of fresh water. "Wash the sweat from their brows, change the dressings now and then, and try to look serious and competent. Believe me, that's all most doctors do."

She took her two children by the hand and left the stinking infirmary with Simon and the hangman as the astonished patrician gazed after her.

Together the family climbed the steep lane up to the monastery church to find a quiet place to talk, but they soon found that wouldn't be easy: The noon mass had just concluded, and crowds of attendees came streaming toward them. Magdalena noticed the number of pilgrims was significantly larger than the day before. There were still five days left before the Festival of the Three Hosts, but already the streets around the monastery were as crowded as at a church fair.

The pilgrims seemed to come from everywhere. Magdalena heard many strange German dialects—of which she knew only Swabian and Frankish—and saw that many pilgrims from individual villages stayed together in tight groups. There were poorly dressed day laborers, solid middle-class workers, and fat patricians who stepped delicately over steaming piles of horse manure, looking disgusted and holding up their trousers. Often someone would start singing a hymn, and the others would join in.

"Come sinners, come now, see the true son of God . . ."

Simon and the hangman took the kids on their backs to make their way through the crowds more easily. The air smelled of incense, fried fish, and dust from the road, and somewhere a boy was crying for his mother. Still, all the singing and praying made Magdalena feel peaceful.

"How did you ever find us in this crowd, Father?" Magdalena asked as they walked through the mass of people up to the church.

"I went down to see cousin Graetz," the hangman grumbled. "At first there was just a dumb, red-headed farm boy there who didn't want to let me in, but then Michael came along with his knacker's wagon and told me my good son-in-law was caring for the sick even here in Andechs."

"Does Graetz know why you're here?" Simon asked anxiously. "Perhaps for the time being it's better —"

"How dumb do you think I am? As far as Graetz knows, I'm here on a pilgrimage. That made a lot of sense to him — he said I needed it." Kuisl clapped his hands impatiently. "But now enough of this chitchat. Tell me what happened to ugly old Nepomuk and what — for heaven's sake — you have to do with all of it." He looked around angrily. "Damn crowds. I know why I never go on pilgrimages."

"I think I know a place where we'll be undisturbed," Magdalena replied with a grin, thinking about how much her father hated big crowds. That's why the hangman always dreaded a public execution. "Follow me," she called to the others, "there's something I wanted to show you, in any case."

Crossing the crowded church square, with its piles of stones and sacks of mortar, she headed toward the little gate she'd discovered the previous night. Followed by the others, she took the narrow path on the other side of the monastery wall, which led shortly to a chapel in the forest. The noise of the crowd receded; they met no one but a grim-looking woodcutter; then finally they were alone. The children crawled happily around the remains of a stone wall, and Simon gave them some pine cones and beechnuts to play with.

"This is where I heard the music yesterday," Magdalena said softly.

"What damned music?" Kuisl growled. "Speak up, girl, before I have to put the thumb screws on you."

Magdalena sat down on a fallen tree trunk not far from the chapel and started to recount what she and Simon had learned in the last three days. She told her father about the two dead men, the bloodbath in the watchmaker's workshop, and the automaton that had vanished along with its master. Then she told him about the two attempts on her life.

"Someone by the wall here took a shot at me," she said finally. "The strange thing is that I didn't hear a shot, just a hissing sound."

"A hissing? Maybe it was a bolt from a crossbow ..." Her father scrutinized the trees around them, stopping suddenly in front of a beech where he scratched a bullet out of the bark with his finger. He frowned and held it up for them to see. "This is fresh," he grumbled, "a rather high caliber. Are you really sure, girl, you didn't hear a shot?"

"Father, I may be stubborn, but I'm not deaf."

"Strange." Kuisl rubbed the heavy, misshapen piece of lead in his callused fingers. "There's actually only one weapon this could come from, and it's very rare and valuable. I saw it only once, in the war."

"So it was Nepomuk," Simon interrupted excitedly. "After all, he was a mercenary and—"

"Nonsense." The hangman spat on the ground in disgust. "When this happened, Nepomuk had already been in the dungeon a long time; you told me that yourself. So stick to the facts. These little monks are dubious characters, and if they themselves aren't involved, they're just trying to find someone to blame."

"Just the same," Simon objected, "your friend Nepomuk is keeping something from us. Evidently he was carrying out some experiments with Virgilius before the watchmaker disappeared."

Kuisl rubbed the side of his huge nose, thinking. "Then I should no doubt have a serious talk with Nepomuk."

"And how do you plan to do that?" asked Magdalena. "Are you going to just knock on the dungeon door, say you're the Schongau hangman, and ask whether you can torture the prisoner just a bit to hear what he has to say? Andechs is under the jurisdiction of the court in Weilheim, don't forget. If the governor learns you're snooping around his district, you'll quickly wind up on the rack yourself."

"Give me a moment. I'll come up with something," Kuisl grumbled. "I always think of something. Now let's go visit my cousin Michael," he said, turning toward the gate. "The children are hungry, and so am I. You'll see, it's a lot easier to think with a full stomach and a good pipe to smoke."

They walked out onto the church square still teeming with pilgrims. The workmen had now roped off an area near the south wing in order to continue the construction work without interruption. Many pilgrims were looking up anxiously at the holes in the charred roof; some of them grumbling because the main door to the church had been blocked briefly. Simon watched a group of angry pilgrims gather around the entrance.

"It's taken me a week to walk here from Augsburg," an old man complained. "A whole damned week. And now they won't even let me into the church. This is a disgrace."

"Let us pray that the monastery is restored to its full splendor in time for the Festival of the Three Hosts," a richly dressed patrician said worriedly. "It doesn't look ready now. Will we have to march among the sacks of mortar and blocks of stone? I've paid my tithes . . . and for what?"

"We've thought about returning home to Garmisch," a little old woman added in a trembling voice. "First there was that fever going around, and now they say some kind of monster is haunting the monastery."

"A monster?" asked an old man next to her with a shudder of delight. "What do you know about it?"

"Well, people say . . ." the old woman began, but she paused as a procession of Benedictines came out a side door of the church. Singing loudly, some carried smoking censers that they swung back and forth. The crowd fell to its knees and the monks strode past them with heads held high. Simon recognized the abbot among them, as well as the fat cellarer, the novitiate master, and the hook-nosed prior, Jeremias. Just before the monks entered the main building of the monastery, Simon noticed how the prior gave him a look of disgust. Then the monks disappeared inside.

The medicus rubbed his forehead, trying to sort out his thoughts. The abbot, the prior, and all the others from the monastery council seemed to be hiding something from him. How would he ever learn what that was? This monastery seemed like an enchanted place to which only a few chosen people had access. How could he ever hope to advance to the inner circle? Simon cursed under his breath.

His thoughts were interrupted by another large monk with a cowl pulled down over his face. For a brief moment the medicus thought he was looking at his father-in-law in a Benedictine robe, but then he realized this was only Brother Martin, the large carpenter who'd discovered him and Magdalena at the watchmaker's house the day before.

Suddenly an idea flashed through his head.

Only a few are chosen . . .

He couldn't help but grin. It seemed he'd found a way to learn more about the monks and their secrets. It would take a bit of planning, but then nothing would really stand in his way.

Of course, he knew his father-in-law would balk at the plan.

• • •

Long after the three Schongauers had disappeared, the man remained standing there, his eyes full of hatred.

After listening to them from his hiding place, he finally disappeared into the crowd in the church square. Beneath the folds of his robe, a strange tingling feeling came over him as he watched the large, broad-shouldered man leave. The giant was not at all as stupid as he looked. He would have to watch out for this huge man who'd correctly guessed the weapon used and asked the right questions. Moving quietly, the man scurried behind the monastery wall like a fat toad that had surfaced only briefly to warm itself in the sun. Not until he reentered the dark forests of the Kien Valley did he feel safe again. Nevertheless, he couldn't shake a nagging fear that the plan might fail.

Now there were three of them poking their noses around in the monastery. If he wasn't careful, soon half of Andechs would be pursuing him. This girl had foiled his plans twice. He'd have to make sure she wouldn't be able to do that again. The next time he'd have to proceed more carefully. Perhaps poison, a silent blade in the night, a message that would lead her into a trap . . . There were so many possibilities.

Next time he'd have to make sure his assistant clearly understood how important it was to get rid of this girl. Sometimes the fellow was just a bit too sensitive; feelings were like a poisonous fog surrounding a person, and before you realized it, it could be too late. He himself knew how powerful feelings could be. Too often they left a gaping wound in the soul that wouldn't heal.

From far away, he heard the old, familiar melody and felt how it helped bring back his old sense of security. Nothing could hold him back now — certainly not this rabble from Schongau.

There were only five days left before his dream would finally become a reality.

7

WHAT ARE YOU ASKING ME TO DO? ARE YOU OUT of your mind?" The Schongau hangman was sitting in the knacker's house, having just lit his pipe a second time. When Simon hesitantly explained his plan, the hangman dropped his pipe on the floor, and Magdalena quickly picked it up before her two children could get a close look at the smoking bowl of tobacco. They had already broken a clay jug in the small room and dumped out a box of grain.

"Well, I do think it's the only way we can learn more about this monastery and its residents," Simon replied hesitantly. "And Magdalena is right: if you want to speak with your friend Nepomuk, it certainly can't be as an executioner on a pilgrimage."

"Aha, but as a stinking monk, eh?" He spat on the floor. "Out of the question. I can't even recite the full credo or bow like these priests."

"But you don't have to," Magdalena cooed gently. "A little humility would go a long way. You'll see, you'll make a wonderful monk." She handed her father his pipe and smiled cheerfully, to which the hangman responded with a grunt.

"How hard can it be?" she continued. "Simon simply introduces you as a wandering Franciscan monk who's helping him to care for his patients. Your friend Nepomuk is in jail, and the pilgrimage is looking more and more like a procession of the sick and the dying. Ever since this strange fever broke out, the abbot is happy to have anyone to help. No one is going to ask you to sing and pray—all you have to do is to keep your eyes open."

"A hangman as a *monk*," Kuisl spat out the word with such contempt that his grandchildren crawled back into their mother's lap, terrified. "Out of the question. Even a blind man would see through it. There has to be another way."

Simon looked at Magdalena and sighed softly. He knew it wouldn't be easy to get his father-in-law to go along with the plan. The idea had just come to him when he noticed the hefty Brother Martin in his robe in the procession of Benedictine monks. The robe was a perfect disguise to learn more about the inner circle of the Andechs monks. The Brothers knew Simon already, but his father-in-law seemed a better choice anyway. Grumpy and uncommunicative as he was, he could just as easily pass himself off as a Carthusian monk vowed to silence. At noon Simon told Magdalena about his plan, and since then, she'd been waiting for her cousin, the knacker, and his silent redheaded assistant to leave the house so she could speak with her father in peace and quiet.

Peace and quiet was just relative, however, for the two little ones kept pulling at each other's hair and tossing clay bowls off the shelves.

"Good Lord, Magdalena," Simon flared up. "Can you see to it that the kids are quiet when adults have something important to discuss?"

"Ah, and why doesn't the lord and master of the house do that himself?" Magdalena picked up little Paul, who was crying because his brother had taken away a carved wooden donkey, and put him in her lap. "You could spend a bit more time caring for your sons."

"Everything in its time," Simon replied, somewhat peeved.

"Now we have to concentrate on learning more about a few of the monks." After one more stern look, he turned to his father-in-law again.

"You can see for yourself, we've taken care of everything. What can go wrong?"

The medicus had found a black robe in a box in the monastery guesthouse, and now passed it hesitantly across the table to Kuisl. It was moth-eaten and the hems were somewhat moldy, but at least it was more or less the right size. After Magdalena made a few alterations it would look like a suitable robe for an itinerant mendicant.

"The Minorites wear almost the same robes as the Benedictines," Simon explained with angelic patience. "Nobody will notice that we have made a few little changes; and if you pull the hood way down over your face, not even your own wife would recognize you."

"Leave Anna out of this, you blasted son-in-law," the hangman growled threateningly. "I'm not going to put up with—"

"For God's sake, Father," Magdalena suddenly interrupted, pounding the table so hard that little Paul began to whimper again. "Can't you see that's the only way we can learn more about these murders? It's *your* friend who'll be burned at the stake, not ours." She jumped up and strode to the door with the two boys. "If you like, we can just all go back home, watch the trial from there, and just pray to the savior in the Altenstadt basilica. Simon and I don't have to be here."

"Ah, you forget the abbot asked me to write another report," Simon murmured. "If we both just get up and go now, it will look suspicious, as if we're trying to flee. After all, until recently we were under suspicion ourselves. They'll come looking for us and put us on trial with Nepomuk. To judge by the way the prior keeps staring so angrily at me, he'd rather see me burned at the stake today than tomorrow."

"Just stop where you are, you fresh woman," Kuisl grumbled, beckoning to his daughter, who was still standing at the door. Then, with disgust, he unfolded the torn black robe and examined it. "I'll never in my life fit into that."

"I can let out the seam a bit at the bottom," Magdalena said hopefully, as she returned to the table. "And I've also found a nice white cord big enough to go around your fat belly. Does that mean you'll do it?"

The hangman shrugged. "I'll never get into the monastery wearing this. Never. Forget it. But perhaps the disguise will get me in to have a few words with Nepomuk. Have you two thought about a rosary?"

Simon held his hand in front of his mouth so his father-in-law wouldn't see his smile. Jakob Kuisl was the stubbornest fellow in the whole Priests' Corner, but besides that he was the best friend anyone could have. In his heart, the medicus knew the hangman wouldn't abandon the ugly Nepomuk. With a triumphant gesture he reached under the table and brought out a carved wooden rosary. Kuisl responded with a grateful grunt.

"Now we have to discuss calmly what we're going to say to the abbot," Simon said, relieved. "After all, Maurus Rambeck will have to give permission for a Minorite Brother to care for the sick in his monastery." He pulled a little Bible from his vest pocket and motioned to his father-in-law. "And then it won't hurt to memorize a few psalms just in case you have to pray and don't know how to do that."

The hangman leaned forward and tapped Simon on the chest. "Believe me, boy," he growled softly, "if your beautiful plan fails, you're going to have to pray yourself. Or better yet, you should do it now." He stood up and put on the moldy robe. "If even one little monk recognizes me, we'll be so deep in shit that even the archangel himself won't be able to get us out."

Less than an hour later, Simon and the hangman climbed the steep stairs to the abbot's study on the second floor of the east wing. Magdalena stayed with the children in the knacker's house, where the two children wouldn't let their mother, whom they had missed so long, out of their sight. Before that, the hangman's daughter had lengthened the ripped robe and cleaned off the worst of the dirt. Kuisl was now wearing the black robe of a Minorite with a white cord around his belly, while a wooden rosary dangled from his neck, swinging back and forth like a pendulum. Simon looked approvingly at his father-in-law, who looked in the robe like the incarnate scourge of God. Kuisl would have made a good priest, though Simon doubted anyone could expect much leniency from him. At least he'd keep a firm grip on his flock.

"This robe itches like the claws of a demon," the hangman cursed. "I really don't understand how priests can wear something like this day in and day out."

"You forget that monks often whip themselves and slide through the church on their knees," Simon reminded him with a grin. "To say nothing of fasting. Pain is clearly the pathway to God."

"Or to truth." said Jakob, wiping the sweat from his brow. "Maybe I should use the robe the next time I torture someone."

They had now arrived at the door to the abbot's study. Simon knocked timidly. When there was no answer, the medicus tentatively pushed down the door handle and the tall door swung open. The setting sun shone in softly through the glass windows, casting light on the rows of shelves covering the entire back wall. In front of the shelves sat Maurus Rambeck at his desk, musing over a pile of books. The abbot seemed not to have noticed their arrival.

"Ah, Your Excellency?" Simon said cautiously. "Excuse the interruption, but . . ."

Only now did Maurus Rambeck jump up. A single little drop of sweat landed on a piece of paper in front of him. Hastily the abbot pushed some of the books aside.

"Ah, the bathhouse surgeon from Schongau," Rambeck murmured with a wan smile. Once again Simon noticed how pale the abbot had become since the day before. His right hand trembled slightly as he raised it in a blessing. "Do you have any news about the two tragic deaths, a clue perhaps that will help us?"

Simon shook his head regretfully. "No, Your Excellency, but I'll have a closer look at the corpses today. At the moment I'm too busy with the sick pilgrims."

"The sick ... pilgrims?" The abbot seemed not to understand. Indeed, he seemed lost in his own world of books.

"Well, this fever that's spreading around Andechs," Simon tried to explain. "It's no doubt a kind of nervous fever, although I don't yet know exactly what kind of sickness it is. I'm barely able to keep up with it in any case, as Brother Johannes is not available ..." He paused briefly. "Fortunately I've found a colleague now to help me—naturally, only if you will permit." With a wide gesture he pointed to Jakob Kuisl, who stood next to him with his hood pulled down and his arms folded, looking like a piece of heavy furniture. "Brother ... Jakob. He's an itinerant Franciscan monk very skilled in the art of healing. Isn't that so, Brother Jakob?"

For the first time the abbot seemed to notice Kuisl. He gazed briefly at the large man in the robe, then nodded.

"Very well," he murmured, lost in thought. "We can certainly use all the help we can get."

"Ah ... Brother Jakob would like to take part in the masses and visit the library," Simon continued. "He has heard much about your books, which are said to contain true hoards of information. Isn't that so, Jakob?" He glanced over at his father-in-law and gave him a little nudge with his foot, but the hangman remained silent. "Well, in any case ..." Simon continued, "will he be permitted to visit the rooms in the monastery? You have my word that—"

"Of course. And now please leave me alone." Maurus Rambeck had already turned back to his books, waving his hand as if to chase away an annoying fly. "There's much I have to do."

"As you wish." Simon bowed, not without casting a final glance at the pages of the book lying open in front of the abbot, but all he could see was that it was written in a strange script. The letters were faded and seemed to have been written many years ago. When the abbot noticed Simon still standing in front of him, he abruptly closed the book.

"Is there something else?" Rambeck said in a rasping voice.

"No, no . . . I was just a bit lost in thought." Kuisl still hadn't uttered a word. As Simon pulled him toward the door, he added, "I'll let you know as soon as I learn anything. Farewell for now." He bowed one last time before the heavy, tall oaken door closed behind him.

Outside in the hall, the medicus took a deep breath then turned angrily to his father-in-law.

"When I asked you to pretend to be a monk, I didn't realize you'd taken a vow of silence," Simon hissed. "Thank God the abbot was much too distracted to wonder about a deaf-mute Franciscan."

"What do you mean, deaf-mute?" Kuisl groused. "You talked enough for two. But you're right; something is wrong with this priest," he said, furrowing his brow. "Did you see the book on his desk that he so hurriedly tried to conceal from us?"

Simon nodded. "Yes, but unfortunately I couldn't make any sense of the writing."

"Hebrew," the hangman replied brusquely. "The old language of the Jews. I saw a book like that one time. I wonder what the abbot was looking for in it?"

"Well, Maurus Rambeck was at the Benedictine University in Salzburg for many years and is known for his studies of ancient languages," Simon replied. "Perhaps we just disturbed him in his work."

"Ha! Work? Judging by his looks he's up to his neck in some sort of trouble. He was as pale as someone heading for his own execution—I know about such things." Kuisl ran down the stairway, taking care not to step on the hem of his robe. "So come now before His Excellency changes his mind and wants us to celebrate evening mass with him."

"Where . . . where are you headed so fast, Kuisl?" Simon whispered, running after the hangman.

"Where else?" Jakob Kuisl turned. Despite the darkness under his hood, Simon could briefly see his eyes sparkle. "To see the ugly Nepomuk, of course. After all, we haven't seen each other for thirty years. And in the meantime, you can have another look at the two corpses. Perhaps you can find something you haven't noticed yet."

Kuisl squeezed the pearls of the rosary in his hands as if they were thumb screws. "I swear to you I'll find the person trying to make a scapegoat of my old friend," he said softly. "And by God, then he can be glad I'm not the executioner in this district but just a hangman in a lousy monk's costume."

With the hood pulled far down over his face, Jakob Kuisl stomped off toward the monastery dairy where his friend Nepomuk was still held prisoner. By now the sun was a red ball sinking into the clouds west of Lake Ammer. The air suddenly turned cooler, so that the hangman began to feel a chill under the thin robe. Once more he cursed his son-in-law for this idea, even though he now secretly conceded it might work. In just a moment he'd find out just how good Simon's idea was.

Two watchmen were standing around the entrance to the farm, and Kuisl could see right away they really weren't professionals—likely hunters drafted by the monastery for guard duty. Dressed in green capes, they leaned on their muskets, looking bored and staring into the sky where the evening star was just setting. Torches were burning in iron pots to the left and right of the door. When the two watchmen heard the hangman coming, they jumped to attention.

"Who goes there?" called one of them, a stout man with the beginnings of a bald spot.

"The Lord be with you and illumine your way," Kuisl grumbled and, in the next moment, felt strangely ridiculous. He felt as if the word *hangman* was burned onto his forehead, but the two watchmen relaxed and nodded to him amiably.

"Greetings, Brother," the fat man replied. "And thank you for your blessing, though a chicken leg would also be very welcome." He giggled softly. Seeing Kuisl's white cord, his laughter stopped suddenly. "Just a moment. You are . . ."

"An itinerant Franciscan, indeed," the hangman said, completing the sentence. "The hapless Brother inside there wants to confess. The abbot himself sent me."

"I see, but why doesn't one of *our* monks do that?" the younger watchman interrupted. "And by the way, who are you? I've never seen you here before."

"Because I'm an itinerant Franciscan, you damn fool," Kuisl whispered. He closed his eyes briefly, realizing his words were out of character. The guards looked back at him in astonishment.

"Do you really think one of the Benedictines would take confession from the poor creature in there?" Kuisl continued in a gentler tone. "Don't forget, he killed three of their Brothers. But please go and ask the abbot," he added, pointing to the light in the second-floor room of the monastery. "I was just with him. Brother Maurus is brooding as so often over his old books. Just don't speak so loudly to him—His Excellency has a severe headache today."

"That's . . . that's all right," the fat man said, patting his colleague reassuringly on the shoulder. Clearly he had no desire to pester a busy abbot suffering from a headache. "We'll stand right outside the door," he mumbled. "You won't take off with the monster," he laughed nervously; then he pushed the heavy wooden bolt aside and permitted the hangman to pass. Kuisl took one of the torches from the wall and shuffled into the dark dungeon.

"May the Lord bless you," he grumbled, "and shove your musket up your butt, you wise-ass dirty bastard," he added softly enough that the guards outside couldn't hear him.

As soon as the hangman entered the room, he was confronted with the sharp odor of old cheese and the stench of urine and other garbage. On shelves along the wall stood frayed baskets, and beneath them cowered a figure in a torn robe. When the ugly Nepomuk heard the sound of the sliding bolt, he was startled and struggled to his feet. His face was still swollen from the blows dealt by his pursuers. He blinked at his visitor with his good eye but wasn't able to see much at first due to the sudden brightness.

"Are you sending me a father confessor already?" he croaked. "Then we can spare ourselves the annoyance of a trial, can't we? It's just as well. At least then I won't be put on the rack before you burn me."

"Nobody's going to put you on the rack," Kuisl whispered. "And somebody else will burn for this. I'll see to that."

"Who . . . who are you?" Nepomuk Volkmar now sat up all the way. He held his hand over his eyes to shield them from the bright light so that he could get a better look at the huge Franciscan monk standing before him. Suddenly Kuisl threw his hood back, and Nepomuk let out a cry.

"My God, Jakob," he gasped. "Is it really you? After all these years? Then my prayers really have been heard."

"If you keep shouting like that, you'll soon be saying your last prayer," Kuisl whispered. "For God's sake, keep quiet before the two idiots out there become suspicious." Without further explanation, he started murmuring words in a monotone.

"Ventram porcinum. Bene exinanies, aceto et sale,
postea aqua lavas, et sie hanc impensam imples . . ."

Nepomuk Volkmar was puzzled. "Why are you giving me a recipe in Latin for cooking pig's stomach?"

"Because that's all that I can think of at the moment, numbskull," Kuisl whispered. "It comes from a big old dog-eared volume in my attic. The watchmen think I'm taking your confession, so just keep your mouth shut."

He kept mumbling for a while, speaking softer and softer until finally he fell silent. A broad grin spread over his face.

"You haven't gotten any better looking in the last thirty years," Kuisl finally said, pressing his friend to his broad chest in a warm embrace.

"And you're not getting any thinner," Nepomuk groaned. "And if you grab hold of me like that I won't need a rack." He lowered his head and started to sob softly. "But what difference does it make? If something doesn't happen soon, it would be better if you just crushed me to death right now."

Kuisl let him go and sat down on an overturned wooden crate. "You're right," he grumbled. "We don't have much time for memories — we can do that later over a glass of wine when this is all finished. All right?" He smiled and beckoned Nepomuk to come closer. "But do tell me what happened. Remember that, if I'm to help you, I have to know the whole truth. Up to now all I know is what Magdalena tells me, and she sometimes piles it on pretty thick."

Kuisl summarized in brief what his daughter and Simon had told him that noon. Then he looked expectantly at his friend, waiting for his reply. "Tell me, Nepomuk," he growled. "Do you have anything to do with these murders? You know it is no disgrace to kill someone: the two of us have done that often enough. But the law was always on our side." His face darkened. "The law, or the war."

"Believe me, Jakob, I'm innocent, at least of these two murders." Groaning, Nepomuk settled down on the floor and drew up his legs. "I don't know who killed the two novitiates, but I have a dark suspicion."

"Then speak up, or I'll put you on the rack myself."

The Brother passed his hands through the little hair remaining on his head and took a deep breath. Finally, he started to speak as Jakob sat back and listened quietly. "Brother Virgilius and I have had many discussions in recent years," he whispered. "We have almost become friends, probably because we are interested in the same thing—the study of the unknown, the rejection of unproved hypotheses." The monk smiled dreamily, then continued. "Did not God himself command us to subdue the earth? To do that, we first have to understand it. Even back then in the war, I kept taking notes in my little book—do you remember? Notes on the explosive force of gunpowder, the best way to reinforce trenches, a guillotine for painless decapitations . . . Unfortunately, no one was interested in my plans."

"You were a lousy hangman, but a smart fellow," Kuisl interjected with a grin. "Just a bit too much of a dreamer to kill. You would have made a good scholar, but unfortunately the Dear Lord had other plans for you."

Nepomuk nodded. "Horrible job, hanging people. I thought the war would be a great equalizer, but then I was a damned executioner again, just like my father and grandfather before me." He sighed deeply. "When I found a place to hide out here in the Andechs Monastery, I felt I had finally fulfilled my dreams. My work as an apothecary gave me the chance to study other things." Nepomuk looked around and replied in a conspiratorial undertone. "Especially the studies of the *tonitrua et fulgura*."

"*Tonitrua et fulgura*? Thunder and lightning, you mean?" Kuisl frowned. "What more is there to know about it?"

The Brother's chuckle sounded like the bleating of an old billy goat. "Hah! Do you know how often lightning strikes up here on the Holy Mountain? Do you? Up to a dozen times a year. If you're lucky, only a few shingles get scorched, but often a whole building goes up in flames, or the church tower. Twenty years ago a ball of lightning even whizzed through the church like the devil. God alone prevented worse from happening." Nepomuk's voice almost cracked. "The monks here ring a bell to ward off a storm in hopes it strikes somewhere else; they pray and sing, but no one has ever thought about how to banish lightning — to exorcise it."

"Exorcise?" the hangman replied skeptically. "Now you really do sound like a warlock, Nepomuk."

The Brother shook his head energetically. "You don't understand, Jakob. Lightning is made harmless by attracting it to iron. That's not witchcraft but proven truth. Even the pharaohs knew that in biblical times; I've read it in old parchment manuscripts; we've just forgotten how."

A smile spread over Kuisl's lips. "So that's the reason for the iron bars you had in the forest with you. Magdalena told me about that."

"I always go out in thunderstorms and set them up at certain elevated locations. It works, Jakob. Lightning is always attracted to them." Nepomuk was now so wrapped up in his own words that he jumped up and had trouble keeping his voice down. "I had only a few more experiments to make, and I would be finished. A few days before the terrible fire in the church I tied iron bars like that up in the steeple with a wire leading down to the cemetery. I was sure I'd be able to channel the lightning down to earth, but unfortunately . . ." The Brother broke off and crouched down on the filthy floor, looking discouraged.

"Unfortunately that set fire to the whole church, you stupid ass," Kuisl continued. "It's no wonder your Brothers don't have anything good to say about you."

Nepomuk shook his head. "They . . . they just suspect something without really knowing. The only person I told about the experiment was Virgilius, who was excited about it and kept peppering me with questions. He thought there must be someone for whom my studies would have great value. When he started in on that again two days ago, I was afraid the abbot would learn the truth, so I just threw him out of the house. Virgilius ranted and raved."

"The argument between you and the watchmaker." Kuisl nodded. "I heard about that. That's why the monks think you have something to do with his disappearance. In addition, they found your eyepiece at his house."

"By God, I swear I don't know how it got there. Maybe I left it lying somewhere and someone picked it up to lure Virgilius to his death." Nepomuk held both hands over his swollen face as his entire body began to quiver. "And I have nothing to do with Virgilius's disappearance. On my honor."

"And that accursed automaton?" Kuisl added. "My daughter thinks she heard it somewhere down below the monastery. Do you know anything about that?"

Nepomuk shrugged. "I know only that this automaton was Virgilius's favorite toy. If someone stole it, he'd first have to kill the builder — Virgilius would never part willingly with his Aurora." He wrung his hands in despair. "Someone is out to get me, Jakob. You must help me. I'm more afraid than ever before in my life. You know yourself what I might be facing if I'm convicted of sorcery. First they'll hang me, then disembowel and quarter me, and finally throw my bloody remains into the fire." He looked at the hangman hopefully. "Before it gets to that, can you at least promise me quick, clean death? Promise?"

"Nobody's going to die here if I don't approve," Kuisl growled. "My son-in-law told me they want to wait until after the Festival of the Three Hosts in order not to terrify the pilgrims, so we have a few days to find the real culprit. And as sure as my name is Jakob Kuisl, I'll find him." He stooped down again and looked his friend straight in the eye. "The only thing that's important is that you don't keep anything from me. Can I really trust you, Nepomuk?"

The Brother crossed himself, held up his hand, and swore. "By all the saints and the Virgin Mary, I promise to tell you the truth."

"Then continue praying in a loud voice." Kuisl stood up, pulled the cowl down over his head and turned to leave. "After all, we want our two bumpkins out there to think you're on your way into the purifying fires of purgatory."

> *"Isicia omentata. Pulpam concisam teres cum medulla*
> *siliginei in vino infusi . . ."*

As the hangman continued mumbling Latin recipes, he pounded energetically on the door. In a moment the chubby watchman appeared to shove the bolt aside and let him out.

"Well, did he confess?" the fat man asked. "Did he stab the two youngsters to death, carry off the watchmaker, and copulate with the automaton?"

Kuisl stopped for a moment and stared back at the man from the darkness of his cowl. Suddenly the two watchmen had the terrifying feeling they were not talking to a father confessor, but the Grim Reaper in person.

"The devil tempts men in many ways," said the gruff hangman. "But often he comes in a simple garb. He has no need of sulfur, horns, or a cloven foot, and he doesn't have to make love to an automaton, you idiots. How stupid are you, anyway?"

Without another word, Kuisl shuffled out into the starry night.

In the meantime, Simon was on his way to the underworld.

The medicus had briefly looked in on the sick in the monastery annex who were still being cared for by Jakob Schreevogl. The young patrician had handled his task astonishingly well, enlisting a few of the Schongau group to help. Now a deceptive quiet prevailed in the provisional hospital, broken only by occasional coughs and moans. Two older women had died from the fever, and the medicus still couldn't say what the origin of the illness was. It began with exhaustion and headaches, then fever and diarrhea followed. It affected everyone equally—strong adults as well as the elderly and children.

Simon couldn't help but think of his own two boys. He tried to shake off the thought and concentrate completely on the task before him. On the spur of the moment, he decided to take a closer look at the two murder victims. He could take care of the living in the morning.

Anxiously, he climbed down the steep stairway into the monastery's beer cellar, which could be reached through an annex directly next to the brewery. It was chilly in the narrow passageway through the rock, allowing one to forget that summer had already begun outside. For almost two hundred years, supplies had been stored here deep in the stone bowels of the mountain, since beer couldn't be brewed during the hot summer months. Though Simon had turned up his coat collar, he shivered slightly.

The coolness in the corridors and cellars of Andechs was not just suited for the storage of beer barrels and brewing equipment; the dead often found their temporary resting place here before burial in the monastery's cemetery. The corpses of the two novitiates were handled in the same way—primarily to avoid any unrest prior to the festival. The burial of two victims of an alleged sorcerer and mass murderer certainly would have set off the wildest rumors. On entering the storage cellar, however, Simon could tell that burial couldn't be delayed much longer.

His nose led him past huge six-foot-high barrels standing in niches in the rock. Water dripped from the ceiling, forming puddles on the hard-packed soil. Simon's steps echoed from the rock walls as he moved down the small corridor, holding a torch in front of him. Somewhere he could hear rats squealing.

Finally he reached the end of the corridor, where he found not another barrel but a worn wooden table and two bundles wrapped in white cloth. He took a deep breath, then placed the torch in a crack in the wall and removed the first sheet.

The stench was so strong he had to turn away for a moment to keep from vomiting. Finally, he turned back to the body.

It was Coelestin, the apothecary's helper whom he'd examined closely two days earlier. By now rigor mortis had passed and the corpse was marked with black and blue spots wherever the outer layer of skin had collapsed and the blood had run off. Nevertheless, the wound to the back of his head was still clearly visible; Simon was certain the victim had been bludgeoned by an unknown attacker and then held under water.

After checking and not finding anything else important, he pulled the second sheet to the side. By now, Simon had gotten somewhat used to the stench, but the sight of the dead watchmaker's assistant still made him shudder. Vitalis, at one time so handsome, looked as if the hounds of hell themselves had clutched him in their claws. His head was wrenched to one side, the skin on his back and legs almost completely charred, and his right hand was so badly burned that some of the fingers had already fallen off. The corpse still gave off a caustic burnt smell.

Simon wondered what was powerful enough to set off a fire like that. Ten years ago, he'd seen a corpse after a burning at the stake, but by then, the body had shrunk to the size of a child and was burned evenly all over. Vitalis had suffered burns only on his back, buttocks, and the rear of the thigh. Simon bent down to examine the burn spots carefully, and tapped his finger against the hard, blackened flesh.

Suddenly he stopped short. In some of the cracks in the skin he noticed traces of a white powder whose origin he could not explain. He scratched it with his fingernail and studied the little specks up close. He turned up his nose in disgust — the powder smelled of old garlic.

Was witchcraft indeed somehow involved in this?

As the medicus reexamined the head of the charred corpse, he discovered a dent in the skull at almost the same point as on Coelestin's. He stopped to think. Was the watchmaker possibly killed in the same way? Or had he suffered the wound in a fall? Had Vitalis perhaps been killed by a blow *before* being consumed by the demonic fire?

Just as Simon prepared to examine the wound again, the torch fell out of the crack in the rock face and onto the wet ground where it hissed and sputtered before going out, leaving the cellar in total darkness.

"Damn."

Simon groped blindly for the table so as not to lose his sense of direction. When his hand touched the cold body of the apothecary's assistant, he instinctively recoiled, lost his balance, and hit his head against a beer keg. His fall echoed through the silence, then it again became as quiet as the bottom of the sea.

Simon could feel his heart pounding. Surely he could find his way back to the surface without the torch, but the very thought that he was alone with two corpses in a pitch-black cellar caused his stomach to quiver. Carefully he stood up and was about to grope his way along the barrels toward the exit when he stopped in amazement.

One of the two corpses was glowing in the dark.

A strange greenish glimmer came from the body of young Vitalis, as faint as the glow from a firefly, and it gave the corpse an eerie sheen that made Simon's hair stand on end.

Torn between panic and fascination, the medicus was eyeing the shimmering corpse when suddenly he heard a loud rumble from the other side of the table. It sounded as if somewhere in the mountain a stone golem had come to life.

That was too much for Simon. He staggered back a few steps, then turning around in horror, ran through the darkness toward the exit. Again there was a rumbling. He stumbled, caught himself again, but hit his forehead on the cellar door. Ignoring the pain, he groped for the door handle and, finding it, rushed up the stairway beyond. Once he could see pale moonlight above, he turned around one last time and could still see the glimmer back in the beer cellar. Then he rushed up the stairs, not stopping until he was standing under the starry sky in front of the brewery.

He was back again among the living.

It took Simon a while to calm down enough to think rationally about what had just happened. What he'd seen down below—was it actually witchcraft? His reason tried mightily to reject this thought, but the sight of a shining green corpse was a hard thing to swallow, even for a student of medicine. And what was the rumbling down below? Had the two corpses come back to life to seek revenge on their murderer?

Simon wasn't quite ready to go back to Magdalena and the children. He needed at least a halfway clear head. How he would have loved a cup of his beloved coffee now, but unfortunately the Oriental brew was still unknown in the Andechs Monastery tavern. In any case, Simon had no desire to bump into the Schongau burgomaster or his son there. Kuisl was no doubt still with his friend Nepomuk in the old cheese-making room. So where could he go?

As his gaze passed over the partially lighted windows of the monastery, only one place seemed to offer him some security and enlightenment.

The library.

Since his earliest youth, Simon had loved books. They were lodestars for him, dividing the world into dark and light sides. Perhaps this time books would lead him back to the bright side again; in books he could find explanations for almost anything, perhaps even for a shimmering green corpse. Simon nodded with determination. If anybody spoke to him in the library, he would simply say he was still working on the report for the abbot.

He returned to the main portal, which was still open, and climbed the wide steps to the south wing, where a corridor led to a high, two-winged door.

Reverently he opened it and looked into paradise.

The walls were almost twenty feet high and covered floor to ceiling with walnut shelves filled with books. There were huge, dusty parchment books as thick as an arm, newer folios made of paper, and thin folders tied together with red ribbons. Simon could see golden letters on the backs of some of the books, while others were labeled with delicate scribbles. Some had simple leather bindings. The entire room smelled of fine wood, dust, and that undefinable fragrance that emanates from ancient parchment and ink.

Simon swallowed hard. He had not seen so many books since he was in the Premonstratensian monastery in Steingaden, and that was a long while ago. There was probably more knowledge stored here in Andechs than in the entire rest of the Priests' Corner.

Slowly the medicus walked down an aisle of books, glancing at individual titles. He discovered Paracelsus's *Große Wundartzney* and, alongside it, a complete five-volume edition of Dioscurides's *Materia Medica*. Simon began leafing through them randomly, but when he realized he wouldn't find anything this way, he laid the heavy volumes aside and began wandering through the aisles again.

He was delighted when he came to the end of a row and found a rather nondescript little book at eye-level that evidently dealt with the history of the Andechs Monastery. While he was sure he would find nothing in it about glowing corpses, the events of recent days had made clear to him that this monastery kept more than one secret. Perhaps the key to all these strange events was to be found in the past.

After some hesitation, Simon took the leather-bound book from the shelf and settled down in an upholstered armchair next to a well-polished cherry-wood table. He couldn't say himself why he picked out this book. It was written in ancient, somewhat overly dramatic, Latin, so it took a while for the medicus to feel comfortable with it. But he'd learned enough from his incomplete study at Ingolstadt University to read the book at least halfway fluently after a while.

Strangely, the chronicle began not as one would expect, with the founding of the monastery, but much earlier than that. Simon learned that at first there was a castle on the Holy Mountain belonging to the Counts of Andechs, a mighty family that ruled large parts of Bavaria and even southern Tyrol. At some point, however, the Wittelsbachs seized power in Bavaria and destroyed the castle.

The chronicle spoke in this connection of a "vile, cowardly betrayal" but had nothing more to say about it. Simon couldn't help thinking of Count von Wartenberg, who had been sitting in the tavern the day before with the two Semers. Wartenberg was one of the Wittelsbachs — and hadn't the fat cellarer said the count had the third key? Simon sighed. The more he dug into this, the more complicated it seemed.

A scraping sound startled him. The tall door had opened and the old librarian with the crooked back entered. When Brother Benedikt first caught sight of Simon, he seemed disconcerted, but then he settled back into his usual arrogance.

"What are you doing in here?" he snarled. "The library is for the exclusive use of the monks."

"I know," Simon replied in an apologetic tone. "But you do have an outstanding collection of medical works, and the abbot thought perhaps I might find a clue here. He permitted me to come here to write my report about the strange deaths." That was clearly untrue, but the medicus guessed that Maurus Rambeck had other problems at the moment than to correct his little white lie.

And in fact the librarian seemed satisfied with Simon's excuse. "The medical knowledge of the Benedictines is indeed unequaled," the monk replied proudly. "It goes back to the ancient knowledge of the Babylonians, Egyptians, and Greeks. We were the ones who preserved the knowledge about poisonous and healing plants and kept alive the knowledge of procedures and diagnoses for all these centuries. Surely you've seen the *Naturalis historia* of Pliny the Elder?"

"Ah, I'll confess that I haven't yet—"

"Ah, but see here . . . as far as I know, the chronicles of Andechs is not a medical work." Brother Benedikt had drawn closer and suspiciously eyed the book Simon had just been leafing through.

The medicus's smile was enough to melt ice. "Excuse me, but my curiosity just got the better of me. After all, I don't often have the chance to visit such a venerable facility. How old is this monastery, by the way?"

"Over two hundred years," Benedikt replied. "It was founded by Augustinian canons, but we Benedictines took charge soon afterward."

"Is that so? I would have thought the building is much older. All the cellars, the weathered rock . . ."

"A castle and a chapel once stood here," the librarian conceded, "but the little church that housed the three sacred hosts is long gone."

"And where are the three hosts now?" Simon inquired, curious. "In a few days, they'll be displayed to thousands of pilgrims."

Brother Benedikt looked at him suspiciously again. "Safely stored away, of course, in the sacred chapel until Sunday, when they will be displayed to the pilgrims from the bay window of the church."

"Isn't it strange that these two dreadful murders and the other remarkable events are taking place just before the Festival of the Three Hosts?" Simon said softly. "It almost looks as if someone is trying to ruin this festival."

"The festival will take place, you can count on that." For a moment Simon thought he detected a bit of uncertainty in the old monk's face, but then Benedikt regained his composure. "For hundreds of years, the sacred three hosts have been displayed to the people in a sealed monstrance on exactly this day," he murmured. "They have survived fire, attacks, and the Great War, and they will also survive this damned witchery. No one can steal them, and certainly no one can make them disappear by magic." He straightened up, and his eyes began to shine, as if he was declaiming an ancient spell. "Three keys are needed to enter the holy chapel, and only the abbot, the prior, and a member of the Wittelsbach family can open the room together. So don't worry, the hosts are well cared for and no one will disturb the venerable ceremony."

Simon cringed when he remembered what Magdalena had told him about her visit to the church.

A Wittelsbach has the third key . . .

Hadn't Magdalena observed how upset the abbot had been during the mass? Then he had left with the prior and Count Wartenberg and disappeared upstairs in the relics room. Was there a connection between the murders and the sacred three hosts?

"I'm afraid you'll have to put your medical studies off until tomorrow," the librarian said, interrupting Simon's train of thought. "I'm closing the rooms here now. In my opinion, you should be caring for the poor pilgrims anyway and leave it to the judge in Weilheim to take care of this satanic apothecary." He shuffled over to the door. "Brother Maurus should have called the judge long ago and worried less about the gossip. We just can't allow a sorcerer in our venerable institution. This is a matter that has to be attended to as quickly as possible."

"Speaking of witchcraft . . ." Simon interjected, "Brother

Eckhart said something about a golem. Do you perhaps have any books about that?"

The librarian stopped suddenly and turned around to Simon. "Didn't I just say you need to care for the sick?" he growled. "But now that you ask — yes, there is a book about that here."

"Aha! Could I perhaps have a look at it?"

Brother Benedikt pursed his lips in a narrow smile. "That's not possible; the abbot himself has borrowed that book."

Simon suppressed a slight shudder.

It is the book written in Hebrew on the abbot's table, a book on conjuring up golems.

"You are right," Simon sighed finally and rose with a shrug. "I must take care of my patients." He decided not to tell the librarian anything about his remarkable discovery concerning the novitiate's body. Something warned him not to trust the old man, or in this case, anyone. "The matter should be in the hands of a judge," he confessed remorsefully. "I've taken up too much time with this. Nevertheless, thank you for your explanations."

Without Brother Benedikt noticing it, Simon quickly hid the Adechs chronicle in his jacket and started for the exit. The librarian's words had awakened his interest in learning more about the monastery's past. He clenched his fists determinedly and put on a droll smile as he followed the monk out the door. Simon had the annoying habit of becoming curious about whatever he was told to stay away from.

What mystery is hidden behind these walls — or beneath them?

Stiffly, Simon descended the stairway as Brother Benedikt continued to eye him distrustfully, and didn't breathe a sigh of relief until he was outside. His heart pounding, he took the chronicle out from under his robe and wiped his sweat from the leather binding. Then he broke out in a broad grin.

At least he'd have something to read tonight.

• • •

After Magdalena had put the children to bed, she sat down, exhausted, in the main room of her cousin's house to relax from the tribulations of the day and absent-mindedly stirred a cup of steaming mulled wine. She'd been singing bedtime songs to the children for almost an hour, and now she was hoarse, as one might expect. Three-year-old Peter in particular couldn't fall asleep and kept asking for just one more. After being away from the children the last three days, they now clung to her all the more. At least her sickness had passed, even though her stomach still felt a bit queasy.

Magdalena wished she could share her feelings with her husband, but as so often, Simon was completely wrapped up in his own plans and thoughts. She sighed softly. Especially now, she wished she had a little support. She was still wearing a bandage around her neck where the silent bullet had grazed her the night before, and though the wound seemed to have healed well, she remained fearful that the stranger might strike again. Or was Simon perhaps right . . . had she just imagined all this? Was the stranger in the belfry perhaps just some drunken monk she'd disturbed in his befuddled condition? And was the shot in the dark nothing more than a ricocheting bullet from a hunter's rifle?

Lost in thought, Magdalena took another drink from her cup of wine. The knacker Michael Graetz had gone off to the tavern in Erling for a mug or two of beer, and her only companion was the silent Matthias, huddled down on the bench by the stove across from her. Once again she noticed what a handsome young man he was. He was perhaps in his early twenties, and with his powerful arms, black apron open in the front, and red hair, he looked a bit like one of the drifters who would occasionally pass through Schongau to sing songs and perform magic tricks.

Graetz had told her that the redheaded lad couldn't speak because marauding soldiers had cut out his tongue when he was a child, and for this reason she didn't expect him to approach her. It was strange to be seated in a room with someone staring at you, however, without even being able to say a word.

"Don't you want to go down to the tavern with your master?" Magdalena ventured, just to have something to say. "It was a tough day, and no doubt your throat is dry."

The silent helper shook his head, and a gurgling sound came from his throat. He was pointing at Magdalena's cup of wine.

"*Ahh dahh ring . . .*" he stammered.

"You don't drink?" she replied.

Matthias beamed, seeing he was understood.

"And why not?"

The handsome fellow seemed to think a bit; then his face turned into a threatening grimace as he spread his fingers out like claws.

Instinctively, Magdalena moved off to one side. "Ah, it makes you sick?" she asked hesitantly.

Matthias sighed and rolled his eyes as if he were drunk. Finally, he reached for a pitcher of water and drank it in one long gulp.

"*Aaah.*" he exclaimed, rubbing his stomach like after a good meal. "*Aach eer . . . ush eer.*"

"You're right," Magdalena murmured. "Alcohol sometimes changes men into beasts, lustful beasts, or snoring bears." She laughed self-consciously, and the good-looking assistant stared back at her unambiguously. Suddenly she felt the heat and closeness of the room closing in around her and stood up, blushing.

"Say," she began somewhat awkwardly, "do you think you could keep an eye on the two sleeping kids for a little while? I'd like to get out for some fresh air, and since you're not going to the tavern . . ." She smiled at him, and for a moment Matthias seemed befuddled, trying to sort things out in his mind, reaffirming Magdalena's impressions that the knacker's assistant was not only handsome but unfortunately a bit dense. He didn't seem es-

pecially enthused at Magdalena's suggestion, but finally he nodded.

"Then . . . until later," she said softly. "And thank you very
much."

She quickly tossed on a scarf, stood up, and left. Outside, in
the cool night air, she almost had to laugh at herself. What in the
world was wrong with her? Evidently, events of the last few days
had rattled her so much that now even a mute knacker's boy
could throw her off her stride. The children, too, had upset her
more than she'd expected while their father was busy with more
important things.

Magdalena took a deep breath, then decided to go up to the
monastery and search for her husband. It annoyed her that
Simon was gone again in the evening, leaving her to care for the
children. He really should have returned some time ago; perhaps
she'd even meet up with him on the way.

The distant singing of drunken men wafted through the cool
night air, and in the fields around the village little fires were
burning. Many of the pilgrims spent the night outside, and by
now several hundred people had set up camp at the foot of the
Holy Mountain.

Steering clear of the fires and the warm and inviting lights of
the tavern, Magdalena climbed up the steep pathway toward the
monastery, and was soon enveloped in silence. The stone wall
around the monastery where she and Simon had sat in the warm
sun yesterday noon had now become a black strip silhouetted
against an even darker background. There was a cracking of
branches in the bushes on either side of the path, and once Magdalena even thought she heard footsteps. She hurried along the
path, finally passing through a gate and entering the monastery
grounds. Here too, in contrast with the loud activity during the
day, quiet prevailed. Somewhere she heard a single bell sound.
Two drunks coming from the monastery tavern approached her,
but they, too, stumbled silently past.

Finally she reached the square in front of the church and started looking for Simon. Just where could he be? He was only going to pay a quick visit to the abbot with her father, but that was at least three hours ago. Had the two of them paid a visit to the ugly Nepomuk in the dungeon?

Magdalena's mind wandered as she stared at the piles of stone and sacks of lime lying all around the square. Workers had put up scaffolding on the walls and front of the church to make repairs to the roof. A wailing tomcat scurried across the boards in search of his mate, and Magdalena looked up, smiling, to see the animal disappear through a crack in the wall of the belfry.

It suddenly occurred to her that she still didn't know what the strange device was up in the belfry. Should she have another look now? Perhaps she could find out if her fall from the belfry was really just a foolish accident.

Magdalena resolutely opened the church portal a crack and slipped inside. The church was empty. She reached for one of the dozens of flickering candles on a side altar and carefully climbed the steps to the balcony. From there, a rickety, partially repaired winding stairway led up into the tower.

Magdalena walked as best she could on the interior side of the steps, carefully placing one foot in front of the other. At least the darkness offered her the advantage of not knowing what was just a few yards ahead of the flickering candles and spared her the dizzying sight of what lay below. With heart pounding, she climbed step by step until she finally reached the upper platform with the three bells. Carefully she raised the candle and looked around.

"What in God's name . . . ?" She held her hand over her mouth to keep from screaming.

The stretcher with the metal clamps, as well as the iron stakes, had disappeared.

To be sure, she walked around the entire platform, but the strange construction had indeed vanished into thin air. All that remained was a piece of wire protruding from the ceiling, dangling in the wind.

Magdalena cursed softly. Someone must have removed the stretcher in the last two days. Now she would probably never find out what the apparatus was. Grumbling, she kicked one of the heavy church bells, but the heavy iron bell hardly moved a fraction of an inch. Then she climbed down and quietly left the church, but not without bowing one last time before the main altar and the two statues of Mary.

Please excuse the lateness of my visit, Holy Mother of God, she prayed to herself. *But you, too, probably want to know what's going on up in your tower. Or have you known about all this for a long time?*

As Magdalena stepped under the scaffolding in front of the main entrance, she could sense something moving. At that moment a large, heavy object fell toward her. Instinctively, she jumped aside in time for a shapeless object to graze her right shoulder. There was a whoosh as a waist-high sack of lime landed next to her on the ground, bursting open and pouring its contents across the pavement.

Everything happened so fast that Magdalena scarcely had time to catch her breath. Her heart pounding, she leaned against one of the uprights of the scaffold, staring down at the sack from which a cloud of dust rose now into the bright, moonlit night.

Was that just another accident? Softly she cursed herself for sneaking through the church in the darkness. Good Lord, she had two little children who needed her, and here she was poking her nose around, looking for some madman.

"Is everything all right?"

The voice came from the right, by the church entrance. A monk approached, but not until he was standing almost in front of her did she recognize the novitiate master Brother Laurentius.

"I heard a noise," he said, "and do hope nothing has happened. For God's sake, you're pale as a ghost."

"Pale as lime would be the right expression," Magdalena groaned, pointing to the burst sack at her feet. "That huge thing almost killed me."

The Brother looked up anxiously. "It must have fallen from the scaffold. I said just this morning that this area had to be roped off. As if enough hadn't already happened in the last few days." He sighed, then looked at Magdalena severely. "But you really shouldn't be hanging around the church square at this hour. What in heaven's name are you doing here?"

Just as she had the evening before in the church, Magdalena noticed Laurentius's finely wrought facial features. His fingers were long, with clean nails that glimmered faintly in the darkness.

"I'm . . . looking for my husband," she stammered. "He's the bathhouse surgeon from Schongau who's taking care of the sick people here. Have you seen him, by chance?"

At once the monk's expression brightened. "Ah, the bathhouse surgeon who is taking care of the sick pilgrims free of charge?" he asked. "A true Christian. You can be sure he has earned his place in the Heavenly Kingdom."

"Thank you, but I think he'd prefer to spend the next few years here on earth," she replied, pulling her shawl tight around her shoulders. "And in your monastery, that's not so easily done at present."

The Brother cringed. "You're right," he murmured haltingly. "This is a dreadful time—first the young Coelestin and then . . ." His voice broke and he turned aside.

"Were you very close to the watchmaker's assistant, Vitalis?" Magdalena asked, concerned.

Brother Laurentius nodded, his lips tightly pressed together. Only after a while did he answer. "I'm the novitiate master here. All my charges are dear to me, as I'm responsible for the education of each individual." He sighed. "But with Vitalis it was something else. He was very . . . sensitive. He often visited me in the evening and poured out his heart." The priest's long eyelashes began to flutter, and Magdalena saw a tear run down his face.

"Did Vitalis have difficulties with his master?" she asked, curiously.

The young monk shrugged. "I don't know. Toward the end he was very reserved—something must have happened. The last time we met he seemed to want to tell me something, but then he decided to remain silent. It was probably Aurora who made him so anxious."

"Aurora?"

"Yes, his master's automaton," Laurentius explained. "Vitalis thought the puppet was alive. He often told me that she moved on her own at night, hissing and whispering, almost like a human being, and he felt she was following his every move."

Magdalena shook her head. "A dreadful thought."

"Indeed. Vitalis thought the puppet was hiding some horrible secret, and on the night before his gruesome end he told me, 'She will kill him—and all of us.' " Brother Laurentius nodded, lost in thought. "Those were his exact words: 'kill us.' Now it seems his prophesies have been fulfilled. God knows what this creature did with poor Vitalis and his master who has vanished." He hastily crossed himself and bowed. "It's quite late, only a few hours before morning prayers. Let's hope and pray this witchery will end soon. God be with you." With these final words, the novitiate master turned and left.

Magdalena stared after his dark form as he vanished into the night, then hastily climbed down the steep path toward the village. She fervently hoped that Simon had returned by now. This monastery seemed more and more sinister to her, and for a long time she couldn't get the automaton's soft melody out of her mind.

A shrill, unending glockenspiel.

Half an hour later, Kuisl, Simon, and Magdalena had returned to the knacker's house and were sitting around the stove in the main room thinking about the events of the last few days. The hangman had lit his pipe for the third time, and the whole room filled with clouds of smoke from the tobacco and the wet wood burning in the stove. Kuisl's cousin Michael Graetz still hadn't returned from his visit to the local tavern, and his silent assistant seemed to have disappeared, even though Magdalena had asked him to stay and watch the children — a good opportunity finally for the three to discuss everything that had happened.

"Experiments with lightning?" Simon asked, incredulously. "Your friend Nepomuk actually was studying lightning?"

Nodding, Kuisl took a deep drag on his pipe. He was still wearing the filthy monk's robe, which clung to him like a wet sack and seemed to itch all over. "He was trying to capture lightning," he grumbled, after he'd finally finished scratching himself. "Not such a bad idea, when you think of how often it has struck just in our little Schongau. Nepomuk took a wire and ran it down the church steeple to the cemetery, and the lightning actually did strike there. But unfortunately, it also set the whole tower on fire."

"Just a moment," Magdalena spoke up. "The day before yesterday I saw a wire like that there, but also a strange sort of stretcher. When I went back again tonight, it was gone; only the wire was still hanging from the ceiling."

She had met Simon on the way home and, until now, hadn't told him or her father anything about the sack of lime that had fallen next to her. In the meantime, she was no longer sure herself whether her constant fear of attack was her imagination run wild, and now, especially in the warm light of the knacker's cottage, everything seemed to her like a distant fairy tale.

"Perhaps the stretcher in the belfry wasn't Nepomuk's at all, but belonged to someone trying to copy his ideas," Simon said.

Magdalena frowned. "And who would that be?"

"No idea," Simon replied, perplexed. "The entire inner council seems very peculiar, above all the abbot himself. Your father and I surprised him reading a book about conjuring up golems." He waved his hands back and forth vigorously, trying to dispel the smoke. "Whoever it is, we're too late. The stranger has clearly disposed of all the evidence because things were getting too hot for him. And now—" Simon coughed, then turned angrily to his father-in-law. "Damn, Kuisl!" he shouted. "Can't you just *once* stop that awful smoking? How can anyone think straight in all this smoke?"

"I can, for one," the hangman growled. "You should try it yourself sometime; it might make things a little clearer for you. I just had a few really interesting ideas." He grinned and took an especially deep drag on the pipe. "Nepomuk told me, for example, that Virgilius had told him about a stranger—someone who would be interested in the experiments with lightning, he thought."

"The abbot," Magdalena interrupted. "Perhaps he needs a powerful lightning flash to bring his golem to life, and he wanted Virgilius to help him."

The hangman spat into the reeds on the floor. "Nonsense. There's no such thing as a golem. I believe in hard iron, a well-tied noose, and the evil in men, not a man made of clay. Golems are nothing but horror stories made up by priests to scare people." He shook his head stubbornly. "It's too bad Virgilius went up in smoke and we can't ask him about this stranger anymore."

"Ahem ... apropos fire." Simon cleared his throat and paused before continuing. "Please don't think I'm crazy, but I've made a very strange discovery, and slowly I'm starting to wonder whether there's something to this talk of witchcraft." Hesitantly, he told the others of his strange experience with the glowing corpse in the Andechs beer cellar and his own hasty retreat.

"Did you say it was a white powder, and the corpse glowed in a green light?" Kuisl finally asked.

Simon nodded. "It was a very dim glow, like a glowworm. I just can't make any sense of it."

"But I can," the hangman replied dryly. "I've heard of a phenomenon like that."

"Well?" Simon sat up attentively. "What is it?"

Kuisl grinned at his son-in-law. "Well, what do you know? I'm afraid I've not had enough to smoke today to figure that out. My mind isn't working fast enough, and unfortunately I'm not allowed to smoke any more in here . . ." Calmly he pulled a louse from under his robe and stuffed it into his glowing pipe, where it burst.

"Father, stop this nonsense and tell us right away what you know," Magdalena hissed. "Or I'll tell Mother that you already had three pipefuls today."

"Oh, all right, all right," the hangman replied, waving her off. "It's probably phosphorus."

"*Phosphorus?*" Simon looked at his father-in-law incredulously. "What in God's name is phosphorus?"

"*Phosphorus mirabilis.* An element just recently discovered by a apothecary in a city named Hamburg, you worthless scholar," Kuisl barked. "You should have hung around the Ingolstadt University a little longer." He leaned back smugly and took a deep draw on his pipe. "Actually, the apothecary, like so many others, was looking for the philosopher's stone, but what came out was a glowing substance, namely phosphorus. I read about it in one of my books by Athanasius Kircher. It has a faint green glow in the dark, but it also has another extremely dangerous property."

"And that would be . . ." Magdalena prodded.

The hangman folded his arms in front of his broad chest. "Well, it burns like tinder. You only have to place it out in the sun, and once it catches fire it can't be put out and inflicts horrible wounds."

"Do you think that poor Vitalis was doused with this . . . this phosphorus?" Simon whispered. "But why?"

"Maybe because someone is trying to make the priests believe in witchcraft?" Kuisl grumbled. "Didn't you say yourself that Vitalis's skull had been smashed in? Perhaps someone bludgeoned him and then spread phosphorus on the corpse to make his death look like witchcraft. Then they quickly found a scapegoat—Nepomuk."

"But his eyepiece," Simon objected. "It was found at the crime scene."

"Anyone could have put it there," Magdalena interrupted. "My father is right. An automaton disappears, a watchmaker seems to have been swallowed up by the earth, and an assistant is horribly burned—all designed to look like the work of the devil, and all to stir up fear? If you ask me, this stranger is stopping at nothing, and now all of Andechs is in turmoil." She hesitated briefly. "The question is, who would benefit from panic breaking out here among the pilgrims?"

Simon was staring through the clouds of tobacco smoke at the cross in the devotional corner when he suddenly slammed his hand down on the table. "I have it!" he shouted.

"Good Lord, Simon," Magdalena whispered. "Please be quiet. You'll wake up the children."

"It must have something to do with the Festival of the Three Hosts," said Simon, now in a quieter voice. "Someone wants to interfere with this festival. Already some of the pilgrims are thinking about returning home. They've heard of the horrible murders and are afraid of the automaton that is said to be prowling the halls of the monastery. If this continues, the festival may not even take place at all — in any case, it won't be a happy festival, pleasing to God."

"But why would anyone do something like that?" Magdalena asked skeptically. "What would anyone have to gain from it?"

Simon sighed. "I'm afraid we don't know enough yet about the monastery to answer that question. But we can change that." With a grin, he pulled out the leather-bound volume he'd been carrying under his jacket. "I . . . uh . . . borrowed this chronicle from the library; perhaps we'll find an explanation here. After all, the sacred three hosts are the most important relic here in Andechs."

"Then go ahead and read it, but I'm going to take a rest from this foolishness." Kuisl pulled his stinking, sweaty robe over his head and tossed it into a corner with disgust. "I just hope this nonsense will be over soon."

At that moment, the door creaked and swung open. Michael Graetz entered, his face red and enveloped in a cloud of alcohol. The Erling knacker had evidently had a few too many beers and wavered slightly as he looked around in astonishment.

"Pinch me," he finally mumbled with a thick tongue. "I think I just saw a huge monk through the window right here in this room, and now he's magically vanished."

"A monk? In your house?" The hangman laughed. Only to Magdalena's and Simon's ears did it sound a bit too loud. "My dear cousin, a priest would climb up onto a manure pile before he'd pay a visit to the homes of dishonorable people like us." Kuisl pointed to a closed chest along the wall next to the devotional corner. "And now let's see if you have something to welcome your family. That would really be something to drink to."

A few rays of light escaped through the closed shutters of the knacker's house, but the person outside huddled in darkness. He crept around the hawthorn bushes separating the house from the forest and peered carefully through their thorny branches.

The man clenched his fists so hard his knuckles turned white. The master would be angry, very angry. He'd failed once again, even despite the master's warning that this curious young woman could spoil the entire plan. She was snooping around too much — that's all there was to it — and what was wrong in taking a life if it would save many others?

The man took a deep breath to try to regain his composure. He had seen so many men die pointless deaths in the Great War that a shield of ice had formed around his innermost self, and only rarely did he feel any emotion. It was terrible that he felt this way about her. Perhaps it was her beauty that caused his weakness, or perhaps her laugh, which he heard coming from the house at that very moment. He had wanted to throw the sack of lime directly at her, but at the last moment, a higher power had moved his hand slightly to one side, just as it had pressed the flintlock a fraction of an inch to the right the night before.

The man behind the hawthorn bushes whimpered softly as he dreaded telling the master of the foiled plan. The master would rage and rant, and worse: he would no longer love him.

Still moaning softly to himself, the man crawled back into the forest where he was soon swallowed up again in the darkness.

The man would have to confess his guilt.

8

Jakob Kuisl sat in the last row of the choir
stall with his hood pulled far down over his face, observing the
other monks.

The hangman whispered a soft curse not in keeping with his
sacred surroundings. In the early hours of the morning, Magdalena had persuaded him to attend morning mass and keep his
eyes open. That damned woman had inherited his own stub-
bornness. After a long discussion, Kuisl eventually grumbled his
assent in playing this foolish masquerade one more day. Inwardly
he had to admit that his curiosity was awakened, and in any case,
his best friend's life was at stake.

Attentively, the hangman looked around the church, which
was filled to the last seat. Children wailed, a number of people
were coughing and sniffling, and somewhere he heard a door
slam shut. The mass should have started more than a quarter of
an hour ago, and the many hundreds of pilgrims in the congregation were murmuring restlessly.

The monks in the choir stalls, also visibly irritated, whispered among themselves, and the hangman gathered from the
bits of conversation that they were all waiting for the abbot and

the prior, who was to lead the service today. When Kuisl looked down he noticed that the count's seat was empty, as well. His wife was struggling to control their noisy children and kept looking to the church portal, as if expecting to see her husband enter at any moment.

The hangman leaned back in the hard seat and tried to attract as little attention as possible — an attempt that was bound to fail, if only because of his huge size. Half an hour ago, when he entered the upper balcony, he caused some commotion among the monks until Brother Eckhart, annoyed, finally informed his colleagues that the large stranger was an itinerant Minorite whom the abbot had in fact permitted to stay at the monastery.

By now the excitement over his presence had subsided, and fewer people were staring at him, allowing the hangman to eavesdrop on their conversations.

"This is the first time both the abbot and the prior have overslept the morning mass," a scrawny monk to Kuisl's right was saying, while his neighbor in the next pew, an elderly man with a bald head, nodded in agreement.

"Let's just hope it's nothing more serious," the bald one whispered. "Did you see how pale and breathless Brother Maurus was yesterday evening at dinner? If you ask me, it's this fever going around. God forbid that we have to elect a new abbot soon."

"Well, then the prior would finally get the position he's been seeking for so long." The scrawny monk giggled softly. "If he hasn't caught the fever himself. After all, he's not here either."

"Shh, quiet. Look, they're just coming out of the relics room." The bald man pointed at a low door to the right of the choir stalls, from which the abbot and the prior were just emerging. Kuisl could sense at once that something was wrong. Both Maurus Rambeck and Brother Jeremias looked as if they'd just seen the devil himself. They were pale, and beads of sweat stood out on their foreheads. Rambeck's lips were trembling as he bent down to speak to the old librarian in the first row of the stalls, whispering a few words in the old man's ear, whereupon the latter cringed and also turned white. In the meantime, the prior had turned to Brother Eckhart and the young novitiate master, who raised his hand to his mouth in horror.

The hangman frowned. What the devil was going on here?

At that moment, Count Wartenberg entered the church, letting the heavy wings of the portal close behind him with a thud. He appeared greatly angered and was trembling all over as he walked with quick, energetic strides to his pew and dropped into his upholstered seat. When his wife bent over to him anxiously, he rudely brushed her aside and stared straight ahead in silence. Even far up in the stalls Kuisl could see how the count's eyes were flashing with anger.

What in the world has happened? the hangman wondered. *Has someone else been murdered?*

Just as Kuisl was about to turn again to eavesdrop on the two monks to his right, he noticed that the abbot and the prior, along with the cellarer Eckhart and the old librarian, had headed back to the low door at the other end of the balcony and disappeared in the direction of the holy chapel. The novitiate master hurried down a stairway into the nave and began reciting the mass in a loud, trembling voice.

"In nomine Patris et Filii et Spiritus Sancti, Amen ..."

The pilgrims rose, and the organ behind the stalls began to play. Fervently, the many hundreds of pilgrims joined in singing the Laudate Deo along with the simple monks, who looked around at one another in surprise. Evidently they didn't know what was going on either.

For a brief moment, the hangman remained seated, then decided it was time to act. Coughing and blowing his nose loudly, he rose, feigning sickness. He held his hand in front of his mouth as he pushed his way through the crowds of monks. By now every one of them feared catching the fever from his Brothers, so when the Minorite visitor appeared to be suffering from this damned illness as well, everyone was glad to step aside to make room for him.

Kuisl reached the end of the choir stalls just as the fat cellarer stepped into the inner sanctum and closed the little door behind him. The hangman hurried over, paused a moment, and just as the monks in the choir stalls knelt and lowered their heads to pray, pushed down the door handle and silently followed the four clergymen inside.

The voices of the singing pilgrims sounded distant and muffled as the door closed behind him. A little stairway with ancient, heavily worn stone steps led upward, lit only by a torch on the wall. Above him, the excited voices of the Benedictines echoed through the stairwell as if the monks were standing in a vault nearby.

Carefully Kuisl slunk up the few steps. On the walls hung numerous framed pictures depicting the miracles experienced by individual pilgrims. The hangman ignored these, concentrating instead on the voices that seemed to be approaching.

Suddenly he came to a small antechamber. On the far side of the chamber was a heavy iron door reinforced with nails and metal struts. Three colorful coats of arms hung on the portal at eye level, and on the wall next to a chest were three iron bars evidently serving as bolts. On the sides of the door, Kuisl could see the corresponding locks.

The hangman tiptoed the last few yards through the little antechamber, relieved to see that the iron door was ajar. Through a small crack he could look into the room beyond, dimly lit by two tiny barred windows. He held his breath.

The holy chapel, the inner sanctum.

It was shaped in the form of a cube and made of stone, with little niches and shelves on each side. All kinds of objects were stored here — chalices, crosses, and little boxes, some so rusted and covered with verdigris that they seemed to have rested here since ancient times. Straight ahead, the four clerics assembled around a small altar covered with a red velvet cloth.

It took Kuisl a moment to see what was disturbing about this sight: the altar was bare.

The monks standing there seemed to be involved in a violent dispute. They raised their hands, tore at their hair, and kept crossing themselves as if trying to ward off evil. Pater Eckhart, the cellarer, was speaking at the moment.

"But that . . . that's not possible," he ranted. "It's simply impossible that any mortal being could have stolen the monstrance with the hosts from this room."

"But nevertheless, it happened, you jackass," the prior replied. "So let's stop and think *how* that could have happened before anyone outside learns about it. This could cost all of us our heads."

"If I were you, I'd be afraid of losing my head, too," the old librarian murmured. "After all, you had one of the three keys needed to open the room, didn't you?"

The prior's face turned crimson. For a moment he seemed ready to grab the old man by the throat, but then he simply jabbed him in the chest with his forefinger. "Are you trying to say that *I* have something to do with the disappearance of the hosts? Don't forget, you need three keys to open the room. The other two keys are held by Brother Maurus and the count. Do you seriously believe that we conspired to steal the hosts? Is that what you think?"

"Stop this, Brothers," said the abbot wearily. He looked as if he'd resigned himself to his fate and was awaiting the eternal fires of damnation. "We won't get anywhere if we just stand here condemning one another," he continued in a soft voice. "What we need to think about is what to do if the hosts haven't reappeared in time for the festival."

The prior shook his head, as if he still couldn't fathom the situation. "Just how is this possible?" he wailed. "When we opened the relics room with the count last night, everything was in its proper place. And then only a few hours later, the hosts had disappeared. From a room with barred windows locked by three sliding bars with three different keys. By God, I swear that I haven't let my own key out of my sight for a moment." He reached for a chain around his neck with a single key dangling on it. "I wear it even when I'm sleeping."

Now the abbot took his key out from under his robe, as well. "The same is true for me," he said, wearily. "To tell the truth, I have no idea where the count keeps his key, but last night and this morning he was wearing it on his belt."

"Why did you two enter the room again with the count this morning?" the librarian asked. "The room was supposed to be kept locked until the festival."

Prior Jeremias sighed. "Because the count asked us to. He said he had to pray again in the inner sanctum before mass. Do you want to deny the request of a Wittelsbach? You know yourself that we're at the complete mercy of the elector."

"You shouldn't have let him into the room last night," the librarian scolded. "That just put stupid ideas into his head. Why in heaven's name is the count here so early? He normally doesn't show up until the festival."

"That's strange indeed," the prior agreed. "On the other hand, it was actually Maurus's idea to visit the relics room one more time yesterday. Why was that, Maurus?"

"Damn it! Because I had a vague suspicion that something was wrong," the abbot replied in a trembling voice. "And as you can see, my suspicion was correct. But why are you asking me all these questions? *You,* Jeremias, must be happy the hosts have vanished. If word of this gets around, I'll lose my post as abbot, and I know you have been just waiting to follow in my footsteps."

"Slander!" Prior Jeremias shouted. "Nothing but slander. We should have called the judge in Weilheim long ago. Everything is out of hand here. Can't you see you've lost control of everything that's going on?"

"How dare you—" the abbot started to say, but at that moment Kuisl leaned forward, snagging the shoulder of his robe on one of the votive pictures, which brought the heavy frame crashing to the ground. He bit his lip to keep from cursing out loud, but the damage was done.

"Quiet," the librarian whispered. "There's someone out there."

"That's the golem," wailed Brother Eckhart. "Oh, God! He's coming to get us. This is the end for us. Holy Mary, pray for us now and in the hour—"

"Silence, you idiot," the prior interrupted. "Let's just see what's going on out there."

As silent as a shadow, Kuisl slipped away from the wall and dashed down the stairway as the sound of footsteps could be heard behind him. In just a few moments, he made it out the door and took his place again among the monks who were now listening to the homily of the nervous novitiate master.

Kuisl knelt down, folded his hands, and silently moved his lips as if in prayer. But thoughts were already churning around in his head as he struggled to piece together everything he'd learned in the last quarter hour. Events fluttered through his mind like pages ripped from a book and seemed to escape each time he thought he had found two pieces that fit together.

Kuisl gnawed on his lips and ground his teeth like huge millstones. For the first time, the hangman sincerely regretted that monks weren't allowed to smoke during mass.

"There are three sliding bars," Simon said excitedly as he prepared a brew of willow bark in the rear of the foul-smelling hospital ward. "Three bars that can be unlocked only by three different people using three different keys. In this chronicle from the monastery library, everything is described exactly. The holy chapel is probably the safest chamber of holy relics in all of Bavaria."

Lost in thought, the medicus stirred the boiling brown potion while Magdalena spread a salve of fragrant resin onto clothes she would later bind around patients' chests. For a good hour, Simon and Magdalena had been looking after the numerous sick pilgrims. Every last bed in the ward was now taken, yet patients continued to arrive.

With a sigh, the hangman's daughter brushed a lock away from her forehead and stretched her aching back. The mute assistant Matthias had been kind enough to take care of her children for a while and had gestured to Magdalena that he was taking the two youngsters to the beekeeper's to fetch some honey. She hoped he would be more reliable this time than the night before. No doubt the two little monsters were covered with honey from head to toe by now.

"The holy chapel contains a few hundred relics now," Simon continued excitedly, as he poured the brew from the bark through a sieve. He had been up studying the Andechs chronicle half the night. He was pale and had rings under his eyes, but as so often, the study of old books had worked him into a highly excited state. "Among the sacred objects are Charlemagne's cross of victory and the wedding dress of Saint Elizabeth," he recounted excitedly. "But the most valuable things are still the three sacred hosts. They were here when all that stood on the mountain was a castle, and that was many hundreds of years ago. When the castle was destroyed, the hosts were hidden away with other relics and appeared again only much later, as if by a miracle. Ever since then, they have been kept in that room, well preserved in a silver monstrance eighteen pounds in weight, which is probably worth as much as a wing of the monastery."

"What makes these hosts so holy?" Magdalena asked as she spread more of the sticky salve onto the cloth.

Simon wrinkled his brow, trying to remember. "Well, two come apparently from Pope Gregory the Great, who discovered signs from God on them long ago. Later, Pope Leo added another host on which the bloody monogram of Jesus had supposedly appeared. Since the founding of the monastery, many thousands of people have made the pilgrimage every year to the Festival of the Three Hosts to view the sacred objects. It is said that God will hear your prayers if you pray long enough in front of the relics."

"The way you put it, it sounds like you don't really believe in it," Magdalena replied saucily. "Didn't we ourselves come to Andechs to pray to the hosts?"

"To tell you the truth, I was more enticed by the idea of being alone with you without the two children for a whole week. As we were before." Simon sighed. "And now I'm saddled not just with the children but my grumpy father-in-law."

"My father has always found a solution to everything," Magdalena replied. "Be happy we have him."

"Perhaps you're right." Suddenly Simon's face brightened. "At least now I know a bit more about this sickness. I visited the apothecary again this morning to get some medicine. The prior and his people really turned everything upside down trying to find some witch's herbs. Thank God they didn't touch the rest." He grinned. "In Nepomuk's cupboard I found Jesuit's powder, among other things—really the best medicine for lowering a fever. Of course there are other uses for it . . . Then, look what I discovered among his books." The medicus pulled out a heavy leather-bound volume. "Voilà! This huge book is by a certain Girolamo Fracastoro, and it describes quite clearly the symptoms we see here—exhaustion, headaches, fever—but also the red dots on the chest and the grayish color of the tongue."

"Does your Signore Fracasomethingorother say anything about how to cure this sickness?"

"Alas, research hasn't reached that point yet, but—"

"I'm afraid your explanations will have to wait a bit," Magdalena interrupted. "One look at my father's face tells me he certainly doesn't want to talk with us about medicine." She pointed at the door, where Jakob Kuisl had just appeared. Like a great ship at sea, the hangman plowed his way through the low-ceilinged room toward them, looking very out-of-sorts.

"We've got to talk," Kuisl growled. "Something unexpected has happened, and I'm sure it has to do with these murders."

A quarter hour later, Simon and Magdalena sat on a wall not far from the infirmary while the hangman paced restlessly in front of them. He told them briefly about the theft of the three hosts and the conversation he'd overheard in the chapel. To the casual pilgrim passing by, he looked just like an ill-tempered monk lecturing two pilgrims.

"That's dreadful," Magdalena gasped. "If the hosts don't turn up by the time of the festival, people will surely assume they were stolen by the golem. All of Andechs will look like a witch's cauldron."

"I assume that's exactly what this insane murderer wants," Simon replied.

Magdalena looked at him questioningly. "Do you think there's any connection between the two murders, the disappearance of Virgilius, and the theft of the hosts?"

"That would fit in very well with the plans of our unknown evil-doer," Simon replied with a shrug. "This devil clearly wants to sow panic among the pilgrims: first the murders and the automaton and now the theft. The only question remaining is what this madman is trying to accomplish."

Kuisl stopped pacing and wiped the sweat from his brow beneath the hood. "Sow panic? I'm not so sure of that," he grumbled. "Maybe this is all about something quite different. Don't forget, Virgilius said someone was interested in those damned experiments with lightning. I, in any case—"

"Shh," Magdalena squeezed her father's hand and pointed furtively toward the end of the street where two more pilgrims had just appeared: the Schongau burgomaster, Karl Semer, and his son. The older patrician headed straight for Simon, ignoring the two others. At the last minute Kuisl was able to pull the hood far down over his face.

"Fronwieser, it's good I found you here," the burgomaster began in a condescending tone. "I'm sure you completely misunderstood me in our conversation two days ago." With a broad smile Semer reached out to him, but Simon declined to shake hands.

"Well, in any case," Semer continued, smoothing his jacket awkwardly with his hand. "Have you spoken with the abbot recently? His Excellency refuses to see me, and Count Wartenberg also seems quite annoyed. First he comes late to the mass, then he leaves before it's over, slamming the door behind him. Do you have any idea what's happened?"

Simon folded his arms in front of his chest. "I'm sorry, but I'm fully occupied with the infirmary," he replied in a flat voice. "I really can't help you with that."

Semer sighed. "If you can't help me, perhaps you can help my son," he said, pointing to Sebastian, who was standing at his side, his eyes flashing in anger. Clearly Sebastian was suffering even more than his father from having to beg for a favor.

"My son will soon take over the business in Schongau—the business, and no doubt my position on the council," Karl Semer said in a whining voice. "If you help me, it could work out to your advantage, Fronwieser." There was suddenly something threatening in his voice. "But if the deal with the count falls through, if my investments in the upcoming festival should be a loss, then . . ." He paused dramatically. "I can make your life very difficult, mister bathhouse surgeon. Taxes, the permission to practice, a license from the town . . . Do you have such a license, Master Fronwieser?"

"You have the gall to threaten us?" Magdalena snarled. "A lot of other people have tried the same thing." Her voice was now so loud that some of the passing pilgrims turned around. "Just remember, Semer," the hangman's daughter continued in a softer voice, "someday you, too, will need the help of a doctor, and God forbid that my husband gives you the wrong medicine."

"Quiet, hangman's girl." The burgomaster didn't even deign to look at her but stared off into the distance. "Brood of vipers. A woman like you should be thankful she's allowed to marry a bathhouse surgeon. In other places, they would put you in the pillory or burn you at the stake for saying things like that. So what do you say, Fronwieser?" Jutting his chin out aggressively, he turned back to Simon. "Are you going to see to it that the judge holds a speedy trial for the demonic apothecary so that peace and quiet return here? Or would you rather be chased out of town with your dishonorable and querulous woman?"

Simon was preparing a harsh response when he heard a loud cracking next to him. He looked to the side and noted in horror that his father-in-law was clenching his fists so hard his knuckles had turned white. Beneath the hood Kuisl looked like the very personification of the Grim Reaper just before he swings his scythe.

My God, Kuisl, calm down, Simon was thinking. *If Semer recognizes you now, it's all over. Then we'll have another trial, and the Weilheim hangman will punish his own colleague.*

The Schongau burgomaster seemed to have noticed Simon's gaze. Annoyed, he looked over at the huge monk with the hood drawn down over his head, and frowned. "Have we met before?" Karl Semer asked. "I've never seen you in the monastery. Such a large man would have caught my attention."

"An itinerant Minorite helping me with my patients," Simon

stammered before Kuisl could reply. "Brother Ja . . . Jakobus," he corrected himself quickly. "A great healer. We thank God we have him."

The mayor continued staring at the silent monk. "Strange," Semer murmured. "I think I've seen your healer somewhere before." He turned to his son. "What do you think?"

Sebastian Semer shrugged indifferently. "I don't know. All these monks look the same to me."

"So be it." Finally Karl Semer turned back to Simon and Magdalena. He seemed to have already forgotten the Minorite underneath the hood. "But think it over carefully before you pick a fight with me, Fronwieser," he threatened again. "Up to now the Schongau council has approved your bathhouse, but that can quickly change. What would they say in Munich if they found out that the Schongau bathhouse surgeon married a dishonorable woman and he didn't even have the proper permits?"

Simon pretended to concede. "Very well," he sighed. "You've won. I'll speak with the abbot. But now I really must go to take care of my patients."

"Fine, fine." Karl Semer smiled thinly. "I see we understand each other. I'll come back tonight. And now, farewell." Then he pointed at Magdalena in disgust. "One day I'm going to order the father of this hussy to cut out her tongue before she gets you all in a lot of trouble."

Magdalena started angrily, but Simon managed to quiet her with a severe glance.

"I'll . . . I'll see to it myself that she's a little more careful with what she says," he quickly replied. "I promise."

"That's all right, then." With a slight nod, old Semer turned to leave with his son but suddenly turned back to Simon. "Ah, Fronwieser, it just occured to me . . ." he began hesitantly. "Didn't you say your father-in-law would be coming to Andechs? I haven't seen him yet. Has he arrived?"

Simon froze, but tried to keep his voice as calm as possible.

"His . . . his wife is unfortunately too ill. He'll no doubt have to remain in Schongau."

A narrow smile spread across his face. "That's a shame," he replied. "A pilgrimage would surely have done the stubborn old fellow some good. It teaches you humility, don't you think? Everyone needs to know his place in life."

Without waiting for an answer, the burgomaster disappeared through a small door in the wall, leaving Magdalena seething with rage and her father grinding his teeth so loud it gave Simon goose bumps. Beneath the hood, Kuisl's face was ashen.

"Damn patricians," the hangman murmured. "They think we are nothing but dirt. I pray for the day when I get one of them on the rack."

"You coward," Magdalena glared at Simon. "Are you my husband, or what? Why did you cave in to that fat old moneybags?"

"Because I was trying to avoid a bloodbath, you silly goose," Simon whispered. "Can't you understand that? If a fight had broken out, your father would have killed old Semer in one blow and wound up on the scaffold. Damn! Why do you Kuisls always have to be so stubborn?"

Magdalena fell silent but looked at him defiantly while her father laughed softly. Evidently he'd calmed down a bit.

"You're right, Simon," he growled. "You probably just saved Semer's life—and mine."

Kuisl strolled toward the exit of the infirmary. "Brother Jakobus," he laughed. "An itinerant Minorite and healer. Simon, Simon, where did you ever learn to make up stuff like that?" Grinning, he beckoned to the others to follow. "And now your Brother Jakobus will show you how to mix a really good potion for a fever—not the kind of trash a lousy bathhouse surgeon throws together."

. . .

A few hours later Magdalena was frolicking about with her children in one of the many fields of flowers near the monastery. Peter was chasing after a butterfly while his younger brother romped about, pulling up wild flowers and herbs and sticking them in his mouth as his mother watched carefully to make sure none of them was poisonous.

Magdalena breathed in the fragrance of the summer breezes, trying to forget all the worries of the last few days. Simon and her father were still sitting in the knacker's cottage, brooding over the theft of the three hosts. Her father seemed obsessed with plans to rescue his friend Nepomuk, forgetting everything else, including his two grandsons.

Peter and Paul had been tugging at their grandfather's jacket for some time, but when he didn't take them in his lap or toss them in the air, even after they'd pestered him a while, they started in on their mother. Magdalena finally gave up with a sigh and took them outdoors. The walk, she realized, was just what she needed.

Humming softly to herself, she strolled along the forest edge with the children, pointing out a spotted woodpecker and amusing the children by tossing pinecones at a few startled squirrels. The children's laughter was infectious, and Magdalena felt really happy for the first time in days.

But then she remembered the cutting words of the Schongau burgomaster. "Hush, hangman's girl."

Karl Semer had called her a *hussy* and spoke of *a den of vipers*. To him she was just an impertinent, dishonorable slut moving in social circles far above her proper place in life. Semer had respect for Magdalena's father—and probably even some fear—but to him the hangman's daughter was nothing more than a whore. Full of trepidation, Magdalena thought about what things would be like once her father was gone. Would the Schongauers chase her out of town?

Paul's cries startled her from her reveries. He had fallen on a slippery, mossy stone and cut his knee. While Magdalena tried to console him, she took him in her arms and looked around for the older boy. Her heart skipped a beat.

Peter had disappeared.

Frantically, Magdalena scanned the meadow and the forest edge, but the boy had vanished.

"Peter!" she shouted, over the wailing of her younger son. "Peter, where are you? Are you hiding?"

Somewhere a jay was calling, bees were humming, and her youngest child was whining, but otherwise there was just silence. Magdalena could feel herself breathing faster.

"Peter!" she shouted again, running into the woods. "This isn't a game anymore. Are you in here somewhere? Your mom is looking for you."

Clutching her youngest son in her arms, she staggered over some roots, moving deeper and deeper into trees, swallowed up by the forest as if by a silent army of giants. Suddenly she stopped: directly in front of her was a steep, almost vertical slope leading down into the earth. Below she could see rocks, wilted leaves, and dead branches.

Oh God! the thought flashed through her mind. *Don't let him have fallen down there.*

For a brief moment, she thought she saw the body of her son lying like a broken doll among the branches. With relief she realized it was just a rotted branch, but then the anxiety returned. If Peter was not down there, how and why had he disappeared?

Had the golem snatched him?

Magdalena clenched her lips, trying not to scream. Simon, and her father, too, had told her that golems didn't exist, but so many things had happened in the last few days that she herself would have never thought possible. Her heart was pounding so fast now that even little Paul looked at her anxiously.

"Mama?" he asked cautiously. "Mama is crying?"

Magdalena shook her head. "Peter ..." she said as calmly and gently as possible, "he's gone. We have to look for him. Will you help me look?"

"Peter with the man?" Paul asked. His mother looked at him, not understanding. He asked again, "Peter with the big man?"

"With *what* big man?" For a moment, Magdalena was so horrified she nearly dropped the boy. "Tell me, Paul, what man are you talking about?"

"The nice man. He has sweet berries."

"Oh, God." Magdalena's voice turned shrill. "Dammit, Paul! Who was the man who gave you the berries?"

"There, the man there." He pointed to the bottom of the slope where a rock stood almost as tall as a man. Behind it, the laughter of a child could be heard, and in the next moment, Peter appeared, beaming with joy, sitting atop someone's shoulders.

It was the mute Matthias.

Magdalena felt a huge weight fall from her shoulders and relieved tears run down her cheeks as she burst into laughter. How could she ever have imagined a monster had taken off with her son? This monastery was driving her crazy.

"Ah, *that* man, you mean," she said, waving to Peter and Matthias. Peter's trousers were dirty and covered with wet leaves and his shirt had a rip in it, but he seemed otherwise unharmed. Cheerily he waved back.

"Mama!" he cried out. "Here I am, Mama. I fell down, but the man helped me."

"You ... you little brat." Magdalena exploded. She was trying to sound strict despite her relief. "Haven't I told you a hundred times not to run away from me? Just look at you."

"The man helped me," Peter replied calmly, and Matthias let out a loud grunt in greeting. Once again, as Magdalena looked down at the silent knacker's helper, she was impressed at how handsome he was. With his strawberry blond hair and wide chest, he looked almost like Saint Christopher carrying the baby Jesus on his shoulders.

"It doesn't matter who it is," Magdalena chided as she looked for a safe place to climb down the slope with Paul in her arms. "Tonight you're going to bed without your sweet porridge, do you hear?"

Finally she arrived at a somewhat flatter spot, where she could slowly slide down the gentle slope on slippery leaves. When she got to the bottom, she found Matthias grinning. He bowed slightly so she could take her oldest child in her arms.

"You're never going to run away from me again, do you hear?" she scolded, holding him close to her bosom. "Never again."

Silent Matthias was still grinning at her. Then he reached down into his trouser pocket and fetched out a prune, which he held under her nose. Only now did Magdalena notice that the mouth of her oldest child was smeared with prune juice.

"Ah, now I understand," she laughed. "You fell down here and Matthias cheered you up by feeding you prunes. It's no wonder I didn't hear a word from you—how could I, when your mouth was full of sweets?"

Peter snatched the sweet fruit from his mother's hands and ate it hungrily. When Peter's little brother started to cry, Matthias gave him a prune, too, and Paul at once put it in his mouth.

Together they walked along the slope past moss-covered rocks and beeches whose green foliage glimmered in the sun. After recovering from her fright, Magdalena felt almost born again. Now little Paul was riding on Matthias's shoulders while Peter walked alongside holding his hand. The children seemed to really like the silent journeyman. Matthias pointed out birds in the forest, tossed leaves through the air so they came fluttering down like rain, and made funny faces that sent the children into fits of laughter. Magdalena couldn't help but smile.

I hope Simon never hears about this, she thought. *I can't re-member the last time he made the children laugh like this. He just doesn't have enough time for them.*

After a while, they came to a group of rocks that looked like the remains of a circular foundation. Behind these a kind of rocky spire rose up. Peter let go of the man's hand, ran toward the rocks, and started to climb up. Once on top, he tiptoed around the edge . . . but then suddenly stopped, as if rooted to the spot.

"What's the matter, Peter?" Magdalena asked. "Is something wrong?"

"Up there, Mama." Peter pointed at another large rock that, in the distance, looked like the giant head of a troll. The child's voice now sounded soft and anxious. "Look, Mama. There's the witch again. I'm afraid of the witch."

"What kind of witch?" With a pounding heart, Magdalena rushed over to the ring of stones, followed by Matthias and little Paul. Halfway around the circle she caught sight of an old woman in a tattered dress, stooped over as if carrying an enor-mous burden. When the white-haired woman turned to her, Magdalena could see from her empty, milky eyes that she was blind.

"The children," the woman whispered, her voice sounding like the moaning of the wind. "The children are in great danger. Someone is trying to harm them—I can feel that."

"What . . . what are you saying, woman?" asked Magdalena, moving closer to Matthias. "Who wants to harm my children?"

With angry grunts, the big, mute man strode over to the ring of stones and lifted Peter down from the rock. The boy, para-lyzed by fear, couldn't look away from the old woman in the tat-tered dress.

"Evil is everywhere!" the old woman wailed. "I'm guarding the entrance to hell, but evil long ago spread to our houses and homes, and I can no longer stop it. Beware, children. Beware!"

Blindly groping her way forward, the old woman staggered

toward Matthias, Magdalena, and the children, reaching out toward Paul with her long, filthy fingernails. The knacker's apprentice gave her a shove and she fell backward, landing in the wet leaves.

"Woe to you!" she screamed as if she'd completely lost her mind now. "Woe to you! Evil is reaching out: I can hear it rumbling in the bowels of the mountain, I hear its song every night — the end is near."

Dazed, Magdalena took her children by the hand and walked backward, step by step, to the slope where they'd come down. "Listen, old woman," the hangman's daughter said, trying to calm her down. "We wish you no harm. I'm sorry if we've frightened you."

Magdalena kept speaking in a soft, soothing voice as she continued to move away with the children. The woman was clearly insane, but crazy people often spoke curses that came true. That's what older people had always told her, in any case; perhaps there was some truth to it.

The old woman was still wailing, but in the meantime her words had given way to an incomprehensible babble. She lay doubled up on the ground, and Magdalena only hoped Matthias hadn't inadvertently injured her. Magdalena was about to walk back to the woman to see what was wrong when the knacker's assistant took her by the shoulder and pulled her back with a growl. He gestured as if to say the woman was out of her mind and pointed back to the monastery. His gaze conveyed a clear warning — now void of any friendliness.

"Geout. Esser geout," he stammered

"You're right, Matthias," Magdalena sighed. "We'd better turn around and get out before she does something to harm the children. There's nothing more we can do to help here; she's living in her own world."

After a final anxious look, she turned and hurried back to

the slope with Matthias and the children. She could hear the whining old woman for a while, but then only the stillness of the forest. The children were already beginning to laugh again, and in a few minutes, they seemed to have forgotten the strange encounter. In another quarter hour, they had struggled up the steep slope and now stood at the edge of the forest, looking out on the fragrant field of flowers.

Magdalena took a deep breath, feeling as if she'd awakened from a bad dream.

"Who in God's name was that?" she asked Matthias, but the journeyman just shrugged and turned to point the way home.

The four hurried across the meadow toward the monastery wall, where new groups of pilgrims had been circling since early morning, praying loudly. In the midst of one such group, Magdalena spotted her father. This time he wasn't wearing his monk's robe, and he looked tired.

"Where in the devil have you been?" he growled, absentmindedly patting his grandsons' heads. "Simon and I have been worried."

"I was in the forest with Matthias and the children," she said, trying to reassure him. "You men were completely absorbed in your conversation."

"Is that Graetz's journeyman?" Kuisl took a careful look at the redheaded giant. "Well, then at least you weren't unprotected. Nevertheless, I think it would be best for you not to go so far into the forest from now on."

"Ah, I see. You want to lock me up, you and Simon?" asked Magdalena, regaining her self-confidence. "You can forget that," she groused. "I'll go where I want."

For a moment she wondered whether to tell her father about the strange encounter with the mad old woman, but she decided to keep silent. In the present situation, it would just be grist for her father's mill. Instead, she turned to him and whispered,

"You'd better be careful Semer doesn't see you out here, or he'll get some dumb ideas."

"Bah!" the hangman retorted. "I'm no more interested in Semer than I am in a used wad of tobacco." He spat on the ground to emphasize his point. "Now for once, I want you to come where *I* want to go. Unlike you, stupid woman, we two men have been thinking."

"Ah, and what came of that?"

"I'd rather discuss that with you in private, if possible, without the children present." Once more the hangman looked Matthias up and down. "Do you think your strong bodyguard would be able to take the two kids down to the knacker's house and keep an eye on them there?"

"Better than you and Simon together," Magdalena snapped.

The children pouted, but when the knacker's helper finally offered them two more plums, they followed willingly. After the children and Matthias disappeared around the corner, the hangman turned back to his daughter.

"Well?" she asked curiously. "What's your plan?"

Grinning, the hangman unrolled the monk's robe he'd been hiding under his cloak.

"Brother Jakobus and Saint Simon will pay another visit to the relics room," he said with a sneer. "There's something there I have to get a look at again. Do you think a weak woman like you can keep the priests off our backs for a while?"

"If you're looking for a weak woman, you've come to the wrong place."

The hangman sighed. "Then just a woman. The main thing is to keep them gawking at you and not watching us."

With a smile, Magdalena joined her father and headed toward the church. It looked like he was finally onto something.

In front of the church they met Simon, who was awaiting his wife impatiently.

"Can you image how worried——" he started to say, but Kuisl cut him short.

"She was with Matthias, and she's still alive; so let's forget the matter."

"With the mute Matthias, Graetz's assistant?" Simon stared at his wife incredulously. "What are you doing around him?"

"At least he takes care of the two boys, whereas their high and mighty father prefers to stick his nose in books," she groused.

"Just a minute. I'm only doing that because we have a murder to solve here. You said yourself——"

"Calm down, both of you," the hangman interrupted. "You can fight all you want in Schongau, but we're here now to help Nepomuk, and to do that I've got to get a better look at the holy chapel. Now, for God's sake, let's get in there."

He opened the door to the church. At the noon hour, relatively few pilgrims were present. Around two dozen were kneeling and praying in the rear pews with their eyes closed, and closer to the front, near the high altar, a single monk was busy preparing for the next mass. To her horror, Magdalena recognized him as Brother Eckhart, the cellarer.

"Oh, great," she whispered. "The old bastard snubbed me before, and I hardly think I'll be able to distract him now."

"You must at least try," Simon whispered. "It will take us only two minutes to get up the stairway, across the balcony, and to the entrance, and if you can distract him that long, it will be enough."

"Two minutes?" The hangman's daughter raised her eyebrows. "That can be an eternity——but all right, I'll do my best." Magdalena dipped her fingers in the holy water from the font at the entrance, crossed herself, curtsied politely, and moved toward the apse where Brother Eckhart was busy cleaning the communion cup with a cloth. Seeing the young woman approach, he turned away pointedly.

"Oh, Your Excellency . . ." Magdalena started to say, but the cellarer didn't respond. "I wasn't here for the offertory this morning," she said, "but I'd like to donate something for construction of the new monastery." At that, the fat monk raised his head.

"You can give me the money if you wish," he answered haughtily, "and I'll pass it along as a charitable donation."

You'll blow it on booze, you bloated winebag, Magdalena thought, smiling.

"As you wish, Your Excellency," she replied in a naive tone. "But may I ask you something first?"

The cellarer gave her a distrustful look. "Are you the woman I chased out of the balcony recently?" he asked, "the one who wanted to know so much about our relics room?"

"Ah, yes," Magdalena admitted after brief hesitation. "The relics . . . they . . . they mean so very much to me." She beamed ecstatically. "I even dream about the relics. In my dreams, Charlemagne and Saint Elizabeth even come to my bed and speak to me. They tell me when the cattle are sick and when the milk will turn sour, and when I look in the pot the next day, the milk is sour. A miracle!"

"A . . . miracle, indeed. And now let me polish the chalice for the next mass." Evidently the cellarer was accustomed to hearing such stories from the faithful, and his distrust vanished. Magdalena cast a surreptitious glance up at the balcony to see Simon and her father starting up the stairs to the monk's choir. She had to think of something.

"This . . . this painting in the back of the church," she giggled, pointing spontaneously at one of the paintings at the back of the apse, "there is a mouse on it crawling right into the priest's stole."

"You stupid woman. You really don't know anything, do you?" Brother Eckhart descended the steps from the altar toward her, shaking his head. To her great relief, he followed her to the painting.

"What you see here is the famous mouse that led us back to the holy treasure long ago. See? It's carrying a scrap of parchment in its mouth."

Grateful for the diversion, the hangman's daughter leaned in to examine the painting, graying now with age. In the picture, a tiny mouse scurried out from under the altar during mass, holding a piece of parchment in its mouth.

"After the destruction of the castle that once stood here, it seemed the treasure was lost," Brother Eckhart continued. "Monks had buried it in front of the altar in the chapel of the castle, and the hiding place was forgotten. But a mouse pulled a piece of parchment with pictures of relics on it from the hiding place, and the relics were found again. *That* is a miracle." He smiled sardonically. "Now give me your gift for the church and get back to your sour milk."

"Ah, yes, my gift . . ." Magdalena smiled awkwardly, watching Simon and her father out of the corner of her eye. They were standing upstairs at the door to the relics room but were apparently having no luck opening it.

Damn. What are you doing up there? How long do I have to stand here looking like a dumb goose?

Magdalena leaned over and fumbled with her bodice as if searching for a few coins between her breasts. The cellarer stared back, absorbed by this unexpected sight. "Perhaps, uh . . . there are other ways you could be of service to the monastery," he murmured, licking his lips. "And we could pay you. As cellarer, I have the key to the pantry, as well as to some other rooms farther down below where we store wine, bacon, and sausage. There's also a little place there where just the two of us could be together."

"To pray?" Magdalena batted her eyelashes.

The cellarer laughed. "You can also pray at the same time — that won't disturb me."

At that moment, the hangman's daughter was relieved to see

Simon and her father disappear through the open door. Immediately a change came over her face.

"Well, what is it?" Brother Eckhart asked lustfully. "Shall the two of us go away to pray?"

"You know what, Your Excellency?" she snarled, her ingenuousness vanishing. "You're too old for me—and too fat and too ugly. And I seriously doubt you're at all able to do that sort of *praying* anymore. I think I'll just donate in the usual way." She extracted a single rusty kreuzer and tossed it at the feet of the astonished cellarer. "And now farewell. Saint Elizabeth is waiting for me at her next audience."

Turning on her heels, she sashayed out the door, but not without stopping to bow one last time before each of the statues of Mary.

When Simon pressed the handle and realized the door up on the balcony was locked, he suppressed a quiet curse. It looked as if their visit here was for naught.

"Of course it's locked," he whispered. "We should have expected that." He looked down into the nave where Magdalena was just heading to the back of the apse with the cellarer. "We'd better retreat before my wife gets herself into even more trouble."

"You can forget that," the hangman grumbled. "Just make sure nobody sees us, and I'll do the rest." He pulled out a little coil of wire and began poking around in the keyhole. "I do this in the Schongau dungeon sometimes to unlock ankle chains when I've misplaced the keys," he said as he slowly turned the wire back and forth. "This won't take long."

There was a soft click as the door swung open. "Well, what did I say?" he beamed as they slipped inside.

"That won't help you to open the locks at the entrance to the holy chapel," Simon said as they hurried up the winding staircase past the votive paintings. "That's quite a different story."

"Idiot! I know that. I don't want to get *into* the chapel, just have a look at the vestibule."

Simon looked at his father-in-law in surprise. "The vestibule? Why is that?"

"You'll see in a moment."

They entered the little room outside the holy chapel now. Subdued sunlight fell through a single locked window on the north side, and the air smelled stale and moldy. Unlike on Kuisl's last visit, a heavy wooden bar and an iron-reinforced door blocked the entrance to the chapel. Knee-high, waist-high, and eye-level, each of the three bars was secured with a heavy lock.

Simon pointed at the three coats of arms displayed on the door. "The white-and-blue sign of the Wittelsbachs, an eagle and a lion for Andechs, and Saint Nicolas for the prior, holder of the third key," he explained. "That's what it says in the chronicle, but it's still a mystery to me how anyone could steal anything out of such a room. Are there windows inside?"

Kuisl nodded. "Three of them, but they're all covered with iron bars."

"How in heaven's name could anyone steal a heavy monstrance from such a room?" Simon asked, incredulous. "The locks were untouched, you said. And both the abbot and the prior insist their keys were never out of sight. The same is probably true for the count. Was witchcraft involved here?"

"Nonsense," the hangman grunted. "Witchcraft is an invention of the devil used to hide things from our eyes. What we have here is man-made."

"Then there are actually only two possibilities," Simon replied. "Either someone managed to steal all three keys for a night, or the culprit is one of the three men. Then he would only have to get hold of two keys to break in."

"Or perhaps there's some completely different explanation." The hangman carefully inspected the almost empty vestibule.

The walls were covered with votive paintings of miracles, and on the left beneath the window stood a single iron-clad chest. Kuisl bent down and opened it.

"Empty," he murmured, lost in thought. "Perhaps this chest is used from time to time to transport the relics."

Simon nodded. "I read about that. Just during the Great War, the three holy hosts were sent to Munich several times lest they be stolen by the Swedes. Each time they were brought back again."

"And now they've completely disappeared." The hangman closed the chest. "But I think I know now who has them."

"What?" Simon fell silent, his mouth open in astonishment. "You know who has them?"

Kuisl grinned at his son-in-law. "And you don't? If you can add two and two, the matter is as clear as day. Simon, Simon . . ." He shook his head regretfully. "I really don't know what they teach at the universities. They certainly don't teach you how to think."

Simon rolled his eyes. It wasn't the first time his father-in-law had teased him; the hangman really knew more about medicine than he did, even though Simon had studied it. It seemed Kuisl couldn't get over the fact that he couldn't attend a university due to his dishonorable status.

"Then at least be kind enough to let me in on what you've learned," Simon said with a sarcastic edge. "Or must I die clueless?"

"There's one thing I still have to check," the hangman responded curtly. "After all, we want to find out if the thief is also responsible for the murders. Until I know that, you'll have to wait." He turned back to the stairway. "Now let's clear out, before the fat cellarer gets it into his head to come up here to dust off the votive paintings. If anyone sees us up here in the balcony, we'll just say I was praying and you came to find me, wringing your hands on account of a patient. After all, you not only have trouble thinking, but evidently in healing, as well."

Kuisl stomped down the stairs, and even though his back was turned to Simon, the medicus was sure he wore a wide, satisfied grin. Grumbling softly, Simon followed. There were days when he wished he could put his father-in-law on the rack.

It would take Simon much longer than anticipated to finally hear Kuisl's theory.

During the day, Simon continued to care for the sick with Magdalena. They were supported by Jakob Schreevogl, who'd paid a few undaunted day laborers to help them set up beds in an adjacent room. In addition, two maids from the village took charge of seeing there was always fresh water and the necessary herbs. Their only condition was that Simon would have the rooms smoked out with mugwort and St. John's wort. Simon didn't think this lessened the danger of infection in any way, but it was only under this condition that the men and women agreed to help the bathhouse surgeon. None of the monks had yet shown up to help.

Simon continued leafing through the book by Girolamo Fracastoro, hoping to learn more about the mysterious illness. The Italian scholar believed that sicknesses were not, as commonly assumed, spread by bad vapors, but through tiny particles in food, in water, and in the air. Could that explain the plague at Andechs?

As the setting sun cast its last warm rays through the tiny windows of the infirmary, Simon's growling stomach reminded him he hadn't eaten since that morning. He put aside his dirty work apron, splashed some fresh water on his face, and looked around for Magdalena, who was just giving some syrup to a girl who must have been about six years old in order to bring down her fever. Their own children were playing in a corner with a few nativity figurines that a woodcutter had donated in lieu of money.

"I'm dying of hunger," Simon groaned. "Shall we go down to the tavern for a cup of stew and a glass or two of wine? There's not much to do here anyway. The people will keep coughing and spitting up, whether we're here or not."

Magdalena looked anxiously over at Peter and Paul. "I think I'd rather go back to the knacker's house with the children," she said, wiping her hands on her apron. "The boys have been here with all the sick people for far too long, and they should go to bed soon in any case." She pointed at Paul, who was rubbing his eyes. "But you go ahead; I'll be all right."

Simon grinned. "Because you'll be back with your mute helper?"

"Matthias?" Magdalena shook her head with a laugh. "Don't worry about that. You may talk too much sometimes, but I could never stand a man who's silent all the time." She took the two yawning children in her arms and waved once more to her husband as she left. "But he's a handsome fellow, Matthias."

Before Simon could reply, she had disappeared in the growing darkness. The medicus checked a few patients then headed outside, too, where he was greeted by a warm wind. Again his stomach growled. With pleasant anticipation, he was heading toward the tavern below the monastery when he noticed a figure approaching.

Much too late he realized it was Karl Semer.

Damn. I completely forgot about him, Simon thought to himself.

"Ah, my dear friend, Burgomaster Semer," he began, as he shrugged apologetically. "I remember . . . the conversation with the abbot. Unfortunately I haven't yet — "

"You can forget it," Semer interrupted. His malicious smile told Simon he had a rude surprise in store for him. "In the meantime I've had a chance to talk with the prior," Semer continued. "And lo and behold—His Excellency is of exactly the same opinion as I. He sent for the judge in Weilheim this afternoon, and I'm sure the judge will be here tomorrow to give the sorcerer his well-deserved punishment."

"But . . . but . . ." Simon stammered.

"The abbot? It wasn't necessary to ask him." Semer picked at his teeth lazily, removing a long strand of meat. "Trial or not, Rambeck's days are numbered," he continued smugly. "The judge won't be happy to learn that such foul deeds were kept from him. There will be pressure on the monks, and presumably Rambeck will resign on his own. In any case, the prior seems a worthy successor."

Simon bit his lip and stared silently at the burgomaster. He knew as well as Semer did that the judge's arrival would seal Nepomuk's fate. There would be torture, a confession, and finally a sentence. There was no way out.

"I'll . . . I'll write my report to the monastery, as I promised." Simon tried to sound as confident as possible. "There are still many discrepancies to clear up."

"Do that, do that," Semer replied, "Though I hardly believe the judge will attach much credence to the opinions of a Schongau . . . bathhouse surgeon." He screwed up his face into a broad sneer. "But please go ahead and do that. And if you have any thoughts of drawing the trial out, for whatever reason . . ." Semer shrugged disparagingly. "The apothecary won't burn before the festival, in any case. The wheels of justice turn too slowly for that, unfortunately. But at least we'll know then who it was, and peace will once again reign in this monastery. Law and order are a citizen's first duties, master Fronwieser," he said, tapping Simon's chest with his pudgy finger, "and the first rules in doing business, too. And now farewell."

Semer turned and headed for the tavern, where presumably

his son, and perhaps the Wittelsbach count, as well, awaited him.
Despite his corpulence, the burgomaster had a spring in his step
now.

Suddenly the medicus had lost his appetite.

After darkness descended like a dark shroud over the monastery
and quiet finally returned to the little streets, a large figure crept
toward the watchmaker's house. The man wore a monk's habit
and, in his right hand, held a lantern, which he'd covered so only
a small slit of light fell on the ground. He looked around one last
time in every direction before pressing his fingers carefully
against the charred door, which opened with a soft creaking
sound.

The hangman nodded with satisfaction. The monks were so
afraid of this supposedly haunted place that they'd apparently
made no effort to close up or lock the house pending further in-
vestigations. Perhaps, though, this oversight was due to the remarkable events taking place now in the monastery. Kuisl hoped
to find something in this house that would bring all these events
together — the theft of the hosts, the murders, and the disappearance of the watchmaker and his automaton. Kuisl believed he
now knew who'd stolen the relics from the chapel, but the motive was still unclear. Something deep inside him told him the
solution was hidden in the watchmaker's house. It was a strange
tickle in his redoubtable nose that always gave him direction
when his subconscious mind was a step ahead.

Now, too, his nose was itching terribly.

Quietly, the hangman snuck inside the house, moving the
lantern shade just enough to cast a faint circle of light around the
room. At first glance, everything appeared the same as four days
ago when Simon and Magdalena had found the dead watchmaker's assistant here. Tables and chairs lay on the floor, some of
them broken, and shards of broken glass from test tubes and

blackened metal parts were strewn around everywhere. The severed doll head stared up at Kuisl from a corner.

A creaking sound startled the hangman and caused him to look up at the ceiling. Above him, hanging from a string, was the stuffed creature Simon had told him about. For a moment, the hangman and the crocodile eyed each other like two like-minded beings — ugly, mythical creatures that evoked terror in men and inspired grisly stories.

What did you witness from up there, you silent monster? Kuisl wondered. *What in hell happened here?*

He turned the lantern in a circle until he found the burn marks on the door where the young watchmaker's assistant had met his horrible end. Another large burned area in the middle of the room indicated where the fire had eaten down into the wooden floor, and the boards creaked ominously as the hangman walked across them. Squinting in the dim light, the hangman tried to reconstruct what had happened.

Someone had poured phosphorus over the poor fellow. He'd run to the door, trying to flee, but then suffered the fatal blow to his head. That's what must have happened, but where was the automaton, and what had happened to his master? Was he dead?

Kuisl groped carefully through the dark room, looking for some clue. On the back wall wind blew in through a large, smoke-stained fireplace. To the right of that, Kuisl found another room with a small bed, presumably that of the assistant. And nearby, a stairway led up to the second floor, the watchmaker's quarters, Kuisl guessed.

The hangman climbed the narrow, worn steps leading to a corridor with two doors at the end. Behind one was a bedroom with a stool and a chamber pot. The other room was more interesting: it contained several shelves of a well-ordered private library.

Kuisl whistled softly through his teeth. Though he had an

impressive library in his home in Schongau, his were primarily works dealing with the healing arts. The books here seemed to be more of a technical nature.

The hangman pulled out some of the precious tomes and casually leafed through them. There were works by Greek authors — Heron of Alexandria, Homer, and Aristotle — written on parchment and translated into Latin, but also more recent works by Descartes, Cardano, and a certain Salomon de Caus.

The works by the latter were especially well thumbed-through, with many passages marked in red. Leafing quickly through the text, Kuisl learned that Salomon de Caus experimented with steam engines and believed that technical apparatuses could be powered in this way. The hangman regretted now that he'd never had a chance to chat with Brother Virgilius, who seemed to be an interesting man.

Or to have been one, Kuisl thought. *Anyone dealing with such heretical knowledge quickly makes enemies in a monastery.*

The hangman thought about this as he placed the book back on the shelf and took the narrow stairway back down to the first floor, unsettled by the feeling he'd overlooked something. Once again he looked around at the destruction in the room — broken chairs, shards of glass, the puppet's head in the corner, the monster dangling above him and seeming to grin at him . . .

What the devil is wrong here?

The hangman was startled now by the sound of footsteps approaching the house. Quickly he extinguished the lantern and leaned against the wall of the laboratory, completely enveloped in shadow.

The steps were moving straight toward the door when suddenly they stopped. The stranger seemed to hesitate.

For God's sake, what an idiot I am, Kuisl thought. *I left the door ajar; it's half open.*

For a while, there was silence outside; all the hangman could hear was the sound of his own shallow breathing. Then, after a while, he heard the steps receding down the gravel path, moving away from the house faster and faster. Someone was running away.

The hangman rushed to the door, tore it open, and stared out into the night, but there was nothing there now except a cat that turned and hissed at him from atop a wall. In the darkness he could hear someone running over the compact clay soil. A shadowy figure disappeared around a corner, and then there was nothing but silence.

With a suppressed curse, Kuisl stepped outside, pulling the door closed behind him, and headed home. How had he been so stupid as to have revealed his presence there? Kuisl was sure someone had the same thought as he had, and intended to look for a clue in the watchmaker's house. But who? The real sorcerer? A curious monk? A young local lad looking for a thrill? Now Kuisl would probably never find out.

Grimly he stomped down the dirt path to Erling, while two cold, evil eyes shined eerily in the darkness, watching him leave. Then their owner turned away, too, and vanished into the night.

9

THE COACH FROM WEILHEIM CAME SOONER THAN expected.

Shortly after ten o'clock mass a procession of three coaches came up the valley through Erling. A half dozen soldiers with muskets sat atop the first one, looking down pompously at the villagers. Behind them, drawn by two black stallions, came an imposing, well-sprung enclosed coach escorted by four musketeers on horseback on the left and right. The third coach, however, was a simple oxcart with a solid wooden cage nailed to the top, large enough for a man.

It was in this cage that the soldiers would escort the sorcerer back to Weilheim.

"Damn, Simon. You were right," Kuisl growled, spitting directly at the feet of one of the many spectators nearby. The hangman was still wearing his monk's robe, and some bystanders couldn't help but gawk at his great size and sinister appearance. "They'll make short work of Nepomuk," he said angrily. "Why didn't I go to speak with him again?"

After his expedition the night before, the hangman had spent some time alone in the forest. But this time, for once, no sudden inspiration came to him. Simon finally found him at the crack of dawn, sitting alongside a brook not far from the knacker's house and smoking his pipe.

Now the medicus stood beside his father-in-law and Magdalena, trying to get a glimpse into the coach through the gaping crowd. Simon, two heads shorter than Kuisl, had trouble seeing anything at all of the people in the procession. To make matters worse, he was carrying Paul on his shoulders, who kept tugging at his hair. In the meantime, Peter, along with some other boys, was chasing a startled chicken. Only reluctantly did he finally let his mother hold his hand.

"It looks like the district judge has come personally," Simon shouted over the voices of those standing around. "Who would ever have expected that?"

He pointed at the coach, where a pale, plump face with a Van Dyke beard now appeared at the window, waving graciously to the crowd with a wrinkled hand adorned with several glittering golden rings.

"What a vain dandy," Simon continued, in a noticeably softer voice. "I once saw the count at a meeting with our secretary. The old man spends the entire year at royal hunting parties. But His Excellency naturally wouldn't pass up a trial against a sorcerer. People will be talking about it for years to come."

In fact, the Count von Cäsana und Colle spent most of his time in Munich, leaving the work in Weilheim to his administrator—a situation the citizens didn't mind all that much. But today the people of Erling seemed eager for pomp and glory. Rarely did a high-placed nobleman, with his soldiers and retinue, pay a visit to the little town, much less for the purpose of arresting "the warlock of Andechs"—as the former apothecary was now being called.

"They'll have a spectacular public festival in Weilheim on the day of the execution," Magdalena murmured. "So many people."

Her father looked disapprovingly at the noisy crowd. He'd

never been able to explain why people were so elated at the prospect of someone's execution — even though this was the way he made a living.

"Even if the Andechs abbot wanted to, he couldn't stop the trial," Kuisl finally growled. "Cases like these fall under the jurisdiction of Weilheim. The most they ever do in Erling is hang a few highway robbers on gallows hill down by Graetz."

By now, the procession had almost taken on the character of a festival. Many pilgrims had joined the citizens of Erling in marching behind the three coaches, and the coachmen had trouble making their way through the crowd. One yard at a time the procession made its way up the mountain toward the monastery. Children and barking dogs ran ahead and everyone else pointed at the wooden crate, already imagining the fate that awaited the sorcerer.

"In Augsburg they once put a sorcerer into boiling water," an old farmer mumbled in a conspiratorial voice. "He screamed for hours, then cursed to himself as he shot down to hell like a bolt of lightning."

"If they confess first, they're just burned alive," replied one of the passing servants pompously, as if he witnessed a witch trial every day. "Sometimes the hangman strangles them first or wraps a sack of gunpowder around them, but only if he's in a good mood."

A little old woman giggled. "Then I'd say things really look bad for the warlock of Andechs. The Weilheim hangman is one mean guy, you know. He never in his entire life had a good day. When he's got someone on the rack, the poor fellow screams so loud you can hear him all the way to the palace in Seefeld."

The bystanders laughed while Simon felt sick to his stomach. On several occasions, he'd attended a public execution, most of them carried out by his father-in-law, but the upcoming one promised to be particularly gruesome. The medicus knew that sorcerers and magicians could expect the worst punishment.

He'd heard of a case in Munich where the assumed heretic had first been pinched by burning tongs, then put on the wheel, and finally burned at the stake. Magicians were quartered, boiled, buried alive, and in earlier times, even impaled. Evidently, only the complete destruction of their bodies was enough to break their evil spells.

By now the procession had arrived at the church square. The soldiers jumped down from the coach and cleared a path so the Weilheim judge could make his way into the church without being mobbed. It seemed His Excellency wanted to attend mass before turning to the irksome task of picking up the prisoner. In dignified fashion, though trembling somewhat, the sixty-year-old Count von Cäsana und Colle descended from the coach on a little stepladder, his entire being exuding the power he'd been accruing for decades. His belly, bloated by red meat, beer, and wine, was wrapped in velvet trousers; around his neck he wore a stiff ruffle that made his chin stand out and lent him an imperious look. At the church portal, the old man was received by the considerably younger Wittelsbach Count Wartenberg and the prior. Brother Jeremias bowed and spoke a few words of greeting.

"Isn't that actually the job of the abbot?" Magdalena asked. "Where is he, anyhow?"

Simon frowned. "Apparently the balance of power in the monastery changes faster than you can say a rosary. I'm anxious to find out whether the prior tells the judge about the hosts that have disappeared, or whether he just hopes the thief will be found before the festival. Look over there." Simon pointed at three monks who exited the church and were bowing one by one before the two counts.

"Look. It's the librarian, the novitiate master, and the cellarer," Magdalena whispered. "Bosom pals. Now the whole council is here except for the abbot. If you ask me," she continued, "at least one of them has something to hide. They're all learned people, but evil doesn't stop at the doorstep to the universities. On the contrary, the more learned they are, the more outrageous their behavior."

Suddenly her father seemed to freeze beside her. Then he pounded his forehead with his fist. "What an idiot I am," he groaned. "Why didn't I think of that before? I've got to get to Nepomuk before it's too late."

"Now?" Simon stared at him, horrified. "But what about the soldiers from Weilheim? No doubt some of them are already down at the dairy. They'll ask who you are, and then — "

"I have to," the hangman interrupted curtly. "They'll probably move Nepomuk to the dungeon in Weilheim today, and then no one will be able to help. I know the executioner there, and Master Hans makes everyone talk, even if he has nothing to say."

"But what more do you want from Nepomuk?" Magdalena asked. "Are you just going to say goodbye?"

"Nonsense. I have something to ask him, and I pray to God he knows the answer. I should have asked him much earlier."

Simon stared anxiously at his father-in-law. "Asked him what?" he demanded, tapping the hangman on the chest. "You say you know who stole the hosts. So who was it? For God's sake, won't you stop torturing us?"

Kuisl grinned, but there was a sad gleam in his eye. "Torturing is my specialty," he replied softly. "If I need you, I'll let you know in plenty of time. Until then, it's best you know as little as possible, or you might do something stupid."

Without another word, the hangman pushed a few pilgrims aside and turned to leave. Simon and Magdalena watched the huge man stride quickly away — bounding up and down like a ship being tossed about on a stormy sea — and then disappear into the crowd.

"Where's Grandpa?" Peter asked, tugging his mother's hand impatiently. "Why did he leave again so soon?"

Magdalena sighed. "Your grandfather is a stubborn fellow. Once he's got his mind set on something, not even the pope himself could stop him." She bent down and ran her hand through his hair. "Do me a favor, will you? Don't be so stubborn when you grow up." But she couldn't keep from smiling. "Unfortunately, I'm afraid it runs in the family."

As Kuisl ran past the many spectators and pilgrims, he cursed softly to himself. Finally he'd figured out what had been irritating him so much the night before in the watchmaker's house. He could only hope it wasn't too late.

When he finally arrived breathless at the dairy, he was disappointed to see that some of the soldiers from Weilheim had already taken up their posts. The big fellows, in their uniforms and armed with halberds and muskets, seemed far more daunting than the Andechs hunters who'd been guarding the apothecary until just a short while ago. Just the same, Kuisl had to try to get to Nepomuk. He pondered briefly what to do — then decided on the most outrageous option.

Mumbling Latin prayers, the hangman pulled his hood down over his face and approached the four soldiers, who eyed him suspiciously.

"Hey, you! In the black robe," one of them shouted. Wearing a silver-coated cuirass, this one appeared to be the leader of the guards. "What's your business here?"

"I'm looking for Brother Johannes, also called the warlock of Andechs. Is he in this dungeon?" Kuisl tried to sound as much as possible like someone accustomed to giving orders. He stood up straight, eyeing each of the soldiers severely.

"Uh . . . who wants to know?" the captain replied, a bit uncertain.

"Henricus Insistoris from the Augsburg convent of St. Magdalena. The bishop instructed me to examine this case on behalf of the church."

It was such a bald-faced lie that Kuisl could only hope his self-confident manner alone would hoodwink the captain. Dominicans actually wore white tunics under their black robes, and the hangman took the name from an inquisitor he once knew. To fend off any objection, he stomped boldly over to the dungeon entrance.

"What are you waiting for?" he demanded. "Are you deaf or has the sorcerer already cast a spell to make your ears disappear?"

"But . . . but . . . the judge . . ." the captain ventured, hesitating.

"He knows about this. Don't worry; the church will serve only to advise the high court, and everything else . . ." Abruptly the hangman stopped, studying a huge mole on the soldier's unshaven cheek. "This mole . . ." Kuisl inquired, seeming greatly concerned. "How long have you had it?"

The captain blanched, nervously running his hand over the mole as his three colleagues looked at him curiously and whispered among themselves. "Well . . . since my childhood; that is, you could say . . . uh, forever."

Kuisl slowly traced the outline of the mole with his finger. "It reminds you of a raven, doesn't it? I once knew a witch who had a mole just like that. We burned her at the stake a few years ago in Landsberg."

The captain's face turned white. "My God, do you believe . . ." he stammered, but Kuisl was already squeezing past him.

"Leave faith out of it when you're talking of the devil's work," he said casually. "And now open this door. I'd like to begin questioning this suspect. Or shall I question you first?"

In a fraction of a second, the captain had pushed the bolt aside and opened the door to the dungeon. Kuisl entered, blinking as his eyes got accustomed to the dim light inside. Finally he could make out the form of the ugly Nepomuk cowering against the wall in back. When the monk recognized his friend, he sat up, groaning.

"Jakob," he said in a hoarse voice. "I thought you had forgotten—"

"Shhh," said Kuisl, holding his finger to his lips. He turned around and called toward the door: "I will call you if I need a strong hand to help with my questioning. Until then, leave the two of us alone."

Only too gladly, the soldiers closed the door. Murmuring could be heard out front, then a soft command from the captain to keep quiet. The hangman grinned.

"I've always wanted to do that—to carry on like a wise-ass scholar," he said softly. "Not so hard, nothing but fancy drivel, yet people fall for it just the same." He pulled down his hood, grinned, and wiped his face. "Now the four of them outside have plenty of time to check out the moles on their faces. I just hope none of them is smart enough to go and check with the judge."

Nepomuk looked at his friend, horrified. "The judge? Do you mean the soldiers outside were sent by the judge?"

Kuisl suddenly turned dead serious. "I'm afraid I have bad news for you, Nepomuk. They want to take you to Weilheim today. I'm sorry I haven't been able to stop it."

Gasping, Nepomuk collapsed and buried his face in his hands. "Then I'm finished," he whispered. "The Weilheim executioner will torture me. Oh God, Jakob, I'm so afraid. Not of death, but of the pain. We both know what comes next—the rack, the glowing tongs, the fire and sulfur—"

"Just be quiet and listen to me," the Schongau hangman interrupted harshly. "What are you? The son of an executioner or a mouse?" He pulled his friend to his feet and looked him in the eye. "Remember the war, Nepomuk. Remember Breitenfeld. There's always hope."

Nepomuk nodded, staring off into space. He remembered.

Back then, at the Battle of Breitenfeld, almost all of Tilly's army had been wiped out by the Swedes; barely six hundred soldiers remained of forty thousand. Kuisl and Nepomuk had survived by hiding underneath a pile of corpses, where they listened to the screams of wounded soldiers being slaughtered by the enemy nearby.

"You survived Breitenfeld," Kuisl murmured. "And you'll survive this, as well. We hangmen were baptized personally by the devil, and it takes a lot more than cheap magic tricks to send us to hell."

Then he told Nepomuk about the theft of the hosts from the holy chapel and the conversation he'd overheard between the monks. The apothecary listened to him in astonishment.

"If the district judge has even a spark of intelligence, he'll realize there's a connection between the murders and the theft," Kuisl continued. "And you couldn't have stolen the hosts—you would have had to fly out of here through the barred windows."

Nepomuk nodded grimly. "That's just what they'll say I did."

For a while, neither said a thing, and the buzzing flies and the muted conversations of soldiers out in the corridor were the only sounds. They both knew that Nepomuk was right, having seen all too often what an insignificant role reason and logic played in witch trials.

"Do you understand, Jakob?" the apothecary whispered. "This isn't war; this is worse. The war was fought according to bloody rules, but faith is like a mad beast—once it's broken out, it can no longer be controlled."

Again both fell silent. Then the hangman finally let out a curse and kicked a basket of cheese so hard that the soldiers outside temporarily stopped their chatter.

"Just the same, you can't let it get you down, do you understand?" Kuisl finally whispered after making sure none of the soldiers had become suspicious. "At least for a few days. First they're going to show you the instruments of torture, and then they'll gradually increase the pressure. You know how it goes — whatever you do, just don't confess. Once you confess, you're finished."

Nepomuk laughed nervously. "And how are you going to get me out? With a little sleight of hand?"

"Of course not. I'll turn over the real sorcerer to the district judge, but to do that I need to find out a few things, and you can help me with that."

The monk's already prominent eyes grew even larger. "Do you know who the sorcerer is?" he gasped.

"I think I at least know who stole the hosts."

Kuisl led his friend to one of the wooden crates along the wall, sat down beside him, and told him briefly what he'd learned. When he was finished, Nepomuk nodded thoughtfully.

"That's . . . that's incredible," he whispered finally. "But that might just be the way it happened. What can I do for you?"

Lowering his voice, the hangman answered him. There wasn't a moment to waste: outside they could hear the squeaking oxcart approach with the wooden box.

Shortly thereafter, Jakob rose to his feet and looked his friend straight in the eye again.

"Don't give up," he whispered. "Everything will work out. *Dum spiro, spero* — as long as you're breathing, there's hope." Kuisl smiled apologetically. "That's what condemned men sometimes write on the wall of their cells in Schongau. Comforting words, even if it doesn't really help in the end. Let's pray that this time at least it all works out." Then the hangman turned and knocked on the locked door.

"Hey you out there," he barked. "The first cross-examination is over. You can open the door now."

The bolt slid to one side and the captain opened the door,

looking off to one side so Kuisl couldn't see the mole on his face again. The other soldiers also stood back. Evidently each had a birthmark somewhere on his body he was hoping to hide.

"May the Lord illumine our way on our difficult journey through life," Kuisl said, making the sign of the cross. "We shall have to continue this examination in Weilheim, but unfortunately it's becoming clearer that this case involves witchcraft, and perhaps even more than we suspected." He leaned down toward the captain and whispered in a conspiratorial voice, "The devil likes to appear in the form of a monk and of soldiers. Did you know that?"

Holding his head high, the self-appointed inquisitor stomped off with an energetic stride, just as the noisy entourage of coaches, oxcarts, and soldiers came to a halt in front of the dairy. The guards descended slowly and headed toward the tavern for their well-deserved noontime beer. Clearly the transfer of the prisoner could wait until they'd quenched their thirst. None of the men paid any attention to the huge monk who quietly moved past them.

As soon as Kuisl rounded the next corner, he threw off the robe and ran toward the knacker's house in Erling as fast as if the devil were chasing him. He'd been thinking about how he might catch the person who'd stolen the hosts. His assumptions had been correct. Now all he had to do was to lure the perpetrator into his trap.

When he arrived, he found his cousin pushing a dead calf off his cart. "Do you have a pen and paper?" he asked him breathlessly.

The knacker grinned and pointed at the stinking carcass. "If you can wait a few weeks, I'll have the finest parchment for you. What a stroke of luck. I just picked up this animal—"

"Just shut up and give me a scrap of something," he interrupted. "I'm not writing a Bible, just a letter."

His cousin raised his eyebrows. "A letter? To whom?" Suddenly his face brightened. "Ah, your Anna-Maria, naturally. Send my best greetings to your sick wife."

"I'll . . . do that. Now quick, the piece of paper."

Kuisl shuddered at the thought of his wife. Was she getting better, or had the cough gotten worse? But then he turned his thoughts back to Nepomuk. If Kuisl was right, he might be able to save his friend soon and return to his wife in Schongau. He followed the knacker into the house silently, where Graetz proudly handed over the paper, pen, and a pot of ink.

"Here you are," he said. "It belongs to Matthias. When I can't understand him, he sometimes writes things down. I myself can just barely write my name, which is all I need. It's different with you educated hangmen — you flay people, but I just flay animal carcasses." He laughed and went outside again to attend to the dead calf.

Kuisl sat down at the wobbly table and wrote a few lines in neat, straight letters. It was just a short note written hastily on a scrap of paper, but Kuisl hoped it would be enough to lure its recipient out of his hiding place.

He carefully folded the letter several times, then returned to the monastery to deliver it.

It was a message for the sorcerer.

Pursued by a raging beast, Magdalena ran with her children past the barley fields not far from Andechs.

Simon had stuffed ears of the grain in his jacket, and they stuck out of his sleeves like long fingers. Wagging his head playfully from side to side and occasionally letting out a deep growl, he emerged from the low bushes at the edge of the field.

"A bear!" shrieked three-year-old Peter, stumbling over his own little feet. "Father is an angry bear!"

"More like a clumsy dancing bear," Magdalena replied, helping her elder son to his feet. "He's certainly not big enough to be a bear."

Paul looked at his father, as if still wondering whether Simon hadn't really suddenly changed into a monster. He pointed his fingers, sticky with elderberry juice, at Simon, who was kneeling now in front of the children.

"Papa, good bear?" Paul asked anxiously.

Simon nodded and spread his arms out with a broad smile. "The best bear in the whole forest. You don't have to be afraid."

After the district judge had arrived from Weilheim, the four of them had gone for a walk through the fields around Andechs. For the first time in a long while, they were together as a family—without the pilgrims or Simon's grouchy father-in-law, who was once again busy with his own concerns. The mild June sun shone down; there was a faraway scent of burning coal, and high over the fields, a buzzard circled in search of an unwary mouse. The children had been frolicking among the poppies along the edge of the field, but when their father suddenly appeared as a raging animal, the mood changed.

"How can you frighten the children like that?" Magdalena scolded. "Just look at Paul. He's scared to death."

"I'm sorry. I . . . I thought the children would enjoy it," Simon stammered, pulling stalks of barley out of his jacket.

"Bear? Papa is a bear?" Paul asked again, clinging to his mother.

"Hah, does it look like they're enjoying it?" Magdalena replied. "And tonight he won't be able to sleep again."

Simon raised his hands apologetically. "Fine, I understand. It won't happen again. But what's wrong with you?" he asked, shaking his head. "I've never known you to be so anxious."

"You would probably be anxious, too, if some madman kept trying to kill you."

Simon sighed. "Do you still believe that the shadowy figure in the tower and the stray bullet in the forest weren't accidents?"

"For God's sake, that was no stray bullet," Magdalena

snapped back. "How often do I have to tell you that? And that falling sack was also intended for me."

"What falling sack?"

Magdalena hesitated. She still hadn't told Simon about the sack of lime that fell from the scaffolding two nights ago and just missed her. Was she being paranoid? While they watched the children play, she told Simon what had happened. Finally, he turned to his wife with a determined look.

"I still don't know what to think of it," he said softly. "But if you're really afraid, let's go back home to Schongau — today. You'll be safe there."

"And leave my father here by himself?" Magdalena shook her head. "That's out of the question. He's getting older and needs us more than he'll admit even to himself. Besides, didn't you yourself say that you have to finish that damned report for the abbot if we're not to look guilty ourselves? Let's stay here for the time being." She ripped off an ear of barley and pulled it apart. "It would really be a big help to me if the lord and master would spend a little more time caring for his children. Tell the boys a bedtime story now and then and don't spend all your time poking your nose in books and other people's affairs."

Angrily, Simon kicked a big rock at the side of the field. "You make it sound as if I enjoy doing it," he scolded. "But I'm only helping your father."

"If it only happened here in Andechs," she replied, staring straight ahead toward some swallows flying low over the fields, "but it's the same in Schongau. Day in and day out, you care for the sick and forget the healthy. Weeks can go by, and the boys hardly remember what you look like. Sometimes I think you're not really there for us."

"That's my job, Magdalena," Simon snapped back. "Don't forget you married a bathhouse doctor, not a farmer who can spend all winter long in the house telling stories to his children.

People are always getting sick, day and night, at every time of year." He looked at her defiantly, crossing his arms in front of his chest. "If you want, you can take off with that mute Matthias. The children seem to like him more than me, in any case. And without a tongue, he can't gripe, either."

"My God, how can anyone be so mean?" Magdalena turned away in disgust. "This man suffered more as a child in the war than you can even imagine. And he may be mute, but that certainly doesn't mean he's stupid. Just look at my father . . . He talks only when he has something to say, not like your wise-ass scholars who talk just to keep their mouths flapping."

"I told you a hundred times not to compare me with your stubborn father. I'm a doctor and not a hangman."

"And I'm a hangman's daughter." Magdalena stared off angrily into the distance where the children were looking at an empty bird's nest. From here, they looked even smaller and more vulnerable than usual. "And my boys are the grandsons of a dishonorable hangman," she whispered. "Something like that sticks to you like pitch — you never shake it off. Never."

At that moment an indistinct figure appeared at the other end of the field of barley. At first it was barely visible in the blinding sunlight, but as it came closer, it gradually took shape: a huge monk striding through the grain. Magdalena couldn't help but think of the Grim Reaper, coming to mow people down with his scythe.

When Kuisl arrived in front of them, Magdalena noticed a fire in his eyes that she knew only too well. A mixture of pride, disgust, and defiance — the way he often looked before an execution.

"I spoke with Nepomuk and have been thinking about it," he mumbled, crushing a few hulls of barley absent-mindedly between his fingers. "The time has come for us to catch the real sorcerer."

• • •

Down in the monastery dairy, the bolt was thrown back and the four soldiers from Weilheim crowded into the stuffy, low-ceilinged room, looking at the trembling figure at their feet with disgust.

"Get up, you bastard," the leader demanded. "Your nap is over. Now we're bringing you to the dungeon in Weilheim, where the executioner will deal with you. Your elegant coach is waiting for you outside."

The other soldiers laughed. The monk whimpered and thrashed about as they pulled him outside to the oxcart with the wooden cage. Behind them the soldiers' wagon and the district judge's coach waited.

It had been a long time since Nepomuk was last out in the sun, so he had to blink to recognize the district judge himself standing alongside his coach, apparently just concluding a long conversation with the prior. The two approached the monk, who was covered with filth. He'd been lying in his own waste for four days, and he could smell it on himself now.

"So this is the famous warlock of Andechs," said Count von Cäsana und Colle, scrutinizing the apothecary as he would an exotic captive animal. Twirling his gray mustache, he turned to the prior. "It's good you let us know. A matter like this cannot remain just the concern of the monastery, and we must examine everything carefully. I can't understand why the abbot didn't call on the district court earlier."

"His Excellency Maurus Rambeck is a distinguished scholar," the prior replied with a shrug. "But he sometimes lacks a . . . well . . . broader view."

Count von Cäsana und Colle nodded. "I understand. Well, we'll surely find a solution for that."

Until that moment, Nepomuk had listened to the conversation in silence. Now he turned to his former superior. "Brother Jeremias," he pleaded, "you have known me for a long time. Do you really believe I'm responsible for these — "

"What I believe is of no importance," the prior snarled, his eyes suddenly turning icy. "Only the trial will reveal your guilt or innocence."

"But the matter has already been decided," he burst out. "All these people have already made up their minds. You know what comes next, Brother. The executioner will torture me. You must not allow that. Please . . ."

But the prior had already turned away and returned to the coach with the count.

"I have complete confidence that the high court in Weilheim will reach a just verdict," Nepomuk heard Brother Jeremias say. "Can I invite Your Excellency into the monastery for a glass of wine in the Prince's Quarters?"

"I would be delighted, Your Reverence, but I fear we must put that off till another time," the count responded. "We have some outstanding taxes to collect in this area, but I'm sure we'll see each other again soon. Perhaps we can drink the wine then in the room of the new abbot." He laughed, and the conversation grew fainter as the two walked away.

Nepomuk took a deep breath, turning his face to the blue sky where just a few white clouds passed by, heralds of a coming storm. The monk knew this was perhaps the last time he would see such a sky. From here on, only Jakob would be able to help him.

Though Nepomuk prayed fervently that the Schongau hangman's suspicions were correct, he harbored no illusions about his chances of escaping torture and death at the stake. The mob had found its victim. Why should it spend any more time thinking about the real perpetrator—especially if this perpetrator was as influential and powerful as Nepomuk assumed.

Suddenly a calm came over him, his trembling stopped, and he murmured a silent prayer.

"Dear Lord, you are everywhere. Be also in me and make me

strong for what is to come. Give the Weilheim hangman a steady hand, and be a light unto the Schongau executioner on his way. No matter what happens, I ask for your blessing."

"Get up, you ugly toad. The fire awaits you." With a loud crack, one of the soldiers opened the front of the crate with a crowbar, then together they lifted the prisoner onto the cart like a calf going to slaughter and squeezed him inside. Nepomuk could hear them hammering nails into the box; then everything turned dark around him except for a few cracks along the top that gave him just enough light to make out the contours of the box. It was narrow and low around him. He sat crouched over and could smell the strong scent of fresh spruce.

"Giddyup."

As the wagon started to rumble forward, Nepomuk had to brace himself on the sides of the box so as not to be flung back and forth. After a while he could hear a growing number of voices outside, nasty, angry voices.

"Hang the sorcerer! Hang him and burn him! Just like in hell!"

"Hey, little monk, see if your magic can get you out of this box. Or can't you do it?"

"Curses on you, you beast. Holy Mary, punish him with pain, make him suffer and scream at the stake for a long time."

Suddenly something struck the box from outside. This was followed by a hail of stones and then a loud thud. The noise swelled to a roar of shouting voices as more stones came raining down and the mob seemed to lose all control.

"Stop this," the captain of the guards could be heard shouting. "This man will not avoid his just punishment, but it will be the district judge who punishes him and not you."

Nepomuk pulled his legs to his chest and put his hands to his ears to keep from hearing the rest, but he could still feel how the crate was being pummeled.

My God, this box is not a prison at all, it's protecting me, he thought. *Without this box people would have no doubt ripped me to pieces long before.*

A while passed before the pounding relented, then finally stopped completely. Removing his hands from his ears, Nepomuk heard just the squeaking wagon wheels and chirping birds now—thrushes, finches, and blackbirds singing in the forest. A narrow strip of sunlight fell through a knothole in the wood and directly onto Nepomuk's face.

It was a gorgeous day.

But distant thunder announced the coming storm.

Just a few hours later, three cloaked figures moved through the little streets below the monastery, hunched over in the torrential rain striking their woolen capes obliquely and soaking them to the skin. Lightning flashed through the sky, followed immediately by earsplitting thunder. Dusk had turned into pitch-black night, and only a few lights were still burning up in the monastery. Simon looked up anxiously, squinting in the face of the driving rain.

"Couldn't we have left a bit later?" he complained. "What a deluge. If we don't watch out we'll be washed down into the Kien Valley."

The Schongau hangman turned around with a look of contempt. "What are you? A man of salt who will dissolve in the rain? It's just water, not pitch or sulfur; your fine jacket will dry out again, and life will go on."

"It certainly isn't healthy to stomp through the rain in such weather." Simon sneezed, as if to support his point.

"You could have stayed with the knacker in his comfy little house," Kuisl snarled. "It would have been better that way. What a group—a silly bathhouse doctor and my own daughter. I'd feel a lot better if I had a few of my men from the war here now."

"But this isn't a war. We're in Andechs," whined Magdalena,

who, following Simon closely, was barely recognizable beneath her soaked headscarf. "And if you were any kind of a leader you would at least have let your troops in on your plans. Who is the damned sorcerer, anyway?" She was working herself up into a frenzy now. "Damn it all. You've been stringing us along since yesterday. Admit that you like keeping us in suspense."

Kuisl grinned. "Let your father enjoy this moment. Besides, it's dangerous to know too much in Andechs these days. It's for your own good. You'll have to put up with it just a bit longer."

Simon and Magdalena followed the hangman up to the monastery. They forgot their argument earlier that day as soon as Kuisl told them they might that very night unmask the person who stole the hosts. In the meanwhile, the knacker and his mute assistant would care for the two sleeping boys. Magdalena had simply told the two men that she and Simon had to take care of the sick pilgrims, but now, in the silence and darkness occasionally punctuated by flashes of lightning, the hangman's daughter wondered whether it wouldn't have been better for them to stay back in the house on such a night, too.

Suddenly Kuisl turned sharply to the right, and the couple quickly realized where he was headed.

"The watchmaker's workshop," Simon groaned. "What in heaven's name do you think we'll find there?"

"I sent for someone to meet us," the hangman replied without turning around. "I sent him a message, and if I'm right, he'll show up."

"And if he doesn't?" asked Magdalena.

"Then I'll head for Weilheim, give the executioner hell, and rescue Nepomuk from the dungeon all by myself."

Magdalena cringed. "Then let's just hope you're right. I don't want to see my father cut up into pieces, skewered on a spear, covered with tar, and set out on display all around Weilheim."

The front of the watchmaker's house had seemed so inviting

in bright daylight but now appeared gloomy in the rain and dark. Low-lying and tilting to one side, the house—with its garden in front and low wall—didn't seem to fit in with its surroundings. The door looked locked, but when Kuisl gave it a push it swung open with a grating sound.

The hangman removed a lantern from under his cape and gazed at the strange objects before him—the crocodile on the ceiling, the broken furniture, the burn marks on the floor. Everything was just the way he'd found it the night before.

"We're a bit early," Kuisl said. "I've summoned our friend to come when the bells toll eleven o'clock, but I thought there would be no harm in arriving a bit early." He grinned. "Not that we should expect any surprises."

"What friend?" asked Simon, shaking the water from his hair. "By all the saints, won't you tell us? I can't think of anything more fun than to prowl around a haunted house, in thunder and lightning, where one man has been burned alive and another was presumably abducted by a golem."

Without answering, Kuisl motioned his son-in-law to approach the narrow staircase leading to the second floor. "Come now, you coward," he said with a mischievous smile. "I'll show you something you'll like. I promise."

"Your word in God's ear. If I must."

The three of them passed through the assistant's bedroom and up a narrow staircase into the small library Kuisl had discovered the evening before. When Simon saw the books, his mood changed dramatically. His fear vanished as he enthusiastically removed one after the other from the shelves and started leafing through them.

"This . . . this is a real treasure," he gasped. "Just look." He held up a stained folio volume. "The *Opus Maius* of the Franciscan Roger Bacon, with illustrations. It must be worth a fortune. And look here . . . Agrippa's *De occulta philosophia*."

"Wonderful," Magdalena replied dryly. "But unfortunately

we're not here to read but to catch a madman. Put the damned books back on the shelf and stop shouting."

"Fine, fine, I just thought . . ."

At that moment, Simon's eyes fell on the front cover of the *Opus Maius,* imprinted with a golden stamp.

Sigillum universitatis paridianae salisburgensis . . .

"A book from Salzburg University?" The medicus frowned. "But why . . ." Something about the stamp puzzled him, but just as he started to examine it more closely, he heard something downstairs. The door creaked, and a moment later the church bells struck the eleventh hour.

"Ah, our friend has arrived," the hangman said. "I was right after all. Let's go downstairs and greet him."

Kuisl quietly descended the stairs into the assistant's room with Simon and Magdalena close behind. Once downstairs, they tiptoed toward the half-open door of the workshop. Through the small opening, Kuisl saw a light moving quickly back and forth through the room; then he heard a soft, grating voice.

"Virgilius? Virgilius? Are you here?" the voice said. "Do you have the monstrance?"

Simon cringed. The voice sounded familiar, and now he saw the man, as well. A monk in a dark robe stood with his back to them, holding a torch to light the room. His hood came down over his face, and he was bent over like a bloodhound intently sniffing the floor.

"My God, the sorcerer," Magdalena whispered. "That's the man from up in the tower . . ."

Simon placed his hand over her mouth, but it was too late — the stranger had heard her. He briefly turned his masked face in her direction, then ran as fast he as he could toward the exit.

"Stop, you scoundrel!" Magdalena called to him. "You just wait and I'll show you what happens when you try to throw a hangman's daughter from a tower."

She reached for one of the two copper hemispheres on the

ground in front of her and flung it at the departing figure. There was an earsplitting sound, like that of a ringing bell; then the man staggered a few steps and collapsed onto the floor, stunned. The torch rolled to one side, flickered one last time, and went out, plunging the room into complete darkness. Not even the hangman or his lantern was visible.

Paralyzed for a few seconds, Simon strained to see what lay in front of him in the darkness. When he finally made out a vague outline, he reached for the second half of the sphere and ran toward the shadowy figure, which, staggering and moaning, seemed to be trying to stand up.

"Stop!" Simon cried out into the darkness. "In the name of the monastery, you are under arrest."

The dark figure hobbled toward them now, gasping, and Simon brandished the heavy copper bowl in his hand, prepared to bring it down on the warlock's head at the slightest hint of resistance.

The man turned toward the exit, but when Magdalena ran after him, he wheeled around again and struck her so hard she staggered backward.

"Simon, stop him," she panted. "He mustn't get away."

Simon was still holding the half sphere over his head, but as he prepared to throw it, another large shadow appeared in front of the open door.

The Schongau hangman.

"Stop at once!" he called out. "All three of you, or I'll whip you so hard you'll have to crawl through the church on your knees."

With his left hand, Kuisl slammed the door closed, and with his right he raised his lantern, shining it directly in the face of the monk whose hood had fallen from his head during the fight.

When Simon finally recognized the man, he had to clench his jaw tight to keep from screaming.

It was the abbot of Andechs, and he was very angry.

10

Greetings, your excellency," Kuisl ex-
claimed, bringing the lantern close so Simon and Magdalena
could see the pale face of the abbot bathed in sweat.

Maurus Rambeck was panting, his robe was covered with
dirt and torn at the seam, and a thin trickle of blood ran down his
forehead. Nevertheless, he tried to radiate the dignity befitting
his office.

"What . . . what do you scoundrels think you are doing?" he
growled as he rose to his feet, rubbing the wound on his head.
"An attack on the Andechs abbot. Are you crazy? That could
cost you all your heads."

"Or perhaps could cost you your own head," the hangman
replied dryly. "We shall have to see. By the way, if you're looking
for your brother in the flesh, Virgilius, I must disappoint you. He
isn't here. The message was from me."

"Brother in the flesh?" For a moment Simon was unable to
speak. He still couldn't believe the person before him, who
looked like a beaten highwayman, was really the Andechs abbot.
Had they made some mistake? Had everything just been a huge
misunderstanding? If so, they could expect a severe punishment.

They had, after all, almost beaten to death the highest dignitary in the monastery.

"Your Excellency, I . . . I don't understand—"

"Perhaps the abbot himself can explain what he's doing here," Kuisl interrupted. "In my letter this noon I merely introduced myself as his brother Virgilius and wrote that the monstrance and the hosts were hidden here." He spat out loudly. "The fact that His Excellency comes to the lion's den completely unaccompanied reveals that he probably knows much more about this than all the rest of us together. And about the robbery of the hosts. After all, he stole them himself, didn't he?"

Flinching and startled, Rambeck quickly got control of himself again. "What nonsense," he snorted. "What is this all about?" he asked in a threatening tone, turning to Simon. "I demand an explanation, Doctor. I enter this house unsuspectingly as the abbot of this monastery and am attacked by a gang of hoodlums."

"Ah, I wouldn't call us a gang of hoodlums, Your Excellency," Simon replied, still noticeably confused. "The young woman on my left is my wife, and the monk here, as you already know, is Brother Jakobus, a Franciscan who helps me in caring for my patients," he said, pointing to Kuisl.

"To hell with Brother Jakobus," the hangman said angrily. "It's time to put an end to this silly masquerade. I'm the Schongau executioner, and the estimable bathhouse surgeon is my son-in-law."

Now it was Maurus Rambeck who looked completely confused. "Schongau executioner? Son-in-law? But why—"

"We'll tell you about that later," Magdalena interrupted. "For now, I'd really like to know why the abbot is searching for Virgilius."

Kuisl placed the lantern down on an overturned table and crossed his arms. "For God sake, because he's his brother," he grumbled. "I already told you. I learned it today from Nepomuk, one of the few who knew. Virgilius himself must have told him. The two Rambecks were students at the same time at Salzburg University."

Simon groaned softly. "That explains all the books upstairs. They come from the university. Damn, I knew that the abbot was also there for a few years. When I saw the seal on Roger Bacon's *Opus Maius,* I should have connected the two."

"If it makes you feel any better, my dear son-in-law," Kuisl replied, "it took me a while to remember that, as well. You told me that back when we visited the abbot for the first time. Thanks to Saint Anthony, it occurred to me again today."

For a few seconds everyone remained silent, gazing at the Andechs abbot, who stood motionless, his eyes flashing, his lips pursed. All of a sudden, however, a change seemed to come over him—he appeared to shrivel up inside, his authority fell away, and what was left was the shell of a man in a torn robe, as tense and anxious as Simon remembered him in recent days.

"My . . . my brother was always the smarter of the two of us," Rambeck began softly after a while. The initial anger in his voice had now completely disappeared as he collapsed onto one of the few undamaged chairs in the room. "Even as a child, Virgilius couldn't stop asking our father questions. Later we studied together in Salzburg, but then we drifted apart. He was in Paris, London, Rotterdam—places where research was much more advanced than here and science was not just considered some satanic monster." His laugh was tinged with despair. "For my part, I took my vows here in Andechs as a simple monk and later hired Virgilius as a watchmaker. That was supposed to be kept strictly secret, as it would be viewed as nepotism," Rambeck continued, absent-mindedly fingering a signet ring on his finger.

"Unfortunately I had to return to Salzburg soon after that to teach," he continued with a sigh. "I had been singled out for higher tasks while Virgilius remained here in Andechs. When I was named abbot of this monastery a few months ago, it was a hard for the vain prior to accept."

"The way things look now, he'll be the next abbot regardless," Simon replied. "The idea of calling upon the district judge in Weilheim came from Brother Jeremias in person."

Maurus Rambeck nodded. "I know. I wish I could have delayed the trial a bit longer for . . ." He hesitated. "Well, for personal reasons."

"You stole the hosts yourself, didn't you?" the hangman asked in a low voice. "And I have an idea why." He pulled out his pipe and settled into a charred, wobbly chair.

The abbot smiled. "For a dishonorable hangman, you're astonishingly sharp," said Rambeck, delicately touching the bump that had now formed beneath his tonsure. "May I ask how you figured that out?"

"I'd like to know, too," said Magdalena, wiping some smudges and a few remaining raindrops from her face and taking a seat alongside her father on a blackened chair. "I think you've been stringing us along long enough."

It took a while for Jakob to light his pipe from the tinderbox. Outside, distant thunder could be heard as the storm gradually retreated. Not until clouds of tobacco smoke had drifted up to the ceiling and were twirling around the crocodile did he begin to speak.

"It was pretty clear to me that the hosts couldn't have been stolen from that room by just any random thief," he finally replied. "There were no signs of forced entry, and the door was sealed with three sliding bolts that could be unlocked only with three different keys. How could a thief have gotten his hands on all three keys?"

"Evidently he was able to do just that, however," Simon interrupted, puzzled. "If not . . ." Suddenly his face brightened and he slapped his forehead. "Damn, how could I have been so stupid?"

"I wondered the same thing, my dear son-in-law," replied Kuisl. "I always thought you were a little smarter than that."

Simon cast an annoyed glance at him then began thinking out loud again. "The thief didn't need a key because he was one of the three people who entered the holy chapel on Monday evening," he whispered excitedly. "Let me guess, Your Excellency. You were the last to leave the room so you could hide the monstrance under your robe. It was dark, and no one noticed a thing. After the others went down the stairs—"

"Our good abbot simply put the monstrance in the large chest in the anteroom and returned later that night to pick it up," the hangman interrupted brashly. "That's the reason I wanted to return to the holy chapel. I had a suspicion, but it was clear the thief couldn't have carried this heavy monstrance down into the church. That would have attracted attention, so he had to hide it somewhere." Kuisl grinned. "So much for hocus-pocus. The biggest riddles often have the simplest solutions."

Rambeck sighed. "It was so simple that I asked myself afterward why no one noticed," he said, shaking his head. "But all the talk about witchcraft and the devil at work made my fellow Brothers blind to the obvious. They preferred to believe in a golem."

"But don't you yourself believe in golems?" Simon inquired. "Just recently I saw you reading a book about them."

"How do you know . . ." The abbot looked up in astonishment. For a moment Simon thought he saw a hint of uncertainty in his face; but then he simply shrugged. "I'll admit I was upset by the gossip. After all, Virgilius's automaton has disappeared. But a golem?" He shook his head. "An object made of dirt that functions according to the obscure laws of magic? Nonsense. I believe, like my brother, in God and the laws of mechanics."

"Just a moment . . . I can't keep up with this," Magdalena interrupted, casting a questioning glance at her father. "Any one of the three people in possession of the key could have been the thief. Why were you so sure it was the abbot who stole the hosts?"

The hangman grinned and drew deeply on his pipe. "Yesterday when I followed the three monks into the holy chapel, Prior Jeremias told me that Brother Maurus insisted on visiting the relics room again on Monday evening," he said smugly. "There was really no reason for that. The chapel should have been closed until the festival began—unless, of course, someone needed something that was in there."

Simon wiped some dust and broken glass from a stool and sat down facing the abbot. The pounding rain against the bull's-eye window had let up and now only a soft dripping sound was audible.

"Very well," the medicus began hesitantly, turning to Rambeck. "Now we know you stole the hosts, but I still can't make any sense of it. Why? And, above all, what does it have to do with your brother?"

"I have a suspicion," Kuisl said. "But it would be better, Your Excellency, if you would tell us yourself."

The abbot straightened up in his chair and looked at each of them closely with a touch of his former arrogance. "Why should I tell you that?" he blustered. "Virgilius is my brother, very well. The fact that I kept it secret is no crime, and as far as the theft of the hosts is concerned . . ." He paused menacingly. "Who has more credibility here—a no-account bathhouse doctor, a dishonorable hangman and his equally dishonorable daughter, or the venerable abbot of Andechs? Especially since we've already found the culprit. Why shouldn't I simply call the guards at once?"

"Because then there will be no one to help you find your brother," Jakob replied in a dry tone.

When the abbot didn't respond, the hangman leaned forward and looked him in the face, his eyes narrowing to slits and his voice so soft Simon and Magdalena could scarcely hear him.

"That's why you're here, isn't it? Because you hoped to find your brother, who was abducted by the real sorcerer?" Kuisl leaned back and sucked calmly on his pipe. When he starting speaking again, a broad smile spread over his face. "But believe me, if anyone can find Virgilius, it's me. The life of your brother in exchange for the life of Nepomuk. I'd say that's a fair exchange."

From his hiding place, the sorcerer's hate-filled eyes stared at the group sitting around a lantern in the watchmaker's laboratory.

In the flickering light, the man could see how that damned hangman was speaking to Maurus Rambeck, and how the latter fell to pieces. The sorcerer hissed like a snake and rolled his eyes. He had expected more dignity from the abbot, but it appeared he was actually intimidated by this group.

The sorcerer had listened to the entire conversation. This executioner and his family were more clever than he thought at first—though not clever enough for him. Nobody was. His real problem was his helper, who couldn't carry out even the simplest orders. Three times this hangman's daughter had eluded his grasp, but now it was clear she didn't represent the greatest danger, nor did the effeminate bathhouse doctor; it was the executioner himself.

The sorcerer licked his dry lips. He should have disposed of this Kuisl long ago. He was dangerous. A falling sack of lime wouldn't be enough, and a direct confrontation seemed too risky. Damn, this whole Kuisl family lay upon him like a curse.

Suddenly he began to grin. The idea was so good he had to be careful he didn't start to chuckle out loud: there was indeed another way to get rid of all his problems, and it was a shame he hadn't thought of it earlier. He'd have to give instructions at once for his plan to be carried out.

Until then, all he could do was wait.

As invisible as a shadow, the sorcerer continued to eavesdrop on the conversation in the watchmaker's house.

Maurus Rambeck sat as still as stone for a long while as rain trickled down the bull's-eye window in thin rivulets. The church bell tolled midnight, and not until the last sounds had died away did he turn to Jakob again. "Do you think you can find my brother?" he asked skeptically. "You, a dishonorable hangman from Schongau?"

"He may be dishonorable, but he's also the smartest and strongest damned man in the entire Priests' Corner," Magdalena retorted. "If you only knew what my father has accomplished in his life, you wouldn't talk like such a jackass."

The abbot raised his hands apologetically and smiled faintly. "Pardon me, young woman; it wasn't my intent to offend your father." He shrugged in resignation. "What can I do? It doesn't look as though I can exactly choose who's going to help me, and in any case, it seems Brother Jeremias will be taking my position soon."

"If we are to help you, you must tell us more," said Simon, leaning forward in his rickety chair. "Tell us what happened to your brother."

"As your father-in-law already said, he was abducted." Rambeck buried his face in his hands and sobbed softly before continuing. "Some madman has taken possession of him and is threatening to kill him if I don't hand over the hosts."

"In other words, you stole the hosts only to save your brother?" Magdalena asked sympathetically.

The abbot nodded and rubbed his tired, bloodshot eyes. "This ... this sorcerer, or whatever you want to call him ... knew that only I or one of the other two keyholders would be able to enter the holy chapel, so he kidnapped my brother and sent me a message, along with the one I have here."

Rambeck reached under his robe, pulling out and carefully

unwrapping a little package. When Simon saw what it was, he cringed. In the soiled cloth lay a blackened finger, a few tendons still clinging to it. It bore an engraved silver ring, which Simon noticed now was identical to the one worn by the abbot.

"This ring bears our family coat of arms," the abbot whispered. "The Rambecks are an old family, and when we are gone, the family will die out." He looked at Simon in despair. "Do you understand? This madman will stop at nothing. First he killed the apothecary's assistant because he apparently knew too much; then young Vitalis when he came to the defense of his master. I had to give him the hosts."

"How could the sorcerer be certain they were the real hosts?" Simon asked incredulously. "You could have given him anything, and—"

"That's the reason he demanded the monstrance, too; don't you understand, you imbecile?" Kuisl snorted, looking up angrily at the ceiling where the crocodile was still swinging in the breeze. "His Excellency had to bring the sorcerer the monstrance as proof."

Rambeck nodded. "On Monday night right after the mass, I took the monstrance and hid it in the fireplace here in my brother's house. Those were the instructions. Then Virgilius was to be released and the empty monstrance left in the fireplace." He laughed softly. "No one would have noticed a thing. I could have simply placed other hosts in the silver monstrance and smuggled it back into the chapel on the day of the festival, in the same way as I stole it."

"Unfortunately, Count Wartenberg demanded entrance to the chapel the following morning to pray. So the plan was discovered." Simon rubbed his sweaty arms. He'd begun to shiver, and not just because his jacket was soaked from the thunderstorm. Disgusted, he stared at the blackened ring finger still lying in the abbot's lap.

"The madman didn't keep his promise," the medicus finally said. "Your brother is still missing."

"He . . . he didn't come back, nor did the monstrance," Maurus replied hesitantly. "Last night I was here looking for Virgilius, but then I heard sounds and was afraid."

"That was just me," the hangman replied in a low voice. "You should have just come in—it would have saved us all a lot of time and trouble."

"You? But why . . ." The abbot seemed irritated at first but then continued in a sad tone. "When I got your news today I thought everything would work out now, but now it seems all is lost. The monstrance and the hosts have vanished, the position of abbot will go to Brother Jeremias, and my brother is presumably dead." The abbot collapsed on the floor with a sob.

Magdalena took him gently by the shoulder as she would a small child. "You mustn't give up," she said softly. "Perhaps it will all work out in the end. My father has already spared many others from disaster."

"And chopped the head off just as many on the gallows," Kuisl responded. "I just hope you've been telling us the truth."

Rambeck raised his head. "I swear by the Virgin and all the saints. This is the truth, and nothing but the truth."

"Very well." The hangman rose and knocked out his cold pipe against the chair. "Then let's get to work now. Three days remain before the Festival of the Three Hosts. If we haven't found the monstrance by then, there will be hell to pay, and if we haven't caught the culprit, things will look very bad for Nepomuk. The Weilheim executioner is a bastard and doesn't waste much time."

"And my brother?" the abbot asked hopefully.

With his huge right hand, Kuisl picked up the blackened index finger from the monk's lap and examined it carefully.

"A clean cut," he said, in an appreciative tone. "The work of someone who isn't finished with his victim, who doesn't want him to bleed to death. It's quite possible your brother is still alive and that we'll be receiving another piece of him."

The hangman placed the finger carefully back into the hand of the abbot, who had turned a ghostly white. As the hangman turned to leave, his massive frame filled the open doorway, blocking the moonlight, and for a short while the room was plunged into almost total darkness.

Nepomuk Volkmar stared at the walls of his cell in Weilheim, which were stained with blood and feces. He'd been imprisoned in this dreary dungeon for only a few hours, but he already remembered the monastery dairy in Andechs as almost a paradise.

This cell in the so-called *Faulturm*, or Rotting Tower, was a square hole eight paces deep and accessible only by a ladder. After the bailiffs drew up the ladder and closed the trapdoor, Nepomuk crouched in a corner, trying not to think about what awaited him in the next few days. The dungeon was just wide enough for him to stretch out his legs in the filthy straw, which crawled with fleas, lice, and other vermin. The cell smelled so strongly of garbage that Nepomuk felt like he had to vomit for the first few hours.

The worst, though, were the rats.

They came out of dozens of invisible holes in the stone, crawling over his arms and legs and fighting near his feet over a few moldy crusts of bread that the guards had thrown down for him. Nepomuk had never liked rats — there were people who believed they carried disease — and in this dungeon, he came to hate them even more. Their shining eyes made them look evil and intelligent, and their squeals sounded like the high-pitched voices shouting for his painful, slow death.

You are a warlock, Nepomuk. The Weilheim hangman will torture you with glowing red tongs; he'll pull your limbs until they are wrenched out of their sockets; he'll pull out your fingernails one by one; and in the end, he'll commit you to the fire, Nepomuk, and you'll scream as you burn to death.

Nepomuk tried to shake off the nightmare. Sitting in the dark, he'd lost all sense of time. What time was it? Midnight? Dawn? The trip in the oxcart from Andechs to Weilheim had taken perhaps three or four hours at a walking pace through the villages where people stood at the side of the road gawking at the box with the sorcerer. Peeking through cracks in the box, Nepomuk studied the faces of farmers watching the strange procession with a mixture of disgust, fear, and excitement. Many had crossed themselves and made signs to ward off evil.

Nepomuk couldn't help thinking of his last visit with Jakob Kuisl. His friend told him not to give up hope, but how could he find hope in this hell? And what could a dishonorable executioner from Schongau do if the Weilheim district judge personally—not to mention the abbot of Andechs, the prior, even the whole world—wanted to send him to the scaffold? Nepomuk closed his eyes and fled to dreams of better days. It helped him distance himself somewhat from his anxiety, until these memories turned bloody as well . . .

It's winter, near Breisach on the Upper Rhine. He and Jakob are together on a battlefield, surrounded by corpses buried under the snow, forming little mounds on the otherwise barren countryside. All day long they ride through destroyed, forsaken villages and burned cities, where stooped-over men pull oxcarts full of corpses through the streets—victims of the Plague. These men are often the only living things in an otherwise empty world. Nepomuk has read the Bible and knows the prophesies of Saint John. Is this the apocalypse? Sometimes he wonders why he and Jakob don't turn into animals like so many others. It's probably their long conversations in the evening around the fire—about the laws of mechanics, medicine, and morals—that save them, or the many books they rescue from the charred ruins, or the faith Nepomuk feels, kneeling before a desecrated altar in a small village church. While Nepomuk prays, Jakob waits outside. The son of the Schongau executioner doesn't want to pray to a God that permits all this to happen. Jakob says he believes in his reason and the law, and nothing else.

But when Nepomuk finally emerges from the church with his reverent mien, he thinks he sees something like a glimmer of envy in his friend's eyes.

A scraping sound overhead startled Nepomuk from his reveries. When the monk looked up, he saw a slender crack of light that grew larger and larger. Someone was opening the trapdoor, and evidently dawn was just breaking outside.

Even the dim light was enough to blind Nepomuk. Blinking, he held his hand over his eyes. After a while he was able to make out about a half dozen faces staring down from far above, not guards but strangers clothed in the simple garb of peasants and workmen. Some of them thought they'd seen Nepomuk the day before as he was pulled out of the box amid the raucous cries of the mob and led into the Rotting Tower.

"Hey. Is he still alive?" asked one man with a face as round as a full moon. "He isn't moving, and I can't see anything. I want my money back if he's not alive anymore."

"Throw down a rock, and then you'll see," said a bearded man beside him. "But be careful not to hit his head—we'd miss a beautiful execution."

The others laughed, and Nepomuk could hear children cry out among them. When he saw a glowing object hurtling toward him, he quickly dodged to one side, scraping his shoulder on the rough rock wall. Blinded with pain, he screamed as the torch fell to the ground beside him, flickered in the damp straw, and fortunately went out.

"Look how ugly he is," shouted the man with the moon face. "The soldiers were right—he really looks like a fat toad."

"Hey, sorcerer," a woman taunted. "Can you fly? Fly up to us. Or have you lost your broom?"

Once again the crowd hooted and hollered. Nepomuk buried his head in his hands, trying to ignore everything around him, but then another object was hurled down at him. This time it was a heavy clod of clay that hit him on the back. Pain shot through his body. Stones followed, along with a few soggy turnips and cabbages, then a hail of all kinds of projectiles.

"Here, eat this, you fat toad," a woman taunted. "Eat it so you can grow big and strong for the torture."

"Get out of here! Go to hell!" The deep voice that spoke now came from a man accustomed to giving orders. "Just stop. You're going to kill him for me."

The crowd murmured, but the bombardment ended. "We paid good money to see the sorcerer," a bearded man complained. "And now we're not even allowed to throw things at him?"

Nepomuk looked up again. The torch tossed onto the straw had gone out, but in the dim light at the top of the shaft, he could make out the outline of a person dressed entirely in black. His wavy hair, however, was combed straight back and snow-white, as if the man had aged far before his time. He was perhaps forty and wore a tight jerkin that highlighted his broad back and strong arms. He looked into the hole, holding the torch down so that for a moment Nepomuk could look him in the face. The man's eyes flashed red just like those of the rats sharing Nepomuk's cell. He inspected his victim like an animal handed over for slaughter, and Nepomuk instinctively recoiled.

"Still looks to be in good shape," he mumbled. "Thank God." Then he turned to the spectators, who were no doubt jostling him for a better look. "Just don't mess up my work," he growled. "If you kill him, you'll owe me—and I promise it will cost you dearly. Do you hear?"

"Very well, Master Hans," a timid voice replied. "We . . . we won't do that; but he's a sorcerer, after all. Certainly a few clods of earth won't hurt him."

"Nonsense," the white-haired man growled. "Believe me, I know these sorcerers. Once you throw them into the hole, they scream and bleed just as we do, and so far none has ever flown away on me."

He cast one last glance down at Nepomuk as if trying to calculate what he would earn flaying this body, then he shoved the cover back over the hole. The crack of light became smaller until finally the cell was once again engulfed in darkness.

"Come back tomorrow, people," Nepomuk could hear the man's muffled voice say through the rotted wood overhead. "If it's up to the district judge, we'll start the interrogation tomorrow morning, and for one kreutzer each, I'll let you into the yard so you can hear the sorcerer scream."

The sound of footsteps faded until finally the only thing to be heard was the squeaking of the rats.

Tomorrow, Nepomuk. Tomorrow they'll pull out your nails and crush your legs. Sleep well, Nepomuk. Dream of heaven, because what starts tomorrow is hell.

The monk, once a hangman himself, turned on his side and cried like a small child. He knew that what he'd seen in the red eyes of the Weilheim executioner was his own death.

That's how Nepomuk got to know Master Hans.

II

LEAVING THE TURMOIL BEHIND, THE FAMILY hiked along the monastery wall that followed the Kien Valley northeast. The hangman's grandchildren took turns riding on his shoulders, where, rocking like ships on the ocean, they looked down in amazement into the valley—and occasionally pulled their grandfather's hair. Simon and Magdalena walked ahead, and the hangman's daughter, especially, couldn't refrain from looking around cautiously. It wasn't easy to find a quiet place to talk in a pilgrimage site as busy as Andechs.

"I haven't had a moment of peace since I learned that that madman is still running around," Magdalena confessed with a sigh. "Perhaps we should have chosen the church or the tavern for our conversation. At least that's a busy place."

"So anyone could eavesdrop on our conversation?" Simon shook his head. "Until we know who's responsible for these strange events, it's better that as few people as possible know what we're up to. I don't trust anyone in the monastery anymore. These priests are just liars and schemers."

They continued in silence along the weathered monastery

wall. Despite the early hour, pilgrims streamed toward them as they returned from washing their eyes in the healing waters of St. Elizabeth's chapel nearby. The little stream was reputed to cure blindness and all kinds of visual impairments. Simon felt his tired eyes could use a refreshing splash of water, too. He'd been awake until late, leafing through the Andechs chronicle, but found no clue about who might be behind the abduction of the watchmaker Virgilius.

Finally they came to a rusty gate in the wall. Simon pushed down on the latch, and it swung open with a squeak. Inside, long rows of weathered, crooked stone crosses stood amid ivy-covered mounds of dirt.

"The Andechs Monastery cemetery," Simon murmured. "Wonderful. Nobody will disturb us here."

And in fact there was not a soul present in this place overgrown with grass, meadow flowers, and poppies. A few wild pigeons settled down on the crosses, and the children chased after them, laughing. In the middle of the yard, at the edge of an abandoned well, a few salamanders were dozing in the sun. And silence had settled over the area, which seemed both peaceful and surreal after all the pilgrims' noise and commotion.

Kuisl headed for a stone bench not far from the monastery wall, took out his pipe, knocked out the cold ashes, and motioned to Simon and Magdalena to join him. "The best place to hold an undisturbed conversation is among the dead," he said. "Now let's think about how we can help the abbot and Nepomuk."

Simon took a seat alongside his father-in-law while Magdalena found an overturned gravestone where she could keep an eye on the children.

"We still don't know what this madman intends to do with the hosts," Simon began. "So far, it seems he wants to spread fear and anxiety in the monastery. The gruesome murders, the disappearance of the automaton, and now the stolen relics . . ." He sighed. "One thing is clear: if the hosts aren't found in two days, unrest among the pilgrims will only grow. It will be viewed as a bad sign; it's even possible that panic will break out."

"Well, at least for now they think they've found their villain in Nepomuk," the hangman said. "They'll torture and execute him as soon as possible to get this case behind them."

Magdalena angrily tossed a stone at the cemetery wall. "But it's clear Nepomuk couldn't have stolen the hosts," she retorted. "He was already in the dungeon by then."

Her father grunted and calmly continued stuffing his pipe. "They'll just say Nepomuk magically escaped from the prison. Believe me, nobody cares about that. The main thing is they have a scapegoat to keep peace among the people."

"If it wasn't Nepomuk, who else would it be?" Simon counted off suspects on his fingers. "First, of course, the prior. After all, he wants to become abbot, and after what's happened thus far, he'll soon be taking Rambeck's place."

Magdalena raised her eyebrows. "I don't know. All that trouble just to discredit the present abbot?"

"Let me finish," Simon said. "So first the prior; then the old librarian. He behaved very strangely toward me up in the Andechs library. He did everything he could to keep me from poking around. He's a member of the monastery council, and thus also among the inner circle who knows the monastery's secrets."

"You could say the same of the cellarer and the novitiate master," Magdalena groaned. "The circle of suspects just gets larger and larger." She looked up at the church tower where bells were just ringing in the next hour. "But I know one thing now: the man in the bell tower who pushed me was not the abbot. I was confused yesterday by the black robe. It was a younger man — young and athletic."

"Then perhaps it was indeed the novitiate master? This is all just getting more confusing." Simon rubbed his temples, exhausted. "Or perhaps it was some entirely different person and we're heading up a blind alley. Damn!"

"Didn't you see anything in that book that might give us a clue?" Magdalena asked. "You sat there with that book half the night while I sang Paul to sleep three times."

Simon ignored the implicit criticism. "The Andechs chronicle is written in a very ancient form of Latin," he explained. "It takes time, and so far, all I've learned is that a castle once stood here belonging to the counts of Andechs and Meranien. It was later destroyed by the Wittelsbachs, who ruled over Bavaria, as well as Andechs. That's why Count Wartenberg has one of the three keys to the relics room."

"Just a moment," Magdalena interjected. "Isn't it possible the Wittelsbachs wanted to take the hosts? It must anger them that the hosts are still kept in the monastery even though their ancestors conquered this land centuries ago."

"The Wittelsbachs have indeed tried over and over to have the relics moved to Munich," Simon replied. "A few hundred years ago, the hosts were even kept in the duke's chapel for some time. Up to sixty thousand pilgrims were said to have gone there to see them every week—it was a big source of income for the state. But I don't think the count would steal the hosts," the medicus said, shaking his head. "He might have put someone up to it—I'm not sure—but what would be the point of taking the hosts to Munich if they couldn't be displayed there? It would be obvious they were stolen."

"Just thinking out loud," Magdalena pouted. "Maybe you can come up with a better idea."

"Damn. We won't get anywhere like this," said Kuisl, who, until now, had been silently filling his pipe. "We're groping around like a fellow looking for the shithouse in the dark. I'll tell you what we're going to do." He pointed to Simon. "You get more information about this count. Perhaps my daughter's idea isn't as foolish as it seems. And I'll slip into this goddamned monk's robe again and look around the monastery."

"And what about me?" Magdalena asked curiously.

"You'll start taking care of your kids." With his smoking pipe clenched between his teeth, he stood up. "It's about time the little brats learn to behave," he said, pointing toward the children. "It looks like they're digging up a corpse right now."

In fact, the two boys were digging in the earth of a fresh grave with their hands, and Peter had already carved out a rather deep hole.

"Stop!" Magdalena shouted, running toward the astonished children, who had no idea they were doing anything wrong.

"Are you crazy?" she scolded, tearing them from the gravesite. "What if the monks see you brats digging up one of their Brothers . . . ?" She hesitated as she read the name on the wooden cross at the fresh grave.

REQUIESCAT IN PACE, FILIUS VITALIS, 9-14-1648–6-15-1666

The grave of the young watchmaker's assistant.

"Look," Magdalena whispered. "Someone was in a hurry to bury the poor fellow. It can't have been a big burial service."

Beside the excavated mound was a second fresh grave, and Magdalena wasn't surprised to see the name on that wooden cross marked the burial site of novitiate Coelestin, the apothecary's assistant. She motioned to Simon and her father, and together they stared down quietly for a while at the two graves.

"Damn," Simon hissed. "They must have been buried quickly yesterday. I wanted to examine their wounds again, as well as that remarkable phosphorus glow. Perhaps I missed something in my first examination."

Magdalena gave the two boys a slap and ran after them as they started climbing over another burial mound. "It was surely the work of the prior," she shouted as she dashed off. "He doesn't want us poking around here any longer, but he can forget about that."

"You've got your hands full if you want to poke around here," Kuisl grumbled, looking out over the cemetery. "Have you noticed all the suspicious deaths here recently? I count six, or rather seven, fresh graves."

"That's surely because of the damned fever," Simon replied with a shrug. "Just yesterday two pilgrims in my care died, and they were probably buried in haste to avoid any excitement."

"And how about this one?" Kuisl walked ahead a few yards, stopping in front of a fresh grave covered with black, damp soil.

"What are you trying to say?" Simon asked. "Another grave. So what?"

"Have a look at the cross."

Only now did the medicus notice the crooked cross half hidden behind the mound of dirt. Squinting hard, he was able to make out the name on the plaque.

R.I.P., PATER QUIRIN, 12-7-1608–5-2-1666

"I still can't see what you find unusual there," Simon replied. "The man was buried at the venerable age of almost sixty years, and—"

"The ground on top is fresh," Kuisl interrupted. "How can it be fresh when the man was buried more than a month ago?"

Simon stood still a moment with his mouth open wide. "You're . . . you're right," he whispered. "It looks as if the grave was dug just yesterday."

"Or it was excavated again. Look." The hangman pointed to a place alongside the grave. "Here a little grass has already grown back, but beside that the ground is black and moist. And there are tracks here."

"Tracks?" Simon bent down and noticed shoeprints at the edge of the grave, leading into the tall grass some distance off.

Then, the medicus noticed something white shining in the high grass. He bent down and picked up a handkerchief wet with dew and rain. Made of the finest quality silk, it was embroidered with a tiny monogram in one corner.

A.

Simon shuddered when he realized what this letter reminded him of.

A for Aurora.

"My God," he whispered. "Is it possible?" With the handkerchief in hand, he rushed back to the hangman and told him what he'd begun to fear.

"Do you really think this kerchief comes from the automaton?" Kuisl asked skeptically. "That this golem was here last night and dug up the corpse?"

Simon rubbed the wet cloth between his fingers, trying to figure out what it all meant. The cloth still smelled slightly of perfume. "I know it sounds crazy," he said, "but perhaps there really is something to this talk about golems. Perhaps the puppet really is haunting the monastery."

"Nonsense," the hangman scoffed. "I believe in evil, but not in ghosts. Only we humans can be evil; we don't need ghosts for that. You'll see . . . there's an explanation for all this." He drew so hard on his pipe that Simon could hear the crackling embers and sensed his father-in-law seething inside. This was the sound of the hangman deep in thought.

"Now put that damned kerchief away before you drive your wife crazy. She's already scared to death of this sorcerer." Kuisl stomped over to the exit gate where Magdalena was already waiting with the children.

Shuddering, Simon tucked the handkerchief inside his jacket and ran after the hangman. They'd barely made it through

the gate when they ran into the Schongau alderman, Jakob
Schreevogl. The patrician was panting and needed some time to
catch his breath.

"Here you are, Fronwieser," he finally gasped. "I've looked
for you everywhere. Fortunately one of the pilgrims down by
the wall noticed you passing by. You must come with me at
once."

"Are there more sick people?" Simon asked apprehensively.

The alderman nodded. "Indeed, but this time it's no less than
the count's son. Hurry, Fronwieser. The count isn't especially patient. And God forbid that the boy dies in your hands," he said,
lowering his voice. "Many other doctors have been hanged for
incompetence."

Simon followed Schreevogl down the shortest path to the living
quarters in the monastery. Magdalena, her father, and the children were soon far behind, so Simon called back to them to meet
him later at the knacker's house. For better or worse, this was
one house call he'd have to make alone.

The count awaited them in the Prince's Quarters on the third
floor of the east wing—an area set aside for the exclusive use of
the Wittelsbachs. Flanked by two guards, a high doorway opened
onto a corridor decorated in stucco with doors leading to several
rooms. Schreevogl led Simon into the rear room on the right,
which had a full six-foot mirror, a bed with a baldachin, and soft
down pillows. The air was redolent of thyme and mint. After the
days Simon had spent in the provisional hospital converted from
a horse stable, this room was a palace.

The poor die on flea-infested straw, and the rich on down pillows,
Simon thought. *But no matter where they are, people die. Death
makes no exceptions.*

In the middle of the bed lay Count Wartenberg's younger
son under a mountain of blankets and pillows. About four years

old, he was so pale it looked as if the Grim Reaper might carry him off at any moment. His chubby pink cheeks were sunken, his long lashes closed over his eyes, and he trembled all over as he let out little periodic cries for help. The grief-stricken count knelt before him, holding the boy's hand, and when he caught sight of the medicus, he rose to his feet angrily.

"Here you are finally," he snapped, his anger directed more at Schreevogl than Simon while his eyes flashed coldly beneath his bushy eyebrows. "I can only hope the wait has been worth it. In the meanwhile, I could just as easily have taken Martin to Munich for examination by a real doctor."

"In his condition, I don't think that's advisable, Your Excellency," Schreevogl replied in a firm voice. "Besides, Master Fronwieser is one of most competent doctors in the entire Priests' Corner."

"Perhaps in the Priests' Corner," the count replied condescendingly as a strong scent of soap and expensive perfume wafted toward Simon. "In this wilderness of stupid peasants, a traveling bathhouse doctor might easily be thought of as a miracle worker, but in Munich he'd be considered nothing more than a quack."

Simon cleared his throat. The count's arrogance made him flush with anger, but he tried to remain calm. "Your Excellency should feel free to take his boys to Munich if he doesn't trust my capabilities," he replied. "There are certainly trained doctors there who will give the boy a purgative or bleed him for a hefty fee."

Not until that moment did the count notice Simon. Wheeling around, he eyed the medicus suspiciously. Still, for a long while, no one said a thing.

"Would you bleed my son?" the count finally asked.

Simon leaned over the boy, then looked questioningly at the count. "May I have a look?"

When Wartenberg nodded, Simon opened the boy's sweaty shirt and felt for the heartbeat. He looked into the boy's bloodshot eyes and had him show him his tongue, which was just as gray and yellow as that of the other sick people. The reddish dots on his chest were the same, too. Finally Simon shook his head determinedly.

"No, I wouldn't bleed him," he answered confidently. "The boy seems extremely weakened by the fever and needs every drop of his blood to regain his health."

"Interesting." Count Wartenberg rubbed his narrow lips thoughtfully as he continued staring intently at Simon. "But the most famous, reputed doctors bleed their patients all the time to drain the bad fluids. Are they perhaps all wrong?"

"Galen's teachings about the four bodily fluids may be useful in treating some illnesses," Simon replied cautiously, "but with a fever it's better to draw off the heat with cold compresses. At least that's what I do with my patients." He reached down again to feel the boy's pulse, which was as weak as a little bird's. "Heat, by the way, is not harmful. The body is fighting an illness, and that makes his temperature rise. I would give Martin lots of liquids and perhaps a potion of angelica, buckbeans, and elderberries or yarrow and fennel. I'd experiment to see what he responds to."

Count Wartenberg raised his eyebrows in astonishment. "You really seem to know a lot about medicine. Master Schreevogl evidently didn't overstate his case when he recommended you to me today in the tavern."

And got me into this mess, Simon thought. *Thanks so much, Master Schreevogl. If the boy dies in my care, I'll be sent to the scaffold along with Nepomuk.*

But then he remembered he wanted to learn more about the count and his intentions; perhaps divine providence had sent this boy to him as a patient. In the course of the treatment he would surely learn something. In any case, the count's son wasn't much older than Peter, and hadn't he and Magdalena come to Andechs to thank the Savior for saving their own two sons?

"I would gladly treat the sick child," he finally said to the count. "Will you allow me?"

The boy cried out in his sleep as Wartenberg looked on anxiously; he then squeezed the boy's hand and stroked his feverish cheek. "Do I have any choice?" he murmured. "You're right, Fronwieser. In Munich I'm surrounded by greedy bloodsuckers and pompous asses who confuse theory with healing. And I don't think the boy would survive the trip back there, so I'll have to entrust him to your care." He stood up abruptly. "Everything is up to you, and money is no object. If you need money for medicine or any other expenses, let me know. You also have free access to this room day and night." Suddenly the count came so close the medicus could once again smell his strong perfume. "But if the boy dies, I'll have you hanged as a fraud from atop the monastery's battlements as a warning for future cases," he said softly. "And I'll see to it that you'll wriggle and thrash around for a long time. Do you understand?"

Simon blanched and nodded. "You . . . you can depend on me, Your Excellency," he replied. "I'll do everything I can to save the life of your child, but allow me first to make a quick visit to the hospital to fetch the necessary medication."

Count Wartenberg dismissed him with a wave of his hand, and bowing repeatedly, Simon left the building with Schreevogl.

"What have you gotten me into?" Simon hissed at the alderman when they were finally out of earshot. "As if I don't have enough worries already."

Schreevogl squeezed the medicus's hand. "Master Fronwieser," he said, "did you see how red the count's eyes were? This man is just a father anxious about his child, just as I was back then with my Clara. Do you remember?"

Simon nodded hesitantly. Some years ago he had in fact

cured Schreevogl's beloved step-daughter of a similar severe flu with the help of an unusual remedy he happened to have on hand. This time he would have to make do with the usual medications.

"When the count asked me this morning in the monastery tavern whether I knew of a good doctor, I mentioned your name at once," Schreevogl continued. "I had to; I'm sure you'll heal the child."

"Ah, but how about the other patients, who aren't so fortunate as to have a count as a father?" Simon replied angrily. "Who's going to care for the poor while I spoon-feed the spoiled kid with tea and honey?"

"I thought your wife—" Schreevogl started.

"Forget about my wife. She has to watch our two children."

The patrician smiled. "Then your humble servant will have to help out."

"You?" Simon looked at the patrician skeptically. "A councilman serving as a bathhouse surgeon's helper?"

"I'd rather be doing God's work in the clinic than running around the church praying," Schreevogl answered dryly. "And didn't your wife herself say that caring for the sick is not all that hard? Besides, I've even developed a taste for it. It feels . . . well . . ." He hesitated, looking for the right word. "It feels *useful*. At least more so than sitting in a backroom negotiating contracts for the delivery of crockery."

Simon couldn't help laughing. "You're probably right. Caring for the sick is more exciting than that, and I really can use the help." He held out his hand to the alderman. "Then here's to our collaboration, my dear bathhouse assistant. Let's hope this nightmare will soon be over and we can return to Schongau."

Schreevogl's smile suddenly faded, and he crossed himself. "Let's pray together and ask for God's help. This place indeed harbors more evil than a single monastery can cope with."

· · ·

After her father donned his monk's robe and left hurriedly to look around some more, Magdalena wandered aimlessly with her children through the busy streets in front of the monastery. She alone seemed to have nothing to do and was annoyed Simon had taken off so quickly, even though she realized he was the only one caring for the count's son. Still she wished he would spend more time with his family.

With a sigh Magdalena let Peter drag her along to one of the many stands displaying pictures of saints, candles, and little rosaries. In the last few days, shops like this had shot up all around the Holy Mountain like mushrooms out of the ground. They sold small hand-size votive tablets for the devotional corner in homes, overpriced glass pictures of the monastery, candles, rosaries, badly printed Bible verses, and little charm necklaces with prayers for divine intercession attached. Magdalena remembered a conversation with Jakob Schreevogl some time ago in which he told her that both the Schongau burgomaster and the count were doing a brisk business with these religious knickknacks, but if the count's son was really as sick as everyone feared, all this would be for naught for the Wittelsbachs. No one had ever been able to buy off death with money.

Magdalena caught Peter just as he was reaching for a rosary. "For God's sake, keep your hands off that," she scolded. "That's nothing to play with." When she pulled her elder son away from the stand more roughly than intended, he began to cry, and then the younger boy joined in.

"Father! Where's Father?" Paul whined. "I want my father and grandfather."

"I've got to disappoint you," Magdalena snapped. "Those high-and-mighty gentlemen are occupied with more important things now, so you'll have to settle for your mother."

When the crying didn't stop, she reached frantically into her jacket pocket and pulled out a few candied fruits to quiet them down. She continued alongside a flock of pilgrims in gray penitential robes who were singing and praying in the monastery square in preparation for the next mass.

Magdalena clenched her teeth to keep from cursing. She felt so worthless. It seemed that everyone around her had something to do; only she was condemned to care for the children. To make matters worse, she had been feeling ill again all morning but had said nothing to Simon so as not to upset him even more. Secretly she'd examined her tongue in a polished copper dish and was relieved to see no tell-tale grayish-yellow sheen. Whatever was bothering her, then, seemed not to be the nervous fever.

Magdalena was so absorbed in her thoughts that it took her a few moments to notice a hand on her shoulder. Startled, she turned around and found herself looking into the smiling face of Matthias. He rocked his head coquettishly and made a face that caused the children to break out in loud laughter.

Magdalena, too, had to smile. The boys seemed to have really taken a shine to the mute fellow, just as she had, she admitted to herself again.

"Good day, Matthias," Magdalena said brightly, even though she knew she wouldn't receive a reply. "What are you doing? Looking for a nice rosary for your sweetheart?" she teased.

Matthias grunted and rolled his eyes, as if to say all women got on his nerves. Magdalena laughed loudly. She loved the silent assistant's expressions, which reminded her of the magicians who visited Schongau once a year.

"Would you like to go for a walk with me on the meadow behind the monastery?" she asked impulsively. It was still early in the day, the children weren't tired yet, and she wanted to get away from all the people who stank of incense and frightened her with their excessive humility and fear of God. "Come along, we'll pick a bouquet of flowers for your girl, if you have one."

Matthias hesitated briefly, then let out a throaty laugh and took the cheering children onto his broad shoulders. Together they walked through the small north gate, then turned left onto the flowery meadow beside the forest, where the boys chased beetles and dragonflies buzzing around in the tall grass.

Magdalena absent-mindedly picked a few daisies, thinking dolefully, *I should give these to Simon, but that's out of the question.*

When she finally looked up again, she found herself a few yards from a wall that was perhaps six feet high. The rough-hewn stones enclosed a small rectangular area directly bordering the forest, with steep cliffs rising up behind it. The entrance was a rusty gate entwined with ivy and secured with a huge lock. Magdalena had started to walk over to the wall when she heard Matthias approach from behind, grunting and shaking his head in warning.

"Is it forbidden to enter?" Magdalena asked curiously. "Why?"

Matthias thought for a while, then tore up a few weeds, smelled them with a pleased expression, then finally pointed to the monastery. "Urbe uf onstry," he stammered.

"This is the monastery's herb garden?" Magdalena asked. "Is that what you are trying to say?"

When the mute man nodded, Magdalena shrugged. "And why shouldn't I go in? Are the priests always so secretive about their healing plants? Let me tell you, Matthias, in Schongau, I'm a midwife, and I probably know more about the herbs in there than all the monks in Andechs together." She took her children by the hand and led them up to the gate. "Come along, Mama will show you a magic garden."

Matthias shook his head furiously, but Magdalena's curiosity had been awakened. If this really was the monastery herb garden, she was interested to see what was growing inside. Perhaps she'd find a few healing plants she didn't know or were hard to find in the forest.

Magdalena ignored the angry sounds of the knacker's assistant and turned the handle of the gate. She was happy to see it was not locked and opened with a soft squeak. Scarcely had she

stepped inside when she was surrounded by the bewitching fra-
grances of chamomile, sage, and mint. From inside, the garden
seemed much larger than it appeared from the meadow — perhaps due to the many climbing trellises of beans and gourds beside the beds, which turned the garden into a labyrinth. Lizards
dozed in the sun on little walls covered with blooming alyssum,
which seemed like pleasant places to rest. Inside, small beds of
shrubs and herbs were carefully divided according to type. Magdalena recognized the usual healing plants, such as rue, wormwood, and fennel, but discovered other, stranger plants. She
rubbed the aromatic leaves of sticklewort and ambrosia between
her fingers and smelled the intoxicating, overwhelming fragrance of the iris blossoms.

In the meanwhile, the children were frolicking on the little
walls, chasing lizards. Magdalena tried not to lose sight of them.
Even if this garden seemed like paradise on earth, she knew that
forbidden fruits grew in this paradise as well. Many of the plants
here were highly poisonous and used only in small doses for medicinal purposes.

Gradually she moved deeper and deeper into the garden.
The mute Matthias hadn't followed her; evidently something
here frightened him, even though she had no idea what. Perhaps
he was just respectful of the monks who obviously kept a close
eye on their monastery garden.

In the middle of the garden a surprise awaited her.

Behind some rosebushes, she found a stone water basin surrounded by four benches. In the basin itself stood a full-size marble statue of a mythical beast — a bearded man with the hooves
and horns of a goat, his lips pursed scornfully and blowing on a
strange flute. With dead eyes, he looked out at the forest where
steep cliffs led down to the garden.

Magdalena sat on one of the benches and gazed at the statue
in astonishment. She'd never seen anything like it before. The
creature seemed a bit like the devil in the frightening depictions

of hell in the churches of the Priests' Corner, but in contrast to them, this figure had a roguish smile and seemed almost friendly. What in the world was such a statue doing in the monastery?

The hangman's daughter suddenly froze. It was surely just her imagination, but for a moment the head of the statue seemed to turn just slightly in her direction. The creature's smile seemed no longer friendly, but more like that of a goblin looking to play a wicked prank.

And then Magdalena was certain—the statue's head was moving.

The stone devil turned its head toward her. Slowly, unrelentingly, its gaze enveloped her—almost as if it were struggling to tell her something. Had its mouth opened just a bit? Magdalena sat rooted to the bench, wondering whether the creature would suddenly begin to speak.

In the next moment a slender stream of water shot out of the devil's mouth, striking her right in the face.

With a scream, Magdalena fell backward off the bench, and the frightened children turned around to look at her. Her bodice was soaked and her backside ached from her sudden fall into the herb garden, but otherwise she was uninjured.

"I'm sorry, I didn't want to frighten you so," a voice said behind the trellises. "But the temptation was just too great. My brother always enjoyed himself immensely with this performance."

Magdalena turned toward where the voice was coming from and saw none other than the abbot himself walk out from behind the trellises.

"But Your Excellency," she began hesitantly. "I mean . . . how is it that—"

"I came here to think a bit," the abbot interrupted with a smile. "About myself and my brother. Actually pilgrims aren't permitted in the garden, so anyone who enters has to be prepared for surprises like this."

In the meantime, Magdalena had gotten a hold of herself again. Straightening her wet bodice, she took a seat alongside her children on the stone bench.

"Excuse me," she said, embarrassed. "But as a midwife, I was just interested in knowing what sort of herbs grew in your garden. I must say I'm impressed."

The abbot chuckled. "By what? By the herbs or by our faun?"

"Faun?" Magdalena asked, perplexed.

Rambeck pointed at the statue with the horns and goat hooves. "That's what the Romans used to call this creature. A wild man of the forest who loves drinking and dancing. There are people who compare him to our devil, but that's naturally nonsense." He sat down beside Magdalena. "My brother had it brought here over the Alps, and . . . well . . . he changed it a bit," he said, winking at Magdalena. "There's a device for moving the head in any direction, and the stream of water from his mouth works by a complicated system of pumps. But you mustn't ask me for details. Such water devices were always my brother's hobby." Rambeck stood up and took Magdalena by the hand. "Come along. I'll show you something that the children will also enjoy."

They walked together through the labyrinth of trellises and walls until they found themselves in front of a little grotto at the bottom of the cliffs. In the dim light of the cave, Magdalena could make out another basin with around a dozen waist-high statuettes around its edge. Like the faun, they were strange and different—out of place at a monastery. One figure grasped a trident in its hand; another a bolt of lightning; and beautiful women, carrying mirrors and hunting spears, stood beside them.

"The ancient Greek gods," Rambeck declared. "Naturally just imaginary figures, but they add a certain character to our garden. Virgilius designed this grotto, as well as the faun and a few other devices in our little enchanted herb garden—all according to the plans of long-deceased scholars." He leaned in toward Magdalena. "There are those who say that civilization was far more advanced in those days, not only in the healing arts but also in the other sciences. Virgilius loved being here in this remote spot, devoting himself to his hobby—building automata. See for yourself."

The abbot pulled a concealed iron lever inside the grotto, and as if by magic, the figures began dancing around the basin on an invisible track, all to the soft notes of a glockenspiel. The children laughed and pointed their little fingers at the spectacle; only Magdalena felt uneasy, and it took her a while before she knew why.

"That's the music I heard that night," she cried out in shock finally, "When someone tried to shoot me near the wall of the monastery."

"Shoot you?" The abbot looked at her in astonishment.

"The sorcerer, or whatever he is, has already tried to kill me twice." Magdalena told Rambeck briefly what had happened to her in the last few days.

When she finished, he looked at her skeptically. "Do you really believe it's the same person who kidnapped my brother?"

Magdalena nodded as she continued listening to the sound of the glockenspiel. "The same person—even if we don't know why he's so anxious to have the hosts." She hesitated, remembering her conversation that morning with her father and Simon at the cemetery. "Or the same creature." Perhaps there really was a golem or some animated automaton haunting the castle. After pausing briefly, she pointed to the circle of spinning statues in front of them. "Your brother was very interested in automata, wasn't he? All of this here, and the one at home. What did his colleagues have to say about that?"

The abbot smiled. "You can put up with anything—even the devil—if he looks out for you. Virgilius did much for the monastery. He provided running water in the cells and built a furnace that heats most of the building. His glockenspiel and dancing figures often added a touch of lightness to the gloomiest days here." Rambeck stared off into space. "Recently he'd taken an interest in lightning," he said. "Brother Johannes did some research in this area, and they were exchanging ideas. It was unfortunate that lightning struck the steeple again just at that time."

"Ah, I know," Magdalena replied. "A really unfortunate coincidence. It's a shame there's still no way to ward off lightning strikes." She remembered what her father told her about his conversation with Nepomuk, but she decided to keep silent and not incriminate the apothecary even more.

The abbot sighed. "I'm sure Virgilius had a solution for it."

Magdalena tried to steer the conversation in another direction. "As a watchmaker, did he have an enemy in the monastery?"

"One enemy?" Rambeck chuckled. "Superstition is a widespread affliction among monks, and as long as I've been here in the monastery, I've tried to protect Virgilius from it. But there was a lot of gossiping behind his back. Brother Eckhart, our present cellarer, for example, considers even a clock in the belfry the work of the devil." He frowned. "Later, when I was called back to the university in Salzburg, it was our librarian for the most part who made his life difficult, though such a learned man as Brother Benedikt, who has read so much in his long life, surely knew better."

The eleven o'clock bell tolled from the church belfry, and Rambeck slapped his forehead. "What a fool I've been, wasting time here while my colleagues have been waiting. I must return to the sacristy to prepare the liturgy."

Once more he forced a smile. "As long as I'm abbot, I'll see to it that everything follows its usual course. No one will be able to say afterwards that I was a bad superior."

"But what about the hosts and the monstrance?" Magdalena replied. "If the relic hasn't been returned before the festival begins——"

"The relic will be back," the abbot interrupted. "And if not in this monstrance, then in another, with other hosts. It's faith that makes these things sacred, isn't it? Faith . . . love . . . hope . . . These are the Christian virtues to which we must cling."

"You mean the Festival of the Three Hosts will take place the day after tomorrow no matter what?" Magdalena asked.

Rambeck looked astonished. "Of course. It has always taken place. We can't disappoint all the faithful." He sighed. "Though this time I will not be presiding at the mass. The district judge in Weilheim made it clear to me that, in the future, he wants Brother Jeremias to take over more responsibilities in the monastery." He shrugged and turned away. "But really I don't mind. Until my brother's fate has been decided, nothing else seems important."

He pulled another hidden lever on the wall, and the statuettes squeaked to a stop, along with the music.

"I must ask you to leave now," the abbot said.

Leading the way, Rambeck beckoned Magdalena and the children to follow. "It's better for you to come behind me. The garden may be small, but it's a labyrinth nonetheless."

They strode past overgrown trellises and sun-baked little walls until they arrived back at the gate.

"It was a pleasure to meet you, hangman's daughter," said Rambeck, though his thoughts still seemed far away. "Perhaps the next time we can stay and chat a bit longer here in the garden—and not about such gloomy things, but just about herbs and medicines."

Magdalena bowed formally. "Who can say? Perhaps with your brother, too?"

The abbot smiled, but he was staring off into space. "Who

knows? I'll pray for that." Taking out a heavy key, he locked the gate, then turned silently and walked back through the flowering meadow toward the monastery.

Magdalena watched him for a long time, until his grief-stricken figure finally disappeared in the shadows of the church tower.

12

THE ROBE SCRATCHED AND ITCHED, AND JAKOB Kuisl thought he could smell in it the sweat of at least a dozen fat monks. Nonetheless, he pulled down his cowl as he made his way to the monastery. He had changed clothes down at the knacker's house but then immediately returned to the Holy Mountain. The many pilgrims who had camped out in Erling and surrounding villages stepped aside respectfully, only a few stopping to wonder why the Franciscan was mumbling such unchristian curses.

The hangman didn't really know what to look for up at the monastery, but time was running out, and in Weilheim his friend's first interrogation would no doubt begin that day. Burning at the stake would quickly follow. If Kuisl didn't come up soon with a clue leading him to the real sorcerer, the innocent Nepomuk would die a cruel, painful death.

On arriving, Kuisl saw that another mass was about to begin. Now, with the Festival of the Three Hosts fast approaching, there were up to a half dozen masses each day, and the first pilgrims were now heading toward the church portal that was covered with scaffolding.

Kuisl looked up skeptically at the hole in the roof and the

new beams forming the steeple. It appeared the building wouldn't be ready in time for the festival, especially since many of the workers at the site were bedridden with this mysterious fever.

When a large group of Benedictines entered the church, the hangman was about to follow them when it occurred to him this would be a good time to visit the monks' cells. Perhaps he could learn something useful in the monastery's living quarters.

His head bowed deeply as if in prayer, Kuisl hurried through the inner portal to the cloister and, from there, through another open door into the east wing of the three-story building. The hangman really had no idea where the individual monks' cells were located, but fortunately most of the rooms in the monastery were empty now during mass. He saw only one very old, stooped monk sweeping the refectory where the Brothers took their meals three times a day. The old man didn't notice him, so Kuisl continued walking through the corridors murmuring his Latin prayers in a monotone: *"Dominus pascit me nihil mihi deerit, in pascuis herbarum adclinavit me . . ."* *The Lord is my shepherd, I shall not want; he maketh me to lie down in green pastures . . .*

In the distance, he could hear the organ and the singing of the faithful, but these sounds faded as he got farther and farther from the church.

The monastery was a huge building with an inner courtyard that Kuisl could make out vaguely through the high bull's-eye glass windows. He decided to look around first on the ground floor and then work his way up until he had found something, or was caught. Despite his clerical garb and murmured prayers, Kuisl had no illusions about what would happen if the monks discovered him in one of the cells; they wouldn't let him go without a very good excuse.

By now he'd passed through a number of corridors and was about halfway around the building without having found a thing that could help him in his search. He passed the Museum Fratrum — a room the lay brothers used for moments of leisure or

prayer with ornamental stucco cherubs on the ceiling and upholstered recessed seats along the walls; then the kitchen and a tiny
library containing only a small selection of religious documents.

Just as he was about to give up and head to the second floor,
he found himself standing in front of another corridor with small
wooden doors along the sides at regular intervals. In contrast
with the splendor of the rooms he'd just visited, these looked
strikingly plain.

He pressed the handle on the first door and was relieved to
find it unlocked. One look was enough to assure him he wasn't
mistaken. This was clearly a monk's cell.

The barren, cavernous room contained nothing but a bed, a
chest, and a stool alongside a rough-hewn table. Some parchment documents lay on the table next to the wax stub of a candle.
Leaning down, Kuisl realized the document was a manifest of
purchases made by the monastery, including the costs of wooden
beams, nails, bricks and mortar, and a load of stone.

A broad grin spread across the hangman's face. These were
clearly the expense records for the monastery construction. The
cellarer was always the one responsible for management and financial matters at a monastery, and in fact he soon found his signature on the document.

*Greetings, Brother Eckhart. I'm sure you have no objection to
my having a quick look at this.*

The hangman cast a fleeting glance at the documents but
could find nothing more than financial statements and calculations. Finally he turned to the chest. To his great delight, it too
was unlocked and its contents very neatly arranged. He found
another monk's robe, a worn Bible, and a scourge with dry blood
still adhering to lead spikes at the end of ropes. In disgust, the executioner turned the short whip in his hands. In Schongau, he'd
used a similar instrument on several occasions to beat criminals
and drive them out of town. Kuisl found it hard to believe that
anyone would subject himself to this painful punishment of his

own free will. What fantasies were tormenting the fat cellarer so much that he had to drive them out with this whip? The hangman had heard of people who enjoyed torturing themselves like that, but he'd never met any in his torture chamber.

Disappointed, he laid the scourge back in the chest, closed the lid carefully, and returned to the corridor. Then he turned the handle on the next cell.

This door was also unlocked. He entered, closing the door behind him to avoid arousing the suspicion of anyone who might pass by. Looking around curiously, he saw a bare room laid out with exactly the same furniture, but with a table that was empty except for a candle, a quill, and a pot of ink.

When Kuisl went to open the chest on the floor, he discovered that this chest was locked. Prepared for such problems, he reached into the pockets of his sticky monk's robe for the bent pieces of metal the knacker in Erling had made for him.

Pressing his lips tight, he poked around in the keyhole until he heard a soft click. The whole procedure had taken no longer than two minutes. Kuisl grinned as he opened the cover, pulled out another robe, and was enveloped in the faint, almost imperceptible fragrance of rose oil.

Underneath the robe lay a small, thin book written by a certain Ovid. In flowery lettering, its title claimed to be a guide to nothing less than *ars amatoria,* the art of love. Kuisl had never heard of either the poet or the book, but as he browsed the Latin verses, he could see that the contents were erotic. He sniffed the robe and the book with his large nose, but the fragrance of costly perfume came from neither of them. Like a sleuth hound, he leaned over and continued sniffing. The fragrance clearly came from the chest; either it had permeated the wood or . . .

He froze. As he eyed the dimensions of the chest, there was no doubt it wasn't as deep inside as it should be. He poked an iron hook into the slit between the bottom and back of the chest until the wooden bottom gave way and could now be turned up.

Beneath the false bottom, he found several bundles, each containing a dozen letters bound with silk ribbon and releasing the intense aroma of rose oil.

Well look here, dear little monk, Kuisl thought grimly. *Whatever secret you're hiding will be revealed now.*

Kuisl listened carefully for anyone approaching in the hall, but all he heard were the faint voices of the pilgrims reciting the *Credo* in the sanctuary. The mass wouldn't be over for at least fifteen minutes.

Very carefully the hangman pulled a letter from beneath the silk ribbon and opened it. It was a passionate declaration of love addressed to none other than the novitiate master Brother Laurentius. Kuisl quickly scanned the lines down to the bottom.

The signature read: *"From one who loves you more than anything else, Vitalis."*

Kuisl rubbed the perfumed letter between his huge hands, lost in thought. Indeed, the watchmaker's assistant. Evidently Vitalis and the novitiate master had been more devoted to each other than was proper for chaste Benedictines. Had Brother Laurentius perhaps murdered his lover because he was about to betray him? Did he have something to do with the abduction of the watchmaker? In any case, the letters in the secret compartment were deadly in the hands of unscrupulous people. Though Kuisl himself had never executed any sodomite monks, he knew of cases where the poor creatures were burned at the stake or buried alive.

At that moment, he heard steps approaching in the corridor. Quickly, he placed the letters back in the chest, pulled the false bottom back over them, and closed the lid. Just as he was about to rush into the hall, however, he realized he was too late — the steps had approached the door, and he could now even make out bits of conversation between two men. He ducked behind the door and hoped the men would walk by.

Unfortunately they stopped right in front of the door.

"Just what do you think you are doing, taking me out of mass for a conversation?" an angry voice said. "I hope there's a good reason for me to miss Holy Communion, Laurentius."

A soft, tearful voice responded. "Brother Benedikt, I don't know who I can trust. I told you about the automaton's melody."

"And what about it?" came the harsh reply.

"I heard it again in exactly the same place. You know what that means. This puppet is down there somewhere." The delicate voice became so soft Kuisl could scarcely hear a word. "And it's looking for us, Benedikt. It knows what we've done."

Kuisl froze. If he caught the names correctly, the librarian Benedikt and the novitiate master Laurentius were right outside the door. He held his breath and prayed they wouldn't enter the cell.

"I don't know what you're talking about," Brother Benedikt replied. "Anyway, it's been well established now that Johannes committed the murders. We spread the stories about the golem just so nobody would poke around down there during the festival. And now you believe it yourself, you fool."

"And the hosts?" Brother Laurentius laughed despairingly.

"You think Johannes magically stole them while he was locked up inside the dungeon? I tell you that was the golem, Virgilius's damned automaton."

"Nonsense," the librarian shot back. "Perhaps Johannes had an accomplice. How do I know? We've found our culprit, and that's all that matters. The hosts are the least of our problems. We'll just replace them with others, and then we can just go on as before."

"You forget the monstrance — it's missing, too. People know what it looks like."

Kuisl had to be sure the men behind the door were who he thought they were, so he bent down to the keyhole. Through the tiny opening, he could in fact see the old librarian rubbing his gout-ravaged fingers thoughtfully over his lips.

"The monstrance is in fact a bit of a problem," he murmured. "It will be hard for us to find one just like it, but I'm sure nobody will notice in the hustle and bustle of the festival."

"How can you be so cold?" Now Kuisl had a good view of the novitiate master, too, who was striding back and forth in the hall, wringing his hands. "Two men are dead, perhaps even three, and a monster is roaming about. We never should have used the cellars. Now it will all come out."

"Nothing will come out if you keep calm," Brother Benedikt said angrily. "In any case nothing can happen to us. Brother Eckhart and I personally sealed the entrance to the catacombs yesterday with heavy stones—just to be sure. Nobody will find out what's down there."

"You know there are other entrances," Laurentius replied anxiously. "They're recorded in the plans. Can't we seal up those entrances, as well?"

Brother Benedikt shrugged. "That will hardly be possible. The plans have disappeared."

"*Disappeared?*" Brother Laurentius raised his hands, and his face turned white. "Why in God's name have the plans disappeared?"

"Damn it, I don't know," Benedikt replied gruffly. "I had them in my room, with many other books and documents, but when I went to look for them yesterday, they were gone. I suspected one of you, or perhaps Maurus—"

"Oh, God, do you think the abbot has found us out?"

"If that's the case, then he's holding back. Perhaps he's just so distracted by everything else going on that he hasn't been paying attention to it. All the better for us. And now listen to me . . ." Brother Benedikt poked the novitiate master in the chest with his gnarled finger so hard that Laurentius had to take an astonished step back. "You've always made a good profit from our little secret. You built your little love nest down there for Vitalis and always showed up when there were things to hand out. So now just hold your tongue. Whatever is down there will soon die of hunger or flee through one of the holes. Remember, we already have a sorcerer, and that's Brother Johannes. Soon he'll be dragged to the stake, the festival will be over, and then we can just keep doing as before. But only if you keep quiet. Do you understand? Only if you keep quiet."

Brother Laurentius nodded reluctantly. "I . . . I understand."

"Then go back to your little room and rest up a bit. You'll see; you won't hear any more music."

"Perhaps you're right. I . . . I'm tired. This is all a bit too much for me."

Horrified, Kuisl watched as the latch moved down and the door slowly opened. He stepped back against the wall next to the entrance. The voices were now noticeably louder.

"I'm going back to the church now to say you're sick," the librarian said. "After that we can calmly—"

Suddenly he stopped. Kuisl didn't notice in time that his big right foot protruded through the crack in the door.

"What the hell—" Brother Benedikt started, but at that moment, the door hit him hard in the face. Screaming, the monk fell to the floor, holding his bloody nose. The novitiate master also fell back against the wall and watched horror-stricken as a giant man rushed out of his cell toward the exit.

"Stop that man," screamed Brother Benedikt. "Stop that fraudulent Franciscan! I knew from the start we couldn't trust him. He's the devil in human form."

Brother Laurentius took a few cautious steps, but the librarian's last words had clearly made him even more anxious than before. He fell to his knees, made the sign of the cross, and watched as the black-robed giant fled out the door.

After her meeting with the abbot in the monastery's enchanted garden, Magdalena hurried back to the clinic. She couldn't stop thinking about her conversation with Rambeck, his stories of an-

cient gods and rattling automata. She desperately needed to talk
to Simon. Perhaps he'd find time to go for a little walk and she
could leave the boys with Matthias for a while.

On entering the former horse stable, she quickly saw that
even more sick people had arrived, among them some of the masons from Schongau. They rolled about, moaning, on their beds
while Schreevogl went from one to the other dispensing cold
compresses. The patrician had changed noticeably in recent days.
His doublet, once so spotless, was smudged, and there was a long
rip in his trousers, but he seemed nevertheless almost cheerful as
he walked down the rows of patients. He looked up bright-eyed
and greeted Magdalena as she entered.

"Oh, Magdalena," he cried. "You're surely looking for
Simon." Holding a steaming cup in his hands, he pointed toward
the rear of the room. "He's back there mixing some medicine,
but I'm afraid he won't have much time for you."

"We'll see if my husband has time for me," she said, clenching her teeth. It came out angrier than intended.

Carrying both boys in her arms, she squeezed past several
beds and finally found Simon in the back standing beside a table
where he weighed various ground herbs on a little scale, then
placed them into a pot. Concentrating, his eyes narrowed to little
slits and his eyebrows twitched nervously. He had just carefully
measured out the greenish powder onto the scale with a little
spoon.

"Simon, I have to talk to you. The abbot—" she began.

The sudden sound made the medicus jump and spill the
powder on the table.

"Damn, Magdalena," he cursed. "How can you startle
me like that? Look what you've done. Now I have to start weighing it all over again. You know yourself how precious angelica
root is."

"Forgive me for talking to you; I'm only your wife," she replied snippily. "I thought the gentleman might perhaps have

time to take a little walk with me and his children — if he even remembers that he has children. Here, may I introduce you?" she said, holding the two boys out toward him. "This is your father."

Simon stared at her blankly, his thoughts apparently far away. "A walk?" he mumbled finally. "Do you have any idea what I'm doing here? If I can't heal the count's son, we'll never take a walk again — because I'll be dead. And at this moment his life — and mine — hang in the balance."

"Simon," Magdalena said, this time in a more conciliatory tone, "don't you think all this is too much for you? The matter of my father and this sorcerer, the murders, all the sick people, and now the count's son. A walk could do you a world of — "

"Once this is over, I'll walk with you and the children to the moon, if you want." He looked at her with tired, reddened eyes. "But until then you'll somehow have to get along without me. I'm sorry, but this here comes first." A brief smile crossed his face. "In the meantime, by the way, I've continued reading the book by Girolamo Fracastoro, and it's extremely interesting. I think I'm almost at the point of solving the secret of this illness. If I only knew — "

"Master Fronwieser, come quickly. We have a new patient."

Shrugging, Simon turned away and hurried toward the entrance, where Schreevogl was just bringing in an old woman who was barely able to stand. She kept mumbling prayers and was coughing heavily.

"Bring her back to me, Schreevogl," Simon called. "Someone died here last night and there's a bed free."

With clenched lips Magdalena watched as her husband laid some dirty straw-filled pillows down on the bed and then returned to the table to resume his weighing.

"Three ounces each of barberry and buckbean, two ounces of angelica . . ." he murmured without looking up. He seemed to have forgotten Magdalena already.

The hangman's daughter stood there silently for a while, holding one child in each hand. She squeezed them so hard they began to whimper. After a while, she turned away and led them toward the exit.

"Come, you two," she said in a tired voice, staring vacantly ahead. "Papa has no time today. He has to help other people. We'll see if Matthias can play with you."

A dozen miles away in Weilheim, the torture began.

At noon the bailiffs opened the hatch to Nepomuk's dungeon and let down a ladder. The monk briefly considered just refusing to go, but then they no doubt would beat him and drive him up the ladder rung by rung. He therefore decided to willingly climb up the blood- and dirt-soiled ladder toward the light.

Nepomuk blinked in the bright sunlight falling through the narrow windows of the tower. After his eyes had grown accustomed to the light he saw four guards and Master Hans. The Weilheim executioner brushed back the snow-white hair from his forehead and looked his victim up and down with piercing red eyes, as if trying to guess how much pain the criminal would tolerate.

"The Weilheim district judge wants to dispose of this matter as soon as possible," he said in a pleasant voice that seemed out of character with a white-haired monster of a man. "That suits me; I'll just get my money sooner. Take him away." Master Hans beckoned to one of the guards carrying a pole almost fifteen feet long with a ring of iron spikes on front. Nepomuk had never before seen such an instrument.

"Since the monastery informs us you are a sorcerer, we will do everything necessary to make sure you can't touch us," Master Hans explained briefly. He opened up the spiked ring at the end of the pole, placed it around Nepomuk's neck, and carefully closed it again. As soon as the spikes dug into Nepomuk's skin, the first drops of blood appeared. The monk realized that if he put up the slightest resistance, the spikes would dig deep into his flesh and split open his throat like dried-out leather.

"Let us proceed," Master Hans said, slamming the trapdoor over the hole. "The tongs are no doubt glowing red by now."

As the guard tugged briefly on the pole, Nepomuk stumbled forward a few steps and almost fell into the spikes before catching himself again and staggering forward carefully behind the men like a yoked ox. They dragged him down a long corridor lined with dungeons behind whose doors he could hear wailing and moaning. At one point, Nepomuk saw a crippled hand with only three fingers waving to him through one of the barred openings.

Master Hans walked alongside Nepomuk, looking straight ahead and humming an old familiar tune that Nepomuk knew from his days as a mercenary.

"I was once a hangman in the war," Nepomuk groaned as he stumbled forward. "I executed some deserters, one of them a witch—a crazy old woman. I never thought she was one, though." He turned toward the executioner hopefully. "Look at me. Do you really think I'm a warlock?"

Master Hans shrugged his powerful shoulders. "What I think or don't think is of no importance. The high and noble gentlemen believe it, so I will torture you until you finally believe it yourself."

They were now descending a winding stone staircase. Through a window, Nepomuk could see the hills and forests outside Weilheim, covered with green beeches and oaks swaying gently in the summer breeze. The tower dungeon was at the west end of the city wall, so on the left Nepomuk caught sight of the Alps. It was a gorgeous day with a dry wind, the kind that gave someone the feeling he could see forever. Then the window disappeared and the stairway continued winding down into the depths of the fortress.

"I come from a hangman's family in Reutlingen," said Nepomuk, once again addressing the Weilheim executioner. "The Volkmars. It's quite possible the same blood flows in our veins." He struggled unsuccessfully to grin as the spikes cut into his neck. "After all, we dishonorable hangman are all related more or less, aren't we, cousin?"

This time Master Hans didn't even look up, but stopped suddenly, grabbing Nepomuk between the legs so hard that he doubled over, writhing in pain. The voice of the Weilheim executioner echoed through the rocky fortress. "Listen, sorcerer, you can whine and cry all you want," Master Hans said softly, "you can shout your innocence from the rooftops or, for all I care, curse me up and down. But for God's sake, stop kissing my ass. I don't give a damn if you're related to me or to a broomstick. I have a family to feed, and I'm saving my money one kreutzer at a time to buy my citizenship someday. So don't expect pity from me."

Master Hans let go of the monk's genitals and gave the guards a signal to go on ahead. Then he started counting off on his fingers as Nepomuk lay on the floor writhing.

"For torturing you I'll get a full three guilders," Master Hans figured. "For burning you, ten. If I rip out your guts first, the council will certainly give me a bonus. And I can get good money for your blood, fingers, and eyes, too. I'll make a powder from them that will offer protection from all kinds of magic spells. People pay good money for that."

Finally a perverse smile passed across his face. "You're my big prize, sorcerer, don't you understand?" he hissed. "Something like you I get only once every few years. So shut your mouth and move your ass, and stop trying to be my friend, *cousin.*"

Master Hans spat on the floor, opened a heavy door reinforced with thick wooden beams at the end of the stairwell, and entered.

"You no doubt know most of the tools here," he said matter-of-factly. "What luck that I can torture a colleague. That spares me all the explanation."

Nepomuk looked around. His whole body began to tremble. A warm stream trickled down his leg, and he was overcome with shame.

They'd arrived in the torture chamber.

13

SULLEN AND BROODING, SIMON HURRIED ALONG
the shortest path from the monastery to the clinic. He noticed
neither the twittering birds in the trees nor the pious pilgrims
singing. For the moment he'd even forgotten his argument with
Magdalena. His thoughts kept returning to the count's sick son.

He feared that if he didn't come up with something soon, his
career as a medicus would end soon on the monastery battlements.

He'd spent the entire morning at the bedside of the young
Wittelsbacher, but the boy's fever hadn't receded a bit. Even
worse, the medicus had discovered the same red dots on the boy's
chest that many of his other patients had and which Girolamo
Fracastoro had described in such detail in his book. Simon knew
that the likelihood of dying from the fever was especially high
for children, and that this fact also dramatically affected his own
life expectancy: Count Wartenberg didn't seem like the type to
retract a threat of hanging a convicted quack. Just to be safe,
Simon left Schreevogl in charge of the sick boy and asked him to
report at once any change in the boy's condition.

The boy was not Simon's only problem. As the medicus

made his way through the crowds of pilgrims in the narrow lanes below the monastery, he couldn't help thinking of his angry wife. Since their confrontation in the clinic yesterday, Magdalena had been as silent as a clam; she'd spoken with him as little as possible and otherwise devoted her time to caring for the children. Why couldn't she understand that he had no other choice?

A sudden uproar near the clinic jolted Simon out of his gloomy reveries. The medicus quickened his pace and soon caught sight of a group of monks crowding around the entrance and wailing loudly. They were carrying something large, and soon Simon recognized it as the body of a man either dead or badly wounded. His colleagues struggled to drag him into the clinic like a slaughtered pig while a crowd of pilgrims in front kept growing, trying to catch a glimpse.

"Out of the way, people," Simon cried, pushing the onlookers aside. "I'm a doctor. Clear out of here."

Only reluctantly the people stepped aside and allowed the medicus to enter. Simon pushed the door closed and secured it with a heavy beam. Angry shouts and wild pounding could be heard outside.

"Has the golem found another victim?" asked an anxious voice through the door. "It was the golem, wasn't it?"

"I've seen this man's wounds," a woman bellowed. "I swear to you, they weren't inflicted by any worldly thing."

"Go home, people," Simon shouted, trying to calm the crowd. "When we know something definite, we'll be sure to let you know. There are sick people in here; you don't want to get infected, do you?"

This last argument seemed to silence the nosy crowd. After a few more angry shouts, the mob withdrew, grumbling.

The Benedictines heaved the injured man onto the closest empty bed, and Simon rushed to his side. The other patients stared fearfully at the new patient, and finally the medicus, too, was able to have a look. He started when he finally recognized who it was beneath all the dirt and blood.

It was none other than the novitiate master Brother Laurentius.

Simon realized quickly that the monk didn't have long to live. His breathing was shallow, his cheeks sunken like those of a dying man, but most shocking, wounds covered his entire body. The robe had burned in many places, and beneath it were black patches of what had once been human flesh. Simon remembered seeing this kind of injury before, after some dark, immeasurably evil creature had attacked young Vitalis with that hellish phosphorus powder.

The burns were in fact so severe and numerous that the medicus wondered how it was possible that Brother Laurentius was still alive. He groaned softly and seemed to be trying to mouth some words. It took Simon a while to realize the monk was asking for water. Apparently he was still conscious.

Simon quickly reached for a flask of diluted wine and poured it carefully, drop by drop, between the lips of the injured man.

"What happened?" he asked the Benedictines standing around as they crossed themselves again and again and fell to their knees.

"We . . . we found him in the forest," one of the Brothers whispered. "Down in the Ox Gorge in the Kien Valley, alongside . . . this thing." He pulled out a torn sack covered with spots of dried blood.

"And?" Simon asked, pointing to the closed sack. "Have you looked to see what's inside?"

Another very young monk hesitated, then shook his head. "We . . . we don't dare. It's something heavy, perhaps one of those iron bars Brother Johannes carried around. Surely Laurentius was curious, opened the sack, and a burst of fire . . ."

"Just give it to me, you superstitious jackass." Simon grabbed the sack impatiently, then opened it cautiously. When he saw what was inside, he stepped back. "My God," he whispered. "How is it possible?"

Curious, the monks approached. When they finally realized what was in the sack, they fell to their knees again and crossed themselves several times.

Inside the dirty sack glistened an elegantly wrought silver monstrance shaped like a church steeple. Two angels hovered to the right and left of a small dome that contained three round sealed vessels.

Three vessels for the three sacred hosts.

"Blessed are thou, Jesus Christ. The holy monstrance, the holy monstrance. It is here among us." The monks prostrated themselves on the ground, murmuring prayers, and the patients — at least those who were conscious — joined in the jubilation. Only now did Simon realize that the simple Brothers and pilgrims didn't know that the monastery's most valuable relic had been stolen a few days ago. For them finding the monstrance in a linen sack alongside a critically injured man was simply a sign from God, though they couldn't say whether it augured good or evil.

"Get the abbot and the prior," one of them shouted. "They must see the miracle with their own eyes."

The youngest monk opened the door and ran out toward the crowd, which was still waiting. "The monstrance. It's inside, a miracle. It flew all by itself from the holy chapel into the forest. A miracle!" he kept shouting.

Simon sighed and closed the entrance with the heavy beam again. Before the hour was up, all the faithful from here to the Hoher Peißenberg would hear about the strange finding. Well, at least the precious piece had appeared again, though it wasn't completely clear what role the novitiate master played in this.

Simon hastened again to the bedside of the critically injured patient, who was now in a state of semiconsciousness. When Simon bent over him, Laurentius suddenly opened his eyes and began to mumble. Simon leaned far down over the monk's lips, trying to understand what he was saying.

"The . . . the automaton . . ." he gasped. "It's down below. Fire . . . Fire . . ."

Simon could feel his heart pounding as he thought back on the white monogrammed handkerchief at the cemetery. Was it possible a living golem was haunting Andechs? Trembling, he placed his hand on Laurentius's forehead. It was burning. Perhaps the monk was just delirious.

"Are you speaking of Virgilius's automaton? What do you mean by 'down below'?" Simon asked impatiently. "Did you find the monstrance down there? Say something."

"The . . . the automaton . . . He had it . . . It belches white-hot fire . . . flames shoot out toward me, hellish flames, the fires of purgatory rage through the darkness . . ."

The voice of the novitiate master became weaker and weaker. Finally he fell completely silent and his head rolled to one side. Simon felt for a pulse, but it was barely perceptible. The medicus doubted Laurentius would survive the hour. The burns were simply too severe.

"In the name of the church, open this door!"

Simon spun around at the sound of impatient pounding at the door. One of the monks had already pushed the beam aside. The door swung open, and in stepped the prior and the old librarian. To Simon's great surprise, there was no sign of the abbot.

The two church officials hurried toward the monstrance, which two concerned monks had already placed atop a chest. Brother Jeremias fell to his knees in front of the simple wooden chest as if it were an altar and raised his hands toward heaven.

"Holy Mary, Mother of God, let us give thanks for this miracle," the prior began in a droning chant. "Nefarious thieves have tried to steal the holy monstrance, but they have been punished by the fires of purgatory." He pointed at the unconscious Brother Laurentius, then made the sign of the cross.

"Finally their evil plans have come to light," he continued, his voice cracking. "Brother Johannes and this wretched novitiate master have brought calamity down upon the monastery, but God himself has judged them, and all has turned out for the best. Let us give thanks for that. Amen."

"Amen." A chorus of monks and patients joined in the prayer of thanks as Simon, confused, looked back and forth between the monstrance and the severely injured Brother Laurentius. Was the novitiate master really the thief they'd been looking for? Had he stolen the hosts and abducted the abbot's brother? And where was Maurus Rambeck, for that matter?

When the voices of the faithful had finally fallen silent, Simon turned to the prior and said in a soft voice, "Actually, I expected to see the abbot here. It must be of interest to him, after all, that the monstrance was found in the forest with the novitiate master, whom you consider the principal suspect."

"The abbot is resting," the prior replied coolly. "He hasn't been well recently, as you surely know. I considered it best not to awaken him."

And make yourself look like the great savior of the three holy hosts, Simon thought to himself. *You scheming bastard, you'll really do anything to become the next abbot as soon as possible.*

"Why are you so sure that Brother Laurentius was trying to steal the hosts?" Simon replied.

The old librarian, who had stood silently alongside the prior till that point, cleared his throat. "Well, that's obvious," he said so loudly that everyone standing around could hear. "The sack with the monstrance was found beside him, and he has wounds that could be inflicted only by some unearthly force."

"Incidentally, the same wounds suffered by the young novitiate Vitalis," Simon interrupted. "Did the Good Lord also strike him down in his anger?"

Brother Benedikt glared at him. "Don't jest," he threatened. "But think of the Revelation of Saint John. What does it say?"

He paused dramatically to let his booming voice reverberate through the room. "*And the angel took the censer, and filled it with fire of the altar, and cast it into the earth: and there were voices, and thunderings, and lightnings, and an earthquake.*"

The librarian fell silent for a while to let his words take effect on the monks and patients. Not until a reverent silence had come over the room did he continue in a stern voice. "I actually wanted to keep this a secret, but circumstances no doubt compel me to bring it to light now. The monastery council has suspected for a long time that the ill-fated Vitalis had . . . an unnatural relationship with his novitiate master."

Shocked voices resounded, but Brother Benedikt raised his hand to demand silence. "Yes," he continued, "the two were accursed sodomites, so it's quite possible the Lord or one of his angels punished the two heretics with holy fire."

"Ah, and the Lord no doubt drowned the novitiate Coelestin, just for good measure?" Simon interrupted, furious.

"Oh God, no. What are you thinking?" Brother Benedikt remained calm, letting a hint of a smile pass over his lips. He evidently enjoyed humiliating the impious bathhouse surgeon in public. "Poor Coelestin was no doubt simply killed by his master, Brother Johannes, after discovering Johannes's plan to murder the watchmaker. The two, as we all know, argued often. Johannes simply couldn't bear the fact that Virgilius was the better scientist, so he killed Virgilius and drowned Coelestin, who had gotten wind of his scheme." Benedikt raised his hand like a lecturer at his podium, while the other monks hung spellbound to his every word. "And thus the case is solved," he concluded in a loud voice. "It turns out there were two crimes. Vitalis and Laurentius were engaged in sodomy and were punished by God himself. The novitiate Coelestin, as well as Virgilius, didn't die by magic but at the hand of a nefarious murderer."

"A murder you can't prove," Simon interrupted. "The body

of the watchmaker was never found, after all. Is he perhaps still alive?"

Now it was the prior who smiled. Brother Jeremias passed his tongue over his lips, obviously enjoying the moment before dealing his final blow. "I'm afraid I must disappoint you, my dear bathhouse surgeon," he replied smugly. "Virgilius's pathetic remains have reappeared. Brother Johannes had thrown them into the well at the cemetery, where they were just discovered this morning. You may go and have a look for yourself, Master Fronwieser," he said, gesturing toward the door. "Brother Benedikt will be glad to accompany you. We can thank God that this case has finally been solved and this miserable snooping around can stop."

The prior walked reverently over to the monstrance, bowed deeply, and finally, holding it high, strode out the door where the relics were greeted with great jubilation.

The three holy hosts had returned to the bosom of the church.

The well was located in the cemetery next to the monastery.

Simon thought back on his visit there the day before. The cemetery, with its weathered stone crosses and ivy-covered burial mounds, exuded an air of tranquility in stark contrast with the noisy bustle outside its walls. The sun shone warm and bright on the many faded inscriptions on the gravestones, and the grass grew thicker and lusher along the paths than anywhere else in the area.

They say bones are a good fertilizer, Simon thought. *How many monks have been buried here in the last few centuries?*

They'd laid out the corpse in the grass next to the well and spread a shroud over it. Flies buzzed around the bundle, which was so small Simon expected to see a child beneath it rather than a grown man. When the librarian carefully pulled the cloth to one side, the medicus realized why.

The entire body of the man before him was so badly burned

it had curled in on itself and shriveled up like a prune. What was left of the mouth was open as if in a final scream, and the teeth gleamed a sickly yellow. Brother Benedikt stooped to pick up a burned piece of wood. Only on second look did Simon realize it was Virgilius's walking stick with the ivory decorations. Its silver handle was still recognizable, though it was twisted out of shape now and covered with a layer of soot.

"That should be proof enough," he exclaimed with disgust, casting the stick into the flowery meadow. The two Benedictines who accompanied him stepped aside in shock. "I'm glad we've finally solved this gruesome murder," the librarian continued. "People no longer need to fear a golem living in a dungeon, an automaton in a crypt, or anything else. In his hatred of his colleagues, Brother Johannes simply incinerated the automaton along with its creator and threw them both into the well. Let us return now and allow the dead to rest in peace."

"Who found the body?" Simon asked.

The librarian smiled. "You may be astonished to hear this, but it was the abbot himself, who, along with one of his assistants, came upon the corpse this morning. You certainly don't doubt his word, do you? Then let's finally leave — "

"Just one more moment." Simon bent over to examine the charred corpse briefly. Unfortunately the individual body parts were so disfigured it was impossible to tell whether there'd been any injury prior to death. The face looked like that of a crudely carved wooden figure that had been cast into the fire and no longer resembled the living Virgilius at all. While examining the twisted right arm, however, Simon noticed something about the hand.

A finger was missing.

The finger with the ring that the abbot showed us the night before last, Simon thought. *Then this really is Virgilius's body. Did Nepomuk really kill him?*

He looked up into the smiling face of Brother Benedikt.

"You knew the monstrance was stolen a few days ago, didn't you?" the librarian asked Simon. "Evidently Abbot Maurus told you, the old fool. Is that so?" When Simon remained silent, the monk shook his head. "Why in the world would he do that? All hell would have broken loose if the word had gotten out. Well, everything worked out well in the end: the monstrance is back, and the festival can begin tomorrow."

"Do you seriously believe that Brother Laurentius stole the relics?" Simon asked.

Brother Benedikt shrugged. "Who knows? Does that really matter now that the monstrance has appeared again? Who cares who really stole it? The main thing is that the people have a culprit. Aside from that" — he said, shaking his finger — "it was an open secret among the monks that Laurentius was a sodomite, so he has received his just punishment."

Simon eyed the old monk suspiciously. Evidently Brother Benedikt really didn't know that it was the abbot himself who'd stolen the monstrance with the hosts, or that the abbot's brother, Virgilius, had been abducted. Was all this just a game of make-believe? Could the librarian be the sorcerer who abducted and killed the watchmaker to get ahold of the hosts?

Suddenly Simon had an idea. He cursed himself for not having thought of it earlier. Perhaps there was a way for him to find out whether Brother Benedikt knew more than he let on.

"Did you examine the containers in the monstrance to make sure the hosts were really there?" he asked curiously.

Brother Benedikt didn't bat an eye. "We'll do that, of course, at the appropriate time," he said in a flat voice. "But you can rest assured they're there — the containers are sealed."

"Wax seals can be forged," Simon replied.

The librarian snorted. "You have a lively imagination, bath-house surgeon. Now excuse me; I have to prepare for the next mass. It will be a great service of thanksgiving in honor of the return of our three holy hosts. You are warmly invited to attend."

He turned and left with his head high—a little old man who nevertheless had an authoritative air, fostered by years of book learning. The other monks who had been standing around silently picked up the cloth containing Virgilius's corpse. It seemed as light as a child's. Praying softly, the Benedictines carried Virgilius's remains to the funeral chapel at the edge of the cemetery.

They wouldn't need a very large coffin.

Incense swirled up like a cloud toward the church ceiling as the chorus of the faithful joined in with the organ's mournful melody and the entire space seemed to tremble.

From his vantage point, the sorcerer watched the many pilgrims opening and closing their mouths like bleating sheep. Open and close, open and close . . . It was astonishing that so many stupid farmers, so many narrow-minded, simple people, could engender such energy. The sorcerer could feel their faith flashing through the church like lightning through a thundercloud. So much power concentrated in a simple baked good: three ancient, crumbling oblates of water and flour.

The three sacred hosts.

Finally he had them in his possession. His plan had worked, though not quite as smoothly as expected. Still, all the dead strewn along his path had been necessary. All that mattered was the result of his efforts.

As the deep bass notes of the organ rumbled through the church, the sorcerer could once again see the fire before him and hear the cries and pleading of the dying. He realized now that he felt sorry for those who had to die, especially those who had died in severe pain. Their constant pleading almost awakened pity in him.

But only almost . . . What were a few deaths really in view of what he planned? Man could be God; all he needed was faith— and that was something stronger here than anywhere, except perhaps in Altötting, St. Peter's in Rome, or in Santiago de Compostela. And central to this faith here on the Holy Mountain were the hosts.

As the sorcerer recited the kyrie eleison with the many faithful around him, he himself felt overwhelmed by faith.

Mea culpa, mea culpa, mea maxima culpa . . . Kyrie eleison . . .

Yes, he, too, had sinned. Tears welled up in his eyes when he thought of *her.* She had vanished from his life so long ago, yet he believed in her, and this faith would bring her back to life again.

If only those damned Schongau busybodies weren't around

The sorcerer clenched the prayer book so hard his knuckles turned white. They were close on his heels—he could feel that—and his assistant brought him more shocking news every day. They were evidently close to solving the mystery. He'd given his assistant clear orders, but all he got were new excuses. Was he too cowardly or just too softhearted? For now the sorcerer needed him, but he would have to find a more reliable servant soon.

It wouldn't be much longer—he was just waiting for the right conditions. He'd once almost reached that point, but what he was hoping for didn't happen. He felt it couldn't be much longer now, though, and until then he'd have to be patient.

Once more the organ rose to a mighty, shrill, earsplitting swell so loud that, for a moment, he imagined he could hear the screams of his dying victims as they pointed at him, castigating and accusing him.

But then the organ stopped, the incense drifted away, and the faithful rose from their pews and headed for the taverns in the surrounding villages—to eat, drink, and fornicate. Faith vanished, leaving nothing but stone and wood, an empty building with no trace of anything divine.

The sorcerer arose, crossed himself and exited through the narrow church portal among the other pilgrims and monks.

The image of the charred corpse still on his mind, Simon headed back to the clinic. The pilgrims leaving the church were laughing and talking loudly, but he hardly noticed them as he continued mulling over the events of the last few hours. He wished he could speak with his father-in-law about them, but Kuisl had disappeared the previous day around noon. Simon wasn't particularly worried. The old man often disappeared overnight in the forest when he went to collect herbs — though not in a forest possibly haunted by a madman.

Simon had no doubt the madman was still on the loose. Brother Benedikt's dramatic words about God's holy anger were nonsense. But where and how in the world had Brother Laurentius come into the possession of the stolen monstrance? And what part did the automaton play in all this? The medicus quickened his pace. Perhaps the novitiate master would be well enough now to at least say a few words.

Entering the clinic behind the monastery, Simon looked for Jakob Schreevogl. Now that Simon himself was mainly responsible for the count's sick son, the patrician's help was indispensable. Then he remembered that Schreevogl was with the count.

But in his place was another man.

A huge figure bent over Laurentius with his back to Simon. It looked as if he was trying to strangle the patient with his huge hands. The medicus ran toward the stranger and pulled him around by the shoulder.

"For God's sake, stop —" he shouted, but then held his hand up to his mouth in shock. "Good Lord, Kuisl," he gasped. "It's you! Where have you been all this time? You scared the hell out of me."

"You scared me, too," said the hangman, glaring at his son-in-law. "I thought for a minute you were one of the damned guards. Since when is an executioner and healer forbidden to examine an injured person?" He cast a sympathetic glance at the unconscious novitiate master. "Of course it doesn't look like much can be done to save this fellow here, not even by me."

Simon noticed that Kuisl was no longer wearing his Franciscan robe but his own clothing. "Don't you think it's dangerous to walk around here like this?" he whispered, pointing to the far end of the room. "We have a few Schongauers here, and they might recognize you. If the church learns that a dishonorable hangman—"

Kuisl interrupted him with a brusque wave of the hand. "To hell with the robe," he grumbled. "Anyway, they're looking for me in that robe."

"They're what?"

"First tell me what the novitiate master is doing here and why everyone out there is blathering on about a miracle," the hangman replied. "Who knows, maybe putting your story and mine together will give us a complete picture."

"As you like, but let's go to a corner," said Simon, lowering his voice. "Most of the patients are too weak to understand anything, but one never knows."

They withdrew to a quiet corner of the room where some mildewed boxes and barrels were piled up. Looking around at the dozing patients and whispering, Simon told Kuisl about finding the injured novitiate master and the monstrance. He also told Kuisl how Virgilius's charred corpse had been found in a well by the monastery. The hangman listened silently, stuffing his pipe. Once he'd finally managed to light it with a burning pine chip, he pointed his foot toward the unconscious Laurentius.

"This fellow here, by the way, is why I disappeared yesterday noon. I thought it best to disappear in the forest for a while." He took a deep draw on his pipe and told Simon about the conversation he had overheard between Brother Benedikt and Laurentius and about his hasty flight from the building. He also mentioned the love letters he'd found in the novitiate master's chest and the old plan the librarian had lost a few days ago.

"In any event you'll no doubt have to snoop around without me from now on." Kuisl finally grumbled. "That's actually fine by me. The old robe smelled like one huge gassy priest."

"Damn," Simon exclaimed. "We seemed so close to solving the mystery. It looks as if everyone in this monastery has something to hide." He counted off on his fingers: "Nepomuk and the dead Virgilius had some heretical ideas; the abbot stole the hosts, even if for honorable reasons; the prior is an overly ambitious schemer; the novitiate master a sodomite — and now the librarian, too, appears to be hiding something in the basement of the monastery."

"You've forgotten the cellarer, who obviously was helping him in all this," Kuisl interrupted.

Simon rubbed his sweaty brow, trying to piece it all together. "What in God's name can the two have concealed down there? And where is the hiding place? If I understand Laurentius correctly, he did see this automaton in the corridors of the monastery."

"They've sealed the entrance in any case, and the plans showing how to get there have suddenly and mysteriously disappeared." Kuisl grinned. "But wait — in your enumeration of these scoundrels and charlatans, you forgot the Wittelsbach count. We still don't know what role that perfumed poodle is playing in the whole affair."

Simon sighed. "For now, Wartenberg is quite convincingly playing the role of the anxious father. If I can't heal his son soon, things really look bad for me."

"The most important thing at the moment is to get this fellow to speak." The hangman pointed at Brother Laurentius, who lay on his bed breathing in short gasps. "He's the key to all this. If Laurentius can tell us where the monstrance comes from and who beat him so badly, we can probably solve the mystery." He took another deep draw on his pipe and looked up at the ceiling absent-mindedly. "I'm afraid certain people don't want him to talk."

"What do you mean by that?" Simon asked, confused.

"What does that mean?" Kuisl laughed softly. "If you were the murderer and learned that your victim was still alive — what would you do?"

"Oh God," Simon blanched. "Do you think — "

"I think that Laurentius's life isn't worth a speck of fly shit if someone doesn't keep an eye on him." Kuisl rose and headed toward the exit. "And I'm afraid that's something only you can do. The church higher-ups know my disguise as a Franciscan now, and it would be too dangerous for me. And as the Schongau executioner, I can hardly sit here and care for the sick."

"You want me to do that? Impossible." Simon shook his head vigorously. "You forget I'm looking after the count's son. And Magdalena is all in a huff because I'm never around to care for the children."

"They'll get over it. Anyway . . ." The hangman stopped in the doorway and looked into the sunlight. "During the daylight, the sorcerer won't dare show up; too many patients are awake. If he strikes, it will be at night. You can calmly go about caring for your patients during the day and keep watch over the novitiate master at night. It would be best to rub his wounds with an ointment of bear fat, marigold, and chamomile." Raising his hand in a wave, he added, "Now farewell, bathhouse surgeon. I've not had anything to eat since noon yesterday — except for the berries and mushrooms I found in the forest."

Simon wanted to tell his father-in-law one more thing, but Kuisl had already disappeared. Groaning softly, the exhausted medicus sat on the edge of Laurentius's bed and stared down at his seriously injured patient.

"Wonderful," he mumbled. "Marigold and chamomile ... I'm going to need some medicine myself."

Wearily he searched his bag for just one more coffee bean. He always carried a little emergency supply of the exotic bean to help him to fight exhaustion and concentrate, but now he realized that, sadly, he'd ground up the last of them the day before. Still, he found something else at the bottom of his bag. A little clay jar he'd picked up at the apothecary's house and overlooked in all the excitement.

Jesuit's powder.

He removed the cover and studied the yellowish powder. Imported from overseas, this medicine could work wonders in reducing fever, but unfortunately the amount here was just enough for one dose. That's probably the reason Simon forgot about it. Now he rubbed his fingers in the dry powder and stared at the gasping novitiate master.

Should he give Laurentius the medicine? Perhaps the monk would talk once more before he died. Or should he save the powder for the count's sick son? Simon imagined the little boy in front of him, the same age as one of his sons, a trembling little creature in the count's much-too-large four-poster, his eyelids fluttering like the wings of a tiny bird.

After a few seconds Simon made up his mind. He closed the lid and put the jar back in his pocket.

A figure was standing in the shadows of the stable wall, watching as the hangman strode away.

The man rubbed his knuckles nervously, cracking them one after the other. What he'd just overheard would interest his master. The man still hadn't carried out his order; something in him was reluctant to do so. It just felt so . . . wrong. With this news he might be able to appease his master, though he knew the master would never give in. And wasn't he always right? Hadn't he always been concerned for his servant's well-being? Didn't he promise him that everything would work out?

The man took a deep breath and crossed himself. The master had told him how important faith was—that faith could heal him, too. Soon his time would come. One more job to do, and they would reach their goal.

After eavesdropping on the conversation in the clinic, he believed, however, that his master would have another job for him. What was it the sullen giant had just said?

I think Laurentius's life isn't worth a speck of fly shit . . .

The man stopped briefly to think about that, then shook his head, leapt over a low wall, and finally disappeared behind the stables.

It was time to report to his master.

It was early evening when Magdalena sat on a bench in the main room of the knacker's house, singing her children to sleep in a soft monotone.

> *Little Jack sat by the stove, fast asleep.*
> *His trousers caught fire and up he did leap . . .*

Excited shouts could be heard up on the Holy Mountain, but the noise disturbed neither the hangman's daughter nor the two boys. The little ones stretched out comfortably on branches near the stove listening to their mother. Peter still had his eyes open, but they were already glassy; Paul dozed, sucking his thumb and dreaming.

The hangman's daughter cast loving glances at her two boys. What could they be dreaming about? Something beautiful, she hoped—flowering meadows, butterflies, perhaps the enchanted monastery garden they'd seen yesterday.

Perhaps about their father?

Her face darkened when she thought of Simon. Since yesterday she'd spoken with him as little as possible, but he didn't even seem to notice. It was always the same. When her husband was with patients, neither she nor the children could get through to him. She didn't ask for Simon to stay with them all day, and she also realized that he was stressed by the difficult situation here in Andechs. What she missed was a loving glance, a few kind words with the children. She wished he would take them into his arms now and then, but Simon was as if behind a locked door in another world, and she didn't have the key.

So Magdalena had spent both yesterday and today alone with the boys, strolling through town with them. She let them throw sticks in the brook nearby but always watched that they didn't wander too far. She was still gripped by fear of the sorcerer and the automaton.

The door creaked as Matthias entered the room. Outside Magdalena could hear the squeaking of the knacker's wagon, so she knew Michael Graetz had picked up a new animal carcass from one of the farmers.

When the mute assistant saw her, he smiled and raised his hand shyly in greeting. Magdalena returned the smile. She had gotten accustomed to the presence of the redheaded giant, and even if he didn't speak, she liked having him around. He was loving with the children and made them laugh with all his funny faces. Softly, in order not to wake the boys, Matthias walked to the table and poured himself a glass of water, which he gulped down thirstily.

"Damn it all, where have you been, you good-for-nothing?" It was the voice of Michael Graetz, who had just entered the room, a knife dangling from his blood-spattered apron. The short knacker crossed his arms and glared furiously at his assistant, who was almost two heads taller.

"A cow died on the Kins' farm and I had to do all the dirty work myself while the fine gentleman went for a leisurely stroll through the forest. If I catch you just once more . . ."

Only then did Michael Graetz see Magdalena and the two sleeping children. He continued in a somewhat softer voice. "Please go outside and burn the entrails behind the house. I've already skinned the animal. Now hurry up, you worthless slacker, before I tan your own hide."

Matthias cringed as if he expected to be beaten, then grimaced and began to whimper.

"Oh, it's okay," the knacker grumbled, now a bit calmer. "Just do what I tell you, and next time leave me a message when you're going out."

When the mute assistant left, Magdalena looked at the knacker quizzically.

"He can write? Matthias can write?"

Michael Graetz grinned. "Someone who can't speak has to make himself understood some other way. Heaven knows who taught him—maybe the monks he always hangs around with." He wiped the sweat from his brow with a corner of his bloody apron. "My father taught me how to write a bit," he said, "but Matthias is a hell of a lot smarter than he looks. He can write down the words of the four gospels as easily as if they were recipes."

"You once told me that Croatian mercenaries cut out his tongue when he was a young boy. Is that true?"

Graetz nodded. "As true as I stand here before you. They raped and killed his mother and hanged his father right before his eyes over on the gallows hill in Erling. Half the village had to come and watch as a warning to the other peasants. It's a miracle the boy didn't lose his mind. He's lived with me ever since he was twelve, as no one else wanted him. He was wandering through the forest until I took him in." He laughed softly. "The best place for mute human garbage like him to live was with a dishonorable, filthy knacker."

Magdalena glared at him. "Don't say that. Nobody is ever going to say my children are dishonorable and dirty."

Michael Graetz cut himself a slice of bread from the table. "What are you going to do about it, hangman's daughter?" he asked with a full mouth. "Peter is never going to become a bishop, even with his beautiful eyes." He choked briefly with laughter. "Maybe you can send him here to be my apprentice."

"You just wait and see, Graetz," she snapped. "My boy is going to amount to something, as sure as my name is Kuisl."

"Believe me, my dear," the knacker said sarcastically, pulling the pitcher of water to him. "The Kuisls and the Graetzes will never amount to anything. Ever. Not in three hundred years."

At that moment came a knock at the door so loud it sounded as if someone were trying to kick it in.

"Open up!" shouted an angry voice that Magdalena thought she recognized. "In the name of the monastery, open this door at once before I have this pigsty torn down."

"For God's sake, all right, all right," the short knacker rushed to the door and pressed the latch. Two hunters in green hunting costumes stormed in. Magdalena recognized them as the same men who had been guarding Nepomuk in the dairy a few days ago. They were armed with lances, and small crossbows hung from their belts. Behind them came a foppish youth and a potbellied older man whom the hangman's daughter knew all too well: the Schongau burgomaster, Karl Semer, and his son, Sebastian.

Squinting, old Semer scrutinized the scantily furnished room before speaking. "Where is he?"

"Where is who?" Magdalena was puzzled. "I don't know whom you're talking about."

"Your father, you dumb goose," Karl Semer walked up to Magdalena and glared at her. "Do you think I don't know what you're up to? A stranger dressed as a Franciscan monk slipped into the monastery yesterday—a spy. He probably even stole documents from the monastery before running off. The prior told me everything." He moved even closer, so close that Magdalena could smell his pungent sweat. "And do you know what else the prior told me? This fraudulent Franciscan was over six feet tall, a bear of a man with a hooked nose like nobody else in the Priests' Corner. I know your father is behind this. Admit it."

Magdalena appeared calm, but inside she was seething. She hadn't seen her father since the morning before, and evidently he'd been caught snooping around the monastery. She could only hope nothing had happened to him.

"Nonsense," she replied coolly. "Why would my father be here in Andechs? Perhaps he's on a pilgrimage? An executioner?" she scoffed. Michael Graetz stood there silently, his arms crossed, and she hoped he wouldn't betray her.

"Ha, hangman's girl, you lie whenever you open your filthy mouth," the burgomaster growled. His son's lips curled into a faint smile, and Magdalena could feel him looking her up and down.

"Your own husband tipped us off," he continued. "A few days ago in the tavern he boasted of how his father-in-law would straighten out things in Andechs."

"Then my father changed his mind. In any case, he's not here. You two can come and have a look under the bench." Magdalena turned to her children who were awake now and had started crying. "And now goodbye. As you can see, I have better things to do than stand here listening to idle talk."

The two hunters were still standing in the doorway with their lances, but now they looked uncertain. Evidently old Semer had promised them they could arrest the false monk in the knacker's house and reap a handsome reward for it, but all they found was a rude woman with two screaming brats and a grim-looking knacker in a bloody work apron.

"What's this all about, Alois?" Michael Graetz growled. Obviously, he knew one of the hunters. "Is this any way to behave, to just come crashing into the house of an honest man, shouting wild accusations?"

"I'm sorry, Michael, but—" the man started, but Karl Semer interrupted.

"This isn't a house, it's a pigsty," he shouted. "And I'm not going to let myself be criticized by a filthy knacker, especially when he's lying. There's no question that Kuisl was here, and somewhere, we're no doubt going to find that damned Franciscan robe."

In the meantime, young Semer had been wandering through the room with visible disgust, carefully examining things. Finally, he stopped in front of a windowsill where he found a small leather pouch that looked familiar. When he tipped it over, little flakes of tobacco fell to the floor.

"Aha, and what is this here?" Sebastian Semer shouted triumphantly. "I know only one person who smokes this stinking weed, and that's the Schongau hangman."

"Then you're sadly mistaken," replied Magdalena without batting an eyelash. "I like to smoke a pipe now and then myself. It's good for digestion, young councilor. You should try it sometime; then you wouldn't have so much gas."

"You smoke it, too? A woman?" It took Sebastian Semer a while to pull himself together. "That's . . . that's a damned lie."

"I can attest to it," the knacker answered quietly from his corner. "She smokes like a saber-rattling Saracen."

"Then . . . then you're lying too. I'll—"

"Me? Lying?" Now Graetz's voice became louder, as well, as he struggled to be heard over the screaming children. Despite his rather small stature, the knacker approached the confused youth threateningly and reached for the knife hanging on his waistband. "Even a filthy knacker has a sense of decency," he trumpeted. "You're calling me a liar? Who the hell are you, anyway?"

"Uh, this is the son of the Schongau burgomaster," Magdalena said, trying to calm him down as she rocked the two crying boys in her arms. "I'm sure we can clear this all up."

"Then the son of the Schongau burgomaster should go back

where he came from," grumbled Graetz, only slightly mollified. "In any case, he's not welcome here."

Open-mouthed and trembling slightly, Sebastian Semer turned to his father. "Father, did you hear what this—"

Karl Semer waved him off angrily. Though he seemed about to explode, he managed to get control of himself. "Very well, hangman's girl, we'll leave," he said softly. "But if I find your father anywhere in Andechs, I'll have him arrested and interrogated on suspicion of breaking into the monastery and of blasphemy. And then we'll see who's more stubborn—the hangman from Schongau or the one from Weilheim. I've heard that Master Hans is a tough fellow. He'll be glad to take on a colleague who's been going around causing mischief dressed as a Franciscan monk." Semer's eyes narrowed to slits. "Who knows, perhaps your father even has something to do with the watchmaker's corpse that was fished out of the well this morning."

Magdalena looked at him, perplexed. "Virgilius's corpse was found? But . . ."

The burgomaster chuckled. He clearly enjoyed seeing the self-confident young woman finally a bit unsettled.

"That's the truth. Evidently, that damn apothecary burned him and then threw him in the well. The prior, who will probably soon be the new abbot, just told me about it. So the matter is clear." Semer smiled maliciously. "Your father has been snooping around here in vain. This apothecary will be burned in Weilheim as a murderer, and we can soon all go about our business again." He bowed stiffly. "And now I must really say goodbye before I get sick from the odor in here." Turning up his nose, Karl Semer turned and beckoned to his son, who was still standing there alongside him, trembling with anger. "Come on, Sebastian, this is no place for people like us."

Holding their heads high, the Semers left the knacker's house with the two perplexed hunters as Magdalena and Michael Graetz watched silently.

"I'm afraid you owe me some explanation," the knacker said once the footsteps had finally faded away. "Why isn't your father here, when he clearly is here? And what is this matter with the fake Franciscan monk? I remember that I, in fact, saw someone in my house who looked like that." He winked at Magdalena. "I don't mind lying to these puffed-up old buzzards because they've offended our family, but I'd still like to know why that old show-off was so angry."

"That's . . . that's a long story," Magdalena sighed. "Let me put the children to bed; then I can probably explain a few things. In any event, it seems everything was all in vain. Now that Virgilius is dead, we can no longer count on the abbot's help. And Nepomuk will be burned at the stake."

She took the two boys into the bedroom, sang them a lullaby, then returned to the main room, where she sat down at the table beside the knacker.

"So . . ." she began hesitantly. "Where shall I begin?"

"Start with your father," said Graetz. "What in the world is that stubborn old fool up to this time?"

Neither Magdalena nor Graetz noticed someone eavesdropping outside. When the man had heard what he wanted, he quietly slipped away through the hawthorn bushes.

His heart pounding, Simon entered the Prince's Quarters in the monastery's upper story.

Jakob Schreevogl had reappeared in the clinic half an hour before to tell Simon the condition of the count's son had become critical. The medicus had checked some of his other patients before hurrying off, not without first reminding Schreevogl not to let the still-unconscious novitiate master out of his sight. Surprised, the councilor had nodded, then bent down to wash Laurentius's burns with a damp towel.

As Simon entered the room of the sick boy in the Wittelsbach family tract, he saw right away how urgently the boy needed attention. He was deathly pale, groaning and rolling in his sleep from one side of the bed to the other, and his heart was racing like a tightly wound spring recently released. Simon put his hand on the four-year-old's red-hot forehead. The count and his young wife sat on the edge of the four-poster canopy bed. She'd obviously been crying—her eyes were red and her makeup was running. She was wearing a tight-fitting, fur-trimmed silk dress, which Simon considered inappropriate for this visit to the bedside of her deathly sick son. Like her husband, she seemed to have a liking for too much perfume.

"Good Lord, can't you do something?" the countess cried out as Simon felt for the pulse of his young patient. "Give him medicine; bleed him if necessary. I don't need a doctor to hold my child's hand."

"Your Excellency, I'm only listening for a heartbeat," replied Simon, trying to calm the overwrought woman.

"By holding his hand? How do you do that?"

"Josephine, let the man do his job," the count urged her. "He was recommended to me by one of the Schongau aldermen."

"That fat fellow you're doing business with?"

"No, someone else. At least I have a good impression of him. I think the bathhouse surgeon knows what he's doing, perhaps more than our sinfully expensive doctors in Munich." The count glared menacingly at Simon. "And he knows what will happen to him if he fails."

The countess rubbed her tear-stained eyes. "You're . . . you're right, Leopold," she sighed. "It's just this . . . sitting around not being able to do anything that's driving me out of my mind." Simon looked at her out of the corner of his eye and wondered whether she'd ever had much on her mind.

"Well?" Wartenberg asked harshly. "Is there hope, bathhouse surgeon? Be honest, please."

The chances of your son surviving are so slight that a single pilgrimage probably won't suffice, Simon thought darkly. *But I can scarcely tell you that, because then you'll be measuring me for the right-size noose.*

"The most important thing for us to do now is to lower the fever," he said. "I found a little Jesuit's powder a few days ago in the apothecary here. It's very rare and expensive, but I'll give it to your son."

"Jesuit's powder?" the countess inquired, horrified. "What sort of witch's brew is that?"

"It's the bark of a tree that grows in the West Indies, Your Excellency. It cured a countess suffering from fever there, and it ought to help your son, as well."

"A countess?" Wartenberg's wife chewed on her painted lips. "Very well, then you may proceed with this . . . uh, whatever it is."

Simon took the jar with the inauspicious-looking yellow dust out of his medicine bag, carefully poured the powder into a little phial, mixed it with wine, then finally dripped it into the boy's mouth. Secretly, he was happy he'd almost forgotten the powder the last few days and hadn't used it already. Now the appropriate moment seemed at hand—the tiny dose might just be enough for a child.

"With God's grace the fever should subside," Simon said after emptying the phial. Then he packed up his medicine bag. "Now we must wait and pray your son is strong enough to overcome the sickness himself."

"Pray! You always just say pray." The countess raised her hands. "This whole place does nothing but pray, and still my little Martin is dying."

"Be still, Josephine," the count whispered. "You are blaspheming God."

"And so what if I am? I always told you we shouldn't come to this filthy hole of a monastery. Someone else could have brought the key. Why in God's name did the elector assign you to bring . . ."

"Good God, I told you to hold your tongue."

Clearly the count hadn't intended to speak so loudly, and Simon could sense they were hiding something from him.

Leopold von Wartenberg eyed him suspiciously. "Did you want something else?" he asked harshly.

"Ah, yes, I do have one more question," Simon said to change the subject. "Has your son done anything out of the ordinary? Did he eat or drink anything he wouldn't otherwise? Something that could be the cause of this sickness?"

The count seemed to forget his distrust for a moment, struggling to remember. "Actually no," he finally answered. "We brought our own cook with us who prepares our food in the monastery kitchen." Suddenly he paused. "But three days ago, we had supper in the tavern in Andechs because our cook had gone to Herrsching to buy fish. The food in the tavern was simple but not bad. We had marinated leg of venison with dumplings and braised turnips. Very tasty, though a bit tough."

"Leg of venison, I understand." Simon nodded. Something about the answer made him prick up his ears, though he couldn't say exactly what.

Finally he reached down one last time to feel the little boy's pulse. It was still fast, but at least the child seemed to be sleeping calmly now. Simon rose, exhausted.

"I'd be very grateful, Your Excellency, if you would let me know of any change in his condition," he said, bowing deeply. "For better or worse. And now, farewell. Unfortunately, other patients are waiting."

Count Wartenberg dismissed him with a brusque wave of his hand, and Simon bowed repeatedly as he backed out of the room. Outside in the hall, he could hear the countess sobbing again.

Exhausted, the medicus rubbed his temples, trying not to think of the long night still awaiting him at the bedside of the novitiate master. Perhaps he could ask Schreevogl to take over at least the second part of his watch. He would tell him simply that the condition of the young monk was so grave he needed constant care.

As he slowly made his way toward the exit down a hall hung with Gobelin tapestries, he thought again of the strange exchange of words between the count and his wife. Evidently Wartenberg was sent on a mission by the elector. But why? And what was so secret about it that it couldn't be discussed in front of a stranger?

Simon remembered that the count had arrived more than a week early to deliver the key to the relics room. There was really no need for him to arrive until the next day for the Festival of the Three Hosts. Why had he come so early? And what sort of business was he involved in with the Schongau burgomaster?

When the medicus arrived at the high portal leading from the prince's quarters to the ordinary rooms, he stopped. The guards stood on the other side of the portal while the count and his wife still sat at the bedside of their sick son. Simon looked at the individual doors leading off from the hall with curiosity. Should he dare have a look around here?

Heart pounding, he tiptoed over to the first door and pressed the latch. The room was unlocked. Casting a hesitant glance inside, he spied an open wardrobe and dresses, colorful scarves, and fur caps scattered around the floor, a sign that this must be the countess's room. Quickly he closed the door and turned to the second room.

This was what he was looking for.

A huge table of polished cherry took up almost the entire far end of the room. On top, inkpots and quills stood beside a pile of documents and rolls of paper. To the right of the table was a bookshelf reaching to the ceiling, and an armchair. The light of the afternoon sun filtered through a high window across the table and the documents scattered across it.

The medicus could feel the hair on the back of his neck stand on end. This was clearly the count's office.

He looked into the hallway once more. He could hear the countess sobbing in the sick room while her husband murmured some words of consolation. Hesitating briefly, Simon slipped into the room and hurried to the table. Frantically he searched the documents, which were all written in Latin and clearly dealt with the monastery's relics. Instinctively, he stopped.

What in the world did the count have to do with the relics?

Simon discovered a list of dozens of items in the holy chapel, among them the victory cross of Charlemagne, the stole of Saint Nicolas, and a *sudarium* from the Mount of Olives.

Other ancient parchment rolls here dealt with the history of the Wittelsbachs and of the monastery. Hastily, Simon scanned the ones telling of the earlier castle of the Andechs-Meranier, its destruction by the Wittelsbachs, and the founding of the monastery of Andechs. He learned of the miraculous discovery of the relics that had been hidden during the storming of the castle and had come to light only centuries later, thanks to a mouse. He read of the increasing crowds of pilgrims, and he read that the relics had often been hidden or spirited away in times of war. None of this was really news to Simon, who had read it all before in the small Andechs chronicle. New, however, was another parchment sheet lying among the others on the table.

A map.

Torn on the edges and burned in places, the map clearly showed the outlines of a castle, with corridors that branched off into labyrinths and ended in several marked exits. A few trees sketched in around the castle suggested a forest, and below that there seemed to be a lake and some rocks indicating cliffs. After a while Simon was able to decipher a few hastily scribbled words.

Hic est porta ad loca infera . . .

"Here is the gateway to the underworld," he mumbled. "What in God's name . . ."

He was just bending over to examine the map closer when a sound caused him to spin around. Footsteps in the corridor. In a panic, the medicus looked for some way to escape, but the only way out was a large glass window at the back of the room. He ran toward it, turned the knob in the middle, and opened it. Looking down, he could feel his legs wobble under him.

God, don't let this be the only way out of here.

Two stories below was the deserted courtyard. Beneath the window, a narrow ledge—about a hand's-breadth in width—ran along the entire front of the building.

The footsteps in the hallway came to a stop just outside the office door. Simon crossed himself one final time, then stepped out on the ledge, closed the window, and moved one step to the right so he was not visible from inside. And not a second too soon, for in the next moment, he heard the latch being pressed and someone entering the room.

I hope he doesn't notice that the window is ajar, Simon thought. *If the count closes the window, my only option is to jump or knock politely and ask to be hanged.*

He heard the easy chair in the office being moved aside.

He's sitting down. The count is sitting down. Holy Mary, Mother of Jesus, don't let him nod off. I can't stand being out here that long.

Simon tried not to look down, but out of the corner of his eye he could see the ground fifty feet below seemingly reaching up to him. He sensed he was going to pass out, and his legs felt like rotting wood beneath him. An invisible force seemed to pull him toward the abyss.

Just as he was about to lose all hope, he heard the scraping of the armchair again, then the door to the corridor squeak closed.

Simon waited a few seconds, then worked his way carefully back toward the window. Casting a sidelong glance into the room behind the glass, he finally pushed the door open with a gentle, silent swing. He tiptoed back into the room and closed the window again. His jacket was soaked in sweat, and his knees so weak that walking on the parquet beneath him felt like wading through a deep swamp.

With three deep breaths, he hurried silently to the door where he first listened and then rushed out into the empty corridor. A few moments later, Simon hobbled past the guards at the door and nearly tumbled down the stairway.

"Everything . . . Everything is fine," he shouted, his voice cracking, though he tried to sound more or less normal. "Just a bit tired. Now let's all pray for the little count. Good night."

"Did you see how ashen the bathhouse surgeon was?" the fat watchman asked, as Simon disappeared down the stairs. "If you ask me, he caught an infection from the little one."

"Shady quack doctor," the other hissed. "I'll bet the count will have him hanged if that blasted fever doesn't get him first." He sighed, scratching himself hard between the legs. "It's really time for us to get out of this hellhole."

Simon staggered out into the courtyard and looked up at the ledge where he'd stood just a few minutes before. Just the sight made his head spin again. Deep in thought, he walked through the inner gate leading from the courtyard into the narrow lanes in front of the monastery, where he was immediately engulfed in an unending stream of noisy pilgrims.

His head was spinning, due only in small part to his experience on the ledge. What sort of map had he seen on the table in the count's study? Was it the same the librarian was so eager to find, the map showing the way to the monks' subterranean hiding place? And what was the strange reference to a door into the underworld?

The more the medicus thought about it, the more he was convinced that Leopold von Wartenberg was somehow implicated in the strange events taking place in the monastery. The count was clearly involved in the matter of the relics, and had been sent there personally by the elector for some mysterious reason. Besides that, he had a map presumably showing the corridors in the basement of the old castle—the same ones haunted by a golem, and the same ones where the effeminate novitiate master had almost met his death.

Simon pushed his way past the pilgrims as he hurried back to the clinic, where he'd last left the Andechs chronicle. In his free time, he'd leafed through it again and again, and now he positively had to read the little book to the end. Perhaps there was something in the little book pointing to what the count was searching for here. Or was the count himself the sorcerer?

As Simon entered the clinic, he was met by a dejected Jakob Schreevogl. The whole clinic stank of urine and garbage, Schreevogl's jacket was smeared with sweat and dirt. The stress of the last few days was clearly visible in the face of the Schongau councilor.

"We have another death to announce," the patrician said softly.

Simon's heart skipped a beat. "Not Brother Laurentius, I hope?"

Schreevogl shook his head. "It's one of our Schongau masons, Andre Losch. God rest his soul." He sighed deeply. "I still can't believe it. Andre was such a bear of a man. Three days ago, he was carousing with the other master masons in the tavern and suddenly—"

"Just a moment," Simon interrupted. "In the tavern, you said?"

Schreevogl nodded. "That's right. All three were brought here with high fevers, along with the Twangler brothers, but Andre's case was the worst."

Simon remembered now what had been bothering him during his conversation with the count. Leopold von Wartenberg mentioned his family had also dined in the monastery tavern.

And only now did it occur to the medicus that other patients had been there as well — not just Losch, but little Martin and the Twangler brothers, too.

Evidently many of the more well-to-do pilgrims had eaten there, and Simon could see now that the sickness seemed to especially affect those with means to eat there.

He chewed his lower lip as he turned this over in his mind. Did the fever have some connection with the tavern? What could it be?

Suddenly he had a terrible suspicion.

"Master Schreevogl," he said, turning to the councilor. "Could you do me a favor?"

"And what would that be?"

Quietly, so as not to waken the patients and start a panic, Simon told him.

Schreevogl nodded, moved toward the door, then turned again to address the medicus. "If you're really right," he said softly, but with a dark undertone, "then at least one head will roll here, and this time it won't be the poor apothecary's."

Nepomuk Volkmar cowered in the pitch black of his cell, staring at his bloody fingers. Some were missing their nails, and the bloody stumps throbbed with a hellish pain.

In theory, the apothecary was happy he was unable to see anything in the darkness — at least that relieved him of the torture of seeing his battered body. But new waves of pain kept coursing through him, and he knew that such agony would be his constant companion from then on.

Master Hans had done a thorough job the day before. After he showed his victim the instruments of torture, as prescribed by law, he put Nepomuk in what they called the interrogation seat, a chair covered with spikes. His arms and legs were secured by iron clasps lined with spikes; even his feet were placed on a board of spikes. As the seated prisoner felt the spikes slowly cutting into his flesh, the pain followed quickly.

After two hours of torture in the interrogation chair, Nepomuk still hadn't confessed to any witchcraft, so Master Hans started pulling out the apothecary's fingernails with a set of long tongs.

It was then that Nepomuk's screams were audible even in the square in front of the dungeon.

But despite all the pain, the monk had remained strong, closing his eyes, praying, declaring his innocence, and thinking about the words of his friend Jakob Kuisl.

No matter what happens, don't confess. If you confess, it's all over.

How could anyone not confess, knowing this was only the beginning? That far worse torture would follow until he finally collapsed, wailing, and confessed to witchcraft? Nepomuk had watched some tortures at his father's side — his father, the executioner of Reutling — and knew that victims yearned for death at some point. When they were finally dragged to the scaffold like animals to slaughter, there was often not much left of them but broken bones.

Would he be able to keep silent after he, too, had been reduced to a whimpering bundle of flesh, yearning for his own death? How long would it take?

Finally after hours of torture, he'd been dragged back to his cell. When the trapdoor slammed shut over him, he could only wait in the darkness for the next horror. Sleep was out of the question, so as the hours dragged by, Nepomuk tried to console himself with memories of better days. The melody of a fiddle; the rhythmic beat of drums before battle; the wild parties with the other mercenaries; the many practice battles with his only real friend, Jakob Kuisl; their conversations on long winter nights in burned-out barns or in the protection of storm-buffeted, half-ruined castles . . .

"Where is your God, anyway?" Jakob asks as Nepomuk rubs the dirty rosary between his fingers. "Is he dead? I can't see him; I can't hear him."

"You can only believe in him," Nepomuk answers.

Jakob laughs softly, turning a sizzling rabbit on the spit as fat hisses and drips into the flames.

"I believe in hard iron," he says finally. "In laws, and in death."

"God is stronger than death, Jakob."

The son of the Schongau executioner watches his friend for a long time, then stomps off silently into the night.

The next day they string up a half dozen outlaws together. As the bandits writhe about in the trees above, Jakob suddenly looks over to his friend as if still expecting an answer from him.

Nepomuk remains silent.

"Hail Mary, full of grace, the Lord is with thee . . ."

Sitting in his cell, mumbling softly, Nepomuk recited the eternal words of the rosary, hoping to rekindle an old faith that seemed to be slowly escaping through tiny cracks in the walls.

"Blessed are thou amongst women, and blessed is . . ."

A creak of the trapdoor above him caused Nepomuk's heart to race. He knew they were coming to fetch him for another session. His tongue became as dry as a bone, and he suddenly felt himself start to shake.

In fact it wasn't long before the ladder was lowered down again. Since he was too weak to climb unassisted, one of the watchmen descended and tied a rope around his waist. Then the men overhead all pulled together, hauling him up like a fish wiggling on a hook.

"Save your strength," a familiar voice said. "You'll need it." It was Master Hans, standing next to the trapdoor above with his arms crossed, looking like a white-haired avenging angel. With bloodshot eyes, the Weilheim executioner examined his victim, then checked him all over for broken bones. Nepomuk knew that Master Hans, like so many other executioners, was also considered an excellent healer. It was his job to ensure the prisoner was fit for further torture.

"Listen up," Master Hans began, almost sounding compassionate as he probed Nepomuk like a piece of raw meat. "You know I make good money every day I torture you, so I should really be happy you held up so well yesterday. On the other hand . . ." He studied Nepomuk's swollen, bloody fingers, as if checking over his own work once more. "On the other hand, it's my duty to tell you that your denials are pointless. Believe me, you'll confess eventually — any other outcome would damage my reputation. So don't make it so hard on yourself." He brought his lips right up to Nepomuk's ear. "You said that you yourself come from a hangman's family, so you must know all this better than I, dear cousin."

Laughing, the executioner gave Nepomuk a friendly pat on the shoulder. Then he closed the spiked iron clamp around the monk's neck, and the guards pushed him through a hallway illuminated by torches.

"Today, you'll have a special guest," Master Hans said as he led the contingent down the passageway with a lantern. "Count von Cäsana und Colle is tired of leading the questioning and would prefer to go hunting. So would I, if I had the time and money." The Weilheim executioner shook his head scornfully. "The noble gentleman looked pale as a ghost yesterday when I pulled out your fingernails." Softly he added, "This is nothing for such a spoiled man accustomed to white bread. He was that way the last time, too. The only blood the count can bear to look at is deer's blood."

"Who's coming in his place?" Nepomuk gasped as the iron spikes dug into his neck. He had the quiet hope a more moderate jurist from Munich might be more interested in truth than in magic. The two witnesses were obsequious Weilheim aldermen who would do anything the count asked. Perhaps they could be swayed for the better by a scholar from the city.

"You know him," Master Hans responded after a while. "The count himself chose him for this job, to give him a chance to earn his stripes, so to speak."

In the meantime, they'd reached the entrance to the torture chamber. The executioner opened the door, and the bailiffs pulled Nepomuk into a dark room illuminated only by a crackling fire in an iron bowl. Just as in his cell before, the apothecary was overcome by uncontrollable shaking. His eyes wandered over the interrogation chair, still bloody from the day before, the rack, and the winch with which Master Hans would no doubt be hoisting him up until his tendons snapped like dry ropes.

On the right side of the room was a wide table with an inkpot, some rolls of paper, and a heavy book on top. Three men sat behind the table, two of them the portly Weilheim aldermen whom Nepomuk had met the day before. The two chubby men, wrapped in expensive clothing, glared at him with a mixture of disgust, fear, and curiosity—almost as if they expected the sorcerer to fly away.

The third man sat upright on the chair between them. When Nepomuk recognized him in the light of the crackling fire, he started shaking harder, fell to his knees, and folded his hands in prayer.

"Please, Brother," he pleaded. "You must believe me. This is all an—"

"Don't get any false hopes," the third man interrupted. "I'm no longer your Brother, but your inquisitor. The Weilheim judge assigned me this unpleasant task in view of the need to soon fill a higher position. Our monastery urgently needs a new abbot."

The eyes of the Andechs prior flashed icily, like two marbles, as he turned and nodded to Master Hans. "Executioner," Brother Jeremias said, "we wish to begin the interrogation. The sooner he confesses, the better."

14

SIMON SAT HUNCHED UP ON A ROUGH-HEWN CHAIR
at the bedside of Brother Laurentius, sadly observing the priest's
burned, disfigured body.

The monk's condition was unchanged. The many burns on
his face, back, and legs were festering so that the bandages had to
be changed frequently. The young monk's face was covered; all
that could be seen beneath the bandages were his nose and eyes.
He groaned, and occasionally one of his fingers quivered, but
otherwise there was no sign of life—he looked more like a
mummy now than anything human.

Simon bent over him compassionately and took his hand.
Brother Laurentius seemed to feel the touch, and his breathing
became more measured. Suddenly there was a sound from beneath the bandages—some mumbled, at first incomprehensible
words.

"Brother," Simon said softly. "If you wish to tell me something . . ."

"He's . . . alive . . ." said a muffled voice from beneath the
blankets. "Down in the catacombs . . . I've . . . I've . . . seen him."

"The puppet is alive?" Simon cringed. "But how is that possible? Who's behind this, Laurentius? Say something, please. It's very important."

"The ... hosts. He ... needs the hosts ..." The Brother's mumbling turned into an incomprehensible death rattle. Reaching up with his right hand, he grabbed Simon by the collar and pulled him down so that the medicus could smell his burnt flesh. Disgusted, Simon noticed a strong odor like that of a roasted pig.

"Thunder and lightning! Thunder and Lightning! Stop him before the fire comes down from heaven. The fire!"

With a final scream, the Brother doubled up, his grip around Simon's neck loosening, and fell back on the bed, lifeless.

"Brother Laurentius. Brother Laurentius!"

Simon felt in vain for a pulse. Frantically he pulled a small, polished copper disk from his doctor's bag and held it under Laurentius's nose. When the disk finally misted up, the medicus leaned back, relieved. The Brother was breathing, even if very shallowly. No doubt he would soon pass away; Simon could only hope he would regain consciousness before that and say something. What in the world had Laurentius meant by those strange words?

Thunder and lightning. Thunder and Lightning. Stop him before the fire comes down from heaven.

The medicus took a deep breath and tried to calm down. Evidently Laurentius had seen the watchmaker's automaton in the subterranean passageways of the former castle. His confused mumblings seemed to suggest this automaton or golem was still alive and that it had something to do with the three hosts. The medicus remembered that special magic numbers and incantations were required to summon a golem. Perhaps hosts, as well?

Simon shook his head reluctantly. All that just couldn't be true. Simon was an enlightened person of the new era, the time after the Great War. He believed in mechanics and empirical knowledge, not in magic formulas and golems. But what if science was wrong? What if there really was something like a physical, living devil? Had Virgilius perhaps created an automaton that could move according to the laws of mechanics, as well as think and . . . kill? Had the automaton killed its own creator?

Then burned him and thrown him into a well? How could that be?

Once more Simon checked Laurentius's pulse, which had returned, though it was still weak. The monk had fallen into a death-like sleep; not even the tips of his fingers quivered beneath the bandages anymore.

Other patients moaned from nearby beds, but Simon doubted they'd heard any of this strange talk. Nor had the pilgrims, still singing and praying outside the door. The medicus thought about Kuisl's warning that the sorcerer, or perhaps one of his accomplices, could enter the clinic in the next few hours to kill the troublesome monk.

If he waits just a bit longer, he can save himself the trouble, Simon thought. *Laurentius doesn't have long to live. It's time to give him last rites.*

To take his mind off this, Simon reached for the Andechs chronicle, which he'd wrapped in a dirty towel and hidden under one of the beds. He leafed through the little book until he got to the place describing the old castle. Perhaps he could find some information here about the subterranean passageways depicted on the count's map.

Until now, Simon had read only that the castle had fallen due to "cowardly, vile treason." Another chapter dealt in more detail with this. Evidently the Andechs-Meranier had been the leading family of nobles in Bavaria many hundreds of years ago, until suddenly the Wittelsbachs seized power.

Simon immersed himself in the tiny, spidery flourishes that described how, at a wedding in Bamberg in the year 1208, the Wittelsbach Duke Otto had murdered the Staufer King Philipp, a son of the famous Emperor Barbarossa. Details of the murder were evidently never completely clear — only that Otto was de-

clared an outlaw, arrested in Oberndorf near Kelheim, and beheaded on the spot.

Simon started turning pages, then stopped short. In the investigation of King Philipp's murder, it was not the Wittelsbachs
who were charged with conspiracy, but the Andechs. All their
property was confiscated and given to the Wittelsbachs, among
them the Andechs castle that was stormed after many long battles, and razed. The chronicle described the conquest of the ancestral castle in dramatic detail.

Lost in thought, the medicus was transported back into the
past, to a world hundreds of years ago that came back to life in
the pithy Latin text. As so often when he was reading, Simon became lost in the images conjured up in his mind. Suddenly he
thought he could see the armor glinting in the sunlight, the cries
of the attackers, and smell the blood and horse sweat in the air as
the castle was stormed. Simon was sitting there, in his chair in
the year 1666, but at the same time he was carried back more
than four hundred years. His lips moved silently as his fingers
followed the lines . . .

> *The battlements rise over the mighty fortress high above the*
> *Kien Valley. Atop the parapets, the defenders run excitedly back*
> *and forth while below the Wittelsbach foot soldiers and knights*
> *gather in a clearing along the moat, preparing for the final as-*
> *sault. For weeks they have laid siege to their enemy's castle, cat-*
> *apulting hundred-pound rocks at it and ramming the entrance*
> *again and again as fire, pitch, and sulfur rained down on them.*
> *Their sappers have dug passageways directly under the walls of*
> *the fortress. Many have died, and even more, tormented by fever*
> *and gangrene, writhe in pain in their tents, which look like red*
> *pustules in the cleared forest land.*
>
> *They yearn for the death of their enemy and know the day*
> *of vengeance is at hand.*
>
> *The traitor had cost them a lot of money, but he told them*

*where the escape tunnel was; this was how the beleaguered de-
fenders were able to smuggle fresh meat, flour, and wine into the
castle—not enough to provide for the entire garrison, but
enough to hold out for the last few months.*

That would all come to an end today.

*A small elite group of fighters set out through the tunnel
into the castle. Silently they slashed the throats of the guards,
leaving a trail of blood and gore beneath the castle and up into
the courtyard. Now they can be heard screaming inside the castle, attacking the guards at the gate, shoving aside the three huge
beams that bar the entrance, and finally opening the heavy door,
leaving the way clear for the over three hundred warriors who
have been waiting outside for just this moment.*

*A cry of many voices arises, as loud as if the earth itself were
opening up and calling for revenge.*

And then the killing begins.

*The men who stagger toward them from the castle court-
yard with uplifted swords are also weakened by disease and hunger. Only a few dozen have held out, and they are cut down like
dogs.*

*"Death to all the Andechs!" the attackers cry, their eyes like
those of wild animals. "Death, death, death!"*

*Blood flows over the stone steps, and the men keep slipping
and falling, but driven by their hatred and lust, they wander
from room to room looking for women, wine, food, and treasure. They were promised treasures, but where are the damned
treasures? The Wittelsbach duke told them there were more
precious objects here than in the entire Holy Land. The gold
they could keep; all the duke wanted for himself were the many
relics.*

*They race through the outer court, storm the tower, search
the women's chambers and the burning stables until finally they
reach the chapel in the interior courtyard. A priest stands in their
way, wringing his hands, but they push him aside, then run him*

*through with lances. They beat down the door to the chapel.
This is where they must be, the legendary treasures the duke had
spoken of so often.*

The room is empty.

*No relics, no treasures, not a single accursed coin—every-
thing was hauled away long ago. The men's hatred is immense.
They burn down everything, search the chaos for survivors who
can tell them where the costly relics are stored. But there are no
survivors; they've all been slaughtered. So the men search more
and more frantically, leaving no stone unturned—digging,
cursing, even mutilating the body of the priest—all in vain.*

The relics have disappeared.

*When they finally withdraw, all that is left of the once
proud castle is a smoking ruin, a field of rubble that will soon be
overgrown with ivy and moss. The castle will become what it
once was.*

Silent stone.

*Not until centuries later will a little mouse reveal the
hiding place of the relics. At that point, all the battles, the mis-
ery, the knights in shining armor—all will have been long forgotten . . .*

Only the dream of the treasure lives on today . . .

When Simon put the book aside, he could feel the hair at the
back of his neck standing on end.

Now he thought he knew what the count was seeking in the
ancient passageways beneath the castle. Could treasures and relics still be hidden down there? Some of the relics had reappeared
a few hundred years later, but if this castle was really the seat of
the Andechs-Merianer, it was quite possible many other precious
items were waiting to be found. Were the librarian and his helper
chasing after these treasures? Had they already found them?

Before Simon could finish his train of thought, he was jolted
by a loud wail from one of the beds in back. One of the Twangler

brothers was thirsty. Simon brought him a cup of water while casting a glance at the other patients. Some needed bandages changed, and others needed a drink to help them sleep.

Sleep . . .

Despite the excitement, Simon suddenly felt how tired he was. The events of the last few days—the count's sick son, the quarrel with Magdalena—it had all clearly been too much for him. And now he had to watch a badly injured monk who probably wouldn't survive the next few hours anyway.

Simon rubbed his temples and sat down again on the chair alongside Laurentius's bed. He picked up the little book again but could feel his eyes closing after just a few lines. He struggled to sit up straight in the uncomfortable armchair. The setting sun shone through the tiny windows and cracks in the wooden wall, warming his face, and his head fell forward. No, he couldn't break his promise to his father-in-law and fall asleep—not now. Where, for heaven's sake, was Schreevogl? It seemed like hours ago that Simon had sent him to the tavern. Shouldn't he be coming to relieve him for a few hours? Had Schreevogl forgotten what he'd asked him to find out?

Once more the medicus cursed himself for running out of his beloved coffee beans. He almost thought he could smell the fragrance of the black ground powder mixing with the stench of dirty straw and reminding him of home. Of Schongau in the summer, when the grain stood tall in the fields . . . of Magdalena, his children . . . were they already asleep? Was she still angry at him? He really had to pay more attention to her. All of a sudden, he regretted he'd had so little time for his family in recent days. What did this murder case, the count's son, and all the other sick people really have to do with his life? Sometimes it seemed to him that, in his concern for others and his thirst for knowledge, he forgot what was really dear to him.

When Simon's head fell forward, he dreamed of his two

small sons, of an automaton playing music, and of a castle going up in smoke and flames. He could hear the laughter of children and the rushing of a distant river. Seconds later, he was fast asleep.

He didn't notice the figure quietly opening the door and tiptoeing to the bed of the novitiate master with outstretched arms. The man smiled at the medicus slumped over in his chair and peacefully snoring. The man had waited a long time at the window, hoping the medicus would fall asleep sooner or later.

And now he could finally finish his work.

Brother Laurentius was dreaming, as well, but his were not beautiful dreams. Once again he saw blue flames flickering around his body, he smelled his own burnt flesh, and he heard the sweet melody of the automaton along with his own screams.

Groaning softly, the monk tossed and turned in his bed. Ever since the unimaginable had happened, he'd hovered between sleeping and waking. In his waking moments, the pain surged like acid through his body; then merciful unconsciousness returned, followed again by short moments of lucidity. How many hours had passed since that nightmare? How many days? He didn't know. People came and went around him; they laid cool compresses on his wounds and poured wine and water between his lips, but every time he tried to open his mouth to speak, all that came out of his burned throat was a rattle.

Except for once.

But the Schongau medicus hadn't understood him; he hadn't been able to make out his words; he didn't know the danger.

Last night, in despair, the Brother had wandered through the forests around the monastery. Fear was nagging at him; the crime they committed would finally be exposed. This golem was like an avenging angel pounding loudly again and again on the door of his conscience. Laurentius, who had heard the melody, knew the automaton was going about its work somewhere down below. This creature would never rest until someone went down there and smashed it into a thousand pieces.

And then that someone would discover what they'd hidden down there so well. That mustn't happen.

Brother Benedikt had assured him that the passage to their hiding place had been sealed, but Laurentius knew there were other entrances to the castle. He'd read about them himself in the library. It was a true labyrinth. Sooner or later the melody would lure someone into one of these passageways and the secret would come to light. Then they would all face the fire or be boiled alive in oil. Laurentius had read this punishment was used centuries ago in cases of high treason and counterfeiting, and wasn't their crime worse — much worse — than both these crimes together?

He had to remove everything down there secretly. But how? Brothers Eckhart and Benedikt were watching him like hawks; he could feel their eyes burning into him. Never would they allow him to destroy their life's work.

After wandering for hours through the rock-strewn Kien Valley, Laurentius finally had an idea and found another secret entrance. God Himself seemed to be handing him the key to atone for his crimes. Lying in the hospital bed now, he never thought he would have to pay in this way, with so much pain. Laurentius had passed through all the rings of Dante's inferno and experienced every type of pain, but perhaps things would work out now.

He was awakened by an unfamiliar sound and listened attentively, but all he could hear through the bandages were muffled sounds, then silence. Suddenly a hand clamped down over his mouth and nose, pushing him gently but relentlessly into the pillows.

"Mmmmmmm . . ." Laurentius tried to seize his attacker with his bandaged fingers, but he was too weak; all he could manage was a feeble twitch. The strong hand remained on his face, blocking his air, smothering him. He had to breathe, he simply had to breathe, but he was immobilized, wrapped in dozens of blankets. He couldn't speak or hear or see anything—just this hand over his face that wouldn't let go. Quivering and thrashing about, he was finally able to grab the end of a sheet and clutch it tightly, tugging at it until the material ripped, leaving only a scrap of cloth in his hand. He could feel every fiber of the soft sheet, smooth and firm like a woven tapestry or a freshly fluffed pillow. Memories of his childhood looped through his mind: his mother, his first days as a novitiate.

As he slowly sank into a soft darkness, the urge to breathe subsided, giving way to a feeling of unbelievable relief. Laurentius realized he was dying.

This time he wouldn't wake up.

The murderer arose, passed his hand almost lovingly over the bandaged face, then turned toward the medicus still sunk down on his chair, dreaming of beautiful things with a blissful smile on his lips.

Hesitantly the man passed his hand over the medicus's soiled jacket, up to the expensive but somewhat worn lace collar, and over his cleanly clipped goatee. All it would take was some gentle pressure, a small cut with a knife, and he would have dispensed with one more of the master's problems.

But he couldn't.

As he lowered his arms with a soft sigh, he noticed the little book on the floor in front of him. He picked it up, began leafing through it, and quickly realized what it was.

This would surely interest the master.

Hastily he put the book in his pocket and disappeared as silently as he'd come. He could still hear Simon snoring as he turned the next corner.

"And you really don't know where your father is now?" Michael Graetz stared at Magdalena in disbelief. During the last half-hour she'd told him all that had happened in the monastery up to that point. She told him also about Kuisl's friend Nepomuk and her father's plan to prove his innocence. Graetz had listened in astonishment, shaking his head from time to time, while the children slept on peacefully in the next room.

"I really have no idea where he is," Magdalena replied. "Perhaps he learned something in the monastery and the sorcerer got hold of him."

"Your father?" The knacker laughed. "If half the stories I've heard about him are true, this sorcerer can count himself lucky if he leaves the Holy Mountain in one piece. But we've got to go and look for him," he added, suddenly turning serious. "And you've got to tell Simon, too, before he starts getting worried."

"Simon?" Magdalena sneered. "With all his work, he doesn't even notice when I'm standing right in front of him, and he evidently doesn't care for his children, either. I'm sick and tired of him."

"You mustn't be so tough on him," Michael Graetz said. "My Ani, God rest her soul, always complained, too, when I disappeared for a few days. Believe me, girl, that's the way we men are. We crawl into a hole in the ground and then can't find our way out until someone comes and gives us a hand."

Magdalena couldn't resist a smile. "Maybe you're right, but you men don't make it easy for us."

A soft whine came from the next room, but then the sound died away just as quickly.

"What happened to your own children?" asked Magdalena in the silence that followed. "Have they all grown up and moved out?"

Graetz shrugged. "Most of them died early; only Hans and Lisl lived to see their tenth summer, but Lisl died of the Plague a few years back, and Hans became a drummer boy for a group of dragoons and went off to war." He sighed. "Since the death of my wife, all I have left is Matthias; he's something like a son to me."

"You certainly scold him as if he were your own." Magdalena grinned. "A strapping young fellow. If I wasn't already married I could easily fall for him."

"Then you'd have a husband who wouldn't talk back." Graetz stood up abruptly and wiped his hands on his apron. "But now I've got to go help Matthias with the work, and you really should go back to Simon and put an end to your quarrel. Save your arguments for later. You have a lot more important things to talk about now, and in the meantime, I'll keep an eye on the children." He stopped to think for a moment. "If your father still doesn't show up today, let me know. Matthias and I know some people in the village we can trust, and we can go out to look for him together. I may be a dishonorable knacker, but I won't abandon my family."

"Thank you, Michael, I know that." Magdalena smiled, squeezing his hand. Suddenly she felt ashamed for having said earlier that her children would become something better.

After a final nod, she turned toward the door and hurried down the narrow path toward the monastery, a huge black silhouette now in the setting sun. Magdalena quickened her steps to reach the clinic before nightfall. The shadows of the trees lining the path seemed to reach out to seize her, and she kept looking about anxiously as she ran up the mountain. Finally she arrived, breathless, at the outer walls of the monastery.

She felt somewhat safer here among the exhausted pilgrims arriving at the monastery and seeking a place to spend the night. The next day, for the Festival of the Three Hosts, there would be more happening at the Holy Mountain than all the rest of the year combined. A feeling of joyful expectation was already in the air, mixing with the aromas of fresh-baked bread and meat roasting on the fire. Some merchants had started setting up stands along the monastery walls, and another group of pilgrims bearing torches came up from the Kien Valley.

As Magdalena passed through the outer portal and turned toward the clinic, she felt someone approaching her from behind. She hadn't heard a sound—it was more a feeling, a slight twinge in her shoulders. She turned quickly in the narrow lane, but it was already too late.

Hairy hands covered her mouth and dragged her between two dilapidated sheds. She struggled to scream, but the stranger's grip was too strong. Finally she was able to bite her attacker on the finger.

"Ouch," said a familiar deep voice. "How dare you bite your own flesh and blood, you viper."

"For God's sake, Father," Magdalena scolded, relaxing a bit as Kuisl cursed and released her. "Why do you have to scare me like that? Couldn't you have just said 'good day' like any other reasonable person?"

"While you run around shouting and drawing attention? Stop talking nonsense. In any case, I'm—"

"Wanted," Magdalena interrupted her father. "I know. Semer can't wait to get his hands on you."

"Semer?" Kuisl sucked on his bloody finger. "What do you know about Semer?"

The hangman was wearing ripped trousers, a simple black jacket, and an old coat that Magdalena had known since childhood. She had to smile when she thought of her father in the threadbare Franciscan robe. With his large frame, he would really have made a good monk.

"Karl Semer paid a visit to your cousin," she finally replied.

"Graetz? For heaven's sake, why?"

"If you want to know, just be still and listen to me."

After Magdalena had told her father about the threatening visit from the Schongau burgomaster, Kuisl angrily pounded his fist against the wall of the shed.

"Damn, that's all I needed," he blustered. "Now I know why the hunters and a few other bailiffs were prowling the back lanes around the monastery. Semer probably promised them a nice reward if they catch me. But they can wait for that until hell freezes over." He looked at his daughter, worried. "Did Simon tell you what happened up in the monastery?"

"I was just looking for him. Evidently they found Virgilius dead. Is that true?"

The hangman nodded. "Let's go find your husband. We have to talk about what to do next. I'll tell you all the rest along the way."

As they headed for the clinic, Kuisl told her about the monstrance being found and the dying Laurentius.

"We can only hope the Brother is still able to talk," the hangman said softly. "And that the damned sorcerer doesn't get to him first. Pray that your husband keeps a sharp eye out and doesn't fall asleep, or he'll be sorry he ever had an executioner as a father-in-law."

Magdalena nodded and tried not to think about what her father meant by that. She knew he was subject to sudden fits of temper, but thank God he could calm down just as fast afterward.

They hurried along until the clinic finally appeared before them. The horse stable was already completely enveloped in darkness, with no sign of a light inside.

"I don't have a good feeling about this," Kuisl growled. "Either Simon has eyes like a cat or he's fallen asleep, the idiot."

"Perhaps it's all been too much for him recently," Magdalena whispered, suddenly feeling sorry for her husband. Why did her father always have to be so hard on him?

Without replying, Kuisl reached under his jacket and pulled out a torch, which he lit with a tinderbox he'd brought along. Then he silently opened the door to the clinic.

In the torchlight, Magdalena could vaguely see about two

dozen beds scattered throughout the room. In most, sleepy figures coughed, thrashed about, or lifted their heads before falling
back onto the bed again. In the rear, the hangman's daughter
caught sight of her husband huddled down on a chair alongside
a bed. His chest rose and fell in rhythm.

And he was snoring.

"I should have guessed. Damn!"

The hangman hurried over to the peacefully sleeping medicus and shook him awake. "Didn't I tell you to keep a lookout?"
he growled. "And here you are snoring so loud it sounds like
you're sawing down the whole Kien Valley forest."

"What? . . . ? What?" Simon rubbed his eyes. It took him a
while to recognize who was standing in front of him.

"My God, Kuisl," he finally said. "I'm . . . I'm sorry. But the
last few days . . ."

But the hangman had already turned to the lifeless body of
the novitiate master. He held his ear to his chest, then felt his
pulse.

"Damn," he whispered. "The man's dead. Now we'll never
find out where he found the monstrance and who did this to
him."

"That's . . . that's impossible," said Simon, jumping up and
feeling for Laurentius's pulse. He tore the bandages from the
monk's burnt face and held the little copper disk in front of his
nose. When it didn't fog up, he fell back on his chair, crushed.

"It must have happened just in the last hour," he said remorsefully. "I was reading for a while, then probably my eyes
closed."

"And the sorcerer waltzed in here and killed our only witness," the hangman spluttered. "It didn't take much to do that."

"Do you think it was really the sorcerer?" Magdalena whispered so as not to wake the other patients. "Maybe he just died."
She knew she was just looking for reasons to spare her husband
the wrath of her father.

"What is this here?" Gently the hangman removed a scrap of black cloth from the clenched fist of the novitiate master. "It looks like Brother Laurentius didn't set out for paradise without a fight."

Magdalena bent down to look at the little scrap of cloth. "That might be from a robe," she said, thinking out loud, "or some other piece of clothing. In any case it isn't necessarily . . ." She stopped abruptly to watch Simon, who was crawling around on the floor, evidently looking for something. "What in heaven's name are you doing down there?"

"The . . . the Andechs chronicle!" Simon exclaimed. "It's disappeared. I was reading it just a while ago, and when I fell asleep it must have fallen out of my hand. And now it's gone."

"Isn't that just fine," the hangman growled. "It's not enough that this sorcerer kills our only witness; he steals your book, as well, while you sit there snoring. How stupid can you be?"

"Father, stop tormenting him," Magdalena said angrily. "Can't you see how sorry he is? Besides, couldn't you have stayed here and kept watch? But no, you had to go waltzing through the forest as you so often do."

"Because I'm a wanted man, you fresh little thing. How many times do I have to tell you that?"

Moaning could be heard now from beds farther back in the room. An ashen-faced older farmer with sunken cheeks sat up and stared at them curiously.

"If I may make a suggestion," Simon whispered, getting up from the floor. "Let's continue this conversation down in St. Elizabeth's chapel. There we'll be undisturbed, and I can tell you in more detail what I learned in the chronicle." He ventured a smile. "And perhaps I can in some small way make amends for what happened — and avoid the torture rack."

St. Elizabeth's chapel was located under the monastery church. Built directly into the side of the mountain, it was an unassuming little church that, even on busy days, was a refuge of silence and meditation.

Sometimes pilgrims visited the chapel because water from the little fountain in the apsis was said to cure eye problems, but now, at ten o'clock at night, it was as quiet as the forest behind it. Small candles burned alongside the altar, casting a flickering light on the few pews where the three sat.

"You think the librarian, the cellarer, and perhaps the sorcerer as well are searching for the relics and treasures hidden during the storming of Andechs castle long ago?" asked Magdalena incredulously.

After Simon told them what he'd learned, he shook his head contemplatively. "It says in the Andechs chronicle that the conquerors found nothing—nothing at all," he finally replied. "Not until almost two hundred years later did a mouse dash out of a hole in the chapel with a scrap of parchment in its little mouth picturing some of the relics. And that's how they finally managed to track them down."

"That's right," Magdalena joined in, shivering and pulling her shawl tight over her shoulders. "That's what that disgusting Brother Eckhart told me, but why should there be more down there than what they found at that time?"

Simon leaned forward in the pew. "The chronicle mentions all the relics kept in the holy chapel," he said. "But the count's list contains many more, among them—"

"What is this count's list?" interrupted Kuisl, who had been listening silently until this point, puffing on his pipe. "This is the first I've heard of that. Did the smart-ass nobleman offer to show you around his office? Please stop beating around the bush."

"Patience, patience: I still haven't told you the best part." The medicus raised his hands, grinning, trying to calm Kuisl down. He knew the hangman's curiosity was insatiable. Now it was Simon's turn to torture his father-in-law.

"Of course the count didn't show me around his study," he

finally said smugly. "I had a look around without his permission, and I came across the list and a map—a map, which in my opinion, shows the ancient subterranean passageways and cellars of this castle. It's quite possibly the same map stolen from the librarian, so we have to at least consider the possibility that the count is the sorcerer and that he, and a number of the monks as well, are looking for the hidden treasure."

With evident relish Simon noted how Kuisl and Magdalena stared at him in astonishment.

"You searched the count's study?" Magdalena asked incredulously. "If anyone caught you doing that—"

"Nobody saw me," Simon said, waving off her remark and trying not to think of his escape onto the window ledge.

"And where is the map now?" the hangman asked.

Simon's secret delight at his father-in-law's amazement was quicky dampened. "Uh, unfortunately I wasn't able to take it with me," he replied. "But I remember it well, especially a few scrawled words," he said, trying hard to remember. "*Hic est porta ad loca infera*. That means—"

"This is the portal to the subterranean places," Kuisl mumbled. "I know that much myself, wiseass. That's just what we're looking for, but did you see where the door was?"

Embarrassed, Simon could only shrug. "Uh, unfortunately not. I had very little time and the script was very hard to read."

Beside him, Magdalena sighed and stretched on the hard church pew. "This whole thing is becoming too much for me," she groaned. "Up to now we thought the sorcerer was trying only to find the sacred hosts, and that's why he abducted Virgilius—to extort Virgilius's brother. And he was able to do just that. So what is the purpose of these underground passages? Why does the count have a map of them? And what for heaven's sake are Brother Benedikt and Brother Eckhart hiding down there? This just doesn't make any sense."

Simon was silent, thinking of the handkerchief with the initial *A* that they'd found alongside the grave of the old monk. Kuisl and he hadn't told Magdalena of this discovery so as not to frighten her even more. Was there really a golem brought to life by the hosts, an out-of-control automaton, lurking beneath the monastery?

"I'll bet my executioner's sword that the hosts are no longer in the monstrance," said Kuisl, drawing on his cold pipe. "This sorcerer took them; that much is certain. Tomorrow, at the Festival of the Three Hosts, the prior and the other monks will hold up nothing more than a few dried-out wafers to show the pilgrims. No one will notice a thing."

"And it's easy to blame Nepomuk for the murders of Virgilius and Coelestin. He's probably already confessed on the rack. Damn." Magdalena crossed herself hastily when she realized she'd cursed in the little chapel. "Now that they've found Virgilius's corpse, not even the abbot is on our side anymore. What luck!"

Simon bit his lip. "And the Andechs chronicle has disappeared," he said softly. "Perhaps I could have found some reference to the passageways in it, but as it is . . ." He shook his head, then finally turned to his father-in-law.

"It looks like you'll have to accept your friend's fate," he said mournfully, "even if we find these passageways and learn why the sorcerer needs the hosts. Until we find the real culprit, we can't prove Nepomuk's innocence. And I can't think of anything else we can do to help in the few days before the execution," Simon added, with a shrug.

"I won't give up. Ever." The hangman rose ominously from the pew, his huge body casting a long shadow along the chapel walls in the flickering candlelight. "Damn it. I'm sure Nepomuk hasn't confessed yet. We've known each other a long time, and I can feel it in every bone in my body. You greenhorns couldn't understand that." He stomped toward the exit, then turned around one more time. "I'll tell you what I'm going to do now — I'm going to think it through. I always come up with something. You'll see a man who has been drawn and quartered restored to full health before you'll see me abandon a friend. Farewell."

Kuisl's footsteps could be heard as he strode down the path through the forest along the monastery wall, but soon Simon and Magdalena were engulfed again in the silence of the chapel.

After a while the medicus cleared his throat. "Magdalena . . ." he began hesitantly. "I know it hasn't been easy for you and the children recently . . ."

Magdalena turned away, occupied more with her scarf and her hair. "You can say that again, you stubborn goat," she growled. "I almost thought I didn't have a husband anymore. Matthias was closer to the children than their own father."

Simon felt a wave of sadness come over him. "Listen, I'm sorry," he said finally. "It probably just all got to be too much for me — these horrible murders, your sullen father's constant grumbling, then the count's deathly sick child . . ."

"Is the boy getting better?" Magdalena asked softly.

Simon shrugged. "I gave him the Jesuit's powder I found in the apothecary. Now everything is in God's hands." He sighed. "If he dies, I'm probably going to die, as well, and I don't even want to think about that." A wan smile came over his lips. "At least I have some clues as to where this damned plague is coming from."

"What do you mean?" Magdalena inquired curiously.

As Simon sensed that her anger was subsiding, a sense of relief washed over him. They could do almost anything if they stayed together.

"Well, I *think* I know how the plague started," he said finally. "It doesn't bring the dead back to life, but at least if we know, then we can do something. I hope very much that Schreevogl has learned some more about it."

In whispered words he told Magdalena of his suspicion. As he spoke, she moved closer and closer to him until finally she snuggled against his shoulder.

"And do you think that's how all these people got sick?" she asked hesitantly.

Simon nodded. "There's a lot of evidence suggesting it. I read about similar symptoms in the book by the Italian, Fracastoro."

"Then let's just hope we're on the culprit's trail soon." She drew closer, and Simon could feel how she was shivering. Though it was the middle of June already, nights were unusually cold, and he took his jacket from his shoulder, wrapping it around her.

"Let's go back to Graetz's house now and sleep," he said, helping her up from the pew. "Tomorrow is the Festival of the Three Hosts. I don't know why, but I'm certain the festival has something to do with all the strange things happening around here—as if the sorcerer has been waiting for just this day."

"Then it's definitely best for us to get a good sleep." Magdalena squeezed his hand, and together they left the chapel, stepping out into the cool night air.

"Tomorrow I'll have another talk with the abbot," she said, looking up into the starless sky. Clouds obscured the moon; somewhere a screech owl was hooting. "I think he likes me. Perhaps he'll help us look for the real culprit even if it's clear his brother is no longer alive." Suddenly she stopped.

"Do you hear that?" she asked her husband. "That tinkling sound?"

Simon listened briefly, then shook his head. "It's nothing—just the wind and the pounding of your anxious heart." Laughing, he pulled Magdalena away from the chapel toward the lights of the monastery. "Come now; you're seeing ghosts behind every tree."

Somewhere far below, the automaton followed its unending,

unchanging course. If Simon hadn't laughed so loudly, perhaps he would have heard the music, too.

The prior bent forward, clinging tightly to his horse's back, as he rode the lonely, dark country road back to Andechs.

A gust of wind howled through the few remaining hairs of the prior's tonsure, thunder rumbled across the lake, and a wolf howled in the distance, but Brother Jeremias was too engrossed in his own thoughts to hear any of this. The questioning of Brother Johannes hadn't gone as expected. The Weilheim executioner had pulled out three more fingernails, crushed his thumbs, set him on the so-called Spanish Donkey, and finally pulled him up in the air with a winch, his arms bent behind his back. Still, the stubborn monk hadn't confessed. He'd mumbled his prayers and carried on about someone named Jakob who would come to help him. Brother Jeremias wasn't sure whom he meant by that. Saint Jakob was the patron saint of pilgrims. Did this simpleton really think he'd get help from that saint?

In the evening, they finally suspended the questioning. The next day was, after all, the Andechs Festival of the Three Hosts, famous throughout all of the German Empire. Christian brotherly love simply forbade pulling fingernails off on such a day, so they'd have to put it off until the next day.

Cursing, the prior dug his heels into the sides of his horse, spurring it on. There was so much left to do. The abbot had told him the morning before that he would assign him, Jeremias, the duty of conducting the festival mass. The prior smiled wanly. Evidently the old man had already accepted the fact that someone else would be in charge soon. It was therefore all the more important for Brother Johannes to confess — not only because the Weilheim judge had made it very clear that a successful interrogation was required before the prior could be appointed abbot, but also because Jeremias needed a scapegoat. This miserable affair had to be put behind them as soon as possible. There had been much too much snooping around already. That bath-house doctor from Schongau was driving him crazy, and Brother Benedikt had told him also that the phony monk had been searching the rooms in the monastery. And that the map had now disappeared, too—the map, so long concealed, that had been in the monastery's possession for centuries. Had someone already gotten wind of them? The prior had a terrible suspicion.

As the howling of the wolves drew closer, Brother Jeremias finally realized he was in danger. This sounded like no less than the whole pack that had been striking terror into people's hearts in the forests around Andechs. Grimly the prior grasped the reins and slapped the horse on its hindquarters. "Giddyap, run, you old mare, if you care for your life."

Jeremias bent forward over the saddle to offer as little resistance to the wind as possible. When he was made abbot, he would send men out to deal with these beasts once and for all. And there were some things in the monastery that would change. For a long time, Jeremias had been dreaming of tearing down the old building and bringing in skilled tradesmen from Wessobrunn, and from the other side of the Alps, to build him a new monastery like the neighboring ones at Steingaden and Rottenbuch—bigger and more impressive. He wouldn't allow the Holy Mountain to look like a storm-ravaged ruin dating back to the Great War. But to do that, he needed money, lots of money. The prior smiled.

Soon money would be no problem; in a few years, his dream would be realized—as long as nothing unexpected happened and their little hiding place wasn't discovered . . .

If only for this reason, Johannes had to confess. For the good of the church. So that peace and order would reign again.

The wolves were so close now that Brother Jeremias could see their eyes shining in the dark. He could feel the horse tremble beneath him, its coat dripping with sweat. Soon the path would head up the steep slope of the Kien Valley and the horse would have to slow down. The wolves were gaining on them; the prior could hear the howling and panting closing in.

With a wild cry, he suddenly whirled around, pulled an ivory-handled flintlock pistol from under his robe, and fired. The shot flashed through the darkness, and there was a loud report followed by howling. The wolves pulled back.

Breathing heavily, the prior put the pistol back under his robe and concentrated on the path in front of him. It was now so dark between the trees he could scarcely see branches that had fallen across the path. He trembled. The Weilheim judge had given him the weapon and gunpowder just the day before, a personal gift meant to seal the bond between them. Never did the prior think he would have to use the pistol so soon, but now, feeling the cold iron of the barrel beneath his robe, he noticed he'd really enjoyed using it.

He had . . . enjoyed it. The cool feel, the recoil, the tortured cries of the wolves . . .

Reaching for the weapon again, he turned around, but the wolves had disappeared.

A shame.

After what seemed an eternity, the lights of the houses at the foot of the monastery appeared. The prior slapped his horse one more time, and finally, bathed in sweat, he reached the outer gate, which the gatekeeper opened with a respectful nod.

After Jeremias had dismounted, he reached down again to touch the cool weapon between his legs. He smiled and absentmindedly crossed himself.

Perhaps he would be able to use the pistol again sometime soon.

15

Shortly before the noon bells, pilgrims gathered on the square in front of the church, though many had been there since dawn. Amid the tightly packed crowd were brightly colored flags showing the coats of arms of many cities and villages. Simon stood wedged among a few pale, exhausted city people from Munich and a crowd of pilgrims from Augsburg who kept reciting the Lord's Prayer and Ave Maria endlessly in their Swabian dialect. By now, over a thousand pilgrims must have crowded into the little square, and below the monastery even more were pressing up the narrow road. The pilgrims kept looking up toward the bay window of the church where the Three Holy Hosts were to be displayed at noon.

Jakob Kuisl stood alongside Simon, yawning. As so often in the past, he'd spent half the night wandering through the forest, thinking, and hadn't returned to the knacker's house until the early morning hours. In his black coat, the hangman tried to seem as inconspicuous as possible amid all the worshippers—which, in view of his size, was a rather hopeless undertaking. Nevertheless, Simon had been unable to dissuade him from attending the "Weisung," or display of the hosts. Later they planned to attend mass, then join the crowd of pilgrims and monks circling the church with the monstrance. Both men still hoped something would happen that day to help them in their search.

Simon rubbed his reddened eyes sleepily. He'd been summoned by Count Wartenberg in the early morning hours. Though he was convinced he was heading for his own execution, his fears had proven groundless. The Jesuit's powder seemed to have worked. The boy's fever had broken, and he was clearly on the road to recovery. When, once or twice, the count gave Simon a sidelong glance, the medicus feared his search of the study the day before had in fact not escaped notice. And when the count patted him on the shoulder, Simon had to be careful not to wince.

A sudden pain brought the medicus back to the present—a pilgrim had accidentally stepped on his foot. Simon suppressed a curse and turned to whisper to his father-in-law. "What are you going to do if someone recognizes you now?" After Magdalena told him of their unhappy confrontation with the Semers, Simon reckoned that the hangman's cover would be blown at any moment. "You could at least have put on a less conspicuous coat. Didn't you say yourself that the monastery bailiffs are out looking for you?"

"Nonsense," Kuisl growled, pulling his collar a little tighter. "They really have better things to do today than to look for some no-account Franciscan monk. Just see for yourself what's going on here." With a sweep of his powerful arm, he indicated the crowds of pilgrims all around singing hymns and growing larger by the minute. The smell of incense was so strong it almost made him dizzy.

"We can only hope the sickness going around isn't as contagious as I feared," the medicus murmured, "or all of Bavaria will catch it."

Indeed, pilgrims seemed to have come from the farthest corners of the electorate and beyond. Simon could hear dialects

from Swabia, Franconia, the Palatinate, and Saxony, and even a
few foreign languages. The thought that the pilgrims might
carry the disease back with them to their cities and villages made
the medicus queasy. With everything going on, Simon still hadn't
had time to ask Jakob Schreevogl what he'd learned the day before in the tavern.

"Damn. I think it's a good thing Magdalena isn't here with
the children," Kuisl said. "The kids would be trampled to death
or get lost." Restlessly he shifted from one foot to the other, and
Simon couldn't repress a smirk. He knew from long experience
how Kuisl hated large crowds. He preferred the silent forest,
with just a few birds chirping in the trees.

"Magdalena wanted to talk with the abbot again," Simon replied. "Perhaps he knows something that will help us in our
search."

"Today? No chance." The hangman spat on the ground, just
missing a little old woman nearby who glared back at him. "Why
would the abbot have time for someone like Magdalena at the
Festival of the Three Hosts?"

"I had a long talk with her last night," replied Simon. "She
met Maurus Rambeck recently in the monastery garden, and he
told her the prior would have the honor of presenting the hosts
this time."

"An abbot who passes up the most important festival of the
year?" Kuisl screwed his eyes up suspiciously. "Isn't that a bit
strange?"

"The matter with his brother really upset Maurus Rambeck.
It's completely understandable if he doesn't feel like conducting
a mass." Simon shrugged. "In any case, Magdalena hopes to meet
with the abbot again today in the monastery garden. He seems to
be there quite a bit."

Kuisl sneered. "And he wants to have a nice chat there with
none other than my daughter? Dream on, son-in-law."

"Your daughter, as you know yourself, is very persistent,"

Simon said with a grin. "I have no doubt on Judgment Day she'll even get an audience with all the archangels, if only she leaves them alone after that."

A murmur suddenly went through the crowd. Simon looked up to see the prior on the balcony below the little bay window. Though the roof was still covered with scaffolding, the work on this important part of the monastery was already finished.

With a sublime mien, Brother Jeremias raised a silver object. The pilgrims on the square below fell to their knees, lowering their heads reverently. From the corner of his eye, Simon watched the old woman next to Kuisl turn up her eyes and tip to one side, where her elderly husband took her in his arms tenderly. Shouts and cries could be heard everywhere.

"The sacred hosts. Jesus, Mary, and Joseph, the sacred hosts. God bless us all."

Simon and the hangman fell to their knees, too. The medicus could feel a warm tickle pass through him at the sight of the praying masses. The hair on the back of his neck stood up, and his eyes teared up in the heavy clouds of incense. He had never been an especially devout person, especially in contrast to his wife, whose idea it was to go on this pilgrimage. But now, among the crowd of young and old who had traveled so far to view the three consecrated oblates in the silver bowl, a shiver ran through him, too. Even Kuisl seemed moved. His eyes narrowed to little slits as he stared up at the balcony where the prior had just spoken the benediction.

"Benedicat vos omnipotens Deus, Pater,
et Filius, et Spiritus Sanctus . . .
In the name of the Father, son, and holy spirit . . ."

The crowd bowed even deeper, prostrating itself on the ground; some cried, while others laughed hysterically or beat their backs and chests wildly.

Only Kuisl continued staring up in fascination at the balcony.

"Impressive, isn't it?" Simon whispered. "So much faith . . . one could almost—"

"Spare me the nonsense," the hangman interrupted. "I know only too well how the Catholics attacked the people of Magdeburg with spears and swords, their eyes gleaming and hands dripping with blood. If anyone wants to pray, he should do it in the silence of the church and not carry on like people at a county fair." He pointed up at the monstrance the prior was still holding up like a flaming sword. "I'll bet the real hosts aren't in there, in any case."

Simon grinned. "And I thought you had just had an epiphany."

"What God and I have to discuss we will do alone, privately. You can believe—"

Suddenly there came shouting nearby that sounded different from the other pious cries. Simon was startled to see two men approach through the crowd, flanked by four Andechs hunters armed with spears and crossbows.

The fat man in their midst was none other than the Schongau burgomaster, and at his side, his son grinned triumphantly at the sight of the hangman.

Quickening their pace, the two were only a few dozen yards away from Simon and Kuisl.

"Ha, Kuisl! I knew it," Karl Semer shouted so loudly that many of the pilgrims turned around to look. Even the prior up on the balcony paused briefly in his benediction.

"Rotten hangman," the burgomaster shouted. "Your head sticks out of the crowd like a flagpole, and this time you won't get away. Seize the heretics and the false monk."

The bailiffs pushed their way through the protesting crowd toward Simon and Kuisl.

"Well?" Simon hissed. "I warned you, but no, you wouldn't

listen. The two troublemakers must have seen you from up there," he continued, pointing at windows in a wing of the monastery where some of the better-off pilgrims were housed. "What in heaven's name shall we do now?"

"What else?" The hangman pushed aside some of the pilgrims in the crowd, forming a little passageway. "We'll run, and we'll see who's faster—the Schongau executioner or the fat old burgomaster and his bowlegged son. Remember, I was a hangman when that puffed-up little windbag was still shitting in his diapers."

Cursing softly, Simon ran after him as the Semers' wild cries rang out behind.

Magdalena strolled cheerfully with her children through a fragrant field of flowers behind the monastery. The sun had reached its zenith and shone down warmly on the fields, sending the last of the morning dew skyward in a soft haze.

She was humming quietly to herself. At breakfast in the knacker's house, Simon had been noticeably attentive. He'd stroked her hair from time to time, letting her know he still loved her. After all their years together, all the arguments and worries, he seemed to be the right man for her, after all.

Despite Simon's warning about possible infection, Magdalena had finally visited the clinic that morning with the children to help Jakob Schreevogl care for the patients. She intended to be there for the presentation of the hosts, but when she saw the huge crowd, she decided spontaneously not to meet Simon and her father until later, at the mass. First she wanted to see whether she'd assumed correctly that the Andechs abbot would indeed spend some time in the monastery garden that day, as well.

"Water! Lots of water! The man will squirt Mama until she's all wet," Peter shouted, holding her hand and hopping up and down excitedly as the stone wall at the forest edge finally appeared.

Grinning, Magdalena recalled how, just two days before, the mythical creature spat a cold stream of water in her face and how she, in a rather unladylike fashion, fell backward on her rump.

"Oh, but this time the man is going to make *you* all wet," she said, teasing the boy as she pressed the latch on the gate. Secretly she worried that the iron gate might be locked this time, and was pleased when it opened with a soft creak.

Just as on her last visit, Magdalena smelled the exotic fragrance of herbs and flowers. The children ran ahead, shouting, and had soon disappeared among the climbing vines, little walls, and flower beds. From time to time, Magdalena could hear them giggle, and a smile passed over her face. This really was an enchanted place, like one of those forest clearings where fairies and sprites danced—a world far removed from the horrors taking place outside the garden gates.

Expectantly, she approached the middle of the garden where the faun stood staring back at her between a few stone benches, just as it had the last time, with a fresh grin.

On one of the benches sat the Andechs abbot.

He appeared deep in thought, and for a moment, Magdalena thought he might have even fallen asleep. But then Rambeck, aroused by the shouts of the children, raised his head and turned toward Magdalena. When he recognized the hangman's daughter, he smiled wearily.

"Ah, the young lady from Schongau who's so interested in herbs," he said, gesturing for her to take a seat beside him. His eyes radiated a dark melancholy that Magdalena didn't remember from her last visit. "Do have a seat, and tell me which healing plant you would recommend for melancholy. Certainly you know some magic herbs."

"Well, valerian, St. John's wort, and melissa can help with melancholy," Magdalena replied, bowing slightly before sitting down beside the Andechs abbot. "But best of all, as far as I know, are friends and a good conversation."

Maurus Rambeck laughed bitterly. "I'm afraid I don't have any friends at the moment, so we'll have to settle for conversation."

"Your Excellency," Magdalena began hesitantly, "I'm terribly sorry about what happened to your brother. I—"

Rambeck waved her off. "It's perhaps better this way—it at least puts an end to the waiting and worrying. The last time we spoke I already suspected Markus was dead."

"Markus?" The hangman's daughter frowned.

"That used to be his name. When he became a monk, he took the name Virgilius, after the famous Salzburg bishop and scholar." The abbot crossed himself hastily. "We were both old men. Now, in God's unfathomable will, he has passed away before me, and I will follow him someday."

"You were very close, you and your brother?" Magdalena asked cautiously.

The abbot nodded. "Markus was the younger of us two, and as a child, I often had to take care of him. He always had crazy ideas." A narrow smile appeared on his lips. "That ne'er-do-well simply dropped out of the university in Salzburg and started drifting around . . . Rome, Madrid, Paris, Alexandria. He was even in the West Indies. I thought I'd never see him again, but then one day he showed up here at the monastery, and I did what I could for him as a simple monk. He seemed . . ." The abbot hesitated, "well, to have pulled himself together again. But I was wrong."

The abbot paused for a long time, staring into space. "Sometimes I think all this struggle for knowledge doesn't really make us happy," he said finally. "On the contrary, it moves us away from God, from our simple, childlike faith. Markus never had that faith, not even as a monk; he was always restless and at war with himself."

The sound of bells could be heard far off, mixing with the singing of the faithful.

"Do you hear that?" the abbot asked. "People singing and praying, and they are happy. They don't need automatons or music boxes, and they don't want to hear that the earth is a sphere revolving around the sun in an endless universe. All they want is to eat, drink, love, and believe." He sighed and stood up. "But perhaps we're living in a new era; as people struggle increasingly for knowledge, they move farther and farther from God."

Lost in thought, the abbot smoothed down his robe, stared for a while at the grinning faun, then turned from the statue, shaking his head.

"I'll tear down these idols," he said softly. "As well as the statues of the Greek gods in the grotto that spin around, playing that cheerful music. Things like this turn us away from the true faith. Perhaps that will bring an end to the curse."

Nodding once more to Magdalena, he moved toward the exit slowly, like an old man. "Farewell, hangman's daughter," he murmured as he opened the gate. "I'll join the others now in the square as a simple believer and pray. You should do the same."

He looked up one last time, tears shining in his eyes. "Don't stay too long in this garden," he warned her. "Believe me, something terribly evil is lurking here."

The gate creaked closed, and soon the abbot's footsteps died away. From far off, the sound of the singing pilgrims rose and fell in unison, in a monotonous hum.

Magdalena pulled herself together and looked at the faun. It grinned and appeared to be looking back at her, almost as if it wished to tell her a secret.

Forget the old fool. Stay here with me. I'm not evil, only a stranger. Just like you, hangman's daughter.

Despite the warmth of the June morning Magdalena began to shiver. The fragrant herbs and flowers, the little walls, the climbing peas and beans suddenly didn't seem as friendly and in- viting as just a few minutes ago. The nasturtium seemed to writhe about like a snake, and the lizards scurrying over the stones cast sly glances at her; indeed the entire garden suddenly seemed strange and threatening. And something else was troubling her.

She heard the humming of the bumblebees, the chirping of the sparrows in the bushes, the rustling treetops in the nearby valley, and the splashing of a distant fountain.

What she didn't hear were her children.

My God. Don't let it have happened.

"Peter? Paul?" she cried anxiously into the rampant greenery. "Where are you?"

There was no answer—only the peaceful hum of bumblebees.

"Children!" Her voice took on a shrill tone now. "Mother is looking for you. Say something!"

Still no answer. Magdalena picked up the hem of her skirt and ran along the little walls, past the climbing trellises that formed a labyrinth here. She slipped, skinning her knee, but felt no pain. Only one thought swirled through her head.

The children are gone. The sorcerer has the children.

She continued calling out. Several times she thought she caught sight of a shadow darting behind a bush or climbing trellis, but when she approached, there was nothing there but more gates and bushes—all the way to the walls at the end of the garden. She ran to the grotto where the statues of the ancient gods were standing in a circle, but the children weren't there, either.

Finally she hurried to the front gate and ran out into the flowery meadow. The gentle, soothing songs of the faithful could still be heard at the monastery, now mixed with the high, shrill voice of a single monk. The presentation of the three sacred hosts was nearing an end.

"Peter! Paul! My God, say something!"

Magdalena looked around frantically for the heads of the little children amid all the tall flowers and wild grain in the meadow; she cried and fumed as tears of desperation and fear ran down her cheeks.

But her children were nowhere to be found. Finally, after turning around to glance at the enchanted garden one last time, she ran back to the monastery. She had to find her husband and her father. Perhaps they could help. Perhaps the two children had simply run over to the church looking for their grandfather. Perhaps everything would be all right. Perhaps.

Deep down, Magdalena knew her children were lost.

The church square overflowed with people as Simon stumbled over a sack of mortar left behind by the workers; behind him he could still hear the angry shouts of Karl Semer.

"Stop! Stop those two! They are dishonorable liars and charlatans!"

The medicus held his breath. The many pilgrims around him seemed puzzled. A moment ago, they'd been engrossed in devotions to their god; now reality intruded in the form of two men struggling to make their way through the crowd. Simon could see the bearded head of the Schongau executioner bobbing up and down among all the pilgrims about twenty steps in front of him. The hangman simply shoved the astonished bystanders aside like stalks of corn in a field, and because of his size, he made faster progress than the slender medicus. Simon could hear people shouting at him in astonishment, but no one tried to stop the huge man.

"Kuisl, wait for me, for God's sake. Just wait!"

Simon cursed under his breath as he got up, pushing aside a heavy man blocking his way. Next to him, a woman shrieked as her rosary fell from her hand.

"Excuse me, I didn't mean to—" Simon started to apologize when a young man punched him in the face.

"You fresh little pansy, who do you think you are, pushing

my fiancée?" the broad-shouldered young fellow growled. He tried to grab the medicus by the collar, but Simon wriggled away, finding a narrow path through the crowd. He was horrified to see that his distance from his father-in-law had grown. By now, Kuisl had reached the edge of the square and was about to flee through the little gate down into the Kien Valley.

"Kuisl! Wait!"

Breathlessly Simon rushed past a group of pilgrims from Landshut, bumping into their praying leader and sending him sprawling and shouting to the ground with their banner. The richly embroidered flag, which weighed at least thirty pounds, fell on two old women, covering them like a huge bed sheet. Out of the corner of his eye, the medicus could see the two women wailing and struggling to get free from the heavy banner.

Finally Simon reached the wall separating the church square from the forest. Looking back, he was relieved to see that the two Semers were also having trouble making their way through the dense crowd. He was about to heave a big sigh of relief when he spied two of the Andechs hunters coming toward him. The bailiffs had decided not to try to make their way through the crowd in the square but to run around the edge, where there were fewer people. Now the men ran toward Simon, grinning. One already had his crossbow in hand, and the other lowered his spear menacingly.

"In the name of the monastery, stop at once," the guard with the crossbow ordered.

Simon paid him no heed but turned and ran toward the gate through which Kuisl had just disappeared. There was a soft whirring sound, then a bolt slammed into one of the trees directly above him.

And all this because, once more, my stubborn father-in-law won't listen to me, he thought grimly. *Now we're probably both being sought as false monks. The Weilheim executioner won't have to complain about a lack of work.*

Simon slipped through the open gate and turned right onto the path along the monastery wall. Soon he saw St. Elizabeth's Chapel in front of him and a path leading down a steep slope into the forested Kien Valley on the left. Turning around, he was horrified to see the hunters had followed him, joined by four others, and were approaching in long strides.

The path continued along the edge of the gorge; to his right were fields and farmland. Where should he go? If he ran out into the open country, the hunters would shoot him down like an animal, but the way into the forest was blocked by the gorge. If he continued running along this path, the bailiffs would likely catch up with him soon. Unlike the slender Schongau medicus, they looked strong and athletic; laughing and shouting, they seemed to enjoy the hunt.

"Look how he runs," shouted one, alarmingly close by. "Like a rabbit, a frightened little rabbit. Hey, stop, you coward! We'll catch you anyway!"

The path now took a turn, and for a brief moment, Simon was out of their line of sight. As he desperately looked around for a place to hide, a hand shot out from behind a rock at the edge of the gorge and grabbed him by the collar. Waving his arms around helplessly, he was dragged behind a huge boulder.

"Damn, just what the—" was all he could say before hairy fingers grabbed him by the throat, silencing him.

"Shut your mouth and stop flailing around. You dance around more than a billy goat."

Simon relaxed when he recognized the voice of his father-in-law. Crouching behind the rock, they were dangerously close to the gorge: only a few fingers' breadths stood between them and the steep gorge falling a hundred feet down to the river. Kuisl continued to hold Simon tight in his grip, but looking down at the steep slope at his feet, Simon raised no objection.

"Didn't I tell you to stay away from the presentation of the hosts?" Simon gasped as he tried to get a firmer footing on the narrow ledge. "Now we're both wanted, and I really don't know how I'm going to get out of this *mmmmmm.*"

The hangman held his hand in front of Simon's mouth as the steady pounding of the bailiffs' footsteps approached along the path. Simon could hear their breathing, and for a moment, he felt like an animal at bay. But then they passed, and soon Simon and Kuisl could hear only the twittering of the birds.

Kuisl had closed his eyes. Now he turned silently to Simon.

"There were only two of them," he whispered. "No doubt the other two are looking for us behind the other boulders along the path. They'll be here soon. We have no choice but to head down into the gorge."

"Down?" Simon looked at him in horror, pointing at the cliff that fell off steeply into the gorge. "Do you mean down there?"

"Of course, you idiot. Where else? It isn't as bad as it looks. There are little trees you can hold onto all the way down."

Simon couldn't help thinking of the window ledge outside the count's office where he'd been standing the day before. Now he would have to tempt fate again. He was a good swimmer, and narrow subterranean passageways were no problem for him, but he'd always had a great fear of heights. And this one was particularly high.

"This . . . this is at least sixty feet up," he objected, looking down suspiciously into the dark gorge, whose bottom was only vaguely visible among firs and beeches.

"Come now," the hangman said under his breath. "Shall I tell Magdalena you met your end as a yellow-bellied coward on the gallows?"

"All right then . . . very well."

Simon turned to face the cliff and slowly slipped into the gorge. Once he'd found a foothold in a crack in the rock, he reached out for a small fir growing on the slope, then took a step toward a ledge farther off.

"If you keep going like that, you won't reach the bottom

until St. Martin's Day," Kuisl said, watching him from up above. "Hurry up. After all, I have to come down behind you."

"I'd be glad to let you go first, my dear father-in-law," Simon hissed.

"So you'll fall down on top of me? Thanks very much, but I'd prefer to stand guard for the time being up here."

Simon took a deep breath, then started climbing down the cliff again. He was beginning to get the knack of it—in fact it wasn't as hard as he'd feared at first. There were plenty of ledges, bushes, and trees to hang onto.

When he got about halfway down the cliff, he took a break, wiped the sweat from his brow, and looked up, where he could just make out Kuisl as a dark little figure between the rocks.

Still gasping, Simon reached for another little fir when suddenly he heard a loud ominous crack.

The tree above him gave way.

Another crunching sound followed; then Simon slipped. The earth below him gave way as pebbles and small rocks fell noisily down into the gorge. Up above, he saw the angry face of his father-in-law.

"Watch out, you idiot," Kuisl hissed before realizing how desperate Simon's situation was. The medicus only had the small fir to hold onto, and bit by bit, the roots were pulling out of the cliff. The bottom was still fifty feet below.

"Wait, I'll—" Kuisl began.

But at that moment, the rest of the root ripped out and Simon fell downward, screaming and thrashing wildly.

The landing was less painful than he feared. The forest floor was covered with old leaves, and a gentle slope at the bottom ensured the landing wasn't too abrupt. He turned head over heels a few times, rolling like a little human avalanche into valley and finally coming to rest next to a large beech.

Carefully Simon checked his arms and legs. Nothing seemed

broken, though his jacket was ripped in several places and there were some scrapes and bruises on his face and back.

Just as he was about to call back that everything was all right, he heard cries at the top of the cliff. Squinting, he could see vague movements far up on the ledge where Kuisl had been standing. More shouting followed, along with what sounded like clanking weapons. Evidently there was fighting up there.

"Kuisl! My God, Kuisl!" he shouted. "What's happening?"

In the next moment, it occurred to him how stupid his question was. Evidently the hunters had found the hiding place and were engaged in a fight with the hangman. And Simon was standing down below, where he couldn't do a thing.

After waiting at the base of the cliff for a long time, not knowing what to do, he heard another shout, and moments later, a body came tumbling down, landing right in front of him. Simon cringed. Before him lay one of the Andechs hunters, his head twisted at a strange angle from the fall, a crossbar bolt embedded in his shoulder. He quivered briefly one more time, then his eyes took on the glassy sheen the medicus had seen so many times on dying men.

Wonderful, Simon thought. *Now we'll be sought not just as charlatans and false monks but as murderers, too. And all I wanted to do was to go on a pilgrimage.*

"Damn, Simon, run. Run to Magdalena." Kuisl's voice boomed down into the valley and tore him from his thoughts. Simon looked up once more, but the figures had disappeared. Presumably the fight had moved back onto the path. Some of the hunters could already be looking for some way to get down to him.

Simon hesitated. Should he really abandon his father-in-law? Of course, he wasn't much help to him down here either. Kuisl was right—they had to warn Magdalena. After this, the guards would surely be looking for her, as well. Were the Semers perhaps already on the way to the knacker's house? Magdalena had suggested they all meet there again after the mass.

One last time Simon looked at the battered, twisted body of the Andechs hunter at his feet. He stooped down, closed the corpse's eyes, and said a short prayer.

Then he ran through the dark valley past firs, beeches, and steep cliffs. He planned to make a wide circle around the monastery to reach Andechs and the knacker's house. Perhaps it wasn't too late.

Simon worried less about his father-in-law. This wasn't the hangman's first fight. No, Simon's greater worry was that, in this situation, the hangman might commit a few more mortal sins.

Like a bear held at bay by a pack of hounds, the hangman stood on the tall rock, kicking at the hunters to fend them off.

The bailiffs had arrived just moments after Simon slid down the slope. They must have been somewhere close by and heard Simon's shouts. Now three of them surrounded the boulder and lunged at Kuisl with spears; the fourth ran back toward the monastery, Kuisl assumed, for reinforcements.

As he continued kicking, he could see out of the corner of his eye one hunter put down his spear and reach for a little crossbow at his side. Kuisl cursed softly — up here on the rock, he was an easy target for a marksman; he'd be brought down like a wounded boar. Kuisl had no time to think, though. At the same moment, another bailiff was climbing up the rock with a dagger.

Cautiously the man got up onto the slippery, moss-covered boulder and tried to stab Kuisl in the side with his long-handled knife. The hangman dodged, grabbed the bailiff by the waist, and lifted him, screaming and thrashing about wildly, toward the archer: a living shield. At the same moment the bolt whizzed toward him, hitting the man in the shoulder. The hangman cringed as he felt a searing pain around his waist. He thought he'd been hit by a bolt, as well, but then he realized he'd only pulled a muscle and knew his back would be hurting for a day or so.

Damn, he thought. *I'm getting too old for this nonsense. It's time for the young folk to deal with these bailiffs, robbers, and insane murderers.*

Kuisl released his hold, and the injured guard fell to the ground, slipping toward the cliff only a few feet away. Frantically he tried to dig his fingers into the rock, but the porous stone began to crumble. For one last moment the hangman could see the horrified face of the injured man, and then he fell, shrieking, into the gorge.

By God, I swear I didn't want that to happen, Kuisl thought. *But, unfortunately, no one will believe that.*

He called down loudly to Simon to run as fast as possible to warn Magdalena, but he had no idea whether the medicus even heard him, or whether he was injured or even dead. Moments before, Simon had shouted something, but since then, Kuisl hadn't heard a word. But now Kuisl had no time to lose. The archer on the path below was cranking the handle, winding another bolt into his crossbow, which Kuisl figured would take just a few seconds.

Shouting, he hangman leapt from the boulder and charged the three men. They instinctively withdrew, and this short moment gave him enough time to dash off down the path toward the monastery. Another bolt whizzed past his head before he reached a bend in the path and was out of his pursuers' sight for a moment.

There was no one on the path in front of him, but close behind he could hear the shouts of the three bailiffs. It would be just a matter of seconds before they would appear behind him again.

As he looked around anxiously, he spotted a nearby alder tree, just on the other side of the wall, with a thick bough projecting over the path.

Kuisl sprinted, jumped up, and clutched the branch, which creaked menacingly under the sudden weight. Then he pulled himself up, clenching his teeth, balanced himself on the branch, and ran over the fifteen-foot wall of the monastery. Without looking down, he jumped over the side, his black coat fluttering like the wings of an enormous bat.

And not a moment too soon.

As Kuisl rolled down the embankment wet with dew, he could hear furious shouts from the other side of the wall. Had they seen him jump? He held his breath, but the men kept running, and soon silence returned.

Breathless, the hangman looked around. He was in the monastery cemetery. Graves with wooden and stone crosses dotted the broad grassy area toward the monastery, and in the center was a round well that he remembered from his previous visit — the same one from which they'd fished the burned corpse of the watchmaker two days before.

Crouching over, Kuisl ran along the graves while organ music sounded from the church. Evidently the service of thanksgiving to honor the sacred hosts was underway.

Once more the hangman observed the fresh graves of the two novitiates Coelestin and Vitalis; and not far from there, the mound marking the grave of the third older monk who had died more than a month ago. The footprints had disappeared, but the earth still looked as fresh as if it had been turned over just a few days before. Kuisl thought about the handkerchief with the initials that he and Simon had found next to the grave.

Was it possible a bloodthirsty golem had defiled the corpses here?

He shook his head as he continued past the well and a few more stone crosses, finally arriving at the oldest section of the cemetery. The crosses here were crooked, weathered, and partially covered with ivy. Faded Roman numerals indicated which people had passed away many years ago.

Kuisl remembered Simon's stories about the destruction of the castle. It wasn't until two hundred years later that the Augustinians had founded this monastery. Later still came the Benedictines. Some of the graves here must have dated from that period. Or were there perhaps other, even older, graves?

Again his gaze wandered over the cemetery's crosses and circular well. As so often happened when he was about to come upon some connection, some missing piece of a puzzle, something troubled him. But whatever it was, it was still beyond him, in his subconscious, and had not yet come to the surface.

The graves . . .

Sighing, he finally gave up. There were too many other things to clear up at present. He could only hope that Simon had managed to escape and warn Magdalena in time. Kuisl absolutely had to speak with the two of them. Perhaps by that time, whatever was rumbling around so deep in his subconscious would come to light. But how could he get in contact with his daughter and son-in-law? He couldn't go back to the knacker's house. Surely the two Semers would be lying in wait for him there with a few guards. So where should they meet?

Kuisl thought about this for a moment before breaking out into a wide grin. The perfect place had just come to mind.

If Magdalena was really his daughter, she'd know where to find him.

Nearly blind with anxiety, Magdalena ran across the field of flowers, along the gorge that led down into the Kien Valley.

Her children had disappeared. Perhaps this lunatic had already seized them. Some madman had already tried to kill her several times, so why wouldn't he go after her children, as well? Magdalena still hoped the two boys had just run off and were playing somewhere nearby. She worried most about the steep rock slope nearby and decided not to tell Simon and her father yet, but to first have a look along the edge of the gorge.

"Peter, Paul? Can you hear me? Are you here?" Her voice echoed across the deserted valley. Wherever she looked, she saw rocks and ragged boulders that looked like petrified trolls amid the stunted pines and spruce, like man-eating ogres whom God had punished long ago for their transgressions.

Did the trolls eat my children, as well?

She continued past some thorny bushes blocking her view into the valley. Looking down, she saw one of the Andechs hunters dressed in green several yards below, running toward the monastery along a path that skirted the edge of the gorge. She was about to call for help when the man encountered two other bailiffs. Gesturing wildly, the little man stopped to tell them something, but from where she stood above the trail, Magdalena could understand only a few words.

"The false monk . . . chasing . . . fleeing with this bathhouse doctor . . . need reinforcement . . ."

The false monk? The bathhouse doctor?

Magdalena could feel the hair on the back of her neck standing up. She knew only one false monk and one bathhouse doctor in Andechs: her father and Simon. What in God's name had happened? Evidently her father had been found out, and these men were chasing him and Simon.

She crouched down behind one of the hawthorn bushes and waited. She couldn't hear a word of their conversation, but all three of them went back in the direction the first bailiff had come from.

Magdalena's head was spinning. Did she dare to keep calling for the children? It was possible the hunters would hear her and recognize her. As they knew she was the wife of the Schongau bathhouse surgeon, it seemed a better idea to steer clear of the bailiffs.

Anxiously she gazed across the valley one last time. She saw rocks, trees, bushes, dead wood . . .

But no children.

Practically numb with despair, Magdalena bit her fist. The pain helped her to think clearly, at least for a while. She needed help, and the only two people who came to mind other than Simon and her father were Graetz and Matthias. Taking a deep breath, she turned and ran back across the meadows and fields until she arrived at the dirt path to Erling. Her heart was pounding in her chest and every breath was painful, but still she ran on and on. Finally, after what seemed like an eternity, she could see the knacker's house between two other farmhouses at the forest edge.

Suddenly she stopped.

Suppose the hunters had already been here? The two Semers at least knew that the Kuisl family was living here. Still, the ramshackle cabin at the forest edge seemed quiet—there was no one in the little vegetable garden; only a few goats were tethered there, grazing in the meadow next to the stable. Smoke rose from the chimney, suggesting someone was home.

Magdalena struggled to make up her mind, then finally ran toward the house. She had no other choice. She would never find her children by herself. Hesitantly she knocked on the door.

"Graetz, are you there?" she asked softly.

She was about to knock a second time when the door swung open and the knacker appeared, visibly shaken.

"Thank God, Magdalena," he cried with relief. "You're finally back. Hurry, come in." Graetz looked around suspiciously in every direction, then pulled the hangman's daughter into the bedroom and barricaded the door.

Magdalena was horrified to see the chaos in the little room. The table, bench, and chairs were knocked over; the large heavy chest in the corner had been broken into; and torn clothes and broken dishes lay strewn all over the room.

"Those fat moneybags from Schongau were just here with two bailiffs," Graetz said right off, pointing at the destruction all around. "They left no stone unturned here. No stone!"

Magdalena could see the veins in Graetz's brow turn red and swell up, and his whole body started to tremble. "Asked me where your father and Simon were. But I didn't tell them a thing. I told them to first prove that Kuisl had stayed here." His face turned red with rage.

He picked a chair up from the floor and sat down, exhausted. "They can do this to us poor people," he wailed. "They took off with all my wife's dowry, God rest her soul. She'd turn over in her grave if she knew that."

"Graetz," Magdalena said, still struggling for breath from her long run. "I need your help. The . . . the children are gone."

"The children?" The knacker looked at her, puzzled. "What do you mean, they're gone?"

Magdalena had to struggle to get ahold of herself as tears ran down her sweat-stained cheeks. "I . . . I was over in the monastery garden with them," she blurted out. "They were playing in the garden, and then suddenly they were gone. I think they've fallen in the gorge, perhaps, or . . . or that this madman has abducted them."

"Do you mean that sorcerer? Why would he do anything like that?"

In short, broken words, Magdalena told the knacker about the attacks on her and about what she feared.

"I think the sorcerer doesn't like our snooping around here," she said excitedly. "He tried to kill me a few times already, and now he's probably taken my children."

Just as Graetz was about to reply, someone pounded on the door again. The knacker cringed.

"Good Lord, I hope it isn't those scoundrels again," he cursed. "Be careful. If they're still looking for your father, be prepared for a few unpleasant questions. It would be best for now if the bailiffs don't even see you."

He motioned to Magdalena to slip into the next room, but the hangman's daughter just shook her head.

"If it's really them, let it be," she said softly but with determination. "Just let them in. They won't keep me from looking for my children."

Shrugging, Graetz went to the door and opened it a crack. When he saw who was standing there, he breathed a big sigh of relief.

"Ah, it's just you, Matthias. Come in. We have —"

Suddenly he stopped short. Looking down, he saw that Matthias was holding a folded note in his hand. The assistant's face was expressionless; only his lips trembled slightly.

"What's wrong, Matthias?" Magdalena asked, moving closer. A wave of apprehension came over her. "What's that in your hand?"

"*Mmmm . . . aaa . . . eena.*"

She looked at him, confused.

"What are you saying?" she asked.

"*Mmmm . . . aaa . . . eena . . . Mmmm . . . aaa . . . eena,*" he kept saying in a monotone, then walked up to her hesitantly and handed her the note. Only now did Magdalena understand he was trying to pronounce her name.

"The . . . the letter is for me?" she whispered, her heart beating wildly.

The mute assistant nodded and handed her the letter with a slight bow.

Opening the letter, she found only a few scribbled words, but they were enough to knock the wind out of her. She fell back onto the chair, as white as a ghost, staring down at the note.

It was a short, evil poem.

Sleep, baby, sleep, your mother likes to peep.
She snoops and noses far and near;
   that's not so good for baby dear.
Sleep, baby, sleep.
Bye, baby, bye, your grandpa likes to pry.

If he won't let this habit be, the sorcerer will strangle me.
Bye, baby, bye.

"What's wrong, Magdalena?" Graetz stepped closer, looked over her shoulder, and made out the few words while the hangman's daughter sat there, petrified.

"My God," Graetz gasped finally. "You were right. This madman has indeed abducted the boys." Angrily he turned to his assistant. "Where did you get this letter?" he shouted. "Tell me right now who gave it to you."

Matthias opened his mouth, struggling to be understood. *"Aaa-annn,"* he said.

"A man?" Magdalena asked hopefully. "What kind of a man, Matthias?"

"Aaaarrrzzer Aaannn. Aaaaarrrrzzzer Aaaann."

"Confound it! Speak clearly!" Graetz said, furious. "Who was it?"

"I'm afraid we're not going to get very far like this," said Magdalena, swallowing hard. She was so concerned about her children that she could hardly think straight. Once more she studied the black lines. The letters were smudged; a few drops of ink had run down the paper leaving spots that reminded her of blood.

Sleep, baby, sleep, your mother likes to peep.

Suddenly Magdalena remembered that, even though Matthias couldn't speak, he could write. Frantically she looked for a quill pen and an inkpot among the clutter on the floor. When she finally found them both undamaged in a corner of the room, she turned the paper over and handed it to Matthias with the writing implements.

"Write on the back who gave you the letter," she asked him.

Matthias nodded and smiled wanly; then he scribbled a few lines on the stained note and handed it back to Magdalena.

Quickly she scanned the words he had written in an elegant, flowing script.

A man wearing a black robe and a hood gave me the letter at the entrance to the monastery. He told me to bring it to the daughter of the hangman from Schongau, but I don't know who the man was.

The tall, thickset man looked back at Magdalena expectantly, like a little dog looking for some praise.

"Thank you, Matthias," Magdalena said finally as she folded the note and tucked it in her skirt pocket.

"Can it have been a monk?" she asked. "After all, he wore a black robe. Tell me, was it one of the Benedictines?"

The assistant shrugged and grinned sheepishly. *"Ahnaa reallli..."*

"You don't know, you idiot?" Graetz chimed in impatiently. "But the voice—did you recognize the voice?"

Matthias seemed to be struggling inside, rocking his head of red hair back and forth. But he didn't say another word.

"Good God," Graetz fumed, grabbing his assistant, who was almost two heads taller than he, by the collar. "If you don't open your mouth right away—"

"Let him be," Magdalena interrupted. "Clearly he doesn't know, and you can't beat it out of him. We'll just have to think of something else." Her lips tightened and a renewed determination flashed in her eyes. This so-called sorcerer had abducted her children to silence her and her father. Unconsciously she clenched her hands into tight little fists. At least now the uncertainty had passed. She knew what had happened to the two children—and she could act.

"First I have to find my father and Simon," she finally said in a near whisper. "Father will know what to do; he has always found a way out."

"But what if the bailiffs have already picked him up?" said Graetz.

"Father?" Magdalena smiled wearily. "It would take more than a few dumb Andechs hunters. I'll bet anything that he and Simon have escaped. The only question is where they are now." She stopped for a moment to think. "People are searching for them all over Andechs, and they wouldn't come here to Erling. So there has to be a place outside the village that both my father and I know . . ." Suddenly her face brightened. "Of course. It's possible," she cried out. "In any case, it's the only place I can think of where we can all get together for a quiet chat and certainly no one will disturb us. In Schongau, I sometimes meet him there, too."

She turned to the puzzled knacker and asked him the way.

Graetz nodded hesitantly. "If I know your father, you could be right. He was always a bit . . ." He grinned in embarrassment. "Well, strange."

He quickly explained how to get there, then turned to his assistant, who was standing off to one side looking sad and depressed, and patted him on the shoulder.

"Don't take it the wrong way, Matthias," he said, trying to cheer him up. "I didn't want to offend you. You'll see, the children will show up again, and then you can play with them. Everything will turn out all right."

A smile spread over Matthias's face. He wiped his huge hands on his knacker's apron, then bowing clumsily several times, backed out the door.

"A poor fellow," Graetz sighed. "What he might have amounted to if those mercenaries hadn't cut out his tongue." Then he turned back to Magdalena. "I'm going now to visit a few people nearby whom we can trust," he said in a conspiratorial tone. "The gravedigger, the shepherd, the barber down in Herrsching, the coal-burner down at Ramsee . . . all of them dishonorable." He laughed briefly. "There are more of us than most people know, and together we'll find your family."

Magdalena squeezed his hand. "Thank you, Graetz. I'll always be grateful to you for this." Then a fierce look of determination came into her eyes. "And now I'm going to look for my father," she said softly but firmly. "Believe me, that damned sorcerer will come to regret ever picking a fight with the Kuisls."

Magdalena headed toward Machtlfing, a small village about two miles away. She avoided the main road and stayed in the shadows of the blackberry and hawthorn bushes as she hurried along, her skirt blowing in the wind. It was early afternoon, and the sun was almost uncomfortably hot. Towering thunderheads appeared in the west; a storm was brewing.

Graetz had described the hill to her exactly. It lay partially hidden in the forest behind the so-called *Bäckerbichl,* or Baker's Hill, but even though the knacker had given her only a rough idea of where it was, she couldn't have missed it. On the crest of the hill surrounded by low-lying bushes were the decaying remains of a wooden frame. At one time three stone pillars had stood here in a triangle connected by wooden beams. One of the beams had fallen to the ground years ago and was rotting away now, and a second leaned precariously against a weathered column. Nevertheless it was easy to see what this structure had been many years ago.

Magdalena was standing in front of the Erling gallows hill.

The path was overgrown with weeds and bushes, and she struggled to make her way to the top. Graetz had told her that this had been an execution site since time immemorial, though nowadays hangings were done in the nearest large town, Weilheim, where the district judge resided. Only during the Great War were deserting mercenaries and rebellious farmers occasionally still strung up here. Now, Magdalena couldn't keep thinking of the father of mute Matthias, who had been hoisted into the air, writhing and twitching in view of his son. "Riding the wind" is what people called such a degrading scene. Sometimes death took up to a quarter hour.

Magdalena hoped fervently she'd find her father and Simon up here. Both of them knew about the Erling gallows hill, as Graetz had often told them about it. Only a short distance from the highway, it served as a warning to travelers. In recent times, though, bushes and small trees had started growing on the hill. Since the rotting corpses of thieves and highwaymen often dangled from the scaffolding for months, the stench, especially in the summer, was so strong that no one wanted to live there; the nearest house stood hundreds of yards away. The gallows hill, moreover, had always been thought to be cursed, so people avoided it—making it a perfect place, therefore, for a secret meeting. Magdalena prayed her father had thought the same way.

Full of anticipation, the hangman's daughter struggled the last few yards to the crest of the hill. A few hungry crows sat on the rotted beams, looking at her distrustfully. Finally, they took flight and, cawing loudly, headed toward the Kien Valley. Thorny blackberry bushes had grown over the rotted wood, bees hummed, a rabbit hopped off into the underbrush, and suddenly Magdalena understood why her father sought out such places to meditate.

The hectic hubbub of human activity suddenly came to a halt here. The ghostly silence created space for dreaming, meditating, and deep thought.

She looked around but couldn't see anything unusual. A wagon rumbled along the back road a few hundred paces to her left, and in the distance she could see the monastery in the milky blue sky of early afternoon. Had she been mistaken?

Suddenly she heard a rustling behind her. She turned around

to see the Schongau hangman standing alongside a hawthorn bush, casually brushing thistles off his coat. He had appeared like a ghost out of nowhere.

"Father," she cried with relief. "I knew I'd find you here."

"Smart girl." Kuisl grinned. "You're my daughter, after all. We have to talk. I . . ." Seeing fear in her eyes, he stopped short.

"What happened?" he asked, approaching her warily.

"Peter and Paul . . . They've disappeared." She had trouble not screaming. "The sorcerer has abducted them."

With trembling hands, she pulled the note from her skirt pocket and handed it to her father. When Kuisl read it, his hand closed so tightly around the paper it seemed he was trying to wring blood from of it. His face was ashen, and his voice soft and flat.

"He'll regret that," he whispered. "By God, this scoundrel will regret it. No one abducts the grandchildren of the Schongau hangman unpunished."

Magdalena sighed and struggled to get ahold of herself. "Wild threats don't get us anywhere either," she said with determination. "First we have to put our heads together and decide where the children might be. I just can't understand how they could disappear so suddenly. One moment they were in the garden, and then in the next . . ." Suddenly she looked around. "And where is Simon? And what have the two of you been up to? Half of Andechs seems to be looking for you two now."

"Unfortunately we lost sight of each other," the hangman grumbled, looking a bit embarrassed. "Those damned Semers recognized me in the church square."

He told her about the presentation of the hosts, their flight afterward, and the fight at the edge of the gorge.

"But Simon is alive," he concluded, trying to calm her fears. "I heard him calling from down in the gorge." But then he frowned. "Strange that he didn't show up again later."

"Perhaps the bailiffs picked him up," Magdalena said, shaking her head. "In any case, we've got to think of something. The sorcerer made us an offer if we stop looking for him . . ."

"And do you trust him?" Kuisl spat contemptuously on the ground. "After everything this madman has done? He won't help us at all. He'll never let the children go. Not even if we promise to return to Schongau at once. He's taken his hostages, and when he has what we wants, he'll wring their necks like two young rabbits and laugh."

"You . . . you mustn't say that," Magdalena was close to tears again. "If it's true, then my boys are lost."

The hangman stared into space, cracking his knuckles. Magdalena knew this habit all too well, one of his usual rituals before an execution.

Or when he was thinking hard.

"If the children are still alive, they'll be crying and whining," he finally said softly. "He'll have to take them someplace where no one will hear them. I'm sure that scoundrel is somewhere in those passageways beneath the monastery—a perfect hiding place if you have two screaming youngsters. And if he doesn't come to us on his own and hand them over, then we'll have to go to him." Once again he cracked his knuckles. "We've got to smoke him out like a badger in its hole, or send the dogs in after him. I'll chase this sorcerer until his guts hang out his mouth."

"Even if the children are somewhere down there," Magdalena replied, running her hand through her black hair despairingly, "you forget we still don't know where the entrance to these passageways is. It seems it was shown on Count Wartenberg's map, and it's a shame my husband didn't bring it with him; all he can remember are those strange Latin words. *'Hic est porta ad loca inferna'* . . . whatever that means. It's enough to drive you crazy."

"What did you just say?" The hangman stared at Magdalena now as if she'd turned into some strange creature of the forest.

"What do you mean?" she asked, puzzled. "It's enough to drive you crazy, because—"

"No, no. The Latin phrase before that."

"*'Hic est porta ad loca inferna.'* Why? That's the sentence Simon told us about."

"No, that's not right." The hangman broke out in a smile like that of a young boy who'd pulled off a prank. "You misquoted. Simon told us the words on the map were *'Hic est porta ad loca infera.'* That would mean, *'This is the entrance to the subterranean places.'* But you just spoke of the *'loca inferna.'* It's possible your scatterbrained husband misread it—after all, the writing was a bit hard to decipher. Why couldn't your sentence be correct?"

A slight premonition came over her. "And . . . what would my sentence mean?" she asked softly.

The hangman picked at his teeth for a while. He loved to torture people by drawing out his answers. He'd been doing it to Magdalena since she was a child.

"Magdalena, Magdalena," he grumbled finally. "I thought I had taught you a little Latin. *'Hic est porta ad loca inferna'* means *Here is the gateway to hell.*" Once more he passed his hand through his scraggly beard, before continuing smugly. "And as the good Lord will have it, I think I know where this gate to hell is." He smiled. "What do you say, hangman's daughter? Are you ready to descend into the underworld with me?"

For what felt like the tenth time, Simon slipped on wet leaves, skidding down one of the innumerable slopes in the Kien Valley.

He felt like a bug in a sandpit. Wherever he looked, huge boulders towered up behind the beeches and firs, and between them thickets of thorny shrubs barred the way. Slopes that at first appeared gentle suddenly turned into deep morasses. Simon's jacket as well as his expensive petticoat breeches from Augsburg were torn in several places, and his boots oozed with mud. No

doubt they were ruined, just like the rest of his expensive clothing. But that was the least of his problems.

The medicus was lost.

He'd intended to go just a bit farther down the valley and
then make a wide circle back to the knacker's house in Erling,
but again and again, his way was blocked by boulders, steep
slopes, and swampland, and he was forced to make detour after
detour. Now he had completely lost his bearings in the dark
forest.

Simon looked around in despair. Somewhere high above, he
could hear the faint sound of bells ringing; that had to be the
monastery, but the direct path up the slope was too steep. Moreover, Simon was trying to avoid running into the guards again.
On his left, Kien Brook plunged into a natural basin and, from
there, farther down into the valley. On the right, cliffs rose up,
and the longer Simon looked at them, the more they seemed to
be man-made. The walls were too smooth; some of the rocks
near the top resembled battlements, staircases, and walkways.
The whole formation reminded him of a huge, ancient castle, or
perhaps the remains of a castle that had long fallen to ruin.

The castle of the Andechs-Meranier?

Simon shook his head. In the gloomy light of the forest, his
imagination was already playing tricks on him. Some of the
boulders had seemed like petrified gnomes, towers, or dragons.
Exhausted, he passed his hand over his dirty brow, cursed, then
moved on.

Why did he have to get lost? By now the bailiffs had surely
reached the knacker's house and found Magdalena. What would
they do with the daughter of a man wanted for burglary and possibly murder? Surely the men had more in mind than to politely
ask questions and let her go. The two Semers, in any case, were
itching for revenge after the knacker and the hangman's daughter had shown them the door during their recent visit.

Simon hurried along, turning southward where he suspected Erling had to be. Unfortunately progress along the path in this direction was especially difficult, and he often had to fight his way through knee-deep piles of leaves, bushes, and dead wood. It almost seemed the thorny branches of the thistles and blackberry bushes were reaching out to grab him and hold him back.

Simon cursed and was trying to tear himself once more from thorns when he looked up and suddenly saw an especially impressive boulder towering above him. The huge stone was at least forty feet high with a gnarled linden tree growing on top. Not far from it was a circle of stones looking almost like the remains of a huge castle stronghold. There was a faint odor of smoke in the air.

The medicus held his breath. Fire meant that people were nearby—perhaps the Andechs hunters or highwaymen looking for an easy target to rob here near the monastery. In any case, Simon hoped to avoid them.

He listened intently but couldn't hear anything suspicious, just the twittering of the birds and the constant rustling of the treetops.

He was about to move on when he suddenly heard a strange noise that sounded neither human nor animal in origin.

It was a sad melody coming from a music box, a long-forgotten love song echoing strangely from the cliffs in the middle of the forest.

Astonished, the medicus stopped in place. This was the same sound he'd first heard a week ago in the watchmaker's house, the same song Magdalena had told him about. She'd heard it while walking along the path in the forest below the monastery just before she'd been shot at. It was the sound of the automaton.

Simon stood still for a while before daring to move. The soft sound seemed to coming from behind the column of rock. With bated breath, he crept along the wall until he finally came to an entrance to a cave. In front of the cave were the smoking remains of a fire, a dirty wooden bowl, and a clay cup, but nothing more. Simon listened.

The sound clearly came from inside the cave.

His heart began to race. Was it possible? Had he in fact found the entrance to the subterranean passageways beneath the castle? And what should he do now? He was on the way to warn Magdalena, but this was presumably the hiding place they'd been seeking for so long: the sorcerer's hiding place.

The hiding place where Brother Laurentius was turned into a piece of charred flesh.

Simon hesitated. He was alone; if anything happened to him, there would be no one to help. Certainly it would be better to go to Erling first and look for his father-in-law. They could come back here together and . . .

And if I can't find the hiding place again?

Simon stared ahead, weighing the options. The fire had burned down and seemed not to have been stoked for several hours. The person guarding the cave must have left some time ago. This would probably be a good time to at least have a quick look.

Carefully Simon pulled a half-burned branch from the fire to light his way into the cave. The entrance wasn't large, just a yard or so wide, and empty except for a few piles of dirty, smelly straw. He stooped down and stepped inside for a closer look.

He groped his way through a corridor, damp and blackened by smoke, looking for anything suspicious. In one corner lay a crumpled and tattered woolen blanket, and on his right, at eye level, there was a small, faded picture of the Virgin Mary. Finally, on one of the piles of straw, Simon found a crucifix made of two twigs tied together and a chain with shimmering pearls, which seemed strangely out of place in this squalid setting. Was this cave a sort of chapel? Who lived here? In the darkness before him, he heard the sad melody of the music box again, much closer now than just a few minutes ago.

As he held his makeshift torch out in front of him, he could make out the entrance to a tunnel through the rock in the back wall.

That's where the melody was coming from.

With a pounding heart, he entered the narrow passageway. There was no straw underfoot now, just hard-packed soil, and the ceiling was so low he had to stoop. Soon he came to a place where worn steps led downward. Simon decided to go only a few more yards and then turn around and look for Kuisl. His assumption had been correct—this was in fact the entrance to the ancient castle catacombs.

He couldn't resist a smile. The hangman had cursed him for falling asleep at the bedside of the dying Laurentius, but now he could show his father-in-law that he was useful after all. He would guide him down here, and together they would—

It took Simon a moment to realize what had interrupted his stream of thought.

The music had stopped.

Now, he heard shuffling footsteps approaching from down below.

"Is . . . someone there?" he called hesitantly into the dark passageway.

For a while there was only silence, then a hoarse laugh. Simon squinted, trying to make out something. He realized too late that, even though he was blinded by the light of his torch and couldn't see more than about fifteen feet in front of him, he himself was quite visible.

At that moment, there was a whirring sound and something bored into his neck. Horrified, the medicus dropped the torch, but before he could pick it up again, he felt the ground give way beneath him like quicksand. The corridor expanded into some enormous space, and his legs collapsed beneath him like thin, rotted twigs.

He didn't even feel the back of his head hit the hard ground, though from the corner of his eye, he could see two mud-spattered leather boots walking toward him. The stranger kicked him hard in the head, opening a large wound over his eyebrow. The world slowly closed in around him as blood ran down over his eyes like a red curtain.

Behind that curtain was nothing but darkness.

The sorcerer bent over his victim and tested the artery in his neck. Hearing the calm heartbeat, he stood up, astonished at how differently people reacted to poison. Judging from the medicus's small stature, he'd expected the man to die at once, but this sliver of a man from Schongau had an astonishing constitution. The stranger knew now he'd need at least twice this dose for the hangman.

But perhaps that wouldn't even be necessary.

The sorcerer smiled. The medicus falling into his trap hadn't been part of his plan, but he was glad that from now on he would have to deal only with the executioner and his daughter. And he'd already made sure those two wouldn't get in his way any longer. His helper had set the plan in motion.

Stepping out in front of the cave, he looked up at the heavens. On the western horizon, clouds towered up, forming gigantic castles in the sky. Then there was a vibrant whirring sound in the air that he knew only too well.

The right moment was at hand; now his waiting would finally be over.

Humming softly, he returned to the cave and cast a curious glance at the motionless figure of the medicus staring up at him with glassy eyes.

Did he recognize him?

Learned men had told him long ago that the poison he used made the body rigid, hardened it without interrupting the thought processes. Though the medicus's face was just a frozen grimace, the victim was screaming and raging inside.

Still humming to himself, the sorcerer tied a rope around the medicus's feet and pulled him behind him down the dark corridor like a piece of dead meat.

Surely the children would be happy to see their father, even though in his present condition he was nothing but a stuffed doll.

An automaton, just like the other.

The sorcerer chuckled. Perhaps he would try out a little experiment on the bathhouse doctor.

16

DON'T YOU THINK IT'S HIGH TIME TO TELL ME where we're going?" Magdalena gasped as she ran behind her father through the forested Kien Valley. They had been underway now for more than an hour, but Jakob Kuisl still hadn't told her where they were headed. They had first made a wide circle around the monastery, slid down a slope covered with wet leaves, then continued running through the forest. Fear for her children had released a strength in Magdalena that allowed her to run like a young deer through the underbrush, without stopping. Her skirt was tattered, branches had scratched her face, and for these reasons, she was all the angrier about not knowing where they were headed.

"Be patient just a bit longer," the hangman grumbled without slowing his pace. He'd left his black coat back at the knacker's cabin, but his shirt was bathed in sweat. "It can't be much farther."

With his huge hands, he shoved a dead tree trunk aside like a blade of grass, then jumped over a small brook. When Magdalena tried to follow, she sank knee-deep in the mud.

"You didn't have to come along," he told her impatiently, reaching out to help her. "I have no idea what a helpless woman—"

"This helpless woman just happens to be the mother of two abducted children," she growled. "So stop this nonsense and tell me where we're going."

Kuisl smiled wanly, then with a single powerful movement, pulled her out of the mud and hurried on in silence.

Magdalena followed, grumbling. Her father could be so stubborn! Ever since he'd made that curious remark on gallows hill about the "underworld," they had hardly exchanged a dozen words. First they ran to the knacker's house, but Simon wasn't there, and Graetz didn't know what had become of the medicus. After a long conversation with the knacker in the next room, Kuisl finally decided to go looking for the children without Simon.

At first he wanted to go alone, but Magdalena quickly made clear she'd never forsake her children, so the father and daughter ran through the forest together looking for the madman who had kidnapped the boys. Magdalena was also worried about Simon. Was he lying injured in the forest somewhere? Had the guards picked him up and taken him to Weilheim to be tortured into telling them where the wanted hangman of Schongau was hiding out?

Several times a dreadful thought passed through her mind, as painful as a poison arrow boring slowly but inexorably into her subconscious: *Suppose the children are no longer alive? Suppose the sorcerer has already killed them?*

As she choked up, she ran faster and faster, trying to drive away her terrible premonition.

Suddenly her father stopped, put his finger to his lips, and pointed to a tall rock standing in the trees a stone's throw away.

"We're here," he whispered. "This is the rock I've been looking for. I asked Graetz about it. Since ancient time, the natives have referred to it as Devil's Rock."

Magdalena turned and looked at him, confused. "Devil's Rock? But . . ."

"Porta ad loca inferna," he whispered. "The door to hell. Don't you understand? This is the place where Satan enters and leaves. It wasn't the name that made me think of it, but something else." Kuisl lowered his voice even more and Magdalena almost thought she detected a trace of fear in him. "I was here once," the hangman said.

"Here?" Magdalena looked around. Suddenly the area looked strangely familiar—the trees, the rocks, and farther off, a few large boulders arranged in a circle. She knew this place as well. But in her fear, she'd paid no attention to it.

The remains of a ring of boulders . . .

"Of course," she exclaimed. "The ring of boulders where the children were playing a few days ago. I saw the tall boulder from there."

Kuisl seemed not to have heard her. He looked up toward the top of the steep rock, lost in thought. "I was here with the children when we came to Andechs," he continued softly. "I took a shortcut, and suddenly we were standing in front of this huge rock. There was a cave with an old woman sitting in front, spouting all sorts of gibberish . . ."

Magdalena felt her mouth go dry. "The hermit woman," she exclaimed. "I met her, too, as did Matthias and the children. She was crazy, talking some nonsense about how my children were in danger, and saying this was . . ." Her voice trailed off as she remembered the old woman's words.

I'm guarding the entrance to hell . . .

"My God," she gasped. "The door to the underworld. She talked about it and even warned the children to stay away. But I didn't take her seriously."

The hangman paused for a moment, then nodded. "She told me about the entrance to hell, as well. Like you, I dismissed it as the babbling of an old fool and finally forgot it—until today, up on gallows hill."

He laughed briefly, then picked up the bundle he'd brought

along and pulled out a hunting knife more than a foot long. With a practiced eye, he looked around in the underbrush for a suitable branch and began to carve one into a club.

"No doubt the locals knew about this entrance long ago," he ruminated as he shaved the wood. "Later, long after the destruction of the castle, its actual purpose was forgotten and all that remained were the names — Devil's Rock, Door to Hell, names that can now be found only on faded maps . . ."

He spat angrily onto the ground, weighing the finished cudgel in his hands. "That's the way people are: what they don't understand is the work of the devil."

Once more his gaze wandered up to the tip of the strange rock. Suddenly he sniffed, and his huge nostrils flared. "Can you smell that?" he asked softly. "There's a fire burning somewhere. Let's be careful — who knows whether the old woman is making her porridge right now and will scream so loud that half the Kien Valley will know we're here."

Magdalena took one last deep breath, then darted toward the rock through the dry underbrush and across a small open area. Finally, she and her father moved cautiously along the cold rock face until they could see the entrance.

No one was in sight. A thin column of smoke rose over a cold fire, but not a sound came from inside the cave.

Magdalena relaxed and stepped into the clearing in front of the rock. "The coast is clear," she said, relieved. "So now let's —"

"Woe to you! Woe!"

The shrill voice came from the bushes on the left. Now the haggard figure of an old woman struggled to her feet in the underbrush — the same old woman Magdalena had met just a few days earlier not far from here. Her tattered dress fluttered like the wings of a moth, and her hands reached threateningly to heaven.

"Satan has risen," the old woman screeched wildly. "He's left the underworld, and now along with Beelzebub is searching for innocent children whose guts he can suck out. Repent, by God, repent!"

For a few moments Magdalena stood there petrified; then she rushed up to the old woman and shook her by the shoulders.

"You're talking about children," she shouted. "My children? Tell me, has that madman dragged my children into this cave? Say something!"

The blind old woman looked back at her with milky, empty eyes. "Your children are both good and evil," she mumbled. "Heaven and hell, Jehovah and Lucifer. Beware, hangman's daughter."

"Who . . . Who told you who I am?" Astonished, she took her hands off the old woman's shoulders and stepped back a pace. Was the woman really a prophet? People said hermits got their inspiration from God. But what did these words have to do with her children?

Good and evil . . . Your children are both . . .

"Speak, you foolish old woman. Who lives here? What do you know about the children?" The hangman had approached now and looked around cautiously to see whether the old woman's shouts had attracted any attention.

The old woman smiled, her toothless mouth wide open. "Yes, yes, the devil has the children," she giggled. "His loyal servant Beelzebub took them to him."

"So there are two?" the hangman asked. Magdalena saw a worried shadow pass across his brow. Perhaps her father was thinking about what chance he would have in a battle against two grown men who had no compunction about murder or abduction.

Suddenly the old woman fell to the ground and began to whimper. "I couldn't stop him!" she cried. "The Evil One passes through my cave with pounding footsteps. It whispers horrible things in my ear, but my prayers aren't heard. May God punish me for my fear! I ran away, but I eavesdropped on the Evil One and saw how he snared the little man. He never came out of the cave."

"The . . . the little man?" Magdalena felt her legs starting to give way under her again. It could be just a coincidence, but Simon was indeed one of the smallest men she knew.

"This little man . . . What did he look like?" she asked excitedly.

The old woman cocked her head to one side like an old owl. "He had succumbed to appearances — fancy clothes, useless decorations. Hah! All that will remain of him is a stinking sack of maggots."

Simon! It flashed through Magdalena's mind. *My God, that must be Simon.*

"When was that?" Kuisl asked. He seized the old woman by the collar and pulled her up to look her right in the face. "Tell me right now or prepare to meet your Savior today."

The old woman broke out in raucous laughter. "Are you threatening me, hangman?" she replied, kicking about as the hangman held her up in the air. "You, who have slaughtered hundreds of people? On Judgment Day their souls will come knocking at your door and demand vengeance. Repent, hangman, repent!"

Kuisl released the old woman as if he'd touched a hot stove, and she collapsed at his feet, writhing about like a worm.

"Not an hour has passed since the little man disappeared in the cave," she said finally. "God have mercy on his soul. I saw the monk burn, and Satan will lead the little man through the fires of purgatory as well."

Out of the corner of her eye, Magdalena was surprised to see her father make the sign of the cross. He'd never done that before, or perhaps only on one of his occasional visits to church. Worried, she placed her arm on his shoulders.

"Are you all right?" she asked while the old woman continued to lie on the ground, whimpering and babbling.

Kuisl nodded hesitantly, then brushed her arm aside.

"Come along," he said. "We're not getting anywhere standing here, and if we intend to save your children and now your husband, we'll have to hurry." He pulled a torch from his bag, lit it over the fire that was still glimmering, and headed toward the cave. Dangling on his belt was the long hunting knife and the freshly carved club.

"Satan or purgatory—it doesn't matter," the hangman growled. "The men who have kidnapped my grandchildren are going to find out what hell is really like."

Seated in the library in the south wing of the monastery, the prior and the librarian listened to the agitated Schongau burgomaster, whose story was so unbelievable it could almost be true.

"You really believe the Schongau hangman slipped into our monastery disguised as a Franciscan monk?" Prior Jeremias asked with a furrowed brow.

Karl Semer nodded emphatically. "I swear by the bones of Saint Nicolas, it's the truth, Your Excellency. When I heard you were looking for a large man, more than six feet tall with a hooked nose, I thought of him at once. This slick little bathhouse surgeon and his wife denied it, but at noon my son and I"—he said, pointing to young Sebastian Semer sitting beside him with an arrogant look on his face—"saw the hangman in the church square with our own eyes. He ran away, along with the medicus, and after that, it was almost as if the earth swallowed them up."

The librarian passed the tip of a finger over his chapped lips. "The hunters did tell us about a huge man who fought like a madman," he murmured. "He threw one of them into the gorge like a stone. Are you sure that's your man?"

"Ha! That's him," Karl Semer exclaimed. "Kuisl was a 'double mercenary' in the Great War: he was one of the best soldiers and received double pay. He'll pick a fight with a dozen men." He sighed. "A good hangman, indeed, but unfortunately extremely stubborn and always causing trouble, especially when you least need it. Kuisl likes to snoop around and stir up trouble when it would be better to just let things be." He cast an anxious look at his son and patted him on the shoulder. "Naturally we also want to see an end to this unhappy chapter in Andechs, don't we, Sebastian? To the best of my knowledge the culprit has already been apprehended, and this continuing confusion can only be bad for our, eh . . ."

"Business," said Prior Jeremias, smiling and finishing his the sentence. "It's all right for you to say that. It's no shame to make money, especially since it's for the benefit of the church. We, too, would be happy for peace and quiet to return as soon as possible." He folded his arms and leaned back in his chair. "But what I don't understand is why this, uh . . . Kuisl is snooping around here. After all, he's a hangman, isn't he, and not an official of the elector?" He laughed nervously and looked over at Brother Benedikt, who was leafing through some books and making a point of looking disinterested.

"We confess we don't have any explanation," Semer said, scratching his bald head. "His daughter and son-in-law came with us on a pilgrimage. At first, Jakob Kuisl wasn't with us. Why he came later—"

"What is the man's name again?" the prior interrupted.

"Kuisl. Jakob Kuisl. Why?"

Suddenly Brother Jeremias remembered the rigorous questioning of the apothecary the day before in the Weilheim torture chamber. Brother Johannes kept speaking of a certain Jakob who would come to help him. The prior had assumed Johannes was crying out in his pain to the apostle Jacob, but perhaps he really meant Jakob Kuisl. Why? The talkative Andechs abbot once remarked that Johannes had been a mercenary in the Great War. Did the two perhaps know each other?

Brother Jeremias drummed his fingers nervously on the table. The situation was becoming more and more muddled.

"Is something the matter, Jeremias?" Brother Benedikt asked, looking up suspiciously from his books.

"No, no." The prior smiled nervously. "I'm just a bit tired. The festival and all the preparations are more stressful than one wants to admit." He rose to shake hands with the fat Schongau burgomaster and his pale son.

"Thank you for your tip," he said in an unctuous tone. "It will help us to arrest this false Franciscan monk soon. Who knows — perhaps Kuisl is even collaborating with the sorcerer." With an impatient wave of his hand, he pointed toward the door. "Now please leave us to ourselves. We all have much work ahead of us."

"Very well, Your Excellency." When Semer bowed, the prior was annoyed for a moment that he still didn't have an abbot's ring for Semer to kiss.

Suddenly the burgomaster looked up at him again with a shrewd twinkle in his eye. "Your Excellency?"

Brother Jeremias frowned. "Yes, Burgomaster?"

"You will surely remember that I sold the monastery wax of excellent quality at a fair price — enough to make three hundred candles — as well as finely printed letters of petition from Augsburg . . ."

"What are you trying to say?"

Semer smiled broadly. "I'm certain that many pilgrims will be coming on Ascension Day, and All Saints' Day, as well. Do you already have a supplier?"

The prior sighed ostentatiously, though secretly he was happy the burgomaster wanted to do business with him. The old Andechs abbot was clearly out of the picture. "Rest assured we will think of you," he said benevolently. "Anyone helping the church is doing God's work."

Bowing deeply, the burgomaster and his son bade them farewell, leaving the prior and librarian alone in the great hall.

"Damn it," hissed Brother Benedikt when the steps of the

two Schongauers had finally died away. He slammed the book shut that he'd just been leafing through. "That's all we need. A hangman snooping around. That dishonorable scoundrel is probably the one who stole the map, and now we can only hope the guards pick him up as soon as possible before he finds something down there."

Brother Jeremias bit his lips nervously. "This Kuisl doesn't give up so easily. You heard what they said. And until Johannes confesses, the case isn't closed. It's possible the Weilheim district judge will have the dumb idea of leaving no stone unturned here."

The old librarian glared at him. "What does that mean — until Johannes confesses?" he blustered. "You were there during the torture yesterday. What are you doing there — tickling him with feathers?"

"I . . . I can't understand myself why they haven't been able to break him," Brother Jeremias lamented. "The Weilheim executioner has tried everything, but we have to make sure that Johannes doesn't die on us. That's why Master Hans wants to wait until tomorrow and help him recover a bit." The prior bent over the table now, almost pleading with the old monk. "Damn, Benedikt. We need the confession or there will be no sentence. You know yourself that Carolingian law is very strict in this respect."

"Then you'd better see to it that they finally wring this confession from him," Benedikt answered coolly, "or we could be the next ones Master Hans puts on the rack." Hunched over like an oak that had survived countless storms, he struggled to his feet and stared at the prior angrily. "In my younger days, I took part myself in a number of inquisitions, and with me the offenders always confessed at once. You're too soft, Jeremias."

The prior clenched his fists under the table. Ever since he entered the monastery many years ago, the old man had always driven him crazy with such lectures. Jeremias knew that Benedikt considered himself the better abbot, but his books were more important to him than any position, and for this reason, he depended on collaborators for his secret plans.

Worthless idiots like me.

At one time, they'd mostly seen eye-to-eye on their goals, but still Jeremias had the feeling the old librarian hadn't always taken him seriously. Jeremias reminded himself that he would be the Andechs abbot soon, and perhaps then everything would be different.

A proud old fool can always be put to use washing dishes in the refectory. We must serve God, whatever our position in life . . .

This thought comforted Jeremias. He thought, too, of the pistol the district judge had given him the day before, and of his run-in with the wolves. It had felt good to pull the trigger.

"Do you know that Laurentius is dead?" he suddenly asked the librarian.

The old man nodded. "Everyone knows about that, and then there are these horrible stories about the golem."

Brother Benedikt crossed himself briefly. "May God have mercy on his soul. But perhaps it's better that way. He was a sodomite and, even worse, a coward. He probably would have told the abbot about our plans sooner or later; now he's quiet for good."

For a while, neither spoke, and the silence in the room, with its thousands of books and parchment rolls, weighed heavily on Jeremias. The prior took a deep breath. Sometimes at night he would lie awake in bed, doubting the wisdom of their actions, but ultimately they were serving the monastery.

Everything is God's will.

"I'll tell you what we're going to do," Brother Jeremias said finally in a voice determined to regain control of the situation. "Perhaps Laurentius was right, and it's really too dangerous to leave everything down there now. With Brother Eckhart, we'll clear everything out and hide it in my prior's residence until this hangman is caught or until Johannes has finally confessed. After all, we still don't know what's lurking down there."

"Are you afraid?" Benedikt smiled coldly.

"Nonsense. I just don't want to take any chances, so let's dispose of the stuff today."

The librarian seemed to think this over. "Very well," he finally said. "It's safer, and we can't make any headway now in any case. Now that Laurentius is dead, we lack a skilled worker."

He hobbled to the door, turned once again, and looked questioningly at Brother Jeremias. "I'd really like to know what it was that inflicted such terrible injuries on our dear Laurentius," he said gloomily. "I'm starting to believe in this fairy tale about a golem."

Nepomuk dozed fitfully in the dark hole in the Weilheim Faulturm, awaiting his next session in the torture chamber. He knew this was the end. The next session would be the last — he would confess, and then this nightmare would finally be over.

A short while ago . . . or was it an eternity? — he didn't know . . . Master Hans had come to him with some bandages and jars of ointment. The hangman spread the cooling salves on his arms and legs and applied clean bandages with fragrant lotion, but these medicines could do nothing to make him want to carry on. He'd given up on life; the pain was too great. Next time, they'd probably hoist him up with his hands bound behind his back or break him on the rack.

Until now, Nepomuk had endured the torture only by closing his eyes and once more thinking back on the good times he'd spent with Jakob Kuisl . . .

The aroma of the capon roasting on the spit; the songs of the common soldiers ringing through the camp; a morning horseback ride through the fog; the fat market women and the skinny,

made-up whores on whose breasts you could fall asleep for a few
hours and forget the war; a practice battle with Jakob, swords
clanging together noisily . . . "Can you feel it?" Jakob asks him
with a grin, pinning him against the charred ruins of a house.
"This is God, Nepomuk . . . This life, the screaming, the sing-
ing, the eating and carousing and dying. I don't need any church
to pray in, all I need is the forest and the battlefield . . ."

When Nepomuk smelled smoke, he opened his eyes, knowing it wasn't a capon roasting on a spit but his own flesh burning.

Master Hans had pressed a glowing poker against his right
triceps.

Nepomuk picked up the crucifix he'd woven for himself
from twigs and straw, pressed it against his trembling chest, and
prepared for life everlasting. "The Lord is my shepherd, I shall
not want. He maketh me to lie down in green pastures . . ."

A smile passed over his lips as he thought of his friend. Deep
inside, he felt Jakob had still not abandoned him and was trying
to prove his innocence.

But it was too late.

Early the next morning, Master Hans would come, and it
would all begin again under the supervision of the prior. He
would confess everything they wanted; if necessary, he'd even
confess to murdering his own mother, causing the last thunderstorm and all the dead, two-headed calves in the Priests' Corner.
Everything—if only they would finally stop torturing him.

"Forgive me, Jakob," Nepomuk whispered, kissing the crucifix. "Forgive me, God. I'm not strong enough."

17

THE FIRST THING SIMON HEARD WAS THE CHIRP-
ing of a bird, one so lovely he thought he was in a beautiful garden, if not in paradise.

He tried to open his eyes, but his lids were stuck shut as if
they were smeared with honey. Startled, Simon tried to get up,
but something kept pulling him down. His arms had to be
bound — he couldn't lift them even an inch — and the harder he
tried, the more it seemed to him his limbs were not bound but
somehow baked into a hard cast. His feet, his legs, his entire
upper body, felt like it was under a layer of clay that he couldn't
break through.

*This must be a dream; in a moment I'll wake up alongside Mag-
dalena, bathed in sweat but healthy, and we'll both laugh about my
silly nightmare. Then we'll look in on the two children, and then . . .*

His train of thought came to an abrupt halt when he recalled
what had happened in the hours before. He'd had to run from
the guards with Kuisl; then he fell off a cliff; and finally he found
this cave in the forest, where he heard the automaton's music.
He'd entered the cave, and then . . . What had happened then?

Simon tried to remember, but from that moment on, he just
drew a blank.

Again he struggled to move, but he still couldn't lift a finger.

All the while the bird kept singing; its chirping sounded like that of a nightingale, if somewhat strange and metallic.

Simon tried to breathe calmly. He'd had dreams like this before and knew he would wake up as soon as he could move just a bit. He tensed his muscles until he could feel cold sweat running down his forehead—but all in vain. Making one last desperate try, he was relieved to find his eyelids had opened at least a crack. Light shone through the narrow slits, a harsh light that shot through him and made him wince. Once more he struggled to open his lids, but he felt as if he was trying to move heavy boulders.

Finally, after what seemed an eternity, he managed to open his eyes completely. It took a while for them to get used to the dazzling light, but he could now make out—at first vaguely, then more and more clearly—part of a room. He stared up at a birdcage hanging from the rock ceiling with a little silver-colored bird inside chirping merrily away. Simon's back felt slightly cold; apparently he was lying directly on the stone floor.

With great effort, he rolled his eyes downward and to the side, where he could make out more of the room. Now he noticed a weathered wooden door and bookshelves on either side holding the strangest objects: some appeared to be technical devices, while others were apparently natural in origin. In the torchlight, the objects seemed as eerie as if they'd come directly from hell.

Or is this place hell itself?

A mummified skull no larger than a fist bared its teeth and grinned at him from atop a dusty velvet pillow, while a yard-long curved horn reminded the medicus of the legends about unicorns. Alongside these lay huge, strange animal skulls, one of which had a sort of thorn where a nose should have been. There was also a brownish egg the size of a child's head, carved mussels, jewelry boxes decorated in ivory, a few crystal glasses, but also a golden astrolabe and one of those famous globes that depict the world in the form of a sphere.

Simon wished he could pinch himself, but for that he would have needed to move his hands. He tried to open his mouth to cry for help but could barely manage to raise his lip in a nervous spasm, like a wolf baring its fangs. Grimacing convulsively, he now heard a sound quickly approaching.

The now familiar melody of the automaton.

The music was accompanied by a squeak and clatter, and after a while Simon realized these sounds came from the little wheels of the automaton Aurora, the same one that had been rolling around in the watchmaker's workshop a few days ago. At that time, Simon had found the automaton, and also the music, remarkable, a technological wonder. Now the song sounded so frightening that, despite his paralysis, the little hairs on the back of his neck stood up.

Rolling his eyes, Simon could see the door opening as the life-size automaton rumbled into the room. Aurora still looked as beautiful as the first time they'd met in the watchmaker's house. Her red ball gown fluttered around her copper legs, her hair was put up artfully, and her lips were the color of fresh blood.

The lifelike doll rolled a few more yards, then stopped in the middle of the room as the music slowed, then finally stopped.

With a stiff grin, Simon could move his eyes far enough down to see the automaton. For a brief moment, time seemed to stand still; the only sound was the soft chirping of the bird.

The figure smiled but remained silent.

Finally it began to twitch. There was a cracking and rattling inside it as the upper body of the narrow-waisted dress teetered back and forth. For a moment, it seemed the machine might tip over, but then the lips suddenly opened like the blades of a pair of scissors.

Simon tried to scream, but not a word came out. He could only watch as his worst fears took shape.

From inside the puppet came a squeaking, like that of a clock that hadn't been oiled in a long time, then a high-pitched, gravelly voice sounded.

"Greetings, bathhouse surgeon. I have waited a long time for someone to help me while away the time. You'll make a nice toy, don't you think?"

With that, Aurora had begun to speak.

Shivering, Magdalena and her father ran through the low-ceilinged passageway that led them deeper and deeper into the mountain.

Perhaps a good half hour had passed since they'd entered the cave, though the hangman's daughter couldn't be sure. Down here, time seemed to run slower. In addition, it was pitch black; the only light came from a small, warm circle around her father, who ran ahead with the torch. Behind them, all was engulfed in darkness again.

Until now, they hadn't encountered anything unusual. At the far end of the cave occupied by the hermit woman, a tunnel and a flight of stairs led downward. For a while they proceeded straight ahead, occasionally passing niches holding rotted pieces of wood, rusty iron implements, and whitened bones, but neither Jakob nor Magdalena stopped to examine them. She was sure that her children were down here somewhere — abducted by the same madman who'd been stalking her. And now it seemed this person had also captured her husband.

It upset Magdalena to think that the abductor evidently assumed they knew more about him, but so far they didn't have any idea who the Andechs sorcerer could be. The prior? The Wittelsbach count? Or perhaps someone else they didn't even know?

Magdalena choked with fear for her children and for Simon. She ran along behind her father as if in a trance, hitting her head from time to time on the low ceiling but not feeling the pain. Kuisl also seemed half-crazed; never had she seen him so angry.

"If he's done anything to the two young ones, then God help him," he growled as they again passed a few rotted beams and bones covered with moss. "He'll wish he'd never been born, the scoundrel."

It occurred to Magdalena that the old hermit woman outside the cave had spoken of a helper. Would her father be able to take on two abductors? The Schongau hangman had seen more than fifty summers come and go, and even if tried to hide it, his movements were no longer as effortless as they used to be. When the hermit woman had cursed him earlier, he looked old to Magdalena for the first time.

Suddenly Kuisl stopped. In front of them, two similar-looking corridors forked off. From one, a slightly moldy odor emanated, and from the other, fresh air.

"Now what?" Magdalena asked, turning to her father. "Shall we split up?"

Kuisl looked at her skeptically. "So you can run right into this sorcerer's arms?" he grumbled. "Forget it. It's enough if I've lost my grandchildren and my chicken-hearted son-in-law to this scoundrel, without losing my daughter, as well."

Kuisl thought for a moment, then continued: "These are no doubt the old forgotten escape routes from the Andechs castle." He pointed at a human skull with a bashed-in forehead that grimaced at them from atop a pile of rubbish. "Now at least we know how the castle was stormed. Someone betrayed the defenders and revealed the location of the escape tunnels. With all these bones lying about, it was certainly an ungodly massacre." The hangman held up the torch and looked into the left-, then the right-hand tunnel. "The sorcerer uses these escape tunnels as a hiding place, no doubt," he mused. "But to hide what? In any case it's clear why the unfortunate Laurentius was found with the monstrance in the forest. The sorcerer dragged him here, but the Brother was able to escape and get at least partway back." Kuisl spat on the ground angrily. "If your husband hadn't fallen asleep, then perhaps he would have told us and we'd have known much sooner where to look."

"Your ranting and raving won't get us anywhere," Magdalena replied, annoyed. "Tell me instead which corridor to take."

Her father scowled. "We'll take the one on the right," he said finally, "the one with the moldy smell. It seems to go deeper into the mountain, and besides, it heads directly toward the monastery."

"How can you know down here what direction we're headed?" Magdalena asked, surprised.

With a grin, the hangman tapped his long, hooked nose. "This here always tells me the right direction. I'm like a blind old dog that always finds its way back home."

Without another word, Kuisl entered the right-hand corridor, and Magdalena followed, shrugging. She had given up trying to understand her father. In most cases she had to admit reluctantly that his quirky hunches were right.

The moldy odor became stronger as they proceeded, until finally Magdalena thought she could place the smell: an old chamber pot that had been standing for a long time unemptied under a bed. The stench was so strong now her throat felt as if it were burning.

Turning up her nose, she hurried along behind her father. Were they somewhere near a huge cesspool? Instinctively she looked up at the ceiling, thinking a load of feces might come falling down on them at any moment. The hangman forged ahead with determination, and a few times Magdalena thought she could see him nodding grimly in the dim light.

"The entrance to hell," Kuisl growled. "The old woman in
Kien Valley was right. It stinks here as if Satan were just around
the next corner. At least I think we're close to solving the first of
many riddles."

"What do you mean when you say . . ." Magdalena stopped
suddenly, spotting a faint light reflecting from the wall on their
left, pulsing like a poisonous cloud in the gloom.

"My God, what is that?" she gasped.

"That?" The hangman grinned. "That's one of our riddles,
even if it stinks to high heaven."

He approached the shining light and suddenly seemed to
vanish inside it.

"Father!" Magdalena cried out in horror. "Where are you?"

Her heart pounding, she ran after Kuisl and realized the
shimmering was coming through a narrow passageway. Stepping through a low doorway, she found herself in a basin-shaped
area glowing in a soft green light. She had to look again before
realizing it wasn't the room itself shining, but just a few objects
in it. On the left was a rough-hewn table with an open book on
top, and alongside that, some bowls, flasks, and crucibles, all giving off that strange light. More books with heavy leather bindings stood there, and the table was strewn with small glowing
chunks.

The strongest light came from the opposite side of the room,
where a pile of waste two yards high glowed a ghostly green, as
if hundreds of glowworms were crawling over it. The stench was
so strong that Magdalena thought she was going to be sick.

"Beautiful," Kuisl grumbled. "We've found the latrine in the
old castle."

Magdalena was so fascinated by the glimmering light that it
took her a while to understand what her father had just said.
"The what?" she asked, confused.

"The latrine, or rather the cesspool beneath it." The hangman walked toward the pile and began poking around. Black clumps oozed between his fingers. Looking up, Kuisl saw a round, encrusted hole in the ceiling.

"No doubt there was at one time a secret room up there for Their Excellencies." Kuisl grinned. "On the toilet, we're all the same, aren't we? Nobleman, monk, and knacker."

Magdalena looked at him, puzzled. "But why is everything glowing here? The table, the bowls, these clumps . . . ?"

"This is where the sorcerer made his hellfire," Kuisl replied. "Both the assistant Vitalis and Brother Laurentius had phosphorus poured over them. Remember what Simon saw when he went to inspect the corpses in the beer cellar."

"The glowing!" Magdalena cried. "Of course! You spoke about this phosphorus. It shines in a green light and burns like tinder. But what's a cesspit got to do with it?"

"Because phosphorus is made from urine vapor." Disgusted, he dropped the hardened feces he was holding. "It takes lots of urine. This is probably the urine of at least a dozen generations of nobility. The sorcerer must have found this pit and used it for his purposes."

Magdalena approached curiously with her torch, but her father held her back. "Be careful," he said. "This stuff catches fire faster than you can say amen. And with this much lying around, you could blow up the whole mountain."

Kuisl turned to inspect the table. He glanced at the mortars, flasks, crucibles, and finally the books, picking up an especially worn one at random.

"This one here is written in hieroglyphics and appears to be very old," he mumbled. "Strange, I've never seen anything like it . . ." He put it aside and reached for another, also written in an unfamiliar language. Finally, he turned to a book right in front of him bound in calf's leather. Leafing through it, he whistled softly through his teeth.

"If I didn't know this work was written by a murderer and madman, I would bow down to the man. See for yourself."

Curiously, Magdalena approached and studied the beautiful writing. There were Latin notes in blood-red letters and sweeping initials, illustrations of puppets, individual human limbs, and mysterious apparatuses whose functions were unclear. On other pages, there were strange formulas, calculations, and recipes. It all seemed to Magdalena like Satan's personal Bible.

"Remarkable," Kuisl whispered almost reverentially. "This is a collection of all sorts of mysterious knowledge, something like the *De occulta philosophia* by Agrippa, but much more mysterious. I've never seen anything like it, and whoever wrote it . . ."

He stopped short, pointing excitedly at one of the last pages with illustrations of lightning striking the roof of a house. A sort of rope or wire led along the wall to the figure of a man, and under it were three Latin words: *Tornitrua et fulgura.*

Lightning and thunder.

"Nepomuk's idea of a lightning rod," the hangman exclaimed. "He told me about it in the dungeon, remember? This is just the way he described the rods to me at that time, and these are the same Latin words he used. That can only mean . . ." Excitedly he rummaged through the pile of books until he finally found another notebook, which he held up triumphantly.

"Ha! As I thought," he cried out. "Nepomuk's notebook. I recognize his writing."

Magdalena frowned. The stinging odor made it hard for her to think. "Nepomuk's notebook?" she asked. "But Nepomuk is in the dungeon over in Weilheim. How did that little book get here?"

"Good old Nepomuk told me back then that the watchmaker Virgilius was very interested in the lightning rod," Kuisl replied. "They even argued about it; Nepomuk didn't want to tell anyone. Virgilius, however, knew someone who wanted to know more about it, and evidently that someone also stole the notebook."

"The sorcerer," Magdalena shivered in the cold, moldy air. "But would he kill Virgilius and the two assistants, and make sure Nepomuk would burn for it, all because he was interested in lightning rods?"

The hangman shook his head slowly. "I don't know," he finally responded. "Until now our man has done everything possible to get a hold of the three hosts. How does that all fit together?" He sighed. "A shame the abducted watchmaker was found dead in the well; I'm sure he could have explained it for us."

Magdalena was just about to reply when they heard a distant banging and scraping farther down the corridor.

"It appears we have a visitor," Kuisl grumbled, reaching for the cudgel still hanging on his belt next to the hunting knife. "Well, let's greet our guest properly."

Paralyzed with fear, Simon watched the life-size puppet in the middle of the room move its red lips. It clattered and rattled as the words came out of its mouth, sounding very human.

"This poison is astonishing, isn't it?" Aurora said. Her high voice sounded strangely hoarse, almost squeaking. Simon was sure he'd heard it somewhere before, but in his fear he couldn't remember when or where.

"I brought it back from one of my many travels," the puppet continued. "The poison comes from the West Indies. The natives there use it in hunting, but also against other men. Usually it brings immediate death, but apparently it didn't survive the long trip unscathed—which makes it actually all the more interesting."

Aurora's mouth flapped as if she were gasping for air. "I'm actually considering whether to try my experiment first on you," the automaton said. "After all, you're rather like a lifeless puppet in your present condition, and it would be interesting to see whether I can breathe life into you. But I probably wouldn't have the time. The moment at which nature and faith meet in this unique synthesis is simply too brief."

Once again Simon tried to raise his arms and legs from the cold, hard stone floor, or to at least raise his head, but it was impossible. His whole body was paralyzed; he could see the automaton only out of the corner of his eye. He was so horrified it was almost impossible for him to think rationally.

This is impossible, an insistent, distraught voice inside his head told him. *An automaton can't think and speak, can it? Is this the notorious golem conjured up by its master, Virgilius, who has now become its victim?*

As Simon stared up at the ceiling, where the bird was still chirping, he finally realized what had been bothering him all this time. The bird's call was a series of identical tones, and the silver nightingale wasn't a living creature but just a pretty toy. The lifeless skulls of nameless monsters glared at him from their places on the shelves, and the technical apparatuses among them seemed as cold and hostile as if they'd come from another planet.

Suddenly Simon could hear soft whimpers nearby—cries and moans that were all too familiar to him. His heart skipped a beat when he realized where they came from.

Peter and Paul! My God, my children are over there.

He wanted to call their names, but they literally stuck in his throat—not a sound came out.

"Oh, it appears the two children have awakened from their deep sleep," Aurora said, smiling. "Don't worry, my loyal assistant gave them only a few poppy-seed cakes. After all, I still need the children. You never know what your stubborn grandfather has up his sleeve, do you?" The puppet's voice now became shriller and more hateful—quite out of character with its delicate appearance. "You've brought this all on yourself," it screamed. "Why do you have to stick your noses in things that don't concern you? All I needed was the hosts. But no, you felt compelled to persuade good old Maurus to let you continue snooping around."

As the children's whimpering grew louder, it became clear they were in the next room. Simon listened as Peter started to cry loudly and Paul shouted for his mother. The medicus thought his chest would explode. His children were terribly afraid; they were right nearby, and he couldn't help them.

"The poor little fellows," Aurora's voice sounded full of pity, even though the smile remained fixed on her face. "The little ones are calling for their mother, that bitch. A few times my helper almost got her—once up in the tower, then with the rifle, and finally with the sack of lime. Why didn't she understand my warnings? Evidently she's just as stubborn as her father."

Then Simon had an idea. Until that point, Aurora's face had been just a vague shadow he could see out of the corner of his eye. Now he succeeded in turning his head a fraction of an inch to get a better look at her. What he saw stunned him.

The puppet's mouth moved even when it wasn't talking.

"I think we should allow the two little ones to see their father now," a hoarse voice said close to where the automaton was standing. "What do you think, Aurora? You be good and stay here, and I'll let the children out of their cage. I wonder what they'll say to a father who's become nothing more than a stiff puppet?"

There was a sound of receding footsteps. As Aurora's mouth continued flapping up and down, Simon could see the shadow of a man heading into the next room at the edge of his field of vision.

Aurora crackled, squeaked, and rattled, her lips moving up and down, but she didn't speak.

It had been the sorcerer speaking the whole time.

· · ·

Magdalena held her breath and listened as the banging and scraping started in again. She was still standing with her father in the ancient cesspit of Andechs castle. He'd quickly stashed Nepomuk's little notebook in his pack, along with the book with the remarkable drawings, and now he listened closely, too.

"It's not coming any closer," he said. "It sounds like someone moving a few heavy crates." He turned to the arched doorway and said, "Come, let's have a look. Perhaps the sorcerer is trying to move out and taking his whole laboratory with him."

As they ran down the low-ceilinged passageway, it seemed to Magdalena as if they'd crossed half the length of the Kien Valley. Where might they be now? Under the monastery? Somewhere deep below the forest? She couldn't imagine how her father could keep his bearings in these surroundings. The hangman was clearly too large for these narrow, low passageways. His huge body kept banging against the rock, and his shirt and trousers had taken on the color of lime, dirt, and stone.

Now the scraping sound got louder, until finally it seemed to be directly above them. They turned another corner and came to a sudden stop.

They had reached the end of the corridor.

The hangman's daughter stared at the hard granite wall. A small trickle of water emerged from the stone in front of them, accumulating in a dirty pool at their feet as tiny pebbles fell from the ceiling.

"Great," she panted. "We've come to a dead end. We'd better turn around and —"

Magdalena stopped short as her father put his finger to his lips and pointed up. Turning and looking up, she could see a stone slab in the rock directly above her. In contrast with the stone around it, it was strangely light in color, as if it had been just placed there recently. The dragging sound came from above.

"I think I know where we are," the hangman whispered, pointing at the solid granite all around them. "If this used to be the escape tunnel for the castle, then we are in all probability directly beneath the former cellar of the keep." Briefly he stared into space. "Back in the war, we stormed a castle up in Saxony," he continued in a low voice. "There was so much screaming and butchering. The last inhabitants of the castle were as stubborn as mules and withdrew to the solid rock keep. When we finally broke through after two weeks, we found no one there. They had all fled through a tunnel like this."

"Now what do you suggest?" Magdalena asked impatiently. She didn't like when her father started telling old war stories. "We can hardly attack them as you did back then, with shouts and rattling sabers. Especially since the stone slab overhead looks so heavy."

The hangman shrugged. "Your father is no longer a youngster," he growled. "But as long as I can lift my executioner's sword, I can lift a slab of stone like that. Step aside."

Kuisl stuck the torch into a crack in the rock, looked around for some large stones, and piled them up on the floor of the passageway, getting dirtier and dirtier in the process. When he judged it high enough, he climbed carefully on top and pushed against the stone slab with both hands. With a mixture of tension and horror, Magdalena watched, listening all the while in vain for sounds of crying children. The banging and scraping drowned out everything, however.

"And what happens when the sorcerer, or whoever it is, sees the slab being pushed aside?" she asked her father anxiously.

"Smart-ass woman," Kuisl gasped, as the veins in his upper arms bulged out like little cords and beads of sweat ran down his muddy forehead. "Do you have a better idea? If not, shut up."

After a while the stone plate rose up with a grinding sound, and the hangman pushed it slightly to one side. Then he waved at Magdalena.

"Quick, climb on my shoulders and tell me what you see," he whispered.

After a brief hesitation, Magdalena climbed up on her father's back, just as she had as a child. His shoulders were still just as broad and strong as the yoke of an ox. She wavered a bit, then gaining her balance, carefully stuck her head up through the crack.

"Well?" Kuisl whispered down below. "Do you see the children?"

It took a while for her eyes to get used to the bright light above after the darkness in the tunnel. Finally she could make out a huge circular room with walls of rough-hewn granite. The ten-feet-high arched ceiling was also made of stone. At least a dozen torches illuminated a chaotic jumble of crates, chests, and tables, where a number of mysterious, nondescript objects stood. Three men in black robes, evidently monks from the monastery, scurried around amid the boxes.

Two of them had just nailed a cover on one of the containers and now, groaning and gasping, were dragging it up a spiral staircase hewn into the rock to a doorway just beneath the ceiling. Another man was inspecting the contents of boxes that were still open. All three were turned away, so Magdalena couldn't recognize them. The stone slab was situated in the middle of the room but half concealed behind boxes, so the monks hadn't yet noticed it had been pushed aside.

"Damn. Hurry up," said the shrill voice of the monk standing closest to Magdalena. He was clinging to one of the crates, gasping, obviously exhausted. "It's high time for us to get out of here. Evening mass is beginning soon."

"If you had helped us carry these, we would have finished a lot sooner," said one of the monks standing on the staircase. "Besides, as I've told you a dozen times already, I'm sick of taking orders from you."

"Well, excuse me, but who had the idea of moving the stuff away?" complained the first. "That was you, you chicken-hearted coward." He laughed hysterically, a high-pitched, girlish ring in his voice. "I can hear the golem already; he's coming to get us."

"Stop," cried the second monk on the staircase. He sounded like an anxious, whining child. Magdalena thought she'd heard the voice before. "That . . . that scares me. There's something down there. I can feel it. We . . . we mustn't disturb it unnecessarily." Suddenly he let go of the chest and fell to his knees. The monk on the other side had trouble holding onto the heavy chest by himself.

"Jesus, Mary, and Joseph," whined the kneeling monk. "Maybe the rumors about the golem are true. What does it say in the old stories? It's a creature made of dirt and clay that came to life when a damned Jewish rabbi breathed life into it. Surely the golem feels right at home in these underground passageways. Let's pray that—"

In the next moment the other monk on the staircase cursed loudly and dropped the heavy chest. It tumbled down the stairs, turning over several times before finally landing a few steps away from the stone slab, where it burst apart, scattering bones, broken glass, and shreds of cloth across the floor.

A golden crucifix landed directly in front of Magdalena. It had been dented in the fall, and the surface had peeled away in places.

Beneath it was tarnished green copper.

"The relics," one of the men shouted down in the keep. "The beautiful relics! You superstitious ninny; now all this work was in vain."

The hangman's daughter rubbed the dust from her eyes as her father staggered below like a stubborn packhorse.

"Damn it," Kuisl complained softly. "What's going on up there? Say something."

"I . . . I'm not sure whether one of these three is the sorcerer," she whispered, "but at least we're onto another riddle here in the monastery. The relics—" She froze when she noticed the man closest to her had heard her voice

"What the hell . . . ?" the monk cursed.

The other two men were now staring down at her, as well— gawking at her as if she were a creature from the underworld. When she finally made out their faces in the torchlight, she let out a scream of terror.

They were Brother Eckhart, the prior Jeremias, and the old, stooped librarian.

"That's . . . the hangman's girl," the prior exclaimed, recovering from the shock. "What's she doing here?"

"It doesn't matter; she's seen us," the librarian said ominously. "And that's bad, very bad." He hesitated briefly, then motioned to the fat Brother Eckhart.

"Look for yourself, Brother. It's not a golem, just a damned woman. Take her, and do with her what you did with all the other women." His voice became soft and mellifluous. "Give free rein to your devilish impulses, Eckhart. She deserves it. The prior himself will grant you absolution, and we'll see to it that no one ever finds the sinful woman."

The horror in Eckhart's eyes vanished, giving way to a lewd grin.

"As you command, Benedikt," he replied softly, licking his fleshy lips. "I've already told the lewd woman she has no business in certain places. Those who don't listen have to find out the hard way."

Rigid with fear, Magdalena watched the fat monk slowly descend the stairs, his huge hands reaching out in front of him and his mouth murmuring a soft prayer.

At the same moment, the hangman's daughter could feel herself slowly being raised up from below. Her father was pulling himself up on the edge of the opening. To the three monks in the cellar of the keep, Magdalena must have looked like an angel slowly ascending.

"What in the world . . ." Brother Eckhart started to say. Then he saw the upper body of the hangman, covered with lime and dirt, emerging from the hole, groaning and growling like a wounded bear.

"My God, the golem," shrieked the fat monk, tumbling back several paces. "It's really the golem rising up from the underworld."

Finally Kuisl had hoisted himself up far enough that Magdalena could jump from his shoulders. He pulled himself completely out of the hole then and stood before the monks at his full six feet, his body smeared with mud and clay, brown streaks across his face.

He looked indeed like a creature arisen directly from hell.

The rigid life-size puppet stared down at Simon, who was still struggling desperately to move.

By now he'd succeeded in turning his head far enough on the stone floor to look directly at the door on the other side of the room. His eyes were open, but so dried out they burned like fire. Nevertheless, he kept looking to the entrance where he could hear the soft pitter-patter of little feet. A moment later his two children appeared, their eyes red from crying, their shirts torn and filthy, but otherwise unharmed.

"Papa!" Peter cried out, stumbling toward Simon. He stretched out his little hands as if expecting his father to jump up at any moment and take him in his arms. But Simon could only lie there, his face distorted in a grimace.

"Papa?" Peter stood in front of him now, passing his little fingers over Simon's sweaty brow. The medicus's eyes were still wide open. "Papa, are you asleep?"

Little Paul had arrived now, as well. He crawled onto Simon's chest and pressed his head tenderly against it. Simon always caressed him until he fell asleep, but now he lay beneath his son like a piece of dead meat. Paul began to cry.

"Don't be sad, children," said the hoarse voice from the other side of the corridor. "You have much to learn in your lives. Everyone must die, even your father. But at least come and have a good look at him, and remember him this way. I, too, had to watch over my dearest a long time before God finally took her away from me. This time, however, the trick is on God. Say goodbye, children; it's time for you to go."

The voice became louder as the stranger entered the room, approaching from the side so that Simon recognized his face only at the last moment.

The medicus tried to scream, and this time he was so terrified that, despite his paralysis, a brief, stifled squawk emerged.

The man standing above him did actually come from the underworld.

With a mixture of awe and horror Magdalena watched as her father, smeared with clay and lime, took out his cudgel and advanced menacingly toward Brother Eckhart.

"Where are the children?" he growled. "Speak up, you fat, black-robed rascal, before I send the whole bunch of you straight to hell."

"What . . . what children?" Brother Eckhart was clearly confused. Until this point, he'd been firmly convinced a genuine golem was standing in front of him. Now this golem was posing curious questions, and in the thickest Bavarian accent. Magdalena could see clearly the monk's mind working.

The wizened librarian had ascended the staircase and was now standing alongside Brother Jeremias, looking down incredulously at the scene below. Finally, he began to laugh hysterically.

"Damn, Eckhart," he cried out. "That's no golem; it's the same man I caught snooping around Laurentius's cell — that stubborn Schongau hangman, a man of flesh and blood. I was almost believing that nonsense about a golem myself."

The Andechs prior seemed to have pulled himself together now, as well. He glanced nervously at the door, as if he were considering running away, but then he evidently made a decision. Reaching inside his robe, he suddenly pulled out a pistol.

"Stay where you are, hangman," he shouted down into the keep. "We haven't toiled away all these years to have everything ruined by a filthy country bumpkin. One step closer, and I'll blow you away like a mad dog."

The old librarian at Jeremias's side seemed stunned for a moment by his colleague, but then a thin smile passed over his lips. "Well, well, Jeremias," he purred, "I never thought you had it in you. Perhaps I've underestimated you all these years. Where does an impoverished monk get a hold of such a beautiful weapon?"

"That's beside the point," the prior snapped. "The important thing is that this girl and her father don't give us away. So put down your cudgel, hangman."

Until now, Kuisl had listened to the two Benedictines in silence. Now he lowered his weapon and stepped back. "A nice toy you have there, little monk," he growled. "A genuine Flemish flintlock pistol, if I'm not mistaken. Must have cost a heap of money. Unfortunately, it fires only one shot, and there are two of us."

"Brother Eckhart can take care of the girl all by himself," the prior snarled, pointing at the fat cellarer still standing uncertainly on the floor of the keep. "He's been looking forward to dealing with that girl so long, and we don't want to disappoint him, do we?"

Until then, Magdalena had been standing behind one of the closed crates, observing the three Benedictines. Now she stepped forward angrily.

"Some fine monks you are," she shouted up to the prior on

the staircase. "Is this what our Savior understood by brotherly love? Rape and murder?"

"Silence, woman," Father Benedict chimed in. "You don't understand what's going on."

"I don't *understand*?" Magdalena pointed at the crates around her. In the torchlight, she saw rusty crucifixes lying around on the tables, along with jawbones, colorful glass stones, and cheap tin chalices. "I'll tell you what I understand. You're making counterfeit relics here. I've no idea what you're doing with them, but certainly you're not putting the fake chalices in your own chapel."

The librarian laughed again. "Didn't I tell you, stupid hangman's girl, that you really don't understand?"

Magdalena looked at him incredulously. "Does that mean—"

"I'll tell you what it means," her father interrupted, swinging his cudgel. "The three of them are probably selling the *genuine* relics and putting the counterfeit ones in the holy chapel. Isn't that right? You're selling all the beautiful chalices, monstrances, and crucifixes, and the people in Andechs are praying to tin-plated counterfeits?"

Magdalena looked back again at the tables with the glass stones and rolls of fabric. To the right stood a brazier with a small bellows, and alongside them a few sparkling gold figurines.

"You're . . . you're melting down the chalices and crucifixes?" she cried out in horror. "You're destroying the sacred treasures of Andechs Monastery and selling them as gold bars? Everything up there is nothing but cheap imitations?"

"Stupid brat." The prior rolled his eyes in annoyance. "Of course not everything. Do you have any idea how many relics have been accumulating up there? Hundreds! Nobody notices when one or two relics are replaced by cheap imitations. The bones and cloth are returned. We change only the containers, so to speak, and the contents remain the same."

He smiled broadly and continued pointing the pistol at Kuisl. The weapon seemed to lend him an enormous degree of self-confidence, and Magdalena could positively feel how the prior was enjoying this scene.

"Believe us, we didn't plan it this way," Jeremias continued almost apologetically. "During the Great War, hordes of merce-naries descended on us looking for our relics, and Benedikt and I had to hide them again and again. We hid the treasures deep down below the monastery. Then one day, we happened to find a walled-over section in the beer cellar. We broke through the wall and the passage led us here."

"To the buried keep of Andechs Castle," Magdalena mur-mured. "How many of these underground passageways do you think are still here?"

"We never looked any farther," said the librarian, rubbing his tired little eyes. "It didn't interest us. We were happy to find a good hiding place during the war." His voice turned shrill and hatred gleamed in his eyes. "In any case, our own soldiers were worse than the enemy mercenaries. The elector always de-manded money for his expensive military campaigns.Where do you think we got that? We melted down some of our relics and replaced them with cheap tin and glass stones. Nobody noticed a thing—on the contrary. The worse the war became, the more pilgrims came here, and they didn't care what they were wor-shipping—tin or gold. The only thing they needed was faith."

"And then after the war you simply carried on and pocketed the money yourselves," the hangman snorted. "Greedy little monks. You're all the same." Warily he eyed the muzzle of the pistol, but Brother Jeremias didn't let Kuisl out of his sight for a minute.

The old librarian smiled wanly. "I knew a stupid, dishonor-able hangman would see it that way," he finally replied. "But if you really want to know—no, we didn't pocket the money our-selves. We used it to buy books, valuable knowledge that would otherwise be lost to history, and we're saving it to make this monastery into something great someday. Soon we can begin with our new construction, isn't that right, Brother Jeremias?"

The prior nodded. "The war taught us that faith doesn't need money. What's the point of all the bric-a-brac that just collects dust in the chests of the holy chapel? A few times each year, we display some of them from the bay window of the church and people are happy — they pray just as fervently even if these objects are just glass stones and cheap metal. And they will be even happier when the monastery is decked out in new splendor. Our actions are God's work."

Kuisl laughed out loud. "Damn it, you really think you're doing the right thing, don't you?" he chuckled. "You're so muddled you can't see how removed you are from your Savior. You have one foot in hell and really believe you're working for paradise." Kuisl nodded grimly. "Your kind was always the worst type I had to string up — those who believed to the end that they were just doing good."

"I don't give a damn what you think, hangman," the prior shouted. "We've almost reached our goal. I waited a long time to be named abbot. Everything seemed to be going my way, and then they sent Rambeck from Salzburg University back to the monastery. What a scandal. But under my leadership this monastery will shine again in renewed splendor. And now, Eckhart, grab that woman and —"

Suddenly Kuisl lunged forward, striking the cellarer on the shoulder. The monk grunted with surprise, staggered back, and tipped over a table, spilling glass stones and little bones onto the ground.

"Eckhart, grab him," the librarian shouted. "He mustn't escape."

As the black-robed monk regained his balance, a strange fire gleamed in his eyes, as if the blow he'd received had awakened in him long-forgotten memories of bar-house brawls and beatings.

Magdalena sensed his life before taking on the Benedictine order must have been distinctly unchristian. With his bald head, bullish neck, and flabby but muscular upper arms, he looked more like a waterfront thug than a monk. Growling, he charged Kuisl, who deftly stepped aside. Nevertheless Eckhart landed a passing blow, and Magdalena watched in horror as her father stumbled. Kuisl was just able to grab one of the crates to steady himself.

He's really starting to show his age, she thought. *Only a few years ago he would have wiped up the floor of the keep with the fat monk.*

As if divining her thoughts, Kuisl rose up defiantly, seized his cudgel, and approached the cellarer like an angry bull.

"Say your prayers, brother," he growled. "You won't have to flagellate yourself any more for your sins. I'll take care of that now."

With hateful little eyes, Brother Eckhart gazed at Kuisl and groped for something on a table behind him. With his huge hands, he finally seized a golden crucifix which he held up before him.

"Even if you're not a golem, you come straight from hell," he hissed. "*Vade, Satanas, vade!* Die, you devil!"

With a scream the monk swung the cross, aiming for the top of Kuisl's head, but at the last moment Kuisl dodged, raised his cudgel, and brought it down with full force on Eckhart's skull.

The monk collapsed like an ox struck between the eyes by a bolt from a crossbow. Blood trickled across the dirty floor of the keep as Brother Eckhart twitched one final time, then passed away. The hangman wiped sweat from his forehead.

"You can be glad it's over for you, little monk," he gasped. "The punishment for counterfeiting relics is a much more painful death."

Magdalena, who had been watching the fight from behind one of the crates, was about to rush out to help her father when she was grabbed by the neck from behind and felt something sharp and cold press against her right temple.

"Drop the club right now, hangman," the prior hissed. He'd snuck down the stairway and was now holding the cool barrel of the pistol against Magdalena's head. "Or your daughter will roast in hell even before you."

Kuisl turned toward his daughter, and when he saw the weapon in the prior's hand, he immediately lowered his cudgel. Magdalena could now see fear in her father's eyes.

He had trouble concealing his anger. "Listen, monk," he began, "I don't care what you do with me — I've lived a full life — but keep my daughter out of this."

"Run with the dogs, die with the dogs," Brother Benedikt jeered as he stepped out from behind the prior, looking like a hungry old crow. He glanced down at the dead Eckhart. "That fat rapist is no great loss," he hissed. "He was evil and sick, but we needed him to move the heavy crates. Just as we needed Laurentius. The novitiate master, with his delicate fingers, was the only one who could make convincing counterfeits out of stone and metal." Benedikt sighed. "A real artist. It's a shame we lost him."

"Such a hypocrite," Magdalena snapped as the prior pressed the mouth of the pistol so hard against her temple that a small trickle of blood ran down her cheek. She continued, undeterred. "You probably killed Laurentius yourself because he was afraid and was about to betray you."

"You're wrong, girl," Brother Benedikt replied coolly. "We ourselves don't know who did that to the good fellow." He pointed at the hole in the floor. "There's something lurking around down there. We covered the opening with the stone slab, but you removed it. So tell me. You came from down there. What did you see?"

"We didn't find a golem or a sorcerer," the hangman interrupted in his deep bass voice. "We were just looking for my grandchildren."

"Your . . . *grandchildren?*" The librarian paused briefly then started cackling like a chicken. "Ha! Don't tell me all this is happening just because the dumb girl's brats ran away on her."

"The sorcerer abducted them, you old fool," Magdalena shouted as angry tears ran down her face. "If none of you is the sorcerer, who is? Speak up! Who knows what this madman is doing with my children?"

But Brother Benedikt just continued laughing, his scornful, hysterical cackle echoing loudly through the cellar of the keep. Finally, he stopped and wiped his face. "That's so funny," he replied, breathlessly. "You really believe that one of us is the sorcerer—and all this time, we thought it was one of you. And while we stand here beating up on each other, the real sorcerer goes happily about his business. That's just precious."

Magdalena hesitated. It didn't seem Brother Benedikt was just trying to fool her. "And . . . and you have nothing to do with the hosts that were stolen and have now reappeared?" she asked uncertainly.

"God, no!" The librarian shrugged. "Why should we be interested in a few old wafers? They can't be melted down. But in one regard, I must disappoint you—the hosts still haven't reappeared. The monstrance that the unfortunate Laurentius brought with him from the forest was empty."

"Just as I thought," Kuisl cursed. "The sorcerer had already removed the hosts. What in God's name does he want with them?"

"That, my good fellow, is something you'll never learn," Prior Jeremias hissed, pointing the flintlock pistol directly into Kuisl's face. "You're right. There's only one bullet in the gun, but after we've taken care of you, we'll deal with your daughter. Strange, isn't it, that this is all starting to really amuse me." In a flash, he picked up a stiletto from one of the tables and held it to

Magdalena's throat. "Perhaps we'll take a little time with the girl, but you're on your way to hell now, hangman. Farewell."

As the pistol clicked, Kuisl dodged to one side, but the fatal shot never came.

Horrified, the Andechs prior stared at a crossbow bolt protruding from his upper right arm. His fingers went limp, and the pistol clattered to the ground. The face of the old librarian beside him turned white, and his eyes were glued to the top of the stairway leading to the exit above.

"Don't kill her. I want her alive."

Turning, Magdalena saw four unfamiliar soldiers in uniforms at the top of the staircase. Their leather cuirasses were emblazoned with a coat of arms depicting a golden lion in a black field. Two of the men aimed crossbows at the two Benedictines.

Between the soldiers stood Count Leopold von Wartenberg. "Behold! We've finally found the nest of the relics thieves," he said coldly. "The executioner in Weilheim can really look forward to a good year. Two little execution pyres won't suffice for this dreadful crime."

18

Simon cringed as the man from the under-
world bent over him almost solicitously. His humpback looked
almost like a little animal bulging out of his black Benedictine
robe. In his right hand, he grasped the silver pommel of his walking stick.

This isn't possible, Simon thought. *You're dead. I saw you — a
charred corpse — with my own eyes in the cemetery.*

But unlike the shriveled black corpse the medicus had examined just two days ago, *this* Virgilius was most definitely alive.
His face was twisted into an insane grimace, and he cocked his
head to one side as if observing his patient's paralysis with great
interest.

"Am I mistaken or did I just see a tiny movement?" the
watchmaker said in a hoarse voice. "It would be interesting to see
if the effect of the poison lessens over time, but unfortunately
we'll not be able to continue this experiment."

"*Nnnnn . . .*" For the first time Simon was able to summon
up all his strength and produce a sound. He had to strain so hard
he almost passed out.

"Papa?" Peter asked anxiously. He kneeled with his brother

on the stone floor, both of them running their fingers back and forth across their father's face. "Papa is sick?"

"Your father isn't sick; he's just resting before going on a very long trip."

Virgilius rose and, supported by his walking stick, hobbled over to the puppet still standing in the middle of the room. Its mouth had fallen silent, and the rattling and clicking had ceased, as well. It was nothing more than a lifeless automaton whose mechanism had stopped.

"Here I thought the little bathhouse surgeon would remain stiff forever," Virgilius said regretfully. He turned to Aurora. "I thought I could make a playmate for you, a puppet for the time when you yourself are no longer a puppet. What do you say?" With a playful, surprised look, he gazed at Aurora, as if awaiting an answer. "Do you think me impolite? I haven't introduced you yet? Excuse me; you are absolutely right."

Virgilius bowed slightly in Simon's direction and pointed at the grinning automaton. "My dear bathhouse surgeon: this is Elisabeth, the most beautiful and charming creature I've ever been privileged to meet in my life. I call her Aurora, meaning *dawn*. A suitable name, don't you think?" He smiled, but Simon could see tears in his eyes.

"Shall I tell him a bit about us, Elisabeth?" Virgilius continued. "Really? Very well, as you wish . . ." He paused briefly before continuing.

"I met my beloved Dawn when I was a young student at the Benedictine university in Salzburg, where my older brother, Maurus, also studied. He always chided me for neglecting my studies and spending all my time with Elisabeth. The stupid fellow. Even today, he still doesn't understand what she means to me. She was — no, she *is* my life."

Virgilius paused for a long time, staring vacantly at the dead skulls, the jewels, the astrolabe, and the music boxes on the shelves.

"What are you saying?" he asked, astonished. "Do you really want me to tell this nice, open-minded bathhouse surgeon our little secret? But . . . you know how it hurts me to do that." He nodded with determination. "Very well then, if you say so. I have, in fact, remained silent much too long. It deadens the soul to keep secrets too long, doesn't it?"

Virgilius's face suddenly turned grim, as if dark clouds were gathering behind his eyes.

"Elisabeth died," he said softly. "Just like a rose in winter. It was the Plague that took her from me thirty years ago. I . . . I tried everything at the time, but all my knowledge, all the cleverness I was so proud of, wasn't enough to cure her."

With a sudden sweep of his cane, Virgilius brushed the astrolabe and a few other technical devices off the shelves and onto the floor, where they broke apart with a loud crash that echoed through the subterranean passageways.

"What use is all this damned science if we can't save the one life that means something to us," he shouted so loudly that the children started to cry and clung tightly to their father. Tears rolled like little pearls down the watchmaker's face. "What an evil trick God has played on us by giving us reason but no control. After Elisabeth's death I traveled the entire world—Africa, Arabia, the distant West Indies—looking for something that would give me back my life. But all I brought back was this . . . this rubbish."

Disgusted, the watchmaker took the long pointed horn from the shelf. Simon thought he intended to stab him with it at first, but instead Virgilius just cast it aside carelessly, then proceeded to furiously pound the other shelves with his cane.

"Nothing but rubbish to fill up my little cabinet of curiosities," he ranted. "Nothing but trash! Things that amuse us. But we're unable to create natural, living things themselves. Everything is a cheap imitation of God's works. Everything . . ."

He paused and suddenly dropped his walking stick. In the

silence that followed, all that could be heard was the wailing of the children, who still clung to their father and stared up anxiously at the angry little hunchback.

"I . . . I'm sorry, Elisabeth," he said, again very softly. "I . . . I didn't want to frighten the little ones. Can you comfort them again? I know you can."

He walked over to the puppet and turned a few little wheels in its back. At once Aurora started to play her sad familiar melody again as she rolled around, clattering in a little circle. It looked as if she was going to dance. The children did settle down for a while; Paul even giggled when the puppet winked its metal eyelids.

"I swear by God, I tried to forget Elisabeth," Virgilius muttered, leaning against the wall next to Simon and staring into space. "All those many summers and winters. But I couldn't do it. Outwardly, I was calm and reasonable, but inwardly I was still seething. After many years of travel, my brother obtained this position in the monastery for me. As a foolish watchmaker. Maurus no doubt thought I'd finally been cured of my spiritual distress." He laughed softly. "I started building automata for these dumb monks, toys they could put in their gardens and enjoy. I made a hellish, burning powder, as well as muskets that shot bullets silently, propelled by nothing but air pressure, and chirping birds made of metal. And I did it all to not have to think of *her*. Finally when madness had practically consumed me, I had a stroke of insight that saved me. I built myself a new Aurora. From the deepest recesses of my memory, I built myself an automaton that looked and acted just like her."

Slowly, Virgilius began to rock his head back and forth in time with the melody; then his legs started moving as well. As the hunchbacked little man hobbled around the room, he took the puppet by the arms and spun around with it in a courtly dance.

"One, two . . . one, two . . ." he sang in time with the music.

Simon felt the paralysis beginning to wear off; with a struggle he could even wiggle a few fingers. Discreetly he moved his arms and legs and hoped the crazed watchmaker wouldn't notice.

When the machine's movements and melody finally slowed down and stopped, Virgilius bowed politely to Aurora and uttered a deep sigh.

"Yes, I know, Elisabeth," he said with a disparaging wave of his hand. "This is just make-believe. You say you're not alive, that this clever bathhouse surgeon knows that, as well, but can I tell you what he doesn't know?" He winked at Simon, who could now move his right arm again.

"What he doesn't know is that we've found a way to bring you back to life," he said in a conspiratorial whisper. "That ugly apothecary showed me how. Lightning. Yes, lightning. Even in ancient writings we learn that lightning is the finger of God. For years I've been looking for a force that can breathe life back into you, and finally, finally, I found it." Virgilius closed his eyes and folded his hands as if he were praying.

"What do you say to that, Elisabeth?" he exclaimed. "That this stupid apothecary hadn't quite thought it all through? That something was missing to bring you back to life?" Virgilius cocked his head to one side as if listening with rapt attention for his lover's reply. "Shall I really disclose our greatest secret to this bathhouse surgeon?" He burst into a hysterical giggle. "Because he won't be able to tell anyone anyway? You're right about that."

Virgilius proudly limped to the other side of the room. By now Simon was able to move his head far enough to make out a sort of small stone altar in the corner. On top of it stood a gold-rimmed glass with three tiny brownish discs inside.

The three sacred hosts, Simon realized in a flash. *Virgilius was the one who stole them from the monstrance and brought them here.*

"I observed the clouds, dearest Aurora," Virgilius said, carefully plucking the hard discs out of the glass. "The weather today is most favorable for us, and so soon after the Festival of the Three Hosts. That's a good sign. Tonight, faith will finally unite with science." Virgilius cast a longing though deeply sad look at his stiffly grinning beloved. "Your long wait will be over. You will return to the land of the living."

The watchmaker crushed the hosts to a fine powder with his fingers, and the remains fluttered into the glass.

Huge black thunderclouds were gathering above Lake Ammer, advancing from the west across the water and extending their long, dark fingers toward the monastery. Even though it was just six in the evening, darkness lay over the mountain, silencing all life. The birds took shelter under branches, the foxes and badgers huddled in their holes, and even the wolves drew in their tails and crowded into packs, as if in this way they might better withstand the imminent danger.

High in the sky, the first bolts of lightning appeared, illuminating the clouds that had risen like towers above the lake. Small waves lapping the shoreline were whipped up by a wind blowing down from the Hoher Peißenberg, bringing a freshness to the air and welcome relief from the oppressive heat of this June day. Trees bent in the wind, groaning and creaking. Though they'd withstood many such storms in the past, this one promised to be especially violent.

One that men would long remember.

In the calm before the storm, the first claps of thunder sounded loud enough to burst the world apart. The sound rolled across the land, whistled through the trees, and battered the walls of the monastery.

Then the rain came.

Count Leopold von Wartenberg stood atop the stairway holding his head erect and watching as his soldiers tied up the two stunned monks. When the bailiffs finally turned to Kuisl and his daughter, the count raised his hand. Suspiciously he stared down at the Schongau hangman.

"At first I thought these scoundrels had found two willing accomplices for their counterfeiting scheme," he said softly, as if to himself. "But now I remember how the Schongau burgomaster just today told me how angry he was with his hangman. The hangman, he said, was here on the Holy Mountain despite his dishonorable station, and had been caught snooping around in the monastery. This afternoon, he threw one of the hunters into the gorge while trying to flee." The count raised an eyebrow and looked Kuisl over from head to foot. "From his description, you could be the hangman. Is that true?"

Kuisl folded his arms in front of his broad chest. "I am the one, but I have nothing to do with the dark deeds of these charlatans. I'm only looking for my grandchildren."

Grinning, the count turned to his soldiers. "Did you hear that? He's only looking for his grandchildren. Unfortunately the sweet little things have lost their way in the subterranean passageways—the same ones, by chance, in which the counterfeiters were up to no good." The guards roared, but Count Wartenberg interrupted their laughter with an abrupt gesture. "Nonsense. Do you really think I'll fall for these lies, *hangman?*"

"But it's the truth," Magdalena interrupted. "My children were abducted by this sorcerer. They're probably still down here somewhere and—"

"Just a moment," the count said, raising his hand for silence. "What is all this talk about a sorcerer? If there really is one, then it's this apothecary waiting to be burned at the stake in Weilheim. Who are you, anyway, woman?"

Magdalena straightened up in anger and stuck out her chin. "I'm Magdalena of Schongau," she replied coolly. "Daughter of the hangman Jakob Kuisl and wife of the bathhouse surgeon

Simon Fronwieser. People say we're dishonorable, but we do have names."

"Fronwieser?" For the first time there was a note of astonishment in the count's voice. "The Fronwieser who cured my son?"

Magdalena smiled wanly. "I'm happy to hear that the little lad is doing better."

"Well, he's not cured yet, but the fever is actually going down. Unfortunately I had to leave his bedside a few hours ago on account of these gallows birds." Wartenberg slowly descended the stairs. The two Benedictines were now lying on the ground, tied up, the guards' boots pressing their faces into the dirt so they could hardly breathe. The crossbow bolt was still protruding from Brother Jeremias's upper arm.

"For years we've known that something fishy was going on with the Andechs relics," the count continued as he examined the tables loaded with cheap metal and the encrusted crucible. "There were rumors, stories, but no proof. Nevertheless, we Wittelsbachs couldn't allow the electorate's greatest treasure, which actually belongs to us, to be drained off through dubious channels. The elector asked me to look into this, but I couldn't find anything in the holy chapel, nor could I the second time I asked to be admitted. But then I discovered a map in the librarian's cell . . ."

Brother Benedikt's head quickly shot up. His cheeks were smeared with mud, and blood ran down over his face, but beneath it all, his eyes flashed wildly.

"So you stole my map," he hissed. "I thought the sorcerer did, but it was just one of you Wittelsbach snoops."

"Silence, monk!" The count kicked the old man in the side so that he gasped and writhed about. "Think instead about what the Weilheim executioner will be doing with you soon. The punishment for falsifying relics is torture on the rack, but if you don't hold your tongue, I'll make sure Master Hans pulls out your guts first." He pointed at the lifeless Brother Eckhart whose head lay in a pool of blood. "Your friend can count himself lucky to be spared all this."

Brother Benedikt coughed but remained silent. The prior who lay tied up next to him seemed to have already resigned himself to his fate, closing his eyes tightly as if he were already in another world. He murmured a Latin prayer as the blood oozed out of his wound and formed a dark stain on his robe.

"I'll admit the map made me curious," Wartenberg continued without bothering to look at either of the monks anymore. "So I went looking until I finally found the underground passage leading from the beer cellar to this place. And what did I find at the end? A huge counterfeiting workshop. All I needed to do was to catch the perpetrators in the act. When they slipped away and came down here, we followed them. But two other people were here . . ."

Now he turned back to Magdalena and her father. "Your husband, this little bathhouse surgeon, did good work, hangman's daughter," he said. "For this reason, I'm prepared to listen to you. Also because I want to know how you got here without our noticing it. But be brief and think carefully about what you say."

"Damn it, I'll do that if only for the sake of my children, you pompous ass," she murmured softly enough that only her father beside her could hear. Then in a much louder voice she continued: "The apothecary Brother Johannes is innocent. The real sorcerer is somewhere down below."

Briefly she told him about the ransom note she'd received from the unknown person, and about the search through the underground passages.

"This man abducted my children because he's afraid we were on his trail," she concluded. "He's probably still down there with them. Please, you must help us!"

Leopold von Wartenberg looked at her suspiciously, without a trace of sympathy. "So . . . a mysterious sorcerer is haunting these passageways," he finally said smugly. "What in the world do you think this unknown devil is trying to accomplish with his murders?"

"We don't yet know what his plan is," she replied, "but his victims stood in his way, and they knew something he didn't want to come to light." She stepped up to the count and looked at him, pleading. "Please let your men come along with us, and let's go back down again. My children's lives are at stake. You have a child yourself."

Leopold von Wartenberg paused and seemed to be considering what she'd said. He closed his eyes and rubbed his nostrils for a while before replying. "It's not so simple. I need my soldiers to take these scoundrels away. Besides, there's an enormous storm raging up there at present, and I need all hands to react promptly to any possible fires. It's almost as if hell itself has opened its doors—"

"Good Lord in Heaven, a *thunderstorm?*"

Leopold von Wartenberg looked indignantly at the hangman who had so rudely interrupted him. But Kuisl remained undeterred. "You spoke of a *thunderstorm,*" the hangman continued brashly. "Is it an especially violent one? Tell me!"

"It's the most violent one I've seen in years," the count replied, looking Kuisl up and down like a strange, exotic animal. "The lightning bolts are striking like cannonballs all around the monastery, and we can only pray they don't set fire to any of the roofs. Why do you ask?"

"The lightning bolts," Kuisl exclaimed excitedly. "This all has something to do with lightning. This madman wanted to learn more about lightning from Nepomuk. He stole Nepomuk's sketches, and down in the corridors below we read about lightning again."

He fetched the sorcerer's tattered notebook from his pack

and began to leaf through it furiously. Finally he let out a raucous shout. "We were so foolish," he cried. "So damned stupid! Why didn't we see this before?"

"What are you talking about?" Magdalena asked, perplexed. Her father simply held the book open for her to see. There, she recognized a humanoid figure attached to wires that ended in jagged lines resembling lightning bolts. Beneath the sketch stood a Latin phrase.

Credo, ergo sum.

"I believe, therefore I am," Magdalena murmured.

"Think back," her father said softly, "to the first time you were up in the steeple. That strange apparatus. Didn't it look something like what you see in the sketches?"

"You're right." Magdalena once again examined the lines in the drawing. "It looked like that. But why—"

"What does all this mean?" the count interrupted impatiently. "What kind of book is this and what are you talking about, hangman?"

"Virgilius!" Kuisl cried out. "The automaton builder. He's trying to use lightning to bring his blasted puppet back to life."

"What do you mean . . . ? What puppet?" Wartenberg asked, confused.

"My God, is everyone here so dense? The automaton that disappeared with him, of course. Virgilius took it along and now probably believes he can bring it back to life. It must have something to do with those damned hosts. Evidently he needs them to complete his experiment."

The hangman pointed excitedly at the pages of the open book. "*Credo, ergo sum . . . I believe, therefore I am.* Virgilius evidently thinks that belief in the hosts, together with the lightning, can breathe life back into his clattering, squeaking automaton. What a lot of goddamned madness."

"But father, that . . . that can't be true," Magdalena interrupted, confused. "Virgilius is dead. Simon himself saw his body beside the well in the cemetery."

"Your husband saw a burned body and, beside it, the walking stick of the poor victim. But was it really Virgilius? Think about that, child." Kuisl shook his head grimly and burst out laughing. Magdalena felt how the sudden revelations made her head spin. "Do you mean he . . . he wanted us to *believe* he was dead?" she gasped. "Just as he wanted us to believe he'd been abducted?"

Kuisl nodded. "He abducted himself in order to get his hands on those accursed hosts. He knew his brother would only give him the hosts if he played some sort of trick on him. The severed finger probably came from a corpse, perhaps even from Vitalis, just to frighten Maurus a bit. Everything was planned from the very start. When Virgilius noticed we were closing in on him, he faked his own death to divert suspicion." The hangman rubbed his huge nose, lost in thought. "The fresh grave that Simon and I discovered at the cemetery, the footprints in the ground—everything fits. Virgilius himself dug up the dead monk, burned him with phosphorus until he was almost unrecognizable, and threw him into the well. The footprints beside the grave were his own. And . . ." He hesitated a moment to give the count a chance to say something.

"Do I understand this all correctly? This watchmaker only pretended he'd been abducted?" Wartenberg asked, skeptically. "And now he's prowling around somewhere down in those passageways?"

"That damned Virgilius," screeched the librarian, lying fettered on the floor. "I always knew he would bring misfortune to the monastery. If we'd only taken over the monastery sooner, we would have long gotten rid of that fellow. The only one still standing up for him was the abbot."

"Your opinion is of no importance here," the count snapped,

signaling to one of the guards. "Take these two to the same dungeon the apothecary was in. They'll have until morning there to think about the agony that still awaits them. I'll be along soon."

The bailiffs seized the monks under the arms and dragged them up the stairway like sacks of flour.

"Please, Your Excellency," Magdalena said, "give us at least two of your men to help look for my children down below. I know they're down there somewhere."

"Magdalena, remember what the count just said," her father interrupted. "Up above the very storm is raging that Virgilius was trying to conjure up in his book. He has the hosts, he has the automaton, and believe me, he's somewhere out there. And if I were him, I'd take the children along. There are no better hostages for his plan."

"And . . . how about my husband?" Magdalena could feel tears welling up in her eyes. "Oh, God, I just don't know what to do."

By now two of the guards had disappeared in the corridor with the ranting librarian and the softly praying prior. A long silence settled over the group. Finally the hangman spoke.

"Your Excellency," he began. It was immediately clear to Magdalena how difficult it was for him to say these words. "I beg you, not for my sake, but for the sake of my family: send your remaining men down there to check. With your permission, my daughter and I will go up above where the storm is raging."

"Damn it!" Magdalena burst out. "How often do I have to tell you, you can't tell me what to do. I'm going down below. I know that Simon and the children are down there."

"And I tell you, you're coming with me, and at once."

The count raised his hand. "For heaven's sake, just stop fighting. All right, I agree. You can have two of my men to go down there and look around, even if I put no faith in all these ghost stories."

"Thank you, thank you, Your Excellency." Magdalena bowed

slightly and hurried back to the hole that led down below. "Let's not lose any time."

"Damn it, I said you're coming with me," the hangman growled. "I'm still your father, so stop contradicting me all the time."

But Magdalena had already crawled down into the hole. The two guards stood on the staircase looking uncertainly at the Wittelsbach count.

"What's the matter with you?" Wartenberg asked. "Are you rooted to the spot? Follow that crazy woman right now." Then he turned to Kuisl with a grin. "You should have disciplined your daughter better when she was a child, but now it's probably too late. She's a damned stubborn girl."

"It runs in the family," Kuisl grumbled as he climbed the stairs from the keep with a shrug. "When she comes out from down there, I'll give her a good spanking. Now let's head back to the surface before Virgilius rides away on a lightning bolt, never to be seen again."

Gradually Simon could feel strength returning to his limbs. Though his arms and legs itched as if a thousand ants were crawling over them and his heart raced, he tried not to move. It wasn't clear what Virgilius would do with him if he realized his victim was not as defenseless as he thought. Simon's children still clung to the motionless, stiff body of their father, staring wide-eyed at the strange hunchback before them.

Simon was still trying to figure out how he could have been so easily deceived. The burned corpse in the cemetery well wasn't Virgilius, but the monk from the third fresh grave. The watchmaker had set out the bait for them, and they had swallowed it.

The handkerchief with Aurora's monogram. Virgilius himself must have dropped it there. The footprints were his own. Why had Simon been so foolish as to believe in golems and witchcraft?

Now the watchmaker dissolved the hosts in a glass and poured the cloudy water into a small bottle. He studied it, absorbed in thought.

"Voilà! This is what I call the true *aqua vitae,* the water of life," he murmured. "A potion as strong as dreams, fears, and the desires of thousands of pilgrims. The sacred hosts have been venerated for many centuries, infused with the faith of generations of pilgrims. These crushed wafers are the focal point of one of Europe's greatest pilgrimage sites."

Virgilius laughed under his breath, shaking the bottle so the tiny crumbs in the water began to dance. "Isn't this amazing? Actually it's no more than baked flour, as lifeless as all the other relics. Rusty pieces of metal, worthless bones, and spotted old shrouds that have almost crumbled to dust. But we humans breathe new life into them through of our *faith.*" Longingly he turned his eyes toward the ceiling. "How many years have I been searching in vain for the key to bringing back my Aurora. Just yesterday in the monastery library I came upon an ancient book dealing with conjuring golems and creating life. I made copies, studied numerology, the Talmud . . . and finally I understood."

Virgilius leaned over toward Simon, whose lips and facial muscles had started to twitch uncontrollably. The medicus suddenly recalled the Jewish book he'd seen a few days ago on the abbot's desk. That must have been the work that Virgilius was citing with such solemn fervor.

"Do you know how rabbis instilled life into their mud and clay golems?" the monk whispered, bending down farther over Simon's twitching face. "They placed a piece of paper inscribed with the name of God in their mouths. Then they recited the last paragraph from the story of creation." The monk closed his eyes as if praying. "And God breathed into his nostrils the breath of life; and the man became a living soul," he recited softly.

Virgilius stood up again, giggling. "Do you understand? Only God, not man, can perform this miracle. But we can help.

The Jews understood this far earlier than we Christians. I've studied the scriptures and written my own book. Now, finally, I know what to do."

Humming, he walked over to a closed chest, opened it, and pulled out a silk cape and a bonnet decorated with artificial flowers. Lovingly he placed the cape over Aurora's shoulders and fastened the bonnet atop her wig.

"The great day is at hand, Aurora," he whispered solemnly. "How long have I waited for this. Faith and science, the lightning and the hosts—together they'll create new life." He pulled out a comb and proceeded to tenderly brush his automaton's hair. Smiling awkwardly under its bonnet, the puppet offered no resistance.

"That stubborn apothecary didn't want to listen"—he mumbled as if to himself—"and didn't want to tell me anything more about his experiments with lightning. So I decided to steal his notes and study them in peace. I told Vitalis about my plans, but that stupid apothecary's assistant Coelestin was watching us up in the tower. The nosy little weasel was watching us experiment with wire and a dead goat." The watchmaker's frantic movements became even more erratic as some of the puppet's stuffing started coming out.

"Tell me yourself, Aurora," he whispered. "Didn't I have every right to get rid of him? There was too much at stake. And when that coward Vitalis wanted to go to the abbot, didn't I have to get rid of him, as well? For you! I did it all only for you. Tell me, how can anyone call me a murderer when I've acted only out of love?"

Virgilius's voice cracked. Breathing heavily, beside himself with anger, he threw the comb on the ground. It took him a while to calm down again, but then a thin smile appeared on his lips.

"After I killed Vitalis, the bright idea came to me that saved the day," he continued with a giggle. "The idea that allowed me to dispose of all my cares at once. I poured phosphorus over Vitalis, faked my own abduction, and blamed it all on the apothecary. His eyepiece lay right alongside the documents; all I had to do was to place it beside Vitalis's charred body." Virgilius nodded as if replying to something the automaton had said. "You're right, Aurora. Johannes deserved his punishment, the damned fiend. Just like Laurentius. Why did that nosy novitiate master have to spy on me and discover these passageways? He almost managed to flee with the monstrance, but I caught him at the last moment. I hope that good-for-nothing sodomite burns in hell forever."

With a slight bow, he turned to Simon. "I really have you to thank for this, bathhouse surgeon. Without you, these stupid monks would probably not have fallen for my trap. But with your help I quickly dispatched the apothecary. My thanks to you. You would have been a good new assistant, but unfortunately I have no more time for that." He seized Aurora by her stiff hands and squeezed them hard. "Our new life together begins as yours is ending."

With a sigh, Virgilius turned to the back wall where a rope hung from the ceiling. When he pulled on it, a soft bell rang somewhere.

"Believe me, I don't really want you to die," the watchmaker said. "Just as I didn't really want the death of the others, either; but each time it was unavoidable. Tell me yourself: how can I take a paralyzed person with me? My servant will have his hands full carrying my beloved Aurora."

Humming softly he removed a small chest from one of the shelves that was still intact and spread a white powder on the floor.

"I hope you understand that I must destroy these passageways," Virgilius continued. "My knowledge mustn't fall into the wrong hands, and certainly not those of this stupid, narrow-minded prior who people say will soon be replacing my brother as abbot. I've always produced this phosphorus powder with the thought it could someday cleanse everything here in a great conflagration."

Simon struggled in vain to rise. By now he no longer cared whether Virgilius became suspicious. If he didn't move soon, both he and his children would be consumed here in a truly apocalyptic sea of fire. Simon had seen what the phosphorus did to Vitalis, Laurentius, and the corpse of the monk in the cemetery. The powder already spread on the ground would be enough to turn the room into one huge fireball. Desperately, Simon looked over at Peter and Paul, who had begun to cry again. Virgilius followed Simon's gaze and passed his hand through his thinning hair contemplatively.

"Ah, yes, the children," he said sadly. "Hm, what shall we do with the children? I am an old, hunchbacked man and I'm sure you understand I can't carry the two of them through the passageways. But perhaps one of them?" He smiled slyly. "You tell me — which of the boys shall I take with me? The little one or the big one?"

Once again Simon tried to reply in a croaking voice, but Virgilius interrupted him with an angry wave of his hand. "I have no more time for your babble. I'll take the little one along; he's lighter. The older one can accompany his father on his last voyage."

The monk pulled a cookie out of his robe and beckoned to Paul. Trustingly the two-year-old crawled to Virgilius, reached for the cookie, and let the hunchbacked old man pick him up. "Very well," Virgilius purred, stroking Paul's tousled hair as the child stuffed the treat in his mouth. "I've got even more sweets where that came from. Shall we have the woman sing again?"

Simon watched in horror as Virgilius rocked the boy in his arms. The child was delighted by the singing automaton, which the watchmaker had just wound up again. After a while, heavy steps could be heard approaching in the corridor.

"Ah, my servant," Virgilius said with relief, pulling a lever on the back of the automaton that made it suddenly fall silent. "Enough dancing. I thought we'd never leave." Abruptly he raised his finger, then turned to Peter. "You'll be good and stay with your father, won't you? He needs you now. Do you understand? You won't leave."

The three-year-old boy nodded earnestly as he held his father's wet, cold fingers firmly in his little hand

"Wonderful. Then let's go now, but first my helper and I have to do just a few things."

Virgilius turned toward the exit where a figure drenched from the heavy rain had just appeared. His clothing was steaming in the warmth of the cave, and with the back of his broad, hairy hands he wiped the rain from his face. When Simon finally recognized him, he quivered like a fish out of water, but he could only watch helplessly as his sons opened their arms to the new arrival, greeting him with shrieks of delight.

"See, I always knew my servant had a heart of gold," Virgilius said. "Sometimes it's even an advantage to lack a tongue, to not be able to talk back."

Gasping, Simon stretched out his hand toward the man, but his arm fell limply to the ground.

Standing in the darkness of the cave was the mute Matthias.

Cautiously, Magdalena slipped into the dark hole while the two guards followed, grumbling softly.

It was clear the men could think of better things to do than to descend into the utter darkness beneath the former Andechs castle. Cursing under their breath, they jumped down onto the stones the hangman had piled up there just half an hour before. They lit up the end of the tunnel with their torches and stared anxiously into the darkness in front of them.

"We have to go back quite a way," Magdalena said, brushing the dirt from her hair. "Farther ahead, another corridor branches off that I haven't explored yet. Quickly now; we have no time to lose."

"I can't believe we're taking orders from a dishonorable hangman's daughter," the older soldier complained. He appeared to be sweating profusely under a beaten helmet and an equally battered cuirass.

"You're right, Hans," the other agreed. "How did it ever come to this, crawling around down here like rats in this filth? Did you raise your skirt for the count?"

"Should I repeat that to His Excellency, or would you rather tell him yourself?" Magdalena responded coolly.

"God forbid. I . . . I . . ." the guard stammered.

"Good. Then we can get moving." Magdalena took the torch from the hands of the astonished soldier and trudged on ahead. Cursing softly, the two guards followed while the hangman's daughter tried to hold back her tears and her anger.

It was hard for Magdalena to rein in her emotions. Her heart pounded as she thought about what this sorcerer might have done to her children and her husband, but she had learned from her father that it was sometimes necessary to control one's feelings to reach a desired goal. If she cried and complained now, the men wouldn't follow her. They might take a few steps into the passageway, so as not to disobey their superior's orders, but then quickly return to the surface. So whether she wanted to or not, she would have to keep control of herself.

After they had groped through the darkness for several minutes, the odor of rot and urine grew stronger. The older guard turned up his nose in disgust.

"It stinks here like the devil's latrine," one of them growled. "Good God, what is that?"

"It *is* the devil's latrine," Magdalena said. "But we mustn't worry about that. All we have to do is — "

"Jesus, Mary, and Joseph!" The young guard stopped suddenly, his mouth open wide as he pointed at the light green glimmer in front of them. "Look for yourself. Ghosts! They're luring us to our doom. By all the saints, let's turn around at once."

Angry at herself for having forgotten the shining phosphorus in the old latrine, Magdalena closed her eyes. She should have prepared the men for this. Now they seemed ready to dash off frantically.

"Ah, that's a little hard to explain," she began. "But they aren't ghosts, they're only . . ."

"The dead — who find no rest," Hans wailed, crossing himself and pounding loudly on his cuirass. "What sort of hellish place have you lured us into, hangman's daughter?"

"Damn! Listen to me. My father explained it all to me. It's a powder that . . ."

"Look over there! It's coming from that room," the young guard wailed, pointing at the passage leading to the latrine. "And do you hear that? That music? By God, the dead are having a dance."

In fact, the automaton's familiar melody could be heard far off. Magdalena's heart beat faster. Evidently Virgilius was still down here with his automaton. Were her children and husband down here with him? Listening closely, she tried to make out where the music was coming from — it seemed not to be coming from the adjacent latrine, but from somewhere in front of them, from another passage. She thought she could hear another soft noise now, as well.

The wailing of children.

With a trembling voice, she turned to the guards. "Do you hear that? We're getting closer. Let's move along as fast as we can . . ."

But the passage behind her was empty. The guards had already turned around and were running back toward the keep. All she could hear now was the sound of their running feet echoing through the darkness.

"I'll tell the count about this, you superstitious cowards," she cried after them. "My father will whip you for this until you see stars of every color. He'll . . ."

With a sigh she fell silent and continued trudging through the passageway alone, always listening for the barely audible music and the whimpering children. More than once she cursed the two guards who had abandoned her so shamefully. It looked now as if she was on her own, and the very thought of that made her shudder. She could probably handle Virgilius by herself, but how about the helper the crazy woman had spoken of? Was he down here somewhere, as well?

Magdalena wrapped her shawl around her neck and tried not to tremble. At least she still had one of the soldiers' torches, which would give her about another half-hour of light. She didn't want to think what would happen after that. Only fear for her children and her husband drove her on.

She stopped for a moment and listened intently. Had she just imagined the crying? She picked up her pace, stumbled several times, got up again, gasping, and groped her way down the corridor littered with stones, beams, and scattered bones.

After a while, it seemed that a green glow was coming from the floor of the tunnel, as well. Traces of the white powder that she and her father had seen only in the former latrine appeared here, as well, though she couldn't remember seeing it in the passageway before. Still, she was in too much of a hurry to attach any great significance to this discovery.

After what seemed like an eternity, she came to the branch in the tunnel where they'd previously decided to turn right. She closed her eyes and tried to listen for the soft sound of the music and the crying children, but was distressed now to find she could hear nothing.

All around her, the silence was almost palpable, interrupted only by drops of water falling from the ceiling.

She swallowed hard, then decided to throw all caution to the wind and call out. "Peter? Paul? Are you here somewhere? Can you hear me?"

At first the only response was the soft sound of dripping water, but all of a sudden she heard something in the second passageway that she didn't recognize at first. It sounded like the distant growling of a bear; it was a while before she realized it was someone moaning. A moment later she heard a voice that brought tears to her eyes.

"Mama? Mama? Where are you?"

"My God, Peter!" She raced frantically down the passageway while she could hear footsteps receding in the darkness in front of her. She thought she could see a few shadowy figures far off, but they'd soon vanished.

"Peter!" she shouted. "Is it you?"

"Mama, over here! Here I am!"

The voice of her older son didn't come from where she'd seen the shadowy figures but from somewhere behind the wall. As she rounded another turn, she saw a round entrance on her left framed by large blocks of stone. The moaning was now close at hand, interrupted only by the wailing of her child. She stumbled through the portal to enter a low vault filled with a splendid four-poster canopy bed, a chest decorated with roses and ornaments, and a dressing table—all furniture like that owned by noble ladies in Augsburg and Munich. The cavelike room, covered with dirt and the soot from the torches, looked like a perverse parody of a ladies' boudoir.

What in heaven's name have I stumbled across here? she thought. *Is this the automaton's bedroom? Virgilius must have loved this automaton more than anyone could imagine.*

Frantically she looked around. On the other side of the vault, a second passageway led to another room from which the crying and moaning were coming.

"Peter! Simon, Paul! Where are you?"

Her heart pounding, she entered the second vault—and let out a loud shriek.

The room looked as if it had been vandalized by an angry devil.

Shelves had been knocked down and the floor was strewn with curious apparatuses, broken horns, stones, and bits of bone. Some traces of greenish phosphorus glimmered in the torchlight, and in some places, there were even large piles of it. On a kind of black altar stood a tiny stump of a flickering candle that cast bizarre, dancing shadows on the wall behind.

But all this was only of passing interest to Magdalena. In the far right corner of the room, her husband lay on the floor, his once so fashionable tailored jacket torn to shreds and his face deathly pale and contorted. Alongside him stood Peter, who came running to his mother now with open arms. His clothes were filthy, but otherwise he appeared unharmed.

"Oh God, Peter," Magdalena exclaimed, taking her boy in her arms. "I . . . I was so worried about you. Where is your brother? And what has this crazy man done to your father?"

She set the boy down and turned to Simon, who lay in a strangely contorted position on the bare stone floor, his whole body twitching. He turned his head toward her and struggled to speak, but Magdalena couldn't understand a word that came out of his mouth.

"*Annal,*" he mumbled again and again. "*Annal . . .*"

As she bent down to him and stroked his sweaty brow, his eyes rolled wildly and his fingers splayed out like cat's claws. The entire rest of his body seemed paralyzed.

As she looked at Simon, she couldn't help thinking of a young Schongau farm lad whom her father had tried to cure many years ago. The strapping young man, who had scratched himself on a rusty nail, was overcome by a strange paralysis—

just like Simon now—and shortly later suffered a seizure and died. Magdalena's father had been unable to help him. Did the same fate await her husband?

"My God, Simon," she cried, "what did this madman do to you? And where is Paul? Please say something. I don't know what to do."

"Annal, annal," was all he could say. Still Magdalena had no idea what that might mean. In her despair, she finally turned to her three-year-old son.

"Peter, can you tell me what happened to Paul?"

The boy nodded eagerly. "Paul is playing with Matthias," he said cheerfully.

"With . . . Matthias?" Magdalena gasped in horror. "But . . . but does that mean . . ."

"Matthias and Paul left with the bad man," he exclaimed. "The man said I had to stay here and keep an eye on Papa."

"That's . . . that's very good," she stammered. "You're a good boy, a really good boy."

Magdalena's mind was racing. She still couldn't believe what she'd just heard. Was it possible that the good-natured Matthias, the man she'd so often entrusted with her children, was conspiring with Virgilius? That he was Virgilius's helper?

"Do you know where Paul went with . . . with Matthias?" she asked in a soft voice.

"The bad man said he would show them both the garden," Peter announced cheerfully. Since Magdalena's arrival, his fear seemed to have vanished. "I want to go back to the garden, too. I want to play with the doll."

"We . . . we'll go to the garden, I promise. But first we must get out of here, do you understand?"

Magdalena tried to smile, but she could feel big tears rolling down her cheeks. Her younger son had disappeared, abducted by Virgilius and a man she'd trusted blindly, and her husband seemed to have swallowed a deadly poison. She felt sadder and more forlorn than ever before in her life.

"Annal . . ."

Startled out of her feeling of depression and helplessness, Magdalena turned to her husband again. She was relieved to see he was now able to raise his right hand; the paralysis seemed to not be so serious after all. Then she realized he was struggling to point to something specific: the little altar where the tiny stump of a candle was swimming in a pool of wax. The wick was leaning precariously to one side. Clearly it would fall onto the altar soon and the candle would go out.

"Annal," Simon gasped, and Magdalena cringed. *Candle.*

Beside the pool of wax, she saw granules forming a trail from the altar to the ground and, from there, to some larger mounds of glowing greenish powder.

My God, she realized in a flash. *The phosphorus. We'll all be blown up.*

Annal . . . annal.

The flame flickered, caught in a slight draft and, for a moment, it seemed it might go out.

Then the burning wick touched the powder strewn on the altar.

19

OUTSIDE THE MONASTERY GATES, THE WORST thunderstorm Jakob Kuisl had seen in many years was raging. He could remember being caught in a similar storm as a child. Back then, the wind had carried away entire trees, and lightning had flashed like musket fire across the countryside. This time as well the heavens were ablaze with countless bolts of lightning. Black and violet clouds swirled across a sky that looked as if Judgment Day were at hand.

The thunder overhead was so loud that Kuisl imagined God himself was pounding against the monastery walls with a hammer. In the next instant there was a brilliant flash, another clap of thunder, and hail as large as quail eggs came pounding down on the roofs. The thunderstorm had to be directly over the Holy Mountain now.

For a while the hangman remained indecisively under the archway of the monastery, looking out at the impenetrable wall of rain. From the buried chamber under the keep, Kuisl had first made his way into the monastery beer cellar with the count. The entrance to the catacombs beneath the castle had been concealed hurriedly behind some barrels; the counterfeiters had made little effort to hide the hole in the wall. Since Brother Eckhart was the cellarer, he also was responsible for the monastery's beer supply, and rarely did anyone else enter this cellar.

As Kuisl continued standing at the entrance to the monastery, he wondered whether his suspicions were correct. The rain and wind were so strong that it would be suicide to go out into this storm and expose himself to lightning—especially since he didn't yet know where to go next. Was Virgilius somewhere in the forest? In his house? Atop a hill? Kuisl knew from experience that lightning always struck the highest point, and the highest point here was . . .

The steeple.

He slapped his forehead for not having thought of it before. His fear for the safety of his grandchildren must have frazzled his brain. Virgilius was certainly up in the steeple. That's where Nepomuk had set up his lightning rod, and that, too, is where the crazy watchmaker had been carrying on his experiments since then. Surely Virgilius was up there.

Just as Kuisl was about to leave the church portal, he heard hurried footsteps and could just make out in the darkness and pouring rain a group of men rushing toward the tavern: the count returning with his soldiers. They were soaked through and through; water flowed in streams from their sleeves and trousers, but Leopold von Wartenberg tried to preserve decorum in spite of it all. He was walking quickly, not running, and once he arrived beneath the archway, he looked the hangman up and down suspiciously, as if not yet sure what to do about him.

"I've just gone to check myself that those two miscreants were put under lock and key in the monastery dungeon," he finally said. "The matter is concluded, and the elector can be reassured. As far as you are concerned," he continued after wringing out his long black hair and wiping his beard, "give me one reason, hangman, why I shouldn't have you locked up as well. Just one."

Kuisl grinned. "Perhaps because Your Excellency will soon be in need of a good executioner?"

"I have Master Hans in Weilheim for that. An excellent man. He would break his own mother on the wheel if she was guilty and if he was paid well enough." A thin smile crossed his face. "Perhaps I should ask him to take care of you, as well. After all, you're clearly responsible for the death of one of the Andechs guards. I've been lenient because you're the father-in-law of the bathhouse surgeon who's been caring for my son. And because your daughter seems to be one hell of a woman. But my patience has its limits."

The hangman nodded. "So does mine," he growled. "Listen, the real sorcerer is out there somewhere with my grandchildren. I've got to find them, and now. After that, you can do whatever you want with me." Without another word, he turned to leave.

Stunned, Leopold von Wartenberg stood as if rooted under the archway. Finally he pulled himself together and cast an angry glance at his soldiers, who prudently held their heads down.

"One hour, Kuisl!" he shouted into the howling wind. But the hangman was now no more than a shadowy figure in the darkness. "I'll give you an hour to bring me the real witch. And don't think you can count on my help. One minute longer, and I'll give Master Hans a nice reward for your head. Understand?"

But Kuisl could no longer hear him. As hail drummed down from the sky, he turned right at the church square, where just that noon hundreds of pilgrims had assembled. Now the area looked forsaken. Puddles the size of small ponds had formed on the hard-packed ground, and a few remaining sacks of limestone stood out of the watery scene like little islands. The pilgrims were waiting out the storm in local farmhouses and barns, praying the lightning would spare them.

Kuisl stomped through the ankle-deep water, casting an occasional glance up at the steeple, but he couldn't make out anything suspicious behind the wall of rain. Had he been mistaken? Was Virgilius perhaps still down in the catacombs, lying in wait for Magdalena? Why did his daughter always have to be so stubborn and have things her way? As so often in matters concerning his daughter, Kuisl was torn between fear and anger. In any case, when all this was over, he'd give his daughter a good thrashing.

If she was still alive.

The hangman tried to suppress these gloomy thoughts, once again directing his gaze at the steeple housing the belfry. Carpenters had installed a new roof and patched up porous masonry damaged by lightning, but on one side, a new wall hadn't yet been constructed, leaving only a knee-high truss there as reinforcement.

Just above the truss, Kuisl spotted a shadow scurry by and then vanish in the gloom. Still, this brief moment was long enough to convince the hangman his suspicions were correct.

Someone was up in the tower.

Breathlessly he splashed the last few yards through puddles to the church entrance. The double doors stood wide open, and rain, leaves, and dirt had blown onto the pews. Wind had partially ripped away the makeshift canopy, leaving shreds fluttering like flags in the storm. Water streamed down over the altars, statues, and weathered tombstones in the nave.

The hangman looked around, perplexed. He thought at least a few Benedictines would be here to keep order, but the church was deserted. Were the monks frightened by the storm? Or had they learned that three of their members had been arrested for counterfeiting relics? In the latter case, it was quite possible the Brothers had retreated to their cells lest they themselves be questioned or arrested.

After hesitating briefly, Kuisl hurried past the wet, mud-spattered pews as the wind continued to howl above him. He had no time for idle speculations. If his assumptions were right, his two beloved grandchildren were up above, at the mercy of the hail, lightning, and rain. Virgilius would wish he'd never been born.

Kuisl ran up the stairs to the balcony and, from there, up another stairway into the tower. Even now, after a full two weeks, work was far from finished. The storm whistled through the open windows, and the narrow, newly built stairs up to the belfry were steep, slippery, and groaning in the wind. The higher Kuisl climbed, the more the entire tower seemed to sway back and forth.

When he got just a few yards beneath the belfry, he stopped and listened. Thunder rumbled and lightning flashed, but amid the constant drumming of the rain, he thought he heard a shrill voice. Indeed, as he climbed higher, he could hear it more clearly.

"Hurry up," a man screeched directly above him. "Before the storm passes. Didn't I tell you yesterday to nail the device down? Now the storm has blown it over, and we're losing valuable time."

The only answer was a deep grumble, followed by the sound of a hammer pounding and a child crying.

Kuisl winced. His grandchildren were up there, and the second man was evidently Virgilius's assistant. Cautiously, he crept up the last few steps and stuck his head through the opening into the floor of the belfry.

At first, all he could see were three bronze bells hanging between the iron-clad beams of the belfry. Fresh, new spruce flooring had been put down, but the walls were still covered with soot from the disastrous fire a few weeks before. Behind a knee-high railing on the east side, rain blew into the room through a gaping hole.

Once Kuisl had finally hoisted himself all the way through the opening, he could just barely make out behind the bells the back of a broad-shouldered man who was nailing a sort of bier upright against the wall. The wooden board was fitted with metal clamps like the ones Kuisl knew from torture racks, and a heavy wire dangled from the ceiling, connected with clamps to smaller wires.

To the left of the bier stood three people looking like a surreal caricature of a family in the raging wind: alongside the hunchback Virgilius was a distinguished looking lady with a red cape and blond hair blowing beneath a lopsided bonnet. She seemed strangely stiff, and it took Kuisl a moment to realize she was actually a life-size puppet.

Paul was clinging to the watchmaker's arms, sobbing.

At first Kuisl wanted to rush out onto the platform screaming, but then he stopped to think this through. The risk was simply too great that Virgilius would harm the child, even throw him off the tower. The hangman decided therefore to sneak up close to the group and wait for a better opportunity. Cautiously he crept behind the belfry cage to watch.

After the broad-shouldered man finished his work, he hooked the hammer onto his belt and turned to Virgilius. Kuisl bit his lip when he finally saw the man's face.

It was the knacker's assistant, Matthias.

What a dirty trick these rascals played on you, involving you in this mess, young fellow, the hangman thought grimly. *It would have been better if the Croatian mercenaries had killed you—it would have spared me the job now.*

But Kuisl was astonished by what he saw on Matthias's face. The young man's eyes were strangely empty and red. It almost seemed that what was running over his cheeks were not raindrops but tears.

"What are you waiting for?" shouted Virgilius now against the storm. "Place Aurora in the bier as we discussed." Then he lowered his voice and attempted a smile. "You do want your tongue back, don't you? I can get it back for you. Just as I can breathe life into this puppet, I can give you back your voice, as well. Believe me! If you start doubting now that we are so close to our goal, all will be in vain."

As Matthias approached the automaton hesitantly, he continued to look back at Paul. The boy stretched out his little arms toward the mute assistant, and his cries turned into screams that even drowned out the thunder.

"Damn it, I tell you nothing will happen to the boy," Virgilius shouted when he saw the anxious expression on Matthias's face. He was rocking the child mechanically, but the motion didn't calm the boy down. "He's only my hostage. As soon as all this is over, you can have the brat again. I promise. Now get to work quickly, before the lightning strikes."

Matthias grumbled and nodded, then picked up the puppet with his powerful arms and leaned her against the bier. The clamps snapped shut around her stiff arms and legs; then the assistant attached the thin wires to the clamps and placed another wire around Aurora's porcelain neck like a noose.

Evidently Virgilius had applied makeup to the automaton in preparation for its last great scene, because black and red trickles of makeup ran down her waxen face. Grinning, she looked out at a storm raging in full fury over the church steeple.

"Now all we need to do is wait for the right moment," Virgilius shouted over the noise, dancing wildly like a dervish. "The lightning will enter the wire, pass through my beloved Aurora, and then—"

A loud crack was followed by an earsplitting rumble. The strike, which must have hit very nearby, was so powerful that Kuisl instinctively jumped to one side. From the corner of his eye, he saw that Virgilius, his eyes wide with hatred, had spotted him behind the bells.

"Aha, do you see now why I need the child as a hostage?" he screamed, turning to Matthias. "This hangman and his whole damned family. When you first told me about them, I knew they would give me trouble. Didn't I tell you a dozen times to get rid of that inquisitive woman?"

Now Matthias had seen the hangman, as well. He stood uncertainly in the middle of the platform, surrounded by the raging storm like a rock in the sea. He seemed paralyzed with indecision.

"Get him, Matthias," Virgilius roared. "He wants to destroy our plan. Don't you understand? Think about your voice."

Kuisl stood up behind the belfry, looking calmly into the tearful eyes of the knacker's boy, raising his hands in a gesture of friendship. "You know this is wrong, don't you, Matthias?" Kuisl said, "You can't fool me. I'm a hangman. I've seen many murderers, but you are not one—at least not a murderer of children." Cautiously, he advanced toward the silent assistant, who was still frozen in place. "If you overcome me in a fight, this madman will make short work of the boy—he will throw him from the tower. The boy means something to him only as long as he can use him to blackmail me. And you mean nothing to him, either."

"That's . . . that's not true, Matthias," Virgilius interrupted. "Think how I cared for you when you were young. Haven't I taught you everything, the writing, the experiments, the apparatuses? Haven't I given you a language to use for making yourself understood even without a tongue?"

The watchmaker clung tightly to the screaming and struggling Paul. "Yes, he's crying now," he continued unctuously. "He's afraid—that's understandable—but you, too, were afraid when you came to my laboratory the first time. Do you remember? You were a small, mute child without parents, an outcast, ridiculed by others, and I was the first to give you something that makes you a better person than all these boors. Knowledge. And if you're patient just a while longer, I'll give you back your voice. Aurora, you, and I will be a family. We'll adopt this boy and—"

"Where's my second grandchild, you monster?" the hangman shouted, approaching Virgilius with a menacing look. Paul saw his grandfather now and tried to squirm out of the grip of the hunchback, but Virgilius held him in a vicelike grip.

"Speak up, you crippled scum. What did you do to him?" Kuisl shouted again.

Matthias looked at Virgilius as if he, too, expected an answer.

"He . . . he's with his father," the watchmaker stammered. "He's safe and sound . . ."

There was a growling sound like that of an angry bear as Matthias shook his head wildly. Kuisl could see how the journeyman was struggling with himself. Virgilius, too, seemed to notice it. With the boy twisting in his arms, he approached Matthias, keeping a suspicious eye on Kuisl. For a moment the hangman considered throwing himself at the watchmaker and seizing the boy, but the risk of something happening to Paul was still too great, especially since Kuisl still didn't know what Matthias would do.

"Come and look," Virgilius said to his servant, putting his hand solicitously on the young man's broad shoulder and leading him over to the knee-high barrier above the yawning abyss. "Can you see Erling over there?" he asked, pointing into the raging storm. "The little cemetery at the edge of the village? That's where your parents are buried. Do you remember how often you cried in the years after their deaths? That miserable knacker Graetz paid you and fed you, but a clever boy like you is destined for greater things. You will be a witness to how man creates life. Look at the cemetery."

Virgilius nudged Matthias even closer to the barrier. Something in the watchmaker's voice seemed to reassure him, and reluctantly the servant moved closer, bending over the edge and staring out at the little cemetery that was almost invisible now in the streaming rain.

"All the dead lying there," Virgilius continued gently. "We can bring them back — your parents, too. What do you think? Do you know what would be even better? You could simply go and . . . *visit* them now. Farewell."

The hunchback gave the strapping youth a sudden shove, and Matthias flailed his arms around wildly as he tottered like a mighty oak in the storm. Kuisl could see the watchmaker's hate-filled eyes flashing through the darkness, but before the hangman could react, Virgilius gave his servant another push. Astonished, Matthias grunted, turning his head briefly one more time toward his master, as if expecting an explanation. Then he fell through the flimsy wooden barrier. Without another sound, he plunged toward the roof of the church, landing on a temporary canvas cover which slowed his fall just slightly before it ripped and the journeyman fell with a loud impact onto the floor of the nave.

In the belfry, the only sounds were the wailing child and the steady drumbeat of the rain. With an exhausted expression, Virgilius stared down at the damaged roof while Paul continued struggling in his arms.

"A shame, really a shame," Virgilius said finally, stepping back from the splintered railing. "He was a good pupil, and so . . . closed-mouthed." He smiled weakly and looked up at the lightning that flashed through the darkened sky. "But you're right, hangman. In the end he really didn't mean anything to me; he was a hindrance, just as all the others were hindrances." Suddenly he looked straight at Kuisl, his eyes reduced to narrow slits. "And if you move a single step, your grandson will be such a hindrance, too. Do you understand me?"

The hangman nodded grimly and raised his hands again. "I understand," he said softly. "And what do you intend to do now? Are you going to wait forever for a bolt of lightning? It isn't going to strike just because my friend Nepomuk hung a little bit of wire up here. It could happen today, or in the next storm, or in a few years—your automaton will simply rust away up here."

"Ha! You don't understand anything," Virgilius hissed. "Do you think I would have gone to all this trouble if I hadn't seen that it really works?" He extracted a little bottle from under his jacket and approached the smiling puppet in the upright bier.

"Your simple-minded Nepomuk told me about his experiments with lightning," he continued with a laugh. "I was the only one who knew he'd hung up one of his so-called lightning rods in the tower. And then the lightning actually hit here. *Quod erat demonstrandum*. From that point on, I knew I was on the right path. The only thing I lacked was the *aqua vitae . . .*" He pulled the cork out of the bottle with his teeth and began pouring the liquid carefully into a hole in the puppet's back.

"This water of life will pulse through her artificial veins like blood," he murmured. "Like blood. The lightning will strike, and my Aurora will finally return to me; the waiting will be over."

When the bottle was finally empty, Virgilius threw it out of the tower with a shout. Then with the boy in his arms, he moved to another corner, leaned against the wall, and waited, his lips moving quietly as if in prayer.

"Lightning, water of life. This is craziest nonsense I've ever heard," the hangman scoffed. "Nepomuk's experiments, however, were pure science. Now give me back my boy and tell me what you've done with Peter and my son-in-law. I hope for your sake they're still alive. If not, this thunderstorm will be nothing compared to what happens when I get hold of you."

Kuisl still didn't dare make a move to approach Virgilius or the boy. Matthias's murder had shown him the watchmaker would stop at nothing. So Kuisl's threats were meant only to kill time until Virgilius made a false move. But the monk only gripped the screaming child tighter.

"Don't come any closer," Virgilius snarled. "Many people have already died so my dream can come true, and this little life here is of little importance to me now." He cast a longing glance at the automaton as thunder rolled over the countryside. "Now let's just stand here and wait."

At that moment, a soft tapping could be heard on the steps beneath them: footsteps, slow and deliberate, yet clearly audible over the sound of the pouring rain.

Someone was coming up the tower.

Down in the catacombs of the castle, Magdalena felt paralyzed as blue flames spread quickly across the altar. In a matter of seconds, the entire stone block was engulfed in a blaze that spread to the ground and, from there, in small pathways to the many mounds of white powder.

"Get out of here," Magdalena shouted, grabbing her son. "At once!"

Then she realized with horror that Simon couldn't run. She hesitated a moment, then pointed toward the exit and gave Peter a push. "Run, Peter! Quickly! I have to help your father!"

The boy seemed to understand. Ignoring the flickering blue sea of flames all around him, he ran toward the door and vanished. In the meantime, Magdalena leaned over her husband and started to shake him.

"Simon, you must get up."

Simon groaned and raised his arms slowly, but his legs seemed as if they were tied to the rock with strong ropes. Magdalena realized he wouldn't make it without her help, so she grabbed him under the arms and pulled him up until he was standing in front of her and leaning against the wall, his face as white as chalk. Bluish flames were crackling all around them, eating their way through the overturned shelves and broken mechanical devices, leaving only a narrow path open to the exit.

"You've got to hold onto me," she shouted over the roaring of the flames. "Do you understand, Simon? Hang on to me!"

She turned around, bent over, and pulled his arms over her shoulders, then stood up, gasping, and dragged her husband like a sack of flour through the raging flames.

At five feet tall, Simon was one of the most diminutive men in Schongau; his size was often ridiculed by coarse men in town, especially since Magdalena in fact was a few fingerbreadths taller. Now, however, his delicate stature would prove to be what saved his life. Magdalena felt like a pack mule, but at least she was able to pull Simon step by step from the burning room.

She staggered through the second room with the canopy bed and dressing table, where flames were already licking at the walnut veneer. Finally, gasping, she reached the round doorway as another bookshelf came crashing down somewhere behind her, burying the ivory horn, the globe, and the shiny bronze astrolabe. She was relieved to see that Simon was now able to hold on by himself and that his legs were moving slightly. The paralysis, in fact, seemed to be abating.

Coughing, Magdalena peered into the smoke-filled passageway through which she'd entered just a few minutes ago. She was unable to save her torch from the burning room, but it wasn't really necessary now. Horrified, she saw little fires burning on the floor of the tunnel as well. Virgilius must have strewn the phosphorus powder all over the catacombs, and now Magdalena realized what that meant: as soon as the flames arrived at the latrine where the laboratory was located, everything would explode.

Frantically she looked around for her son but couldn't find him in the clouds of smoke. She couldn't even imagine what might have happened to her second child. She could only hope that Peter had told her the truth and little Paul was somewhere outside with the treacherous Matthias and unharmed.

"Peter!" she shouted, her husband still clinging to her shoulders with his almost one hundred pounds. "Peter, where are you?"

She heard crying and finally a voice. "Mama, Mama, I'm here!"

Magdalena listened intently. The cry hadn't come from the right where the corridor led to the hermit's cave but from the left. Peter had run the wrong way, and she'd have to bring him back as soon as possible. If they spent too long down here, they would all be lost—either they would burn up or the smoke would suffocate them.

Cursing and struggling for breath, she stumbled through gray, foul-smelling clouds, her eyes tearing up from the smoke and Simon's weight practically crushing her to the ground. Nevertheless, slowly, yard by yard, she moved ahead, calling her son's name again and again. "Peter! Peter! Here I am!"

The damp, low passageway turned slightly upward, and after a short while, Magdalena noticed that there were fewer mounds of phosphorus, then eventually none at all. Behind her she heard the crash of another wall collapsing. Clouds of smoke reached out to her like long fingers, but she could feel a draft of fresh air coming from somewhere ahead, and the smoke was thinning out. Evidently Peter had intuitively chosen the right direction.

Turning another corner, she finally saw her son. She cried out with relief but just as quickly caught her breath. The passageway ended there; Peter was pounding frantically on a heavy wooden door without a handle.

"Mama! The garden! I want to see the garden."

"The . . . garden?" She looked at her son blankly. His face was as black as coal and he was coughing, but she didn't see any burns on his body. On the contrary, the three-year-old seemed almost cheerful. Carefully she set her husband down on the ground and examined the locked door.

"Which garden do you mean?" she responded.

"The garden with the jolly stone man who spits water," he said excitedly. "It's behind this door."

"You mean the . . . the monastery garden?" Suddenly she realized how the boys had been abducted. Virgilius must have lured the two from the garden into a hidden passageway there. Anxiously, she examined the weathered wood but couldn't find a handle or a keyhole. The hinges were massive.

"Damn," she hissed. "Another of the crazy watchmaker's infernal objects." She kicked the door, but it felt like solid brick. Nervously she looked back down the steep, slippery corridor from which clouds of smoke were still rising.

"If we can't think of something soon, we'll suffocate here like foxes in a burrow," she mumbled. In vain she examined the rock walls for hidden cracks or holes. Finally, she turned helplessly to Simon, who was lying on the ground behind her.

"Simon, can you hear me? We'll suffocate here. Wake up. I need your help."

Simon groaned and struggled to move as if he was in great pain; finally he managed to turn on one side and sit up. He was panting hard; clearly that little movement had caused him unbelievable effort.

Torn between hope and despair, Magdalena stared at her husband, whose paralysis was slowly beginning to wear off. Would it happen fast enough for him to help her? She doubted that, and in any case, she didn't know what she expected him to do. Snap his fingers and make the door open? The little medicus had so often come up with an idea that saved the day. She prayed now he would be able to walk and speak again as soon as possible. Tears welled up in her eyes when she thought of the unavoidable fate that awaited them both.

Suffocated to death on the wrong side of a door leading into a blooming garden.

"Mama, when can we leave?"

Magdalena awakened with a start from her dark musings and smiled wearily at her son. "We . . . we can't go, unfortunately, Peter. Father is sick and I don't know how to open this door."

"But all you have to do is press on the stone."

"What?"

She jumped up—she'd almost forgotten that Peter had been here before. It was possible the boy had observed how the door was opened.

"Which stone, Peter?" She took him up in her arms and looked him directly in the eye. "Listen now. This is very important. Which stone do I have to push?"

Silently Peter pointed to a square stone about as large as a fist, which protruded a finger's breadth from the wall. Magdalena hadn't noticed it before among all the other irregular stonework, but now it really stood out. The image of a laughing face, etched into its surface, seemed to jeer at her.

"*This* stone?" she asked cautiously.

Peter nodded, and Magdalena pressed the square button. Silently the stone slid back into the space behind it, and there was a click as the heavy wooden door opened a crack. Heavy rain could be heard now on the other side, accompanied by thunder and lightning that lit up the passageway for a moment.

"You . . . you are wonderful, Peter," Magdalena laughed. "For this, you can have honey cakes, as many as you can eat. But first I have to get your father out of here. Come, the fresh air will surely do him some good."

When they turned around, Magdalena was relieved to see Simon had already gotten onto his knees. He swayed like a reed in the wind, but he didn't fall. Breathing heavily, he reached out to his wife.

"I ccccaaaan . . . wallllk all by myyyself," he croaked. "By myyyself . . ."

Magdalena ran to help him before he could fall. "That's what you think," she replied, pulling him up and guiding him carefully to the door.

When the door opened all the way, they found themselves staring into another cave.

Magdalena uttered a brief cry of disappointment. She was sure they'd just entered another underground passageway, but then she felt the wind on her face, heard the rain coming down, and smelled the flowers in the garden. She realized they'd entered the artificial grotto the abbot had shown her just two days before. In the middle was the basin with the statuettes of the Greek gods. The door through which they'd entered the grotto was covered with gray plaster so as to blend in perfectly with the rock.

Peter had already run into the garden and was climbing jubilantly onto one of the little walls as the rain drummed down on him, washing the soot from his face. He waved to his mother cheerfully, seeming to have survived the recent terror unscathed.

Magdalena felt a lump in her throat when she thought of her younger son. Where had Matthias taken little Paul? Was he even still alive?

She was startled by something pressing against her shoulder. Simon was propping himself up against her. "I ccccaaaan . . . wallllk all by myyyself," he stammered again.

Simon let go of her and tottered like an automaton into the garden.

The medicus had walked only a few yards when they heard a mighty rumbling. At first Magdalena thought it was thunder, but then the earth beneath their feet began to shake and large rocks came rolling down the hill into the garden. An especially heavy boulder crashed directly in front of her, burying the basin with the Greek statuettes.

Behind Magdalena, a rumbling could be heard in the passageways below, sounding as if hell had in fact opened its gates. Instinctively the hangman's daughter threw herself down onto the damp lawn and watched as the little grotto behind her finally collapsed.

Hic est porta ad loca inferna . . .

The green fire had finally reached the cesspit below.

Jakob Kuisl and Virgilius held their breath as the footsteps on the creaking staircase approached the belfry. The steps were slow and calm; whoever was groping his way up evidently had time on his hands. Or was he too tired and old to move any faster?

Finally a black hood appeared in the opening. The figure continued climbing until he'd arrived at the landing, his torch bathing the belfry in flickering glow. At last his thin, arthritic fingers pulled back a scarf that had been obscuring his face.

Virgilius shouted out with surprise.

Before them stood the Andechs abbot. His face was as deeply furrowed as parched earth, and his thin tonsure as white as snow. Maurus Rambeck seemed to have aged years in the last few weeks.

"Maurus," Virgilius said. "What are you doing here?"

"Trying to prevent you from causing any more harm," the abbot replied firmly. "If that's still possible. Let the child go." Pointing to the small crying boy, he walked slowly toward the watchmaker.

"Never!" Virgilius shouted. He drew back and held the struggling child over the stormy void. "Stay where you are, Maurus. Even you won't stop me from bringing back my Aurora."

"You're sick, Virgilius," Father Maurus said softly. "Very sick, and this is the end. Accept that; put yourself in God's hands. Don't bring any more sins down on yourself or this monastery."

"But . . . but you helped me," Virgilius pleaded. "You yourself wanted Aurora to come back to me."

"I never wanted that," replied the abbot, his voice rising. "I wanted all this madness to end. Yes, to save you, but also to save the monastery. I see now that was an error."

When Kuisl stepped out of the darkness, the abbot noticed him for the first time. Brother Maurus raised his slim eyebrows in astonishment, and his tired but intelligent eyes flashed with emotion.

"You're here, too?" he asked. Then the monk regained his composure and a faint smile appeared on his weathered face. "I should have expected as much. Your burgomaster is right; you really are an annoying snoop. But what does it matter? It's all over now."

"You knew all along, didn't you?" the hangman retorted. "You knew your brother was behind all this."

Maurus Rambeck shook his head wearily. "Not at first, though I'll admit I had my suspicions. Virgilius had been pestering me for weeks about the hosts. He wanted me to get them for him, just for a while, and he would give them back. Naturally I didn't go along with that."

"Curses on you, Maurus," the watchmaker snarled. He'd moved a few steps closer to his brother, the crying child still in his arms. "All these . . . these problems wouldn't have come up if you'd just given me the hosts. I could have switched them with other ones. No one would have noticed, and Elisabeth would be back with me again."

"Forget about your Elisabeth," Maurus shouted. "Don't you realize that you can't bring her back, Virgilius? She's been dead now for more than thirty years." The old man drew closer to his younger brother, his eyes flashing with anger. "Elisabeth's remains are rotting in some cemetery in Augsburg. Her flesh, her red lips, her tender breasts that you longed for so much have all turned to dust long ago. Only her spirit lives on, but you can't bring that back, either. Only God can do that."

"No! That . . . that can't be! She . . . she must come back to me; she just has to." Virgilius stamped his feet on the ground like an angry child, shaking Paul so violently the boy started screaming. When the hangman advanced, Virgilius ran back to the opening and held the struggling child over the void.

"Get back! Everyone get back!" he screamed. "We're going to wait for the lightning to come from heaven and bring my woman back to me." He held his head out to the sky, opened his mouth as if to drink from the falling drops, and closed his eyes to let the water stream down his face.

"Elisabeth was Virgilius's great love," Father Maurus tried to explain, looking sadly at his mad brother. "Back then, his name was Markus. He was smart, well-read, and extremely sensitive, and when Elisabeth died, it broke his heart. Our parents thought it would pass, and so did I, but instead things became worse and worse until my brother would no longer even get out of bed or eat or drink. A doctor finally concluded that sending him abroad would help him forget." He sighed. "So my wealthy father gave him money, and my brother embarked on long voyages. In fact, he seemed to be getting better; he sent us optimistic news from Africa and the West Indies. We should have suspected the madness was still simmering beneath the surface."

Virgilius started humming a soft melody, the same one his automaton played, but the sound clashed with the crying of the child like a poorly tuned instrument. Kuisl wondered again how he might overpower the watchmaker, but the child was still dangling over the void.

"When my brother came to Andechs and started work here as a watchmaker, I thought he was cured," Rambeck continued, shaking his head. "But then he built this . . . this monster." Disgusted, he pointed at the grinning automaton. "He dressed it like Elisabeth; he even gave it her nickname. It must have been that damned book about golems that sent him over the edge. From that point on there was nothing I or anyone could say to him. He didn't respond to my letters, so not until I returned from Salzburg and assumed the position of abbot did I see how bad the situation was. But then it was too late. All he ever wanted was the sacred hosts."

"And when he didn't get them, he simply staged an abduction and extorted you," the hangman replied harshly. "Admit it, you knew he was behind it."

"I . . . suspected so. When I found the book in our library about golems, it slowly dawned on me what Virgilius was up to." The abbot shook his head regretfully. "I knew I could no longer stop him, but I also didn't want to turn him over to the bailiffs. After all, he's my brother. They would have tortured him and burned him alive."

"So instead my friend Nepomuk has to die," Kuisl growled.

Father Maurus shrugged apologetically. "The whole thing was like a little trickle that grows and grows until a river just carries you away. It was driving me crazy. When you caught me in Virgilius's house, I was on the point of confessing, but I still had hope you might be able to stop him, that I could learn where he was hiding out."

As Virgilius continued humming the automaton's melody, Kuisl watched him cautiously, but Paul was still dangling over the void, crying.

"It wasn't Virgilius who dug up the dead monk in the cemetery; it was you, and you set fire to him and threw him in the well," Kuisl thundered now at the abbot. "You were afraid we'd catch on to what he was doing. Admit it."

"That's true," Maurus smiled. "It seemed too dangerous to have you turn him in to the judge in Weilheim, so I set fire to the corpse of our dearly departed brother Quirin, who'd been suffering from consumption, and placed one of Virgilius's walking sticks beside it. I even cut off Quirin's ring finger so he would look just like Virgilius. After all, a corpse can't commit a murder, can it?" He winked at the hangman. "Tell me how you figured it out."

"It was you yourself who raised my suspicion when you found the body in the well so quickly," Kuisl replied. "Besides, how could a hunchback with a walking stick have dug up a grave? And there were no prints in the ground from a cane. The only thing I couldn't figure out was this handkerchief."

The abbot looked bewildered. "What handkerchief?"

"Alongside the grave we found a lace handkerchief with the initial *A*. My superstitious son-in-law thought it belonged to Aurora."

"Oh, that?" Rambeck laughed softly, shaking his head again. "I must have lost the handkerchief near the grave. *A* stands for *abbot*. Every abbot in this monastery receives such cloths, along with gloves, napkins, and other such frilly things. They all bear this insignia."

Virgilius's humming finally stopped. The hunchbacked watchmaker's eyes were still closed as he held the boy out in the rain like a sacrificial offering.

"I . . . I understand," Virgilius murmured suddenly as if in a trance. "I finally understand. There can be no new life until an old one dies. It all makes sense. You here, Maurus, are the messenger of Christ, and the hangman is a messenger from hell—and then this boy. Above all the boy. God sent him to me."

There was another blinding flash of lightning as Virgilius stepped just a bit closer to the opening. Solemnly, he held the crying child up to the black clouds.

"O, God of vengeance, take this living sacrifice from me and give me back my Aurora," he pleaded.

Then he dropped the boy over the side.

Like corpses, Magdalena and Simon lay motionless on the ground of the monastery garden, while Peter played atop the ivy-covered walls, undeterred by the steady drumbeat of rain. Behind them, the last section of the grotto had collapsed, sealing the entrance to the underworld off forever.

Simon coughed and spat phlegm and water, but the cool rain had helped relieve his paralysis somewhat. Now he could even talk, though the words came out with a strange drawl. In faltering sentences, he told Magdalena what had happened in the passageways.

"He took Paul with him," he gasped. "Along with that damned Matthias. I . . . I knew right away that that fellow wasn't to be trusted."

Magdalena shrugged sadly. "You're right, but that doesn't bring our son back. Even if he's alive, he's out there somewhere in this storm. If I only knew — " Suddenly she jumped up. "Of course. How could I forget?" she laughed. "This damned fear muddles my mind. They've surely gone up to the belfry."

Simon frowned. "The belfry?"

Magdalena nodded vigorously. "Remember, Simon? It must have been Matthias who almost threw me off the tower. I presume I interrupted him setting up everything for his master's great experiment. This time, they intend to carry it out. The lightning will surely strike the belfry."

She quickly stood up and called to Peter, who came running. Anxiously she eyed her husband on the ground. "Can you walk or would you rather . . . ?"

"Stay here while my youngest son is in the hands of a madman?" Simon croaked, struggling to get up. "Are you kidding? I'd rather crawl on all fours to that blasted bell tower."

"Then let's go." Magdalena pulled her husband to his feet, took Peter by the hand, and led them both quickly across the fields and meadows toward the monastery. Simon staggered and stumbled but, with Magdalena's occasional help, was able to walk on his own. So they moved ahead faster than expected.

"You may be right," Simon gasped, pointing at the dark steeple in the distance that seemed to sway slightly in the storm. "If lightning strikes anywhere around here, it would be up there."

Magdalena crossed herself. "God forbid it comes to that."

Storm clouds still hung dark and heavy over the Holy Mountain, rain poured down, the storm raged like a wild beast, and hail flattened the fields of grain.

Along the way they came across splintered branches and fruit trees knocked down by the storm. Clearly the harvest this year would be a disaster and people would go hungry again.

A few minutes later they arrived at the outer monastery wall. Blown open by the wind, the gate was standing crooked on its hinges. Silently they ran through deserted streets, ankle-deep in mud. Here and there, lights could be seen burning in the farm buildings and in the monastery, and though Magdalena thought she saw anxious faces peering out from between the slats of the shutters, she hurried on.

Briefly she thought of asking the abbot or some of the other monks for help. But the Andechs bailiffs were still after Simon, and she had to hope her father in any case was on his way to the church tower with some of Wartenberg's soldiers. No doubt he would have figured out that Virgilius wanted to carry out his experiments up there.

Climbing the final yards up the steep slope, they arrived in the muddy church square and stared up at the tower. Rain fell in their eyes, and though it was only seven in the evening, it was almost dark.

"There!" Simon cried suddenly pointing to a tiny point in the belfry that seemed to be moving. "You were right. Someone is up there. But I can't see who."

Magdalena squinted and held her hand up to shield her face from the downpour, but she could only make out a figure holding a sort of bundle out over the scaffolding. There was no sign of her father or the count's soldiers.

"Whoever it is up there, we must hurry," she said. "If necessary, I'll go alone and you can stay down here with Peter, and I . . ."

Hearing a soft groan inside the church, Magdalena stopped

short and listened. Then she raised her mud-splattered skirt and ran toward the portal while Simon and Peter followed close behind.

The nave was so dark that only the vague contours of objects were visible. Leaves and twigs had blown in through the damaged roof and columns, and the altars and confessional stools stood out from the wet floor like black boulders. A few of the artistic stained glass windows had been damaged by the storm, and the pews were strewn with colorful splinters of glass.

In the middle of the church, a figure lay in a pool of blood. His arms and legs were contorted and twisted like those of a broken doll, and though he was groaning and twitching slightly, he was otherwise motionless. Slowly he turned his head toward Magdalena and she finally recognized who it was.

Matthias.

Magdalena stared up at a gaping hole in the roof and the torn canvas that had been temporarily covering it. The knacker's boy must have fallen straight through the opening. It was a miracle he was still alive.

"You . . . you monster!" she shouted, running toward him. "What did you do with my children? I trusted you, I . . ."

She saw the smiling face of the silent journeyman and stopped short. Even now that she knew Matthias had abducted her children, he looked friendly, helpful. Could he really be in league with Virgilius?

Moaning, he stretched out his hand and seemed to wipe the floor. It took Magdalena a while to realize he was writing something on the mud- and blood-stained surface. She knelt down to read it before the rain could wash it away.

I am sorry.

"Bah, as if that changes anything," exclaimed Simon, who had now arrived on the scene. "He's sorry. This scoundrel has been deceiving us all along and working with Virgilius. He's a criminal and kidnapper, and perhaps even Brother Laurentius's killer. And he was out to get you, too."

But even Simon couldn't keep his son from leaning down and passing his hand through the man's blood-spattered red hair.

"Matthias sick?" Peter asked anxiously.

Magdalena nodded. "Your friend Matthias is very sick," she said softly. "He's probably going to die." She cast an anxious gaze up at the balcony, then at the stairway leading from there up to the belfry. "But before that perhaps, he's going to tell us what's happening there. Do you hear me, Matthias?" She turned to the mortally injured workman. "Who's up there? If you want to make amends, do it now."

Matthias grumbled, then reached for his dirty, torn jacket. Pulling a wax tablet and stylus from a pocket, he started laboriously composing a message.

"This is taking too long," Simon groaned. "In the meantime, Virgilius may kill our child."

"Wait!" Magdalena raised her hand for silence, but she, too, kept staring through the hole in the roof where the tower was clearly visible. "Just a moment. This might be important."

Finally Matthias finished writing. He groaned and handed the tablet to Magdalena, who quickly started reading.

Virgilius and the boy are in the belfry. So is your father and the abbot. No harm will come to the boy. Don't let the boys think badly of me. Only God knows the entire truth.

Magdalena looked sorrowfully at the childish scribbles.

Only God knows the entire truth . . .

When she looked down again, she saw his head had tipped to one side and his eyes were staring rigidly skyward. A few green and red beech leaves floated down from the hole above.

"Matthias dead?" Peter asked anxiously.

Magdalena nodded. She couldn't hold back a few tears forming in the corner of her eyes. "He . . . he is now with our dear

Lord, and we'll probably never find out why he conspired with this madman. But deep inside, I know he wasn't a bad man."

"Not a bad man?" Simon shook his head furiously. "Magdalena, he abducted our children. He's a murderer and a criminal."

"How many murderers has my father executed who would perhaps have been saints in another life?" she said softly. "And how many scoundrels are running around free, dressed in expensive clothes."

She crossed herself, rose to her feet, and straightened up.

"You stay down below here with Peter," she told her husband gruffly. "I'll go up there now and bring my son back. If my father and the abbot can't do it, I'll just have to do it myself. To hell with Virgilius."

Without another word, she ran toward the balcony that lay in the growing darkness.

There was something in the watchmaker's eyes that tipped Jakob Kuisl off a fraction of a second before he released the boy.

An instant just long enough for Kuisl to lunge for the opening. Slowly, as if God had ordered time to stop, the hangman saw his grandson falling. He reached out and just managed to catch the bawling child by the collar. There was a horrifying rip as the clothing started to tear, but then it held. With his arms and legs thrashing about, Paul dangled like a marionette from his grandfather's outstretched arms.

As Kuisl pulled the boy back inside with a loud shout, Virgilius gave him a sudden push from behind. For what seemed like an eternity, the hangman tottered at the edge of the opening. The watchmaker screeched behind him in an inhumanly high pitch. "The sacrifice! You took away my sacrifice. I need this boy so that Aurora can live."

A sudden gust of wind struck the hangman from the front, allowing him to regain his balance. One last time, he glanced down into the gaping void and then, summoning all his strength, threw himself back onto the platform. The boy landed safely beside him and clung tightly to his grandfather.

"It's over, Virgilius," the abbot shouted into the storm. "Give up and return to God. It's still not too late."

"Never!" Only the whites of the watchmaker's eyes were still visible, shining eerily in the gathering darkness as he broke into a defiant laugh.

"God took away what was dearest to me; how can I return to him? He mocked me and forsook me." Virgilius's voice was so loud that it even drowned out the clap of thunder. "I can be my own God. I don't need him. Don't you understand, Maurus? It's faith alone that makes this Christian Moloch so strong. I used my faith to bring Aurora back."

"God alone can create life," the abbot admonished, approaching him with raised hands. "Repent, Virgilius. Let me grant you absolution."

"I curse your absolution. I curse God." Virgilius ran to his automaton, grasped it by its stiff arms, and looked out into the darkened heavens.

"All I need is a single bolt of lightning," he cried, looking up into the clouds. "There will come a day when we realize that lightning, too, isn't divine, but a natural phenomenon we can use for our own purposes." He reached for the wire leading from the ceiling down to the bier, where it branched into other smaller wires. Carefully he checked the connections. "I must have done something wrong. There must be some reason the lightning hasn't hit the steeple yet," he murmured. "Exactly, that must be it. We must work even more carefully if we wish to abolish God. Like a watchmaker. We must—"

Suddenly the stairway started creaking again and footsteps could be heard coming up. Virgilius turned around to stare at the woman who had just appeared in the opening. He couldn't recognize her in the darkness. Her hair was drenched from the rain and she was breathing heavily from the climb up the stairs, but she held her determined head up and chin out. Like an angry, vengeful goddess, she raised her hand to point at the watchmaker, who cried out in delight.

"Aurora . . . is it you?" he asked hesitantly. "Did you finally come back to me after all these years? But . . ." His gaze shifted from the automaton to the woman standing before him in the opening. "How . . . how is that possible? The lightning . . ."

"Go to hell, Virgilius," she snarled.

At this moment, there was a crash so loud that Kuisl thought the tower would split apart. A fraction of a second later, a blue light as thick as a man's arm shot from the top of the steeple directly into the puppet. Virgilius, still clinging to an end of the wire, was enveloped in a bluish aura like a gigantic halo. Flames shot out from his hair, his sleeves, even from his ears, and as he opened his mouth in a shrill, inhuman scream, tiny flames appeared there, as well.

Virgilius twitched and thrashed. His whole body trembled as he continued holding the wire. Then it became a giant flaming torch.

The force of the explosion threw Kuisl back against the side of the tower as everything around him erupted in flames. His ears were ringing shrilly, but otherwise all he could hear was blood pulsing through his head. Coughing, the Andechs abbot crawled toward the trapdoor, his robe ablaze. In the opposite corner, Magdalena clutched her boy in her arms, her eyes and mouth open wide in a scream, though Kuisl still couldn't hear a thing.

He jumped up, rushed to Magdalena, seized her and the child, and pushed them both toward the trapdoor. All around them timbers were beginning to fall from the ceiling. Though Kuisl could feel flames singeing his beard, he didn't stop until he made sure his daughter and grandson made it to the trapdoor over the stairs. Then he climbed down behind them.

When he turned around one last time, he could see Virgilius

still standing like a flaming scarecrow alongside his beloved Aurora. A blackened clump engulfed in flames, he bared his teeth and stared at the automaton he had created. The puppet's wax face was melting like honey, revealing the metal parts and iron beneath.

Her dead mechanical eyes glowed, and for a brief moment it looked to Kuisl as if it wasn't Virgilius clinging to his automaton but the automaton clinging to its creator.

Then more burning beams fell from the ceiling, burying the two.

The hangman rushed down the stairs, away from the chaotic scene above, just a few yards behind Magdalena and Paul. He could hear the wind whistling through the tower, fanning the fire, a flaming hell they struggled to escape as they staggered down the steep stairway. They stumbled a few times but always managed to grab hold of the railing at the last moment.

Arriving breathlessly in the nave, Kuisl felt enormous relief on finding his second grandchild and son-in-law unharmed and waiting. The Andechs abbot stood to the side, coughing, his robe burned up to his knees and his face blackened with soot, but otherwise apparently uninjured.

"That . . . that was the punishment of God," Maurus Rambeck gasped, staring blankly into space. "We've seen the face of God."

"If we don't hurry, we'll see it again soon," replied Kuisl, nudging the others toward the exit. "This fire will destroy the entire monastery."

Standing in front of the church, they watched the burning steeple light up the darkness like a mighty torch. Glowing beams and shingles fell on the church roof below, and soon the entire structure was in flames, threatening to spread to the neighboring monastery buildings.

More and more monks — as well as pilgrims and simple villagers — gathered in the square, staring up in disbelief at the roaring conflagration that continued to grow as the rain gradually eased off.

"This is the end of the monastery," whispered the abbot next to Kuisl.

"Or the beginning," the hangman replied. "Didn't you want to build a new, finer one anyway? If not now, when?"

Suddenly shouts could be heard in the crowd, voices of the count and his soldiers assigning men to various fire brigades. Armed with buckets, people ran like frightened ants in all directions—pilgrims and Benedictines side by side, all trying to control the fire. Kuisl spotted his cousin Michael Graetz in the front row of the crowd with some other dishonorable people. The hangman suspected the battle was hopeless. Wind whipped flames toward the monastery and the outlying buildings, and a few glowing roof shingles were already falling from the far-off brewery.

"Damn it, hangman," cried Leopold von Wartenberg, who had fought his way over to them. "What did you do up there? I'll have Master Hans personally boil you in oil for this."

Unlike the figures around him, who were covered with ash, mud, and soot, the count was still as neat as a pin, lightly perfumed, and untouched by the slightest smudge of dirt. Evidently Leopold von Wartenberg was better at giving commands than at doing things himself. When he raised his hand to strike the dishonorable hangman, the Andechs abbot intervened.

"Your Excellency, this man is innocent," Maurus Rambeck said firmly. The abbot seemed to have regained his former haughty manner. "It was the lightning that struck in the tower, burning my brother to death and destroying the automaton."

"Your brother who is already dead?" The count sneered. "Then it's true what this shrewd hangman surmised? Virgilius was behind all of this?"

Maurus Rambeck nodded. "I'll draft a report first thing tomorrow morning and make a clean breast of it all. But for now, let's all lend a hand. We must at least save the library."

"My God, the library!" Simon hobbled toward the burning monastery, wringing his hands. "All the beautiful books. We must save them."

"Damn it, Simon, stop," cried Magdalena, while both children clung to her singed skirt. "You can't run that fast yet. Come and care for your two little boys instead."

But Simon had already disappeared with one of the fire brigades.

She sighed. "Perhaps it would have been better if that strange poison had affected him a bit longer. Then he wouldn't always be running off on me."

"When will you women finally understand you can't change us men?" the voice of her father grumbled behind her.

He smiled at his daughter, his black beard burned away in spots and little embers still glowing in others. "Your husband loves his children, Magdalena," he continued with feigned severity. "But they're safe now, and at present he has to care about his other beloved things."

"As long as he still remembers his family," she sighed. "Books, books, books are all this dreamer thinks about. I'd better not tell him that a few especially valuable ones went up in flames down in the catacombs, or else—" Suddenly she seized her father by the arm. "My God, Nepomuk's and Virgilius's notebooks. Are they perhaps . . . ?"

The hangman nodded grimly. "They burned up in the tower. In all the confusion, they must have fallen out of my pocket. What a shame." He looked at his daughter seriously, but she noticed a slight flicker in his eyes. Only she and her mother were able to tell when he was lying.

"Believe me, it's better like this," Kuisl continued. "Knowledge like this can always be used both for good and evil. Nepomuk was committed to doing good, but as long as there are men like Virgilius, such books shouldn't be allowed in our libraries. Their time will come soon enough." Without another word he turned to leave.

"Where . . . where are you going?" she cried. "Damn it. Can't you men just say what you're doing and stop disappearing without saying a thing?"

Kuisl turned to her again. "I'm going to the clinic. What else? If Simon isn't there tending his patients, I'll have to do it myself. Or do you just want to let the sick there burn to death?"

With a defiant look on her face, Magdalena fell silent; then finally she broke into a smile.

"Do you know what?" she said, squeezing her children's hands hard as Kuisl hobbled off toward the clinic. "Your grandfather is a stubborn, dishonorable, eccentric scoundrel, but I think the dear Lord loves him just the same."

20

IT WAS LATE MORNING WHEN SIMON STRUGGLED
to open his eyes, feeling almost as if he was still paralyzed. Then
he realized dirt and soot were still sticking to his eyelids. He had
worked until late in the night, along with some Benedictine
monks, to save the books in the library. Simon had been one of
the last to venture into the burning building. As he emerged
from the library at around two in the morning, an especially
large pile of books in his arms, the flaming roof had crashed
down behind him. He'd at least been able to save Athanasius
Kircher's *Ars magna sciendi*, but the Andechs chronicle that Matthias had stolen from him in the clinic was still missing.

Simon lay in bed in the knacker's house, staring out a little
window at the blue morning sky. Birds were twittering, and a
ray of sun fell directly on his face. He still couldn't believe the
monastery had been almost completely destroyed by fire the day
before. Only the tavern and a few outlying buildings had been
spared, and all that remained of the church was the foundation.
When Simon had finally collapsed with exhaustion, the fire still
hadn't been completely extinguished.

Stretching, he was relieved to see he could move his arms

and legs again. They hurt as if he'd been lying all night on a cold stone floor, but at least the paralysis was gone. What kind of devilish poison could Virgilius have given him yesterday?

Virgilius . . .

He shuddered when he thought about the last few terrible days, days he wouldn't forget for the rest of his life. Only the laughter of his children brought his mind back to the present. They were standing in the doorway with Magdalena, grinning, and when they saw he was awake, they hopped onto the bed and began jumping around noisily. They seemed to have coped well with the dreadful events of the past day. Perhaps they were just too little to understand.

"Stop, stop," Simon groaned, trying to chase the boys off the bed again. "Take pity on your poor, sick father!"

"What your father needs more than anything is a bath," Magdalena responded with a smile. "You look like Beelzebub in person," she laughed as she pulled the covers off. "Come on. Graetz put out a fresh basin of water for you on the table in the next room. He asked to be excused because he had to go and see the priest about the burial service for Matthias." Her face darkened suddenly. "He still can't believe that his helper was conspiring with Virgilius. Nor can I, to be honest. Graetz is arranging for a mass to be said for Matthias tomorrow at the parish church in Erling."

She shook her head as if to cast off evil thoughts, then she gave her husband a gentle kick. "Now get up, I said. Everybody in town has been up for hours while you've lolled around here in bed."

"Please, please, I'm coming." Simon stood up with a yawn and rubbed his eyes. "We were able to save most of the books last night, and for that, we should be allowed to sleep a little longer." With a serious face, he turned to his wife. "The church treasures were destroyed for the most part, I assume?"

Magdalena shook her head. "On the contrary, all the relics

were saved. The fire stopped right in front of the holy chapel. Only the wooden bolts were charred."

"By all the saints, that's really a miracle."

"That's what everyone is saying," she replied with a grin. "No doubt that means even more pilgrims will come flocking to the Holy Mountain in the future. The abbot spoke to the pilgrims this morning and already promised them a new, even more beautiful monastery. The workmen in Wessobrunn, as well as those from Schongau, will be busy. Hemerle and a few others want to stay right here."

Simon entered the next room, leaned over the washbasin, and rubbed the worst of the dirt from his face, while Peter and Paul played with a wooden top at his feet.

"Basically, that's exactly what the prior always wanted," he said finally, shaking the water from his hair. "A new monastery. That's why he and the librarian melted down all the monstrances, golden chalices, and reliquaries."

"But they'll keep none of it. Wartenberg's soldiers carted them both off to Weilheim before dawn, where they'll soon be put on trial." Magdalena's lips narrowed. "To judge from my father's description of Master Hans, they'll soon wish they were dead."

"And Nepomuk?" Simon asked.

Magdalena handed him a fresh towel. "The abbot promised to plead for his release, and until then, the torture won't proceed," she replied with a wink. "My father is already on his way to Weilheim to bring Nepomuk the news personally. He was smart enough to take advantage of the chaos here and run off. After all, he's still a wanted man. Maurus will ask that he not be prosecuted for killing the dead hunter, however, as the other guards have apparently admitted to shooting their own comrade with a crossbow."

"Then Maurus will remain abbot of the monastery?" Simon asked.

"Well, it certainly won't be the prior, and there's no other candidate for the position."

"We probably won't stay here much longer." Simon put on his old jacket, still wet from the rain the day before, along with his bucket-top boots, which were slightly burned at the tips. "But there's one thing I still have to do," he said. "I should have done it much sooner, but then all this got in the way. I'll be back again soon, I promise."

With a final smile, he slipped out the door.

"Simon," Magdalena picked up her skirt and ran into the garden after him, but her husband was already far down the path on his way to the monastery. The ground was still wet from the day before, and mist was rising in the bright morning sun. "Wait, I wanted to tell you something! We—"

With a sigh she threw up her hands and turned to her children, who were rubbing their sleepy eyes after a little quarrel. "Your father will probably never change," she said, patting the boys on the heads. "Too bad for him. He just won't find out. We can keep the secret to ourselves for a while, can't we?"

The children clung to her legs, and Magdalena felt a knot burning in her abdomen. With a gentle smile, she turned around and reentered the house.

Even if the church had been reduced to ashes, she would light a candle for Saint Walburga that night.

Still unsteady, Simon hurried toward the Holy Mountain, which looked like an enormous pile of charcoal under the radiant blue sky.

The fires had been extinguished, but all that remained of many of the buildings were blackened skeletons and the columns of smoke rising above them. Here and there, monks and some local residents were looking for the few things that could still be salvaged. The apothecary and the watchmaker's house had also been destroyed by the fire. Simon could see workmen standing in front of many buildings, trying to estimate the damage and calculating how much wood, stone, nails, and plaster would be needed to rebuild. As bad as the fire was for the monastery, the reconstruction was a gold mine for local citizens impoverished by the war. And no one seemed too concerned that the money had been amassed through the sale of melted-down relics.

That, too, is a sort of miracle, Simon thought grimly. *Perhaps even the dear Lord wanted the church's treasures to be redistributed among the people in this way.*

Finally the medicus reached his destination. Before him was the clinic that had been nothing but a foul stable a little more than a week ago. He was relieved to see the damage here wasn't serious. Some of the roof shingles had been singed and there were a few piles of ashes on the square out front, but evidently the sick were already back in their beds.

As Simon approached, the door suddenly opened from within and Jakob Schreevogl looked back at him with surprise.

"You're here?" the patrician said with a smile. "They told me you collapsed last night and were unconscious. I had no idea I'd see you so soon again."

"It appears I'm no longer needed here," replied Simon, entering the large, well-ventilated room and nodding his approval. It had been recently swept, and fragrant reeds had been spread across the floor. Around two dozen patients lay dozing in their beds. All of them seemed well cared-for, and their bandages and compresses recently changed.

"Are you sure you don't want to sell your brick factory and try your hand as a medicus?" asked Simon, amazed. "You really seem to have talent for health care."

Schreevogl shook his head. "I wouldn't have been able to do it without the help of some of the monks. Besides, the worst is behind us, thank God, and the number of patients is falling. I will admit I have enjoyed it, even though it doesn't pay even half as much as owning a business in Schongau. But you surely didn't come just to pay me pay me compliments, did you?" he said with a wink. "You asked me yesterday to look around in the tavern and find out where they get their food. Well, I can imagine now why you had me do that, and I have a surprise for you."

Simon nodded excitedly. "This damned plague *must* have something to do with the tavern. There are just too many patients who ate there before getting sick. What did you learn?"

"You were right."

Simon looked at the patrician, puzzled. "What do you mean? For God's sake, don't make me drag it out of you. Does that mean—"

"The food in the tavern all came from the same supplier," Schreevogl replied with a grin. "I inspected the meat, eggs, and vegetables. Much of it was old, and maggots had even infested some of the meat. The tavern is almost surely the source of the illness."

"But . . . but why did the tavern serve such food?" Simon asked, astonished.

"On the instruction of the prior. The supplier had influential allies in the monastery council. The same man also sold the monastery beeswax diluted with fat and overpriced pictures of saints. It seems there was a big payoff."

His heart pounding, Simon held his breath. "Do I know the supplier?" he whispered.

Schreevogl nodded with a grin. "I suppose you could say that."

"Oh, God, it's—"

"Karl Semer. The abbot cancelled all deliveries from him as of this morning, and Semer will never be allowed to sell anything to the monastery again." The patrician smiled mischievously. "And he will no longer be selling anything to the Wittelsbach count, either. I made sure myself that His Excellency learned about it."

Simon laughed so loud that some of the patients woke up

with a start. "That fat old moneybags," he cried out, shaking his head again and again. "That's what he and his son get for their wheeling and dealing. This will take Semer down a peg or two." Suddenly he turned serious. "I hope this makes him a bit more reasonable in the Schongau town council. He's made some serious threats against me and Magdalena."

Schreevogl shrugged and went to one of the patients to change the dressing on his leg. "Don't worry about that. I can't imagine the Schongau Council would elect him burgomaster again under these conditions. Before that could happen — "

The door flew open with a crash, and Count Wittelsbach stormed in. He wore a stiff red jacket, just as the day before; his handlebar mustache was carefully curled; and as so often, he smelled of soap and perfume. But his eyes betrayed that he hadn't slept much the night before.

"Ah, there you are, bathhouse surgeon," he began impatiently, without so much as looking at Jakob Schreevogl. "I've been wondering where you were. Have you seen your father-in-law?"

Simon looked at him innocently. "I thought he had reported to you about the events yesterday, didn't he?"

"No, confound it, he didn't." Then he waved his hand dismissively. "But basically I don't care what this hangman does. Let the monks deal with him. I've had the entrances to those damned catacombs sealed and the relic forgerers led away. My work here is finished." Then he hesitated briefly. "Actually, I'm not here on account of the hangman but because of my son."

"Is he better?" Simon asked, his heart pounding. "Did the Jesuit's Powder work?"

Leopold von Wartenberg nodded. "Yes, the fever has gone down and he does seem to be getting better. I . . . I have you to thank for that." He straightened up. "Therefore I have an offer to make you."

Simon frowned. "What do you have in mind?"

"We're traveling back to Munich today," he declared. "My family could use a doctor like you. There are still some rooms free in our palace, and the pay would be at least ten times what you're earning now. You could care for my son, take on a few wealthy patients, and otherwise lead a good life. How would that suit you?"

Simon's head began to spin. Was it possible? Could someone like him, who had dropped out of medical school in Ingolstadt and was working as a dishonorable bathhouse surgeon, really settle down and practice medicine in Munich? This was exactly the kind of post his late father had always wanted for him. And the count would certainly know how to help him gain the proper approvals.

"You're hesitating?" the count asked.

"No, no, it's just . . ." Simon shook his head and laughed, but then he looked at the count anxiously.

"And my wife and my children?" he asked softly. "What about them?"

"A hangman's daughter?" Leopold von Wartenberg raised his bushy eyebrows. "A dishonorable woman and two equally dishonorable kids in my house? How would that be arranged?" He stopped to think for a moment. "Very well, I could let you visit them from time to time. They could live in the Tanners' Quarter in Munich and you could send them a little money for a while." The count chuckled. "But love comes and love goes, and I'm sure you'll soon find another woman with a better social standing."

Simon rocked his head from side to side as if he was considering the offer. "Well . . ."

Leopold von Wartenberg winked mischievously at him. "Our coach is leaving from the monastery at noon," he said. "You could travel with our group."

"That's . . . really very generous of you," the little medicus began hesitantly. "But . . . uh . . . I'm afraid Munich will have to get along without me." He straightened up and turned his nose up almost the way the count had. "I'm sorry, but your city stinks too much of perfume; so I wish you a good day and farewell." Bowing slightly, he skipped out the door. Out of the corner of his eye, he could see the count standing in the middle of the clinic, open-mouthed like a carp gasping for air. He didn't say a word.

"We'll see each other in Schongau," Schreevogl called after the medicus. "And give my greetings to Magdalena. By God, she's the prettiest and stubbornest woman in the whole Priests' Corner."

Simon smiled and took a deep breath. The Andechs air still smelled of fire, but also of burning coal, sweat, beer mash, and a bit of incense.

This was the odor of people, and Simon loved it.

Nepomuk was startled when the door to his cell opened a crack. Blinded by the light, he squinted. Early that morning they had fetched him from the hole and locked him in this larger cell. There was no window here either and the straw stank as if it hadn't been changed for years, but he had room enough now to stretch out, he had been given fresh water and a slice of bread, and there were far fewer rats. After the hell of recent days, it almost felt like paradise.

They had intended to continue the torture that morning, and the monk had been praying all night in preparation for his great journey. He knew he wouldn't survive another day of torture. Six of his fingers had been broken, and Master Hans had pulled the fingernails out of the others, one by one. His right shoulder had been dislocated, pain radiated up to the top of his skull, and his arms and legs were covered with burns.

Nepomuk was sure the pain would be over that day. Either he would die from the torture or would, screaming and half-mad, confess to everything they asked. His subsequent burning at the stake would be a welcome relief.

Now the door opened all the way, and Nepomuk saw Master Hans on the threshold.

"Have you come to take me away?" he groaned, addressing the white-haired man with the red eyes who had tormented him over and over in his nightmares. "I almost thought you'd forgotten me."

Master Hans shook his head. His lips were red, and his rat-like eyes seemed to glow in the dark. "The torture has been postponed," he grumbled. "Who knows who ordered that. You seem to have powerful advocates, monk."

"The torture . . . has been postponed?" Nepomuk struggled to get to his feet, but he was too weak. He fell back to the ground, groaning and glaring up at the executioner like a whipped ox. "But . . . but why?"

"Don't ask me. The ways of the noble lords are unfathomable." Master Hans picked a piece of meat from his teeth and flicked it into the putrid straw.

Then he began to curse loudly. "All that work for nothing. I had you almost to the point of confession. But they'll pay me every penny, every penny." He grinned. "And what does it matter? I got a nice delivery today: two new criminals. And you have a visitor."

He stepped aside. Behind him appeared another man who had been visiting his dreams. At over six feet tall, he had shaggy black hair, a dirty coat, and a hooked nose. And he was smoking.

"Well, I'll be damned," Jakob Kuisl growled, drawing on his pipe. "I've got to say Master Hans really did a thorough job. It will no doubt take a week to get a bag of maggots like you back in shape."

"Indeed." The Weilheim executioner at his side smiled. "A masterpiece, but unfortunately your friend was too stubborn.

You could have saved yourself a lot of grief if you had just confessed, but I can also cure you for a price."

Kuisl declined for his friend. "Never mind, Hans. You're perhaps better at torturing, but I can take care of the healing. That requires something the dear Lord unfortunately didn't give you."

"And what would that be?"

"A heart."

Kuisl handed the astonished executioner a few coins. "Take these, and leave us alone for a moment. Get out of my sight."

With a shrug Master Hans shuffled out into the hall, where he tossed the coins in the air and deftly caught them. "You were always too soft for this line of work, Kuisl," he called back into the dungeon. "Too much feeling just leads to bad dreams. What's wrong, Kuisl? Do you have bad dreams?"

Without bothering to reply, Kuisl walked toward his friend crouching on the hard dirt floor in front of him. He pulled Nepomuk to him like a child and embraced him.

"It's over, Nepomuk," he whispered. "It's over."

"Over . . . ? Over?" The fat monk stared at his friend in disbelief. His eyes were still swollen from being beaten by the Andechs hunters, and flies were circling his bloodied lips. "Do you mean I'm . . . free?"

"I'm not able to take you myself," the hangman replied in a steady voice, "but the Andechs abbot swore to me by all that's holy that he will get you out of here soon." Kuisl grinned. "The noble gentleman owes me a favor. Without me, someone would have taken his place as abbot."

A long, shrill shout of pain could be heard in the distance. Nepomuk trembled. "My God, who was that?" he gasped.

"Oh, I'm afraid that was the abbot's replacement. Brother Jeremias and Brother Benedikt have already confessed to everything, but Master Hans hopes to squeeze a few more things out of them. After all, he's paid on commission." For a moment, Nepomuk could only look at his friend with his mouth open. He had to pinch himself to make sure he wasn't dreaming.

"Do you mean the . . . the Andechs prior is over there . . ." he stammered.

Kuisl set him down gently again on the ground. "That's a long story, and I'll tell you all about it, but first let's relax a bit in this stinking hole." With a wink, he took out another long-stemmed pipe and a pouch of wine he had under his coat.

"I thought we could perhaps chat a little about old times," he said warmly. "After all, that's what I promised you the last time we met in the Andechs dungeon. Do you remember?" He offered Nepomuk the pipe and the full pouch of wine.

"To our friendship," he said.

"To our friendship," replied the apothecary.

Nepomuk looked at the hangman wearily, his swollen eyes filling with tears that had nothing to do with the dense tobacco smoke.

EPILOGUE

On Tuesday morning at eight o'clock, Jakob
Kuisl knelt before a plain wayside shrine not far from his hometown. The cross, overgrown with ivy, stood a ways back from the
road so the hangman didn't fear being discovered by anyone.
Kuisl hadn't prayed for a long time, and his words came haltingly. "Our Father, who art in heaven, hallowed be thy name . . ."

He thought of the mad woman in the Kien Valley who had
demanded he seek penance. So much had happened in recent
decades—he had accumulated such a burden of guilt—that a
simple prayer simply couldn't suffice.

But this was at least a start.

"For thine is the kingdom, and the power, and the glory forever. Amen."

The hangman crossed himself, stood up with a groan, and
continued along the road from Peiting to Schongau.

He'd stayed all day with his friend Nepomuk in Weilheim:
they drank and smoked together, and above all, they told stories
from the Great War. Kuisl had cleaned Nepomuk's wounds,
covered them with ointment, and wrapped them in bandages.
From years of experience, he knew the wounds would heal in a

few weeks but the emotional scars would remain. In his dreams, Nepomuk would be haunted by the torture for the rest of his life.

Finally, after the hangman promised to visit his friend again soon, he had set out at a leisurely pace toward Schongau in the shadow of the Hoher Peißenberg. Magdalena, Simon, and the children had gone directly home from Andechs, and Kuisl assumed they would arrive home before him.

When he saw the silhouette of the town gleaming before him in the morning sun, a strange familiarity came over him. People here in the town on the other side of the river had never cared for him, they avoided looking at him, and those who sought out his healing services mostly did so in secret. After buying a talisman, a love potion, or a piece of a noose, they would cross themselves and proceeded to confession. But despite all that, this small, dirty, ugly town was his home.

He had none other.

Lost in his thoughts, he crossed the bridge and took a narrow, shaded path below the city wall. His prayer earlier in the forest had left him with a pleasant, unfamiliar feeling of security. But then his thoughts turned to his two younger children, the twins Georg and Barbara, and whether they had been able to control those rowdy Berchtholdt boys after his departure. Had they performed his duties as executioner — removed the garbage in the streets and carted it out of town?

But above all, he thought of his sick wife, Anna-Maria. Was she still trembling with fever? He remembered her cough had gotten a little better before he left. He'd thought of Anna often in recent days, especially when he became angry or impatient, and wondered what she would do in his place. Anna-Maria could be just as temperamental as her husband, but she always kept a cool head at the critical moment. Especially before executions, which often robbed him of sleep at night, she had always been a pillar of strength and had kept him from getting drunk.

The hangman started walking faster. He passed the outlying

sheds and homes of the Tanners' Quarter, which was crowded between the Lech and the city wall. Now in the early afternoon, many men were out in the streets, hanging foul-smelling leather hides out to dry on poles and frames. Women were standing by the river, washing and chatting. When they saw Kuisl, they turned and whispered among themselves. The hangman was accustomed to such behavior, but something seemed especially strange about it today. Almost as if they pitied him.

What in God's name . . .

Finally he reached his house, which stood somewhat off the road near a large pond. Alongside it was a shed for the knacker's carts, and by the entrance, a lovely garden with flowers, fruit trees, and vegetables.

It was when he saw the garden that he knew that something was definitely wrong.

His wife tended it daily, but now it looked as if it hadn't been weeded for a while. Goutweed and bindweed were growing in the flowerbeds, and slugs were crawling over the wilted, partially brown lettuce. A climbing trellis that had blown over in a recent storm hadn't been set up again.

"Anna?" he called hesitantly. "I'm back. Can you hear me?" But there was no answer from inside the house.

After a while, the door creaked open. As soon as he saw the midwife Martha Stechlin standing in the hallway with a pale and deeply furrowed face, he knew what had happened.

"No!" he shouted, running toward the door. "No! Tell me it's not true."

"There was . . . nothing I could do," the midwife said softly. "The fever was too strong. We took her—"

"No!"

Kuisl pushed Martha aside and staggered into the room. At the large, battered table beneath the crucifix in the corner sat his family, their vacant eyes still puffy from crying. At the center of the table stood a large bowl of steaming porridge, untouched.

The hangman saw Barbara and Georg—the latter having grown a light fuzz on his upper lip—and he saw Magdalena and Simon holding Peter and Paul on their laps. The boys were sucking their thumbs in unusual silence.

They were all there except his wife, Anna-Maria. The worn stool she'd always sat on—where she'd groused, hugged, darned socks, and sung songs—was empty.

Kuisl felt a pang in his heart as painful as if he'd been run through with a sword in battle.

It can't be. Oh, great God, if you really exist, tell me this isn't true. It's an evil prank. I pray to you, and you slap me in the face . . .

"It happened just yesterday," Magdalena whispered in a low voice. "This plague cost many in Schongau their lives, and she was one of the last."

"I . . . I should have stayed here. I could have helped her." His broad shoulders slumped. Suddenly he looked very old.

"Nonsense, Father," said Magdalena, shaking her head vigorously. "Don't you think Martha tried everything? God gives us life, and he takes it away. Death was just too strong. All we can do is pray . . ." She stopped short, tears running down her face as Simon squeezed her hand.

"Would you like to see her?" the medicus asked his father-in-law gently. "She's in the other room."

Kuisl nodded, then turned away silently and moved into the next room. No one followed him.

As if she were just sleeping, Anna-Maria lay with closed eyes in the large bed they'd shared for so long. Her hair was still long and black, with only a few strains of gray. Someone had combed her hair and dressed her in a white lace nightshirt. A few flies buzzed through the room, alighting on her waxen face, and Kuisl brushed them away. Then he knelt beside the bed and took his wife's hand.

"My Anna," he murmured, gently stroking her cheeks. "What am I to do now that you're no longer here? Who's going to scold me when I've had too much to drink? Who will pray for me in the church? Who ..." He stopped short and bit his lip. They'd been married more than thirty years. As a mercenary, he'd brought Anna back from one of the wars, and together they'd grown old. Tears ran down his scarred face—the first tears in many, many years.

He couldn't help thinking again about what the mad woman in the Kien Valley had told him a week ago.

Repent, hangman! Soon misfortune will strike you like a bolt from the blue.

Was this the misfortune that would strike him? Was this the punishment for all the dead who had paved his way through life? Could God be so gruesome?

He heard a faint sound from the neighboring room. Magdalena had come in behind him and placed her hand on his shoulder.

"I ... must tell you something," she began hesitantly. "I don't know if this is the right moment, but I'm sure Mother would have wanted it this way."

Kuisl remained silent, only his raised head revealing that he was listening.

"It's just ..." Magdalena started to say. "Well ... Peter and Paul will soon be sharing the little room upstairs with someone. I'm ... I'm going to have another child."

The hangman didn't respond, but Magdalena could sense his mighty frame begin to tremble.

"Martha examined me, and she's quite sure," she said with a smile. "I was feeling ill a few days ago, do you remember? And now we know why I was constantly nauseated."

Now that she'd broken the news, words poured out like a warm summer rain.

"And this time, Martha thinks it will be a girl," she continued. "What do you think? Would you like to have a little granddaughter?"

Kuisl snorted. It seemed to Magdalena he couldn't decide whether to laugh or cry.

"As if one of you wasn't enough," he grumbled finally.

The hangman squeezed the hand of his wife one final time, then turned and embraced Magdalena so firmly she could hardly breathe.

AFTERWORD

This is the fourth book in the Hangman's Daughter saga and the
first set in my hometown. Perhaps for this reason I'm especially
fond of it. I spent my childhood and youth near the Bavarian
lakes southwest of Munich — the Wörthsee, Pilsensee, and the
Weßlinger See — as well as on the Ammersee (Lake Ammer).
The Andechs Monastery was always a landmark for us, a needle
pointing upward from the hilly countryside at the center of our
little world.

Many of my first stories originated in the forests and lakes of
this region and are interwoven with old sagas and legends of my
homeland. The little town Ellwang, for example, was thought to
have been so remote it was the only village spared in the Thirty
Years' War — the Swedes simply had been unable to find it. And
the abandoned town of Ramsee, whose ruins lie in the forest
south of Andechs, was my model for the village destroyed by the
mercenaries in the third novel in the Hangman's Daughter series, *The Beggar King*.

I can't begin to say how often I've hiked up to the monastery — first as a child to play minigolf, then as a young man to
drink beer, and finally, as an adult for prayer and reflection. The

latter two aren't always easy up there, as the streams of tourists are fierce, especially on weekends. The air there is fragrant with *schweinebraten,* beer mash, and grilled fish on a stick; your children tug at your hand, demanding the ice cream you promised; and noisy American tourists or giggling Japanese stagger about from the strong beer. It's not an accident that the double bock beer, with its alcohol content higher than 7 percent, is no longer served in one-liter mugs in Andechs. I know from experience that paradise begins after three liters, and is quickly followed by the hell of headaches, sweat, and a sour stomach.

But come on a quiet day in midweek, quietly order your half liter of beer, and let your thoughts wander as you look out at the church and the Alps, and you'll understand why the dear Lord chose this spot for his monastery.

One beautiful Tuesday, while I was researching this book in the monastery beer garden, I saw an older gentleman in a traditional Bavarian *Trachtenjanker* jacket reading the newspaper. Suddenly he looked up, grinned with all three of his teeth, and toasted me with the universal Bavarian blessing.

Mei, grad schee is . . . What a wonderful day it is!

I smiled and nodded silently. Then I ordered a second beer and took out my notebook.

My best ideas came to me that day.

If, after reading this novel, you want to undertake a pilgrimage to Andechs, be prepared: a number of things have changed on the Holy Mountain since the seventeenth century. There was a secularization of church property at the beginning of the nineteenth century, a difficult time for this monastery, but even more important, a fire on May 3, 1669, that destroyed almost all the buildings. Only after the fire did the rebuilding occur in the Baroque style you can see on every Bavarian postcard. For those reasons, I allowed myself a bit more freedom in the descriptions here than in previous novels.

To show you that I've nevertheless based much of the novel on historical fact, I've prepared a little monastery guide that will give you enough material for your discussions at the beer garden.

Spoiler alert! Don't read the guide until you've finished the novel!

Or are you the kind of person who reads a book from back to front? Well, the main thing is that you learn about this wonderful monastery, with its long history — and drink a beer or two to my homeland. Just be careful with the double bock beer!

Once again, many people have contributed to making this book possible. First of all, I'd like to thank Elfride Kordwig, who guided me through the monastery and lent me books that gave me a magnificent overview. (And again, apologies for missing our appointment! I had the worst toothache in my life . . .)

I'd also like to thank an Andechs monk who wishes to remain anonymous. He revealed to me some important details about life in the monastery. Further thanks to the local Erling historian Karl Strauß; Joachim Heberlein of the Weilheim Local History and Museum Club; Helmut Schmidbauer from Schongau (above all for the tip about the holy foreskin!); my brothers, Marian and Florian, as well as my father, for medical advice; my mother for the hiking tips and books about our region; my editor, Uta Rupprecht, for every successful battle with words; my agent, Gerd Rumler, for his encouragement; and my wife, Katrin, who fell asleep only once while reading this manuscript and contributed a number of valuable ideas.

And naturally, thanks to my children, who climbed the steep path up to Andechs without complaining (for the most part) when their father had to check one more insignificant detail. Before we go again, we'll get ice cream; I promise!

GLOSSARY

Andechs: This name derives either from the Roman word *dak-sia,* meaning *yew,* or the Celtic word *aks,* meaning steep cliff. The first mention of the word dates from the second century.

Andechs Castle: The Andechs castle was the ancestral seat of the Andechs-Meranier (q.v.). The fortress was built in the second century not far from the monastery, and was almost completely razed by the Wittelsbachs in the first half of the thirteenth century. Whether the fortress was overcome by treason — as in my novel — or was surrendered without a fight is unknown.

Andechs Chronicle: The little *Andechser Chronik,* by Willibald Mathäser (published by the Süddeutscher Verlag in the Sammlung Bavarica), was the model for the chronicle in the novel. It still offers the best overview of the monastery's history.

Andechs-Meranier: After the murder of the king of Bamberg (q.v.), this powerful noble family forfeited its once dominant position in Bavaria to the Wittelsbachs and died out in the mid-thirteenth century.

Apothecary: Constructed in 1763 facing the Andechs Church, the apothecary was closed during the secularization period and serves today as a parish office. Almost none of the former furnishings are preserved. Whether an apothecary was located in Andechs in the seventeenth century — and where one might have stood — is unknown.

Automata: These existed in antiquity, and were in fact all the rage among nobility during the early modern period. Usually they were artistically crafted clocks or music boxes, but there were also human-like puppets, like the Bremer Complimentarius in the seventeenth century—an iron sentinel that could open its visor and salute visitors at the Bremen city hall.

Bamberg Regicide: On June 21, 1208, the German King Philipp von Swabia, of the House of the Hohenstaufen, was murdered by Otto VIII of Wittelsbach, Duke of Bavaria. The wedding of Philipp's niece, Beatrix, to Duke Otto von Andechs-Meranien took place the same day. Oddly, it was not the Wittelsbachs but the Andechs-Meranien dynasty who was accused of the plot. Many details remain unknown.

Benedictine University: This university was founded in 1622 in Salzburg, annexed by Bavaria in 1810, and reestablished as a modern university in 1962. At a very early date, classes were held here in theology and philosophy but also in law and medicine.

Count von Cäsana und Colle: From 1656 to 1688, this Weilheim district judge had jurisdiction over major cases in Andechs—i.e., all punishments involving mutilation, torture, and death.

Curiosity Cabinets: These popular collections of strange objects were common among noblemen in the Renaissance and Baroque eras, and for the most part, were assembled through voyages of exploration. The curiosity cabinets were precursors of our public museums. A good example can be found today in the Castle Trausnitz in Landshut.

Devil's Rock: In my novel, this odd conglomerate rock formation in the Kien Valley serves as the entrance to the cave of the mad hermit woman (q.v.). It's often referred to as "The Devil's Chancel," and some say a hermit's cave was once actually located there.

Elizabeth Fountain: This healing spring was downhill from the church near the monastery wall. The chapel that once stood there was demolished in 1805. Pilgrims used to stop here to rest and wash their eyes.

Festival of the Three Hosts: At this well-known pilgrimage festival at Andechs, which takes place the fourth Sunday after Pentecost, the three sacred hosts (q.v.) are still presented to the faithful.

Friesenegger, Maurus (1590–1655): This Andechs abbot wrote one of the best-known diaries about the Thirty Years' War, which evokes the horrors of this period like no other work. A must for all amateur historians, it was recently republished by the Allitera Verlag in their monacensia edition.

Garden: The real monastery herb garden is located west of and behind the church and is not accessible to the public. Anyone looking for the monastery garden described in my novel will be disappointed; it exists only in my imagination.

Golem: The Hebrew word for *unformed* or *embryo*, this creature was made from mud and clay and, according to Jewish legend, was brought to life by a rabbi to follow the commands of its master.

Hermit: At the end of the seventeenth century a woman named Kuttenmiedl was said to have lived in a cave in the upper Kien Valley. A pious hermit, she often appears in frightening children's stories, and she served as a model for the blind old woman in my story.

Holy Chapel: This chapel on the second floor of the Andechs church houses the three holy hosts and other religious treasures. The chapel is secured with three iron bars, which in earlier times could be opened only with three different keys. During the great conflagration of 1669, the fire miraculously stopped directly in front of the chapel. The interior can be visited today only on a specially guided tour.

Jesuit's Powder: Also called Peruvian Bark or cinchona, this medication was used to reduce fever. Powder made from the bark of the cinchona tree is known today as quinine. The botanical term *Cinchona* supposedly dates back to the countess of Cinchon, who fell ill with malaria in 1639 and was cured by a Jesuit priest.

Jesus' Foreskin: According to unsubstantiated rumors, this is one of the many relics at Andechs—though it's thought to be kept at other Christian sites, too. If you believe the Greek scholar Leo Allatius (who died in 1661), Jesus' foreskin ascended with him into heaven where it turned into the rings of Saturn.

Kien Valley: This forested valley is traversed by hiking and pilgrimage routes. The best-known pathways lead from Herrsching along the Kien Brook and along the edge of the forest over the so-called Hörndl (approximately one and a half hours on foot).

Lightning: There was—and is—lots of it in Andechs. On May 3, 1669, the steeple of the Andechs church was struck during a violent storm. The resulting fire destroyed almost the entire monastery, which had to be rebuilt. For dramatic reasons, I bumped this event up to the year 1666.

Macer Floridus: This was a standard work on medieval herbal medicine that described the medicinal properties of around eighty plants. It was written in the second century by the Benedictine monk Odo Magdunensis.

Ox Trench: This ditch, dug by the monastery, extended down into the Kien Valley and was used primarily during the Thirty Years' War as an escape route for men and animals.

Phosphorus: This chemical element takes its name from the Greek word *phosphoros,* meaning light-emitting. In 1669, the German apothecary and alchemist Hennig Brand discovered it while boiling urine in his search for the philosopher's stone. White phosphorus glows in the dark and is quite flammable. In my novel, I've moved the date of its discovery back a few years.

Pilgrimages: At the end of the Thirty Years' War, there was renewed interest in pilgrimages in Germany. The destinations were Rome and Santiago de Compostela, but also Andechs in Bavaria. In just the years 1622 to 1626, a half million pilgrims visited the Holy Mountain. Today, only a few hundred come each year to Andechs for the Festival of the Three Hosts (q.v.).

Prince's Quarters: These rooms, dating back to at least 1530, were located on the third floor of the monastery and reserved exclusively for the Wittelsbach family.

Rambeck, Maurus: The Andechs abbot from 1666 to 1686, his picture hangs alongside the portraits of other abbots in the monastery library. Contemporaries referred to him as a "walking library." He loved philosophy but, above all, the languages of the Orient. Hebrew was his specialty.

Sacred Treasure: These Andechs relics were lost after the storming of the Andechs Castle (q.v.) and did not reappear until 1388 when a priest noticed a mouse scurrying away during a mass with a piece of parchment in its mouth. Alongside the altar, under a stone slab, a chest with iron fittings was found containing, among other things, the victory cross of Charlemagne, part of Christ's crown of thorns, and the three sacred hosts.

Tavern: The history of the Andechs Monastery tavern goes back to the time of Duke Albrecht III, who founded the Benedictine monastery in the fifteenth century. There, marvelous beer has been brewed since 1455. If you do visit and have too much to drink, just be careful coming down through the Kien Valley, a number of drunks have fallen there.

Thirty Years' War: Lasting from 1618 to 1648, this war was particularly savage in Bavaria, exacerbating the Plague, crop failures, hunger, storms, robberies, and roaming packs of wolves. In some areas, over half the population died, and entire regions were abandoned.

Three Holy Hosts: Andech's most precious relics. Divine signs are said to have once appeared on the three holy hosts, which came to Andechs via a circuitous route and are still kept there in an eighteen-pound silver monstrance in the holy chapel (q.v.).

Tunnels: According to a local historian, a number of excavations in the 1980s revealed the entrance to a tunnel about thirty feet underground near the monastery. Rumors persist to this day about subterranean passages around the old Andechs castle (q.v.), and one such rumor claims an escape tunnel was found leading to a castle in Seefeld, some miles away.

Typhoid: This fever, whose name comes from the Greek word *typhos*, meaning *smoke* or *fog*, is caused by contaminated food and unsanitary conditions. Typical symptoms are a gray coating on the tongue and reddish spots on the chest and belly. It was first described in the sixteenth century by the Italian physician Girolamo Fracastoro, who's now regarded as the forerunner of modern microbiology.

Virgilius: This name was given to a mythical warlock who often appeared in medieval stories as a builder of automata. The name probably goes back to the Roman poet Virgil.

Wittelsbachs: One of the oldest German noble families, they rose to prominence among the Bavarian nobility after the downfall of the Andechs-Meranier (q.v.). The Wartenbergs of my novel are a branch of the Wittelsbach family.